W9-ALN-608

BLAZE

BLAZE

ROBERT LEUCI

AVON BOOKS NEW YORK

This is a work of fiction. Names, characters, places
and incidents either are the product of the author's
imagination or are used fictitiously. Any resemblance
to actual events, locales, organizations, or persons,
living or dead, is entirely coincidental and beyond
the intent of either the author or the publisher.

AVON BOOKS, INC.
1350 Avenue of the Americas
New York, New York 10019

Library of Congress Cataloging in Publication Data:

Leuci, Bob, 1940–
Blaze / Robert Leuci. — 1st ed.
p.   cm.
I. Title.
PS3562.E857B58   1999   99-16670
813'.54—dc21   CIP

First Avon Books Printing: November 1999

Printed in the U.S.A.

FIRST EDITION

QPM   10 9 8 7 6 5 4 3 2 1

www.avonbooks.com

for

Thomas Anthony Leuci
(at this writing, two days old)

In my life story there have been many heroines, and the kindness of women helped me struggle through. I have synthesized Captain Nora Riter, the heroine of *Blaze,* from a number of these fabulous women. I take a moment here to thank just a few:

- Regina Manarin Leuci, the mother of my children, and though we have been physically separated for a long time, Regina remains the queen of silent strength.

- Santina Leuci, my daughter, gratefully a reflection of her mother and, alarmingly, too much the soul of her father.

- Myra Leuci, a confluence of beauty, brains and kindness, the mother of my grandchildren.

- Linda Barban, a synonym for gentleness and beauty, a woman who will always have my respect and affection.

- Ann McKay Thoroman, my editor at Avon Books who organized this work and molded it with quiet faith and kindness and much patience.

- Jennifer Moyer Bell, whose poet's heart and editor's mind have been tremendously helpful. Jennifer has earned my undying gratitude.

- Every writer longs for a good agent; I have had a great agent and friend for eighteen years. The illustrious and extraordinary, Esther Newberg.

For these women and for those who I suppose would prefer not to be mentioned here, thank you.

and for the first time in her life
thoroughly happy-happy in the freedom of her life,
and in the keen enjoyment of the investigation
that broadened its field day by day.

—Mark Twain, *The Gilded Age*

BLAZE

A replay of the final seconds of the Knicks game was on the television set. Volume turned up loud. Alfred had just been punched in the face; his eyes were tearing, his nose dripped blood down onto his T-shirt, and some drops had found their way between his legs, staining the sofa. They had made him take off his sweater, slacks, shoes, and socks. The Knicks lost to Orlando, 110 to 100, another two-fifty down the tubes. Ordinarily Alfred could live with a losing streak, but this one he'd tied into was a humdinger. It was killing him.

"So, Al," the muscled kid named Blaze was saying, "I warned you, ten grand is not wood. Where is it?"

"I'll get it. Didn't I say that I'd have it next week? That's what I said, Blaze, I just said that."

"Next week," Blaze said with a laugh. "You said that last week and the week before." He grabbed hold of what was left of Alfred's thinning hair.

Fat Paulie came in from the kitchen carrying a cutting board.

"What did he say?"

"He said, next week."

"C'mon," Paulie said in an unbelieving manner. He pinched Alfred's cheek, hard, and twisted. Paulie thought it was funny, but it hurt.

Alfred was sitting back on the sofa bed. He was in pain and fright-

1

ened, his breath came on hard and labored, he sounded as if he were snoring.

"You're steaming me, Al," Blaze said. "Paulie, whadaya think?"

"I think you're getting steamed. Where should I put the board?" Paulie said, "there's no place to put it." Blaze shook his head.

"You should have a coffee table in your living room," Blaze said. "Everybody does. You live like shit, Alfred. Like shit."

Alfred closed his eyes and bent his head. When he looked up he could see the television set. Michael Jordan hit a long three, nothing but net. More of last night's highlights, Chicago had won by twenty. Now one of the seven-foot white guys did a reverse dunk, it was garbage time.

Blaze was watching the television, too.

"Who's gonna beat these guys?" he said to Alfred. "I'll tell ya who, nobody."

When Alfred reached to pick up his trousers to get a tissue to stop the bleeding, Blaze punched him on the side of his head. Blaze's ring made Alfred's ear bleed. They're going to do it, Alfred thought, five grand for these teeth and the two morons are gonna knock em out.

"You were warned," Fat Paulie said.

Alfred hunched over and put his face in his hands like a man in deep, dark sorrow. He felt nauseated, he felt as though his lunch and dinner were climbing into his throat, and now he had to pee.

"C'mon," he said slowly, "look at me. I'm no kid anymore. I can't take this. Once, maybe, you know a few years back. Fuck it," he said. "Never mind."

Blaze and Fat Paulie laughed at him.

Alfred touched his ear then stared at the blood on the tips of his fingers. "Man," he said, "what makes you two so nasty?"

They had snatched him out of the Roma Cafe on Court Street in front of a half-dozen customers, one of whom Alfred was sure was a priest. Six people standing around, not saying a word, arms folded across their chests, looking both curious and unconcerned. It was strange, Alfred thought, how so often in his life people looked at him and did not see a thing.

"Nobody gives a shit about you, Alfred. No one's sorry. Everybody knows you're a hambone," Blaze said.

"I'm no hambone," Alfred said. "I know you since you was a little kid and you talk to me like that. Jesus Christ, I'm old enough to be your grandfather, and that's how you talk to me. A hambone?"

2

"What's a hambone?" Fat Paulie said. And Blaze stuck a finger into the cleft of Alfred's chin, saying, "You said you'd get the money from your daughter. That's what you told me."

"I know. I will."

Blaze made a circle with his thumb and right index finger. Taking two fingers of his other hand he slid them through the circle. "Roseann's still fucking that cop? I saw him on the TV last week. Big-time guy, this guy, this guy your daughter's fucking."

Alfred did not answer him.

Blaze grabbed him under the arm and Fat Paulie lifted him by his T-shirt, they got him upright and walked him into the kitchen. Fat Paulie took the cutting board and laid it on the counter. He handed Blaze a meat cleaver that he had removed from a brown paper bag. They both were holding tight to Alfred.

Alfred turned to Blaze in terror. "What in the hell are you gonna do? C'mon, cut it out. Please." A cry broke from Alfred's throat. He hated to hear it. It made him feel small and weak.

Blaze seemed embarrassed, his eyes scanned the room then locked in on Alfred. "Ey," he said, "this bill is six months old. You've run out the string."

Fat Paulie grabbed his wrist; Blaze reached for his thumb. Alfred struggled, causing the three of them to go round and round like some kind of disjointed folk dance.

Finally, they maneuvered Alfred back to the kitchen counter. With all his strength he pushed himself away; screaming, cursing, he tried to bite Paulie's wrist. Blaze raised the cleaver to his shoulder. Alfred began to cry. Fat Paulie yanked his thumb and Blaze chopped it off. Alfred screamed and fell to the kitchen floor. He crawled around, scrambling until he was under the kitchen table. Alfred rolled himself into a ball whimpering like a baby, his remaining four fingers between his thighs.

In a moment Blaze had him by the hair again. "I'm an expert," he told Alfred, "it's a clean cut, you'll be fine." Fat Paulie got down on his knees, took Alfred's face between his two palms. Suddenly Paulie was shouting at him.

"Next week we come for your head. Do you hear me? Go and see your daughter."

Blaze whispered, "Go see Roseann. Are you listening, do you hear me?"

"I'm gonna bleed to death. Christ," Alfred moaned, "it hurts."

3

Then his lunch and dinner came up.

Blaze giggled and slapped him on the ass as if he were a horse. "Fucking degenerate gambler," he said, "useless piece of shit."

After they left Alfred found himself crawling and slipping along the kitchen floor; he remembered hearing somewhere that if you found a limb, put it on ice, and got it real quick to the hospital, the doctors could reattach it.

They'd done it with some guy's dick.

"The Yankees are in Fenway Park and continue their hot streak," the television said. Alfred had bet five hundred on Boston. That was the last thing he heard before he fainted.

When he awoke he was bloody and sore. He made his way to the bathroom and looked at himself in the mirror. When he saw himself, his hand, his face, it all spilled out of him in choked sobs. Eventually he was able to find his thumb in the kitchen sink. He crouched over it like a child and wrapped it in tinfoil. Then Alfred placed his thumb in a coffee mug and protected it with ice cubes. After a while he stopped studying his hand and looked up. Alfred thanked God that it was not his head.

Surprisingly tranquil, Alfred rode in the backseat of a taxi to Coney Island Hospital. He sat on a bench in the emergency room among accident victims and cops who made curious statements about his thumb. After he had waited for about twenty minutes or so, a doctor decided to come and have a talk with him.

"I've been waiting here for twenty minutes," he told the doctor. "Twenty minutes is a helluva long time."

The doctor had dark hair and skin with a soft baby face. His voice reminded Alfred of the voices of English movie actors. "Look around you," he told Alfred, "it's a Saturday night. Please don't give me a hard time."

"You want to hear about a hard time, let me tell you about some of the people I've met."

Alfred gestured with his chin to his hand and then he showed him the coffee cup with his thumb in it. The doctor nodded his head quickly with his eyes closed. "Ooooh," he said, "you must come with me, you must come with me very, very, quickly." He snapped his fingers twice.

In a wheelchair now, some good drugs running into him, Alfred buried his head in his one good hand. I've got to call her, he thought. I've got to tell Roseann that the psycho bastard Blaze knows about that man of hers, that cop. Alfred wondered if that was what you called the chief of New York's detectives, a cop?

A fat nervous orderly with a big round head, puffy cheeks, and no eyebrows wheeled him into the elevator. Alfred saying, "Listen, buddy, can you do me a favor?"

The orderly looked at him with suspicious eyes. "A favor? Like what?"

Questions of reality and perception had come together with the doctor's good Demerol, turning Alfred's brain into a carnival of flashing lights and merry-go-round sounds.

"Before I forget, I want you to write something down for me. Can you do that? Got a scrap of paper or something?"

"I can find one."

The orderly searched his jacket pockets and came out with a notepad and pen.

"Okay, write this: call Roseann."

"What else?"

Alfred grabbed the orderly's wrist, pulled the man's head in close. Alfred whispering now, "Get this down: the Knicks, L.A., the Nuggets, and Seattle."

An uh-oh whistle from the orderly. "A big sports fan," he said.

"That's me, a regular devotee."

Now the drugs were making his head dance to some sleepy music and it must have been showing in his face, because the orderly's tone became soft and personal. "Man," he said, "what the hell happened to your thumb?"

"Lost it in a crap game."

"Say what? You're goofin on me."

"I'm telling you, the guys I play with, you throw snake eyes they tear out your heart and feed it to the dogs."

"I hear ya, crazy people."

"Yeah, crazy people, exactly."

The orderly peered at Alfred's hand. "Fella," he said, "maybe it's time you found new friends and some other form of recreation."

"Absolutely."

5

PART ONE

She sat perfectly still, barely breathing, watching the traffic, knowing that she'd have to deal with this jazz every morning. Each and every lane on Seventy-second Street was jammed, but Nora saw an opening, hit the gas, and went for it. She was able to scoot for half a block.

Traffic or not, it was a gorgeous morning. The first time she had seen the sun for days, this June morning in Manhattan, with a fresh sea breeze coming in off the river. She opened her window and leaned toward the sunlight like a tulip.

Nora yearned to feel lighthearted and airy. Why not? It was spring, time for fresh starts and new beginnings. But what she felt was assaulted, invaded, and used. She did not want to think about it anymore, fight this impossible traffic. She told herself, get there, get it done. But now that she didn't want to think about it, the way the chief had spoken to her kept returning.

Nora was not accustomed to being sent out on a wild-goose chase. As a captain and the lead investigator for the chief of New York's detectives she could, and had, treated subordinates that way. But she was a hotshot investigator, a woman on the rise, a major star at headquarters, and that was supposed to earn you a certain measure of respect.

For a time, stopped at a traffic light, waiting to enter the East River Drive, Nora considered the way Jean-Paul Clement had dropped the case on her. She had said yes to the chief, of course. Yes, indeed, she'd go into Brooklyn and nail the bum. But she had been suspicious and irritated from the get-go. In all senses of the word, the job the chief had given her was bizarre.

Her department car was down and in for repairs, so Nora decided to drive her own car. It was a Mazda, a ruby-red convertible. Heading downtown, she continued to battle the Monday morning traffic along the East River Drive. At the Brooklyn Bridge exit she was suddenly deep in gridlock, thinking: What next?

Earlier that morning Nora discovered that Max, her soon-to-be ex-husband, had invaded her safe-deposit box. Max walked off with some family jewelry and Nora's second gun. Max had been going batty for as long as Nora had been assigned to headquarters and Nora had been assigned to headquarters for a year.

She couldn't figure it; good, solid Max had come apart, section by section. And, what horrified her, what drove her right up the wall, was that she had felt herself sinking, going down the tubes right along with him.

For a time she had shelved the decision to cut her losses and send him packing, some sort of token of female honor, a gesture of defiance. The years she'd put in had to count for something. Her partner, Sam Morelli, telling her over and over, dump this guy, will ya, you're handling this all wrong. Plus, there was her lawyer Vera pointing out that if she didn't get her act together and nail Max, he could get half her pension. Yesterday, the coke arrived at their apartment via Fed Ex. Game time, she told herself, time to pull the pin on this jerk, protect yourself.

Traffic began to inch toward the bridge, blocked by a construction company doing a patch job in the right lane. Nora glanced at the faces of the drivers around her, all of them looking as though they'd dealt with this all before.

In the midst of all this razzmatazz with Max, the chief sends her into Brooklyn. The man practically telling her he had a personal interest in some dipshit named Blaze Longo. A street slug with a taste for mindless violence. Wherever Nora looked in her life right now, there was something to make her miserable.

Crawling over the bridge, at the center now, cars bumper-to-bumper all around her, she couldn't get it out of her mind: Max stole my gun. Jesus.

Nora leaned on her horn, pissed that she didn't have a car with a siren and flashing lights. She closed her eyes and listened to a cadence of horns and shouts, stunned by what she had started.

No one had to tell her that the NYPD regarded cops who lost their gun as careless in the extreme. She'd been around long enough to know that there was a long list of things that could close the gate on a cop's career in this job. A reputation for drinking; womanizing, for men; bed jumping, for women; a disregard for rules and regulations; the proclivity to act before you think. The loss of a prisoner or a gun. Forget drugs, don't even mention the word.

The opinions of the people that ran the department were quick off the tongue, cut and dried: she's a comer; he's a dud. They were cocky, mean and confident men, and the blatant hypocrisy of it all was simply one more thing that made Nora nuts.

Dead still again, Nora sat hands crossed over her steering wheel watching a man in a turban. He resembled a genie that had popped from a bottle to make its way in this world behind the wheel of a taxi. She turned away and when she looked back the turbaned-headed man was smiling.

For a while there was only the sound of the horns, impossible gridlock. Then an opening, a little progress. Eventually the traffic began to move.

Nora had decided that she'd stop at the Brooklyn South detective headquarters before going to the courthouse. See what the 10th Division detectives had on this character Blaze Longo. When she made the left that brought her from Tillary Street to Atlantic Avenue the traffic eased considerably and finally she was able to scoot off in her little red car.

During the past six months, living with Max had been like watching a risky high-wire act. The better part of Nora hoped he'd make it, but the possibility of that long fall and sudden stop had become erotically appealing in a demented sort of way. Yesterday, Sunday morning, when the FedEx guy showed up, bringing a parcel addressed to Max, Nora had opened it. Bingo, there it was, all she needed to send her into orbit. Inside the package she found about two grams of cocaine that had been pressed flat and a note that said, ENJOY. The sender, some shit bird out of Miami, called himself Pedro Pizzaro.

A few minutes later, when Max came strolling in, she laid into him. She shouted, Max moaned, and used con words like love and trust and understanding. She finally had said, "Get your ass out of here."

Max left the apartment in a haze of agitation, on his way, she was sure, to his sweet, little redheaded schoolteacher in Queens.

Nora drove eyes straight ahead, serious, looking at the street and traffic, telling herself, Relax, you'll think of something. There were women who were marvels in the kitchen, some who could create with their hands. Nora figured it was all a matter of natural, inborn talent, a genes thing. As for her, she had always been blessed with exceptionally good luck. She owned a clear head with the innate ability to untie life's knots. It was a gift, some would say, from God. Things will clear, she kept telling herself, you'll nail this Blaze character and get out from under Max, get the gun back, and maybe the jewelry, too.

She thought of times when she was younger and at home and her sister Lilly telling her, "You could walk back and forth across a highway all day with your eyes closed and never get grazed. I think you're a witch, and that's why you'll never truly be happy." With a tone of mild disgust, Nora would tell Lilly, "Because I'm not like you. Not interested in kids and family night at Girl Scouts. Things like that bore the shit out of me. Get it, sis?"

Lilly was content to live a Martha Stewart existence in the solemn silence of the sticks of Rhode Island. Except, Nora had to admit, Lilly's life didn't seem all that bad lately. Living near the ocean, all that peace and quiet, walking to the beach, raising a daughter and a dog. It beat hell out of this traffic, this noise, freaks running all over the street.

Weary and drained, Nora looked up the avenue and it was strange in that instant, how her humor suddenly changed and she came to life.

Across the avenue from where she sat, Nora watched a cop riding at full speed along Flatbush Avenue, one hand holding the reins of his galloping horse, the other swinging a nightstick in the air, like one of the Czar's Cossacks. The mounted cop was in hot pursuit of some dipshit. The guy looked like he had a pig, or a lamb, or a side of beef over his shoulder. And man, oh, man, the dipshit moved like some Dallas Cowboys running back.

Nora knew that there was a huge wholesale meat market just off the intersection of Flatbush and Atlantic. She saw workmen running, too. Men in blue aprons, yelling, pointing, moving purposefully in and out of traffic. Nora folded her arms, resting, watching the show with a feeling of, are you kidding me? She eased her head against the driver's-side window as though something had made her suddenly exhausted. Perfect, she thought, I've crossed the bridge to the dark side of the moon.

An hour and a half earlier, Nicky Ossman stood watching a butcher named Andrew Joey, a man Nicky called AJ, as AJ trimmed a side of beef. Andrew Joey saying, "A pig, lamb, lamb's good, veal even better, but a lamb would be nice."

"Whatever's there," Nicky said, "you'll take it, right?"

Andrew Joey's eyes were bloodshot, as usual. He exuded a faint odor of raw meat, as usual. He wore a soiled white coat with huge pockets, from one pocket hung a blood-stained rag, as usual.

"Of course, veal, veal would be real nice."

"That's a small cow," Nicky said. "Who do I look like, Superman?" He turned around. The butcher shop was empty, the display cases empty, too, save for the crushed ice Andrew Joey had spread along the bottom rack. Sizing up the shop, Nicky had the feeling that nothing here had changed in fifty years: an inch of sawdust on the floor, the worn wood of the butcher-block table, the walk-in refrigerator with a door so heavy that when it swung closed it jarred your bones. The meat hooks, the various-size saws, wooden hammers, cleavers hanging on the wall among the framed photographs of the '53 Brooklyn Dodgers. The Duke, Jackie, Gil, and his all-time favorite, the Reading rifle, Carl Furillo, number six with his cannon of an arm. All before Nicky's time, sure, but Brooklyn legends and great ball players, nothing pretentious about any of them.

Man, he would love to see them play today, see how much money they'd earn today. Kids today who couldn't carry their jocks earned millions. Bullshit .250 hitters today took down more bucks than the entire old Dodger team, Campy included. Pee Wee and the Preacher, too.

"Just don't get nailed," Andrew Joey said.

Nicky turned back to the butcher. Andrew Joey was an unimposing man, weed-thin with huge, horselike teeth, and the thickest of eyeglasses. Considering the way the man went about whacking meat with a cleaver and hammer, Nicky had to wonder how AJ kept his fingers.

"That horse cop still up there?" Nicky asked.

"He was the last time I looked. A lame and his horse, that cop couldn't catch a Jew on Delancey Street."

Nicky reminded AJ that there weren't any Jews left on Delancey Street. "By the way," Nicky said, "I spotted your cousin Blaze going into Paulie's the other night."

"You talk to him?"

"No, I haven't spoken to Blaze, in what? five years. Maybe more."

Andrew Joey, frowning, raised one hand in slow motion. "Do me a favor and don't mention the name around here. That man's acting awful strange lately. I bet he's doing some dipping and sniffing."

Nicky did not answer him.

"Blaze," Andrew Joey said, "came by the other day all pissed-off about something. Foul-mouthed motherfucker, cursing, carrying on in front of my customers. I had to chase him."

Nicky said nothing, just kind of smiled and nodded.

"I taught Blaze everything," said Andrew Joey, "gave him the trade, bought him his tools. He was going to come into the shop, work here with me. I'll tell you something, the man is a box of snakes, but he's one helluva butcher."

"That right?" Nicky told him, "I'm not surprised."

"Yeah." AJ shrugged, sawing at the side of beef, measuring his slices carefully, using his thumb, an inch, an inch. "See," he said, "you put your hands on some easy money. Yeaaah," and then Andrew Joey paused and looked around the shop. "Easy money does it every time. I'll be honest, you're not going to get rich being a butcher, and Blaze, he's got this thing for money. The man loves playing the wiseguy, you know, bad ass, that type of bullshit. Listen to this, he kept his butcher's tools, right. This is the good part, I asked him for the tools, told him I could use a new set. You know what he told me? He said, I need em. You tell me, what in the hell does a guy that runs in the street, a guy like Blaze, what's he gonna do with a set of butcher's tools?"

"I wouldn't even want to guess," Nicky told him. "All right," he said, "I'm off on my mission. I'll see you in an hour." He hoped he did not sound foolish.

Andrew Joey gazed at his empty cases, squinting now, thinking something over, then looked at Nicky. "Of course the price will depend on what you snag. Veal is worth some bucks, beef, too. And lamb—depends on how big. You get a whole lamb I'll give you fifty, seventy-five bucks. Depends on the weight."

"I'm not doing it for the money."

"Not for the money, then why?"

Nicky said, "For the exercise, see if I can still pull it off."

"Pull this off. What are you nuts, the exercise?"

Nicky shrugged.

"Nicky the Hawk."

"That's me."

It was near 10:00 A.M., Nicky was cruising the loading platform of the wholesale meat market, checking out the sides of beef, lamb, whole pigs hanging from hooks. All the activity around the platform threw him into a panic. There were delivery trucks parked and waiting. Rugged workmen in long blue coats were loading trucks, drivers milled about, checking bills of lading, reading the morning paper. He was struck momentarily by the build of the workmen and wondered if they could run.

Nicky Ossman was what you'd call a Brooklyn neighborhood guy, but it pissed him off when people thought of him that way. Anyone speaking to him in person would see it, should see it, since it was there for all to see. The guy was special, a class act. Not the same as those neighborhood lames with nothing stirring in their tiny little brains, Nicky had style. When he walked down the street he knew everything that was going on. There wasn't anything anybody could tell him about Red Hook he didn't know.

You'd make Nicky as a good-looking guy with a soft, city, south-Brooklyn accent with some wiseguy overtones, combined with street-corner shrewdness. The fact was, some would say he was one of those rare human beings who was distressed by the pain of others. And, he worked at improving himself, his image, the way he spoke, with voice and even singing lessons. Nicky harbored an implacable dream to be a film star, the next De Niro or Travolta. He studied acting at the HB Studio and the school for Film and TV. When he made a little score, doing this or that, a few extra bucks in his pocket, he alternated getting singing lessons and dance training. Twenty-nine years old. Not a kid anymore, but not too old.

As far as Nicky was concerned his life was just getting started. He could name you a gang of big-time stars that didn't catch a break until they were in their forties. Two, sometimes three times a month, Nicky was up at four o'clock in the morning, on the F Train and into Manhattan to join the line for auditions in front of the Actors' Equity building. A lot of people in the line were just kids in their teens. Most were ethnic-looking like Nicky, his face a gift from his Swedish, seaman father and Sicilian mother.

Nicky, dressed in jeans, his field jacket, and high tops, moved quickly along the building line of the meat market. He was checking out the hanging meat, deciding. He stood where he was for a moment and closed his eyes, took a deep breath. The morning sun warmed his face, the air was heavy with the odor of sawdust and hanging meats. Only after he stood for a while did he realize how nervous he had become. I'm going to get busted, he thought desperately. I'm going to end up in the joint for this foolishness. Nicky opened his eyes and then closed them again. Traffic was heavy, cars, trucks, vans, parked haphazardly along the avenue, a dog was barking.

Sunday morning, over breakfast, he'd told the boy Tino and his cousin Irma that he was getting slow in mind and body. What's worse, he had told him, he didn't feel strong. I need to work out, he'd said, a little exercise.

"I'm going rustling."

Irma told him in that low voice of hers, "You're kidding?"

"Rustling is just the ticket to get it back up," he'd said.

Tino had been attempting pushups on the kitchen floor, he was lying flat, his arms spread wide, his cheek resting on the yellowing, white linoleum.

"No! No, Nicky," he'd moaned. "Please, not again. It's so embarrassing, my friends spot you and they all go, 'man, we saw Nicky running with meat over his shoulder. Wasamatta you people can't afford to buy food?' "

"Ten o'clock," Nicky told them, "as soon as they hang the meat, I'm there." Irma had dismissed him with a disgusted wave of her hand.

Nicky's penchant for rustling gave Tino and Irma fits. "It's so ree-diculous," Irma said. Tino saying, "Kids do that shit. Why you, why, tell me why? Nicky," Tino shouted, "it's dumb."

Of course they were right. Only, how does someone from the world of Chekhov explain to a woman like Irma and a boy from Red Hook the importance of being in a real drama, the knee-shaking kind? Nicky tried to tell them that he saw rustling as both a physical exercise and a stress-management tool. He'd been doing it for years. It was, by God, the way he got his nickname. Irma had stared at him with that glazed-over look in her eyes when Nicky expounded on the idea that it was essential for an actor to amass as many experiences as possible. He illustrated, and tried to explain in a detached and theoretical way, that he had a responsi-bility to gather creative energy. Lately he'd been feeling zoned-out, not thinking clearly, feeling that he was becoming slow and lazy, losing his edge. He needed something to get the blood to flow.

Irma told him she'd flog his skinny ass with a whip, just the way she did her Thursday, two o'clock client. The tall, skinny, Pakistani intern. That'll get your blood flowing, she'd said, that whip will turn you loose.

Opening his eyes, Nicky made his way along a wall of corrugated iron fencing on which there were a great many posters advertising an African dance group's performance at the Brooklyn Academy Of Music. The fence ended where the loading dock began. Then, spotting just what he wanted, Nicky jumped up onto the loading dock and took hold of a good-sized lamb and snatched it off its hook. As he threw the lamb over his shoulder he experienced a rush that brought a smile to his face. The lamb in hand, hoofs dangling, Nicky ran off.

Nicky charged right into the heavy morning traffic that was flowing both ways along wide Atlantic Avenue. A startled meat-truck driver shouted, then another. The platform exploded with workmen, yelling and in pursuit. Half the men at the loading dock joined the chase, it was what Nicky had expected, all part of the drill. As he neared the intersection of Atlantic and Flatbush, he glanced back and spotted the mounted cop behind him coming on fast. Even with all the snarled traffic the cop was easy to spot, sitting on top of a horse.

Nicky ran full out, followed by the pursuing crowd, the mounted cop closing in. At the intersection, sidestepping through wall-to-wall traffic, he paused again, just for a moment, glancing rearward. The workmen had fallen back, but the cop, to Nicky's dismay, was urging his horse with professional ease around the cars, trucks, and vans. And even from where

Nicky stood the cop looked pissed. Nicky moved with the flow of traffic now, if anything faster than before. But the strain was starting to show: apprehension filled Nicky's features.

A late-model red sports car, a Mazda convertible, pulled up alongside him. The electric window came down. Nicky could see the woman driver. Not bad, he thought, looks like a hippie. He glanced at the car, but kept right on moving.

"Hey!" the driver called out.

"Beat it, lady, can't you see I'm working out here?"

The woman looked at him, then glanced into her rearview. "C'mon," she said, "get in."

"I told you, I'm working out."

"Will you get in the car, you're not going to outrun that horse." She took her sunglasses off and the two of them stared at each other for a brief second, amused.

She was a remarkably good-looking woman, with features that put Nicky in mind of a flower-child goddess. Hardly any makeup at all and these long earrings. A huge thicket of great black hair and, this was important, a beaming smile. Her hairstyle made her look like a woman in a magazine ad of bygone days, of good pot, and psychedelic paintings, of group sing-alongs, communes, and hot morning sex. It had been a while since he had lifted a skirt. He sighed. These were dumb thoughts and Nicky pushed them aside.

The Mazda kept pace and every so often the driver would toot her horn, staring at him like, you poor, dumb, dickhead. Nicky picked up the pace, running full out. Feeling it in his legs, in his chest, his lungs burning. Christ! He could hear the clippity-clop of the mounted cop closing in.

"C'mon," she shouted, "get in." The voice bell-like and demanding.

"Leave me alone, lady," Nicky shouted without looking over. Off in the distance a siren, a sound that he didn't dare acknowledge, a sound he knew meant trouble, not that he didn't have enough already. More than enough. On the other hand, here was this dazzling woman driving a quick little car, offering him a ride, practically begging him to jump in.

It all happened fast. Nicky found himself sitting on the front seat of the Mazda, the lamb on his lap. It was a mistake, he knew it the moment he sat in the car. The woman snapped at him, "Don't let that thing touch my seats." Except, even though he knew it was a slip to grab this ride, Nicky still felt a certain thrill, a kind of excitement about what might happen next. He glanced down at her legs, her skirt hiked up above the knees so she could manage the gear shift. By the rules of his own game, he should not have jumped into the Mazda. And check out the loony chick, he thought, at a traffic light, looking both ways then rolling right on through. Like, who does this woman think she is, blowing off a red light like that?

"Thanks for the lift," Nicky said, "I can get out here. Here is fine, or there on the corner."

Silence from the driver as if he'd said something stupid. Glancing at him now, the woman gave him the once-over, flicking a thumbnail against her upper tooth. Nicky thinking belligerently, I could have made it, another block, maybe two, I'm home free.

She made a sharp U, cutting off traffic, the mounted cop doing rodeo tricks trying to get a fix on her license plate. The woman laughed a sly laugh, a bit tough, and said, I don't believe this shit. Nicky thought a woman who looks like this, talks like that, is not your average flower child. He sat tight and quiet considering some disappearing act, a now-you-see-him-now-you-don't kind of thing. He watched the woman closely, seeing those eyes, great big eyes flashing at him, checking the street, a little angry, not all that happy now to rescue him.

"I've done it before," Nicky told her.

"I bet you have."

Nicky checked her hands, nice hands, good jewelry, no wedding ring, but white, stone-cold white, gripping the wheel so tight. Nicky was beginning to sweat, feeling it inside his clothes. "No, I mean," he said, "I outran that horse before. Really, I have. I'm very athletic." Throwing her his best smooth and flirtatious grin. Their eyes met for a split second, then she turned away pointing the Mazda toward Bergen Street. There was a precinct house on Bergen and Sixth Avenue, a place where Nicky had been an invited visitor on more than one occasion.

"Just drop me at the corner. I don't want to seem ungrateful, but this really is far enough."

"I've got some good news, I got some bad news," she told him. "You call it. Which do you want first?"

Nicky just stared, frozen. An icy cold calm emanated from this woman. She slowed the car about a half block from the precinct. Nicky thinking, what in the hell do you do now, huh? What in the hell is her game? He shrugged and made a face.

"I know that mounted cop," she said with a grin. "He's an ex-Marine with a black belt and no sense of humor. But he won't catch you now."

Nicky managed a frightened, sad, little smile and nervously gripped the lamb as Nora drove right to the front of the station house, pulled up and parked in the number two spot, marked DETECTIVES. "The bad news is, I'm a cop. And you're busted, cowboy. Grand theft lamb, it'll be a first for me."

"Oh, that is disgusting! It's not possible," he said, "no cop has a pair of legs like that. Not at all possible."

Nora reached over and opened the glove box. Taking out a pair of handcuffs. "Ah, yes," she said, "looks can be deceiving, can't they? Look at you, you seem for all the world like a decent guy, bright, good-looking, young, strong. But the truth is you're a petty thief, a schmuck, a dipshit."

Nicky thinking: I can manage the door with my elbow, toss the lamb in her lap, and make a run for it. I can still go for it, make a break.

Three uniformed cops who looked as though they spent all of their off-time pumping iron, stood arms folded, eyes narrowed, staring at the red little car parked in a DETECTIVES-marked spot. Nicky took a deep breath and glanced out the window; freedom seemed a long way off.

"I won't ask you for a break," Nicky told her.

"It never hurts to ask," Nora said. Nicky turned away as Nora draped the handcuffs on his wrists.

"You should be ashamed of yourself," she told him. "A petty thief. Ashamed is what you should be."

"Mea culpa, mea culpa," Nicky said. "Forgive me."

"Up yours. C'mon, get up, get out, get going. I've things to do."

"You're arresting me?"

"I'm not taking you to the prom. Move your ass."

"And a nice ass it is, too, so I've been told."

"Great, you'll be a big hit at Rikers. Get yourself a pair of three-inch pumps and some fishnet stockings, you'll be a star."

Nicky grinned. Thinking, bitch. Thinking, he never did hit it off with hippie-type women.

As Nora and Nicky got out of the car, one of the uniformed cops walked up to greet them, glancing first at Nora then Nicky, checking out the character in handcuffs, a lamb cradled in his arms. The cop was smiling. "Whataya got here?" he asked softly.

Nora was watching Nicky and beyond him the front door of the precinct house busy with cops coming and going. She said to the cop,

"A dis-con and larceny for starters. I'm Captain Riter from the chief of detectives office, my car all right for a while?"

The cop was giving her a funny look, wanting to ask a question, but not wanting to. Finally he said, "Larceny goat, is that what you got?"

"Can I leave my car there?" Nora said flatly.

"I'll let the desk know, but it would help if you had a plate."

"As a matter of fact I have my chief of detectives office plate in the glove box."

"All you need, you won't need anything more than that," the cop said.

"Listen," Nicky said with a grim smile. "Why don't we forget this whole thing and go and get some breakfast, I'm starved."

"Shut up," she told him. "Look," she said to the cop, "I'll only be a few minutes."

Nicky would remember that. *Shut up*. And the look in her eyes.

"No problem," the cop said. "The squad's out, they won't be back until this afternoon. Can I give you a hand with this ape, Captain? You look a bit flushed." A big smile.

It was the old macho-man soft-shoe. The favorite dance of male cops.

"Thanks, but no, thanks," she told him. "I can handle him. But I'll tell you what you can do for me."

"Sure, sure, Captain. What is it?" An even bigger smile.

"Take that lamb, goat, or whatever the hell it is, tag it, and put it someplace for safekeeping."

The cop said, yes, ma'am, took the lamb from Nicky, and moved off.

Nicky moved ahead of her up the steps and into the precinct house. She watched him as she had watched him in the street. She watched Nicky walk up in front of the desk officer, to the railing in front of the desk, watched him turn and look around at the milling cops and clerical staff, the smiling faces of the women in the muster room. The desk officer looked up, surprised. Nora draped her captain's shield on a golden chain around her neck.

It seemed to take the desk officer a minute to understand what he had before him. He turned from Nicky to Nora with a faint polite smile and leaned forward resting his elbows on the desk.

"What can I do for you, Captain?"

Nora explained that she had been on her way into 10th Division detectives headquarters when she ran into this character on Flatbush and Atlantic.

"We heard it over the air, a mounted cop giving chase, that was it, right? A larceny from the market. That one, right?"

"That's it," Nora said.

They looked at each other in silence for a moment. "So what would you like to do, Captain?"

Nora folded her arms and looked at the floor. Arresting this guy would blow off her whole morning. At the same time she didn't think she had many options. The start of a killer day. A dipshit and his goat.

"What's the matter?" the desk officer asked.

"Oh, nothing. Jesus, I have a meeting over at the DA's office at eleven."

"You'll never make it."

She gave him a quick fond smile. "Sure I will. Lieutenant," she said, "have someone bring him up to the detectives, put him in the cage. Soon as I finish up at the DA's office, I'll come back here and book him. How's that?"

Nicky put a hand to his heart. "A cage, you're going to put me in a cage. I'm a human being, not an animal." His voice had a trace of old England. "I simply won't have it."

The desk officer and Nora looked at each other and laughed.

Lieutenant Anton Sierra had been with the department for fourteen years. He'd met his share of knockout, drop-dead-gorgeous policewomen, but this dazzling creature standing before him was a captain. A captain who dressed like a hippie. A combination of awe and dread was written all over his face. Sierra cleared his throat, he stood straight and tall, sucked in his gut, and motioned to one of the muscled uniformed cops, told him to take Nicky into the 124 room. When the cop and Nicky walked off, he swiveled back to Nora, saying, "Listen, if your prisoner has ID and so on, we'll run a name check. If this character has no outstanding warrants, what we can do is give him a desk-appearance ticket, a summons. How's that?"

"Fine by me."

Sierra squinted, and closed one eye, "But if there is anything outstanding, he's wanted, something like that, I'll have to get you back here."

"You can call me at the DA's office. ADA Devlin at the Racket Squad. Call me there and if need be, I'll come back."

"That'll work."

"Good."

Nora walked to the clerical office and found Nicky sitting, playing tic-tac-toe with the uniformed cop.

"Without going into detail, you're going to get a desk-appearance ticket, a summons. You got ID?" she asked him.

Nicky said, "A driver's license, that all right?"

"Sure. Listen," she said, "act your age," she told him. "Get a life."

"Nice meeting you," Nicky said. "See you around the set." And at that moment he meant what he said. He would remember the way she smiled at him saying, "I see you again, you're in deep shit."

"Captain," Nicky said, "it was a game, nothing but a game. I do this for laughs."

"You think it's funny having cops on horseback chasing you all over Brooklyn? You could get someone hurt, killed maybe."

He looked at her in silence and shook his head. After a long moment he said, "Just a game, believe me, I didn't want to see anyone get hurt."

As he faced her in the clerical office, Nicky's thoughts were not of rustling or game playing. This woman made him edgy, gave him a small pain in the stomach, a little thickness in the throat. Earlier, when she was talking with the desk officer, Nicky had run his eye over her. She had put a hand to the back of her neck, lifting all that hair. Nicky thought that maybe she sensed his watching.

"A game, huh?" Nora said.

"A little fun, nothing more than that."

"If it's a game you were playing, you lost."

"The way I see it, I'm a winner."

"Maybe you should look around you. This place doesn't look like the winner's circle to me."

"I met you, didn't I?"

That stopped her.

What for some men would be a momentous act Nicky could do without thinking. Throwing Nora his very best grin he said, "Christ, you are one beautiful woman. But I guess you know that." Nicky held his smile for a long take, then he bent his head and just about then her voice hit him. Nora said, "We meet again, you won't think this is all so funny, smartass."

"May I say something?"

Nora put her hand to her brow as if her head hurt.

"There are certain qualities a person needs," Nicky told her, "to stay in tune with the human race, empathy and compassion. All of us here can see you have an abundance of both."

The cop sitting with Nicky turned away, tried not to smile. Nora stared at Nicky, thinking, only one word for this guy: dipshit, bonehead. That's two, she thought. "You know," she said, "if I weren't so busy, I would take great pleasure in printing you and tossing your ass in the slammer." She continued to look into his eyes, into the blackest eyes she'd ever seen. Dark, hard eyes, been around, seen more than their share, plenty of sexy stuff there and a sparkle, too, a sense of humor. She looked at him and what she saw was everything Nora associated with street guys. With his little-boy grin he was the embodiment of it all, a classic dipshit. This day was getting away from her and Nora was starting to lose all her humor.

Staring intently Nicky said, "Lighten up, Captain, you'll live longer."

Nora stood in the doorway a moment, a hard grin in place, as though she were thinking about it.

Assistant District Attorney Daniel Devlin sat behind a desk in his office working on a hideous-looking hero sandwich of tuna salad with loads of mayonnaise. Nora didn't know which was more unpleasant, the chewing sounds or the look on ADA Devlin's face as he ate. He was all eyes, one blue, one brown, and he kept glancing around the room, staring as he chewed. His body, too, was strange, tall and very thin, a large head with waves of black hair.

Nora explained Chief Clement's interest in Blaze Longo. Devlin nodded, chewing away, not saying anything. Finally he drank down an entire bottle of soda and favored Nora with a sunny, quick, impatient smile, telling her that Blaze Longo was a loan shark and a killer and any investigation having to do with him should be a homicide case, not something for the chief of detectives office.

Nora felt her anger rise. She didn't want to get off on the wrong foot, but Devlin was getting under her skin. Then the telephone rang. Devlin took the call, and said into the phone, "I'll do what I can, Chief." The words barely made it out of his food-packed mouth.

Devlin hung up the telephone, opened his desk drawer and handed Nora a case folder. "We don't have bodies," he said, "but there are missing persons, three that we know of."

Inside the folder were several memos from a debriefing of an FBI informant, and Blaze Longo's arrest record along with a fairly recent photo. The informant served up the names of three people that Longo had made to disappear. "I mean," Devlin told her, "Blaze Longo is nothing more than our usual run-of-the-mill, Red Hook scumbag. I have to wonder what makes him so special that he interests the chief of detectives and his top investigator?"

His voice suggested ulterior motives. Nora was not offended, bureaucrats made her weary and irritated but they rarely offended her. This one was pale with thin lips, and a mean little smile.

Among other things, ADAs like this Devlin hated cops. Irish guy, framed St. John's University Law School diploma on the wall. Daniel Devlin, known to his friends as Dan, Danny, probably had a brother, or an uncle, maybe even a father on the job. Son of an abusive cop, that would explain it.

The funny thing was, smiling Danny had a point. Nora could not imagine why Jean-Paul was interested in Longo. She hesitated, thinking that it was sloppy for Jean-Paul not to have brought her up to speed on this. A quick telephone call, a name out of the blue. No why or wherefore. Devlin was going on about caseloads, stuff like that. Nora didn't say anything, wondering *did* Jean-Paul have an ulterior motive?

It was not unusual for Nora to play special investigator for the chief. She was Jean-Paul's favorite and valued, and she could move behind the scenes. She got a huge charge walking into one of those male-dominated detectives' offices, checking on things, loved to hear voices rise in surprise and anxiety when they found out who she worked for. "The chief himself? The chief of detectives? Whatever you want, Captain, whatever you need."

And Jean-Paul was always dazzlingly grateful. "You're a find," he'd say, "a stand-up guy for a gorgeous woman." Meaning she'd do his bidding, no questions asked. Jean-Paul Clement, after all, was a five-star super chief, one of the handful of men that ran the NYPD. He was also a consummate skirt chaser, and was constantly on Nora's back.

Nora decided that she would not let on to Devlin that she knew nothing, less than nothing about Longo, or why Jean-Paul had an interest in him. "He has that certain quality that tweaks your interest," she told the ADA. "A hyena in the weeds, if you know what I mean? You think Longo's special, don't you?"

"Look, they're all special. Anyway, I've given you everything we have on the guy." Daniel Devlin smiled in a world-weary fashion.

Nora left the DA's office around twelve-thirty and walked along Court Street toward Montague. The midday sun was warm, the air fragrant, a season-changing feel to the noontime breeze. The Botanic Garden, Coney Island, she thought, Nathan's, Sheepshead Bay, Junior's cheesecake—all things considered, Brooklyn wasn't all that bad.

The traffic heading for the bridge seemed fairly light. Nora was looking forward to getting into the office, calling Sam, and telling him about her mother's jewelry, her bank accounts, her gun. Time, she told herself, to put things in order. The question of the chief and this Longo case was a difficult one. She'd have to speak to Jean-Paul at the first opportunity, scope out exactly what he had in mind for this Blaze Longo.

Blaze Longo seemed to be little more than some street slug, maybe a concern to the locals here in Brooklyn, but a minor player, hardly a target for her office. Nora's mind already jumped ahead to working a Brooklyn case. All she could see were problems. Maybe it's Brooklyn, she thought, the smell and history of the place that makes you paranoid.

An attractive young man walked toward her, slowed, then passed her by. He was in his early twenties, tall and thin with a full head of curly blond hair. The young man nodded and smiled at her as he went by. Nora slowed for a second and turned to look back over her shoulder.

She resumed her trek just a tiny bit confused. As she had gotten older younger men were attracted to her. Older men, it seemed, were frightened. Some privately, some openly. She thought it all had to do with middle-aged limp penises, the consequence of confronting a liberated woman who carried a gun. A problem, she suspected, that most younger men didn't experience. Maybe it was all self-deception, she thought, the result of her love life dying. Sexual fantasies, perhaps mixed with the fact that she hadn't made love for the past couple of months. That was all.

Nora did have a pretty face, and she was well formed, with gray eyes and black hair that hung down to her waist. She wore Spanish shawls and long skirts, high-heeled sandals, and boots when the weather grew cold. She loved Indian jewelry, the real stuff, necklaces and bracelets of turquoise, and silver, long, drop earrings. Always full of life, she sauntered around the department like some sort of movement leader, knowing full well that all the cops, sergeants, lieutenants, captains, deputy inspectors, inspectors, and chief inspectors looked at her wondering what she was like in bed.

She was thirty-five, a bright, irascible, tough-talking woman, and not at all ashamed to use her seductiveness to get what she wanted. There was a time a few years back when Nora was a pariah at the gate but now she was inside, one of the boys. Skilled as a psychologist at reading body language, a master interrogator who had the talent to turn answers around and shove them up a suspect's ass. Everyone said that Nora Riter was a comer, a fiery captain who was being groomed for big things.

Suddenly she was thinking about her arrest that morning, that character with his lamb. Nora realized that she did not know his name. She was at loose ends, running on nerves. F'r Chrissake, she thought, you didn't get any information on him at all.

Nora clapped the palms of her hands alongside her head in exasperation. She focused her eyes on the steering wheel trying to track her thoughts: worn down in a flush of confusion, she started the car and headed back to Brooklyn South detective headquarters. Blaze Longo, Max, the good-looking dipshit and his lamb. Her stomach was twisting. Heavy clouds moved in from the west and the sun faded. The day was piling up on her.

Stopped at a traffic signal, Nora reached to the rearview mirror, turned it to get a good look at her face. She stared at her reflection and shook her head the way you did when you'd seen a hopeless case. As she readjusted her mirror, there was a roll of thunder and the rain broke.

Instead of heading to Brooklyn South, Nora turned onto the bridge and headed for her office. Whatever she needed from the precinct she could get by telephone.

Strange how quickly the day had cleared, the rain stopping, the sky now cloudless and turquoise, almost as blue as the sky above Utah, almost. Even stranger because she now could see the moon, white as fine Irish linen, looming, fading, and reappearing across the river over Manhattan.

Nora Riter was driving in light traffic on the Brooklyn Bridge, heading for her office. Getting to see the moon in the early afternoon, she considered, was some sort of omen.

Trying not to feel anxiety about Max, this Blaze Longo case, or the screwball with his lamb, she thought of Sammy.

Nora loved this guy Sammy Morelli. He had been every detective's dream, the perfect partner. The kind of guy who would burn at the stake for you, the kind you say you trust with your life and mean it. As though he were a brother, a friend, better than any lover she ever had, a man she could count on. God knows she had worked with her share of jerks, their sunny expectant smiles telling her they hoped they could jump her bones.

Ten years ago, before Max, Sammy had taken her by the hand when they both worked Public Morals. Since then, Nora had been promoted and transferred three times and wherever she went in the department, she took Sammy. Now, thirty days from retirement into his terminal leave,

Nora had asked him to keep an eye on Max. As soon as Nora asked, it became Sammy's favorite thing to do. Sammy hated Max.

Sammy Morelli was a quiet, compact little man, with black curly hair who looked as though he could run through a stone wall. Sammy told her time and again, "It's over, divorce the bastard. Why the hell do you keep hanging on with this man?"

"Yeah," Nora would say, "you're right, I know, I know."

Except, if she didn't handle it just so, Max could get alimony, and he'd take a shot at a piece of her pension. She'd seen it happen to other cops, good guys and women, too, married to loonies for life, frightened of losing their pension.

So, two weeks back, Nora had had dinner with her lawyer, Vera Ryan. Vera had told her infidelities occurred in most marriages. These days it was no big thing. Christ, you watched TV, read the papers. Some men were total ding-a-lings with needs that most relationships didn't provide. Max apparently needed something Nora could not deliver and so he went out and got it. "Nora," she'd said, "Max is a smart guy and he thinks he's a stud. You have to prepare yourself. As far as divorce court is concerned it's a crapshoot. Some judges can be nutty. Amateurs trust their luck to the courts, judges, and lawyers, you're no amateur. See to it that you nail the bastard. Get me the ammunition, dearie, and I'll whip his ass." The next day Nora had called Sammy.

She arrived at the fourteenth floor of headquarters a few minutes before one. A pair of tough-looking uniformed captains were standing around in front of the chief's office waiting, for what? Nora couldn't imagine, Jean-Paul was scheduled to be out of town for at least two more days. The captains gave her a long and not altogether respectful look.

Nora walked around to her own office on the east side of the building. Once there she hung up her jacket and then glanced at two or three of the Unusual Occurrence Reports that had come in during the night. Then she strolled across the room to the windows. The day had turned bright, it had grown warm with the approach of summer. Arms folded, Nora stood watching as a tugboat fought its way north against the powerful current of the river. A black helicopter rose from the Wall Street heliport and made its way over the Brooklyn Bridge, above the Statue of Liberty, heading, she supposed, for the casinos of Atlantic City.

Once she had brought Max here. Standing together, holding hands, they had watched from her window as the tall ships made their way up the East River. It had been a wonderful moment in a good year. She now stood at the same place gazing out at that same river, the Brooklyn skyline. Nora felt as though she were under siege. Max has my gun, but no bullets, she was certain, almost sure. Ten minutes later Sammy called.

"He's there," Sam told her.

"With the schoolteacher?"

"Same place, same broad, same lunch. The two of them, a goddamn rock-and-roll show. I took about six more shots."

"Anything good?"

"Good, of course, good. I know what I'm doing. Man, Nora, these two go at each other like a pair of minks."

"Terrific." Nora stared down at her shoes, calming herself.

"That all you got to say?"

"Sammy, what do you want me to say? Look," she said, "why don't you just head on home. You've done enough for one day."

"Why don't I just go in there and kick his ass?"

Nora nodded, "Hmmmm," she said. "Naw, go on home."

"I thought maybe I'd come in, have you buy me lunch."

"Fine, I'll be here."

"Whadaya say, how about we go over to that joint Chow Chow's over on Mott Street?"

Nora smiling a little. "You're on."

"You know what? I should give Jimmy Rice a call at Safe and Loft. Have him go over to your place and change the locks."

"I don't know, Sam . . ."

"Whadaya mean, you don't know? Of course, you know." Sam hissed in disgust. "Look," he said, "I'm calling Rice, enough of this shit."

"Maybe you should."

"Ain't no maybes about it. I checked, Rice is doing a ten to six and he owes me one."

"Everybody owes you one."

"True. Well, whadaya say?"

"Change the locks?"

"Tell me the truth. Say Max wants to come home, you take him back?"

"No, Sammy, no. Max is history," she said after a moment. "All right, go ahead, give Rice a call. Ask him if he needs my keys."

"Jimmy Rice is the best locksmith in the country. The guy moves with mystifying speed and slyness. He doesn't need anyone's keys."

Nora laughed, an easygoing, tired sort of laugh, and hung up.

Her office was glass enclosed, not at all private and she was a popular attraction for the detectives and brass who worked out of One Police Plaza. Along the hallway in front of her office the uniformed captains she'd seen earlier walked by muttering, shooting sidelong glances at her.

All these headquarters characters would always find some reason to cruise her. They'd stroll by to take a peek at the famous, knockout captain. Whispering to each other as they went, in that smart-mouth bantering style, You tell me, does this broad look like a cop? Broad spread her legs, got to headquarters on her back, most likely gives the chief pipers. The way he calls her by her first name, both of them always grinning like they had something going. Sure, they'd say, the woman was too delicate and sexy for patrol. But then someone would mention her arrest record in the narcotics division, and the cases she broke and closed in Homicide, and someone else would say, no shit.

Even after a year they'd still come by and wonder if she was half as good as her reputation.

Led Midtown North in closed homicides, that's big, that's major.

Yeah, but look who she had for a partner. Sammy Morelli, one of the best that ever came down the pike. Then they'd really get into it, start blowing smoke, like, How could you work with a broad built like that, looked like that, moved like that. One thing for sure, you couldn't bring that home. No way, the wife would throw a fit, probably cut your nuts off, bring that package home.

Anyway, she looks like some whacked-out liberal broad. Probably made poor Sammy loony, what with moaning and groaning for the poor and deprived. Gorgeous woman or not, she's a boss, and who the fuck would want to work for some smart-bitch, bleeding-heart, liberal boss?

Only . . . man, look at that hair, that face, and forget the ass, that's no white woman's ass. Nora had heard it all a million times.

For Nora, waiting for Sammy was lost time. Straightening up a cleared desk, but something else, too. She felt uneasy carrying Max's cocaine around.

She had played briefly with the idea of turning the drugs over to narcotics. Have Max take a first-hand look at crime and punishment. But she just couldn't bring herself to have Max dragged off in chains. She had decided to deal with Max in her own way, in her own time.

Nora made herself a coffee and walked to her office window and rested her shoulder against the frame. She turned and looked around her office, considering the boundaries of her life. She had once loved this man, this Max Riter, and she could not move the thought from her mind. The notion of all the times they'd spent together, the tough times they'd shared, the times they were able to help each other, encourage each other; the way he stood by her when her mother was sick and dying, even when she was running around like a lunatic trying to keep it together; the doctors, the hospital, the nursing home, the funeral. How she hated herself for the nursing home. Max steadied her, gave her support and encouragement. But that was a long time ago, before he had gone round the bend.

How had it all come together and how did it fall apart? Two months ago Nora had admitted to herself that she truly had stopped loving Max. What she mostly felt then and now was a kind of pity. The guy wasn't right, hadn't been right for a long time. The crazy, out-of-control mood swings. The way he lost weight, always looking tired and worn, and the way he walked around in a kind of stoop. Still, he was her husband, and she had loved him. He had been the kind of man she'd always wanted, or thought she wanted. But the character she'd been living with was not the man she'd once loved. This guy was a fake, all that sorrow in his face, the darkness in his eyes. The lies. She had forced herself to hang in, and what for? She was ashamed of herself for even trying. So ashamed of herself that she didn't tell Max that she knew about his lawyer and the schoolteacher in Queens.

Heartless bitch, he'd called her. When Max walked from the apartment, slamming the door behind him—selfish, heartless bitch, is what he had said.

After a while Nora went to the restroom, where she took the cocaine from her shoulder bag and flushed it away. She fixed her makeup, then carefully appraised herself in the washroom mirror. She looked good, a little tired, but good. After a moment Nora winked at herself. "Hey, heartless bitch," she murmured, "you look good."

''So what are you going to do with the coke?" Sammy Morelli said, taking the seat across from Nora, finger-combing his hair.

She didn't answer him. Sammy shook his head and said, "All right, you open a case, bring the coke over to the lab, get a voucher number. Open a John Doe case, put it in the confidential file. You could do that." Nora puffed her cheeks and blew out some air.

"If not, you'd better throw that shit away."

They were sitting in Chow Chow's, a restaurant in the heart of Chinatown, just a few blocks from headquarters eating some kind of noodle soup.

"Well," Nora said, "this case the chief laid on me looks like a real hummer."

Sam stretched his arms and yawned then looked around the restaurant. "That's what he has you around for, to look into hummers."

"You know, I went over the bridge this morning. I meet with this ADA Devlin, the guy's scratching his head, giving me those looks like, why are you people interested in this? I hate Brooklyn, hate the bridge, hate the traffic, hate the courthouse. Damn zoo. Devlin tells me this character Longo, Blaze Longo, he's a run-of-the-mill Red Hook badass, a neighborhood jerkoff, a nobody. This, the same creep, the chief tells me he has a personal interest in. You figure it."

"Look out."

"My thoughts exactly."

"What sort of case?"

"Sounds like loan sharking, a few of his customers appear to be missing. Blaze Longo, you ever hear of him?"

"No. Then again, if he's out of Brooklyn, he may as well be out of Bosnia as far as I'm concerned. I never worked Brooklyn, don't know anyone there."

For a while Sammy was quiet, engaged in heated hand-to-hand combat with the chopsticks and the noodles.

Sammy dropped the chopsticks and went for the fork. "You put Max's coke in an evidence envelope, sealed it, and so on? You know, like we did in narcotics?"

"Excuse me, I'm the captain, I know what to do with drugs. See," she said, "you have to hold the bottom one like this. You know, like a pencil. Then you can manipulate the top one. Easy, see."

"I'll stick with the fork. Think about it," Sammy said, "how the hell can you tell the chief that you have some coke that came through the mail?"

"Sure, I could." Trying to sound calm, in control. "He knows all about the problems I've had with Max, he'd understand."

"Understand? Yeah, maybe he'd understand. He would hear you out, then tell you to go and lock the bum up. More likely he'd say you should have some postal inspector lock him up. But he'd want him collared, you can bet on it."

"I tossed them."

"You what?"

"I flushed Max's drugs."

"I figured that. How did I know that?" There was a long moment of silence, then he said, "You're not handling this right."

Eating, being still for a few minutes, she played with the thought of having Max arrested. Sammy cleared his throat. Four characters who looked like they just took the walk across Canal Street from Little Italy sat at a table behind them.

"Listen," Sammy said quietly, "it's time you came down on Max. Enough already, enough." Sammy glanced at the four characters in leather jackets, frowning; he turned his head to look at Nora, "These guys familiar?" he said.

Nora shook her head, then sipped her tea.

"Anyway," Sammy said, "this guy you married is nothing but a headache."

"Tell me about it. Only, I don't want him arrested. The man needs help, not jail. It would kill his parents. Lovely people, really nice folks."

"Who would have ever guessed that a nice Jewish boy from Scarsdale could turn out to be such a hard-on."

"It all has to do with luck," Nora told him, "mine, when it comes to men, has always been lousy."

"So this guy, tell me," Sammy said, "Max, your husband, he ever have anything going?"

"He was kind to animals, loved dogs and cats."

"So did Charlie Manson."

She had almost forgotten why she fell for Max. The guy was charming, attractive, and smart, very smooth, especially in bed. The circumstances had been right, she couldn't say no. As a younger woman all her fantasies included marriage, but for years she bounced around, running from one relationship to another, a speedboat without a slip. She tried but simply could not find the right man. Just into her thirties she was without one. And being unmarried in the police world was such a hassle. You fought off unattractive single men and attractive married men, so that when Max came along . . . Now, she was thinking not so much about when it went wrong, but when it had ever been really right. There were those trembles in the shadowed light of the bedroom candle. That counted, for Nora that counted big time.

Sammy took out his pad and pen, began to draw little boxes in big ones. "You own a safe-deposit box?"

"Oh, yeah. He's been there, cleaned me out."

"He had a key?"

"Uh-huh."

"What was in the box?"

"Jewelry, some good things, my mother's things."

"That it?"

"My old service revolver, the .38 Smith."

"You're kidding?"

"I only wish I were."

All New York City cops own at least two guns, some own more. The service weapon, the one carried on duty, had been prescribed for years. A .38 revolver, Smith and Wesson, or Colt. Nora never loaded her old service weapon without remembering a story from a summer a few years back. A uniformed cop had been in a gun fight out in Rockaway, trapped behind a car with his six-shot pop gun. 'The perpetrator was armed with a thirteen-shot automatic' as the media phrased it. The perp waited for the cop to try to reload, then walked across the street, smiling, the cop nervous, scared, dropping his bullets on the ground, his shaking hand unable to slide the rounds into the chamber—father of four, shot dead. Then the PBA's drive to get uniformed cops a more modern weapon, an automatic, to give the cops a fighting chance. Nora was one of the outspoken superior officers in support of the idea. Now she carried her Glock 9mm in her attaché case. A good gun, fifteen-round clips sliding in fast. She had stashed her .38 six-shot revolver in the safe-deposit box.

"You'd better hope he doesn't go out and sell it to some wacko."

"I know."

"You do?"

"Of course."

Sammy was nodding, thinking. Then stopped. "You need to go back to the office and do up a 49 and a 61. Get something down on paper. Cover yourself, babe, do it."

"I'll give it a day or two." Nora said as she poured them both tea. "If I don't have the gun by the time Jean-Paul comes back from his conference, I'll do the paperwork."

"Nora, you have your share of enemies in that building across the street. Don't give them something to beat you with. Don't do that, it's not smart."

"I know, I'll take care of it."

An image came into Nora's mind of the stern men in brass and braid at headquarters. Each one with his own hidden agenda. Nora had learned the hard way to watch out for other captains, her competition for promotion. The backslapping and backstabbing life at police headquarters would make Machiavelli blush.

"So, you got what," Nora said, "three weeks left of terminal leave?"

"That's it, about that. It's a sad thing to see what happens to a cop when he throws in his papers. Freedom, boredom, and then death. My future in a nutshell."

The mental pictures of Nora's own future rose and fell of their own accord, bobbing on the waves of what could be, scary thoughts that were scattered and fragmented. She never gave much thought to retirement. Of being without her work, of being alone. She had few friends on the job, and fewer outside. Despite all the attention she received, in her heart

Nora could not fool herself. She knew the truth. Other than her sister and niece in Rhode Island, she was alone in this world. Sammy said he read somewhere that most retired cops die within five years after they pack it in.

"You know," he said, "it makes sense. Everybody's out of shape, bad hearts, no exercise, years of job stress and bad marriages, drinking, eating lousy food, your heart blows its top."

Nora stared at her soup and tea.

"Let me ask you a question," she said. "We know each other ten years. Now, be straight with me, I'm serious here, be honest."

"Yeah?"

"Ever think of me as a heartless bitch? C'mon, be serious, ever think of me as that?" Nora looked straight at him. "What I mean," she said, "I mean, no one knows me better than you—you know—I seem cold, unfeeling, and heartless to you?"

Sammy kept quiet.

"Well?"

Sammy shrugged.

Nora said, "The hell does that mean? Shrug your shoulders like that, want to tell me what you mean by that?"

"What do you want me to say?"

Nora said, "What are you saying, you saying you see me as a heartless bitch? Is that what you're saying? Because if that's what—"

"Hold it," Sammy said. "Wait a minute, time out. Max the A-hole calls you a heartless bitch and you want me to confirm or deny it. What's wrong with you?"

"Well?"

"Well, what?"

"What am I talking Chinese, you think I'm a heartless bitch, or not?"

"You're no heartless bitch."

"Thank you."

"Then again, no one will ever confuse you with Mary Poppins."

Nora laughed, "No, no I guess not. What the hell am I going to do without you?" she said. "My hero, my star is leaving me."

Sammy's face flushed, he smiled, saying, "If I'm a star, you're a constellation. You'll manage and I'll be around."

"Decided what you'll do?"

"Go to Europe for about eight weeks, when I get back, we'll see. I hate the idea of this PI jazz, it's not me. Then again, what else is there?

I don't see myself working in an insurance company taking crap from some snotty-nose twenty-six-year-old. I'd go nuts."

She said, "I am going to miss you." He nodded and said, "I won't miss you, not for a minute. You drove me crazy."

She smiled. "Did I really?" she said. "Drove you crazy, huh?"

"Well, sort of." After a moment he said, "How come we never . . ."

"Huh . . . ?"

"You know."

"What? Oh, Sammy, you're not serious?"

"What am I, chopped liver? I'm not saying we'd follow through, but we never even discussed the possibility."

She laughed that away, saying, "My mother was right. She told me, you know what she said? she said, men always will think like young boys, their little heads ruling their big ones."

"Yeah, well," Sam said, "it's what makes the world go around."

"What does?"

"Love, affection, sex. Maybe not in that order, but we all hang by those three threads."

"Ten years, and this is the first time I've seen that side of you. I don't believe you, you're a happily married man."

"Not so happy. Anyway, it's not like I didn't let you know."

"The man under my bed."

"Waiting."

"Eat your soup."

Three hours later, in the storied Brooklyn neighborhood called Red Hook, Nicky Ossman arrived home to the sound of the telephone in the kitchen. He made his way through the hallway, worried. Passing Tino's room he could see the boy napping, arms spread wide, feet crossed at the ankles, Tino's head obscured by a pillow.

The phone was one of those old-time jobs that hung on the kitchen wall, heavy and black with a quick dial. The tone was set low, barely audible. Nicky picked it up, thinking, twenty to one it's Irma, and heard, "Where the hell you been? Don't tell me you went rustling, I don't want to hear you went rustling. Whenever I need you you're not around."

Yes, indeed, dear cousin Irma.

"Come over, will you? I need you," she said.

"Afternoon, Irma," he said. "It's about time you got home. Have a good night?"

"Good night? No, I did not have a good night. Don't tell me anything, okay. Just come over."

Nicky looked out the kitchen window, the bright day had faded and now the sky was low and dark. Outside a fine light rain was being blown against the windows. He lived in a 108-year-old tenement and on days like this it seemed to Nicky that the rain was coming in through the walls.

"Give me a minute to check on Tino."

"The door's open, I'll be in the shower. Hurry up, will you?"

Nicky walked back to the bathroom drowsy and irritated, wondering what kind of jam Irma had got herself into this time. In the bathroom he splashed cold water on his face, brushed his teeth and brushed his hair, feeling better—not great, but better. One of these days cousin Irma is going to come home in a bag, he thought. She was pushing it, staying out all night, running around with hard guys, mean fuckers. He looked in on Tino again, the boy was rolling around, maybe just half asleep. The book he was reading lay at the foot of his bed. When you were twelve years old, Nicky thought, did you take afternoon naps?

What time was it, three, three-thirty? Nicky decided that he would tell Irma one more time, enough. Hanging out with those jerkoffs over at Paulie's. Gimme a break.

As he started to leave the apartment, Nicky remembered his watch, so he headed back to the bathroom to get it. Nicky never went anywhere without his lucky watch. A gift from his acting teacher, Norm Streeser, a failed film producer and a personal friend of Martin Scorsese. Streeser had told Nicky that one day Nicky would be a film star. He looked in on Tino again and saw the boy sitting up, watching him. Tino's mouth working as if he wanted to tell him something.

"I've got to go across the hall for a minute, Tino," he said, leaning into the room and speaking sharply. "Get up and wash your face, sleep now you won't sleep tonight. I'll be right back."

Tino blinked, open-mouthed, then rolled himself into his bedding, saying, "I don't feel good. My stomach hurts."

"What did you have for lunch?" Nicky asked walking into the boy's bedroom. "Pizza, right?"

Tino nodded.

"And you drank chocolate milk?"

Tino didn't answer.

"How many times do I have to tell you? You have a delicate stomach, delicate. You don't drink milk with pizza, especially chocolate milk."

Tino waved his hand.

Nicky found Irma in the shower.

When she had phoned he had been tempted to lay down the law, to say, enough of your bullshit, Irma. He had his own life to live, he was up to his ass in problems of his own. But Irma had sounded scared,

44

crazed, and upset, on the edge of crying, and sweet cousin Irma never cried.

Nicky stood in the bathroom doorway and watched Irma shower through the transparent shower curtain. Irma moved the curtain aside and said, "You're my cousin and my friend. Two hundred and fifty dollars, Nicky, a night's pay, you know I can't sustain losses like that, I just can't."

Nicky leaned up against the doorjamb and said to Irma, "Keep this up and your only friend is going to be your shadow. You are wearing me out, babe."

She told him about going over to Paulie's afterhours club around midnight, all these guys shooting crap, high on something. He could barely hear her over the sound of running water. "What?" he said.

"This guy from out on the Hook," she said, "a pal of pea-brain Paulie, he told me he had no money. After I do my thing. I mean, I give the trick the full treatment, thank you very much, the whole tour, a complete ride, and when I ask for the money he tells me to go and fuck off. Made me feel like some street whore off Fourth Avenue."

Irma stepped from the shower and toweled herself off. It was an awkward and embarrassing moment for Nicky. But not for Irma, who stood with her hands on her hips, her breasts staring at him like a pair of pointed bicycle lamps.

"This trick," she said, "had a roll of cash this big, Nicky. I mean, he had the money."

Nicky had known Irma all of her life and thought of her as a kind of off-beat and sweet kid sister. She *was* a kid, twenty-three years old, and, sure, there were some who'd say she was none too bright, but she had a way about her. Almost innocent. Kind of decent and clearheaded. Never looking for trouble but trouble always somehow found her. Nicky figured that Irma either had a high tolerance for the deranged or she was too stupid or too fucking crazy to be scared.

He watched her shake her head slowly, staring at him. That's when he saw her bloodshot eye, and swollen cheek starting to turn blue.

"What happened to your face?"

"What happened to my face?"

"Don't stand there naked and pissed off answering me with questions. Put something on and tell me what happened."

How Irma had got herself into the whore business he couldn't say. But seeing her standing there he could understand why the girl made bucks. Slim and small-boned, a pretty, child's face. He looked at the tuft of blond hair between her legs and thought of all the men that had put their dicks there. It was not a pleasant thought. Still, he held on to it, the thought of all those guys banging away on Irma. Irma, seeing herself as a hair's-breadth away from being a star hooker, with dreams of breaking into the big time. Moving from South Brooklyn to the Dakota, shopping at Saks, eating at Lutèce, giving a little head in limos instead of in afterhours clubs and gypsy cabs. Irma's fantasy.

Irma dried herself and took her robe from the back of the door. She told Nicky it was the worst experience of her life. Rape was what it was, this creep raped her. "If you don't pay a whore," she said, "it's rape, you can be busted." Irma went on, "This guy, this friend of Paulie's, was one mean bastard. And, he had this little dick." Irma holding her thumb now, putting on a little show, wiggling her thumb around like some sort of finger puppet.

"Look, Irma, in your line of work these things happen. C'mon," he tried to console her, "it's three o'clock in the afternoon. You should go to bed and get some sleep."

Irma said, "This guy was an animal, Nicky, he slapped me around."

"Who was this character, you know his name?"

"Blaze, Blaze is what they called him."

"Blaze Longo?" Nicky said. "You screwed the anti-Christ?"

Irma said, "Am I supposed to know what you're talking about? Is this guy a priest or something? He sure didn't act like no priest, and let me tell you, I know how priests act, I've done my share—of priests, that is."

"Did Paulie say anything?" Nicky said, "It's his club. Paulie is responsible for what happens in his club, right?"

"What is Paulie going to say? Paulie didn't go with me, this guy did. This guy, Blaze, with the cash."

"You tell Paulie?"

"Yeah, sure, what's he gonna say? The guy's gambling, he's making money off the guy, he don't care what happens to me."

"There's rules, it's his club, he's responsible."

"So what do I do, sue him?"

"Irma, what do you want me to do?"

"Talk to this guy, Blaze, talk to Paulie, get what's owed me."

"I'm not your pimp, Irma. I've told you a hundred times, don't make me your pimp."

"He slapped me, he slapped me hard."

"Jesus."

"And he kicked me."

"What, where, who kicked you?"

"Here." Irma hiked up her robe and flashed Nicky her butt. "That guy kicked me." She paused and turned away from him, "I don't deserve to be treated like that, like something you use and then kick."

"You figure they're still there? It's getting late."

"Still there? Sure they're still there, they stay at Paulie's till the action dies. They're there, bet on it." Irma laid a hand on Nicky's shoulder, "Go ahead," she told him, "Paulie respects you and if that creep, Blaze, is still around, come out of your psycho De Niro bag, that'll get him. Do the—'You talkin to me, Are you talkin to me?' thing. Scare the shit out of him."

Nicky nodded, his stomach tense.

"You know this guy Blaze?" Irma said.

Nicky nodded again.

"A bad guy, huh?"

Nicky nodded.

"I could tell, a regular mad-hatter. I think we should forget it. I'll take the loss, it won't be the first time."

"He kicked you, huh?"

"Hard, he kicked me hard," she was close to tears again.

"And Paulie knows? You told Paulie?"

"Paulie was standing right there. He thought it was funny, they all thought it was a joke, laughing and pointing."

Nicky studied Irma, turned her around, stared at her butt. His mother used to say, Flesh and blood, you and your cousin are like brother and sister, flesh and blood.

Nicky stood for a long moment in the bathroom, rocking back and forth. When he walked into the hallway, she called after him, "Where you going? Nicky, it's okay, really, it's no big deal. I'll get over it."

He didn't answer her.

"See, look what I did, I upset you now. Nicky, Nick," she said, "I love you, you know that, right?"

"Do me a favor," he said, "don't love me so much. All right, look," he told her, "I have a chicken in the refrigerator, make a soup, everything you need is there. Tino hasn't had a decent meal in days."

47

"Sure, sure, Nicky, I make a great chicken soup. I'm famous for my chicken soups."

"That you are. Among other things, you make a good soup."

It was hard for Nicky to imagine Irma getting kicked around by Blaze and Paulie. He decided that he'd take the walk over to Paulie's club. See what the hell Paulie and Blaze found so funny.

Five minutes after leaving Irma, Nicky hit the street, hands in the pockets of his jacket, chin aimed at Court Street. He walked past the ILA union hall, the fish market, the Roma Cafe. At the corner of Fourth Avenue he turned into the block. Three four-foot women in black were scooting along the street like a flock of penguins heading toward St. Anthony's six o'clock, Italian mass. Their eyes lifted as Nicky went by, smiling. The rain had stopped but the sky remained dark and overcast.

Nicky was not very tall, not short, either. He was of average height, with darkly handsome features, almost sinister. Reddish brown hair and opaque, smoky-black eyes. As his cousin Irma said, You look like a killer, it's not your fault, it's what you look like. I know that sounds the way it sounds, it just happens to be true. You know that.

Although Nicky knew and was known by most of the neighborhood outlaws he steered clear of them, tried to stay out of trouble. As a kid he fantasized about being a gangster, Pacino in *The Godfather*, but common sense told him, forget that shit, it's not for you. Sure, there was money in it—money and jail time. Jail terrified Nicky.

Besides, being a hoodlum meant that chances were pretty good that you'd take orders from morons. And sooner or later you'd get your head handed to you by other morons looking to make a name for themselves. Nicky, on the record as a guy who was in great shape and could handle himself. A guy who would do a safe score once in a while, but never someone else's violence. If Nicky was going to make someone bloody, it would be for his reasons and never for money.

He stood for a moment in front of Paulie's building, considering options. The afterhours club was on the parlor floor of a four-story apartment house much like his own. Four stories of cream-colored brick that went up in the 1890s. Nicky climbed the brownstone steps and walked into the foyer, pushed Paulie's bell, and waited. In recent years Nicky had taken to carrying a switchblade knife. It was a prop, carried mostly for effect. Still, if the need arose, he could use it. The heft of the mean weapon felt somehow comforting in the pocket of his jacket.

Paulie, when he answered the door looked perturbed, tired, and curious. "Nicky, the hell are you doing here?"

"Came by to shoot a little crap," Nicky said; he walked past Paulie into the hallway.

Paulie was a big man, fat. And he walked with that tranquil rolling shuffle peculiar to big men, his eyes slightly downcast, his body concealed by a blue shirt that was more like a tent and hung to his knees.

Paulie looked at Nicky. "Why are you here? You never come over. What the hell are you up to?"

"Paulie, you telling me I can't come in?"

"Of course not."

"I understand that my cousin Irma was here," he told Paulie. "I heard that she did a little comedy skit, broke you guys up. Irma was a big hit, gave everyone a laugh."

"I hope you didn't come by looking for trouble, Nicky. Because if you did, let me give you some free advice . . ."

"Paulie," Nicky said, "free advice is worth what you pay for it. Irma's my cousin, Paulie, you know that. She's like my kid sister. You know that, Paulie."

"Irma makes your heart go pitter-pat, is that what you want to tell me? Who you kidding? She's a hooker, man."

"That's all right," Nicky said.

Paulie nodded and looked away.

"You come over here," Paulie said, "with some evil in your heart you'd better have a gun in your hand, because that man inside is one bad sonofabitch. He violates people, and he's not here alone."

Before Nicky could answer he heard the door to Paulie's club open and a voice say, "What the fuck?" Standing in the doorway was Blaze Longo. Blaze had the look of an all-night loser on his face.

In the land of the South Brooklyn tough guys, Blaze Longo was a snake among snakes. His story charmed the most famous outlaws. Nicky knew he was evil for hire, vicious as they come, the species at its most evolved.

"Nicky the Hawk. Jesus, Nicky," Blaze said in earnest, "what the hell are you doing here?"

"Hey, Blaze, how've you been?"

"Nicky, Nicky, Nicky, man, it's been what, three years?"

"More, more like five."

Blaze looked slim and sunburned, prosperous. His eyes wide open, black, shining bright with the light of cocaine. Still wearing his wild, Mexican mustache, he was a bit of a dude in a green silk shirt turned up at the sleeves, and black slacks. And of course, those boots of his. His hands were large and callused, his fingernails cracked and stained with grease. Blaze spent his days at work in his body-and-fender shop, a place, where it was said, he hurt people. Nicky knew very few men who made him feel any sort of fear. Blaze, whom he had not seen for at least four or five years, was one of them. Seeing Blaze again, the wacko standing there in his steel-toed boots, made him feel anxious and tense. But Nicky knew that Blaze understood he was no pushover and that pleased him.

Nicky moved past Blaze into Paulie's apartment. Paulie was saying, "You two guys know each other?"

No longer packed with swarms of hang-out guys, the club was fairly quiet. Nicky took a stick of gum from his pocket and put it in his mouth as he looked around. The club was a four-room-railroad tenement flat whose interior partitions had been removed, leaving one large space decorated with walnut paneling and a dropped ceiling with recessed lighting that was set dim. There were tables for cards, a roulette wheel, and a crap table. Posters of Las Vegas, Tahoe, Atlantic City, and Foxwood decorated the walls, adding a little color to the otherwise drab decor. The tables were occupied with what he could see, about a half-dozen familiar faces and that many again of people he didn't know.

After his eyes became adjusted to the light he exchanged indifferent glances with the patrons. Nicky felt conspicuous amid the gathering of Italian knits and tasseled loafers and shimmering running suits—the look of neighborhood cool. Along one wall was a banquet table set with sandwiches, a keg of beer, bottles of wine, and a machine that made coffee by the gallon. A stereo was playing. Bobby Darin, doing "Mack the Knife."

When Paulie and Blaze emerged from the hallway they both appeared genuinely glad to see him. Paulie saying, "Blaze and Nicky the Hawk. Man, what a combo that must have been. You two guys worked together, man, what a combo. I can't believe it."

And Blaze said, "Pier 1, the Grand Colombian Line. Used to be real busy, ships coming and going. We were checkers, made a whole lot of money, right, Nicky? We did good."

Nicky grinned, pretty sure Blaze had already told Paulie the whole story. Wondering now if the nutty bastard told him about the wino.

"There was a time I wanted to work the docks," Paulie said, "went to the union hall, talked to Joey Legs, said he'd fix me up. I thought I'd do something with the union, but it wasn't my cup of tea."

"Should have called me, I would have hooked you up," Blaze said.

Paulie shrugged. "Getting back to Irma, Blaze, here, didn't know she was your cousin."

"Is that right?"

"Nicky, what can I say, I figured she was some bimbo. Anyway, Paulie musta forgot to tell me." As he talked Blaze used his eyes and hands to shift his attention from Paulie to Nicky. "Hell, man," he said, "if I'd a known she was your cousin . . ." Sounding amazed.

"Blaze, she's a woman. You don't kick women." Nicky put his finger on Blaze's chest. "It's not nice."

"Nicky, Nicky, fucken Nicky the Hawk, missed seeing you around, buddy." He moved Nick's hand aside. "Okay, tell me, what do I do?"

Nicky paused. "She's owed some money."

"It's true," Blaze said, "you're right, Nicky. What's she get?"

"Two fifty from you, two fifty from Paulie. That second two fifty is a fine, Paulie."

Paulie said, "What're you talking about?" Bewildered. "What fine?"

Blaze laughed, saying, "Pay him, Paulie."

Nicky watched Paulie shake his head, slowly, giving him a stare. Paulie went into his pocket and took out a roll of bills, peeled off five hundred and held it in his hand. Nicky saying, "Very nice of you, Paulie," with that innocent look, Paul Newman doing Butch Cassidy. Except Paulie wasn't listening. He was staring hard at Nicky, trying to back him down with a look. "This is your club, Paulie," Nicky said, "you're responsible for what happens here."

"Give it to him," Blaze said, "what the hell you waiting for?"

Paulie folded the money and handed it to Nicky.

"Nicky," Blaze said, "you remember the wino?"

Nicky didn't say anything.

Blaze said, "Paulie, let me tell you about this guy, this shitbird, ragbag troll lived in a box under the highway at Van Brunt. The troll would creep down to the pier every morning, begging and moaning, you know? Anyway, Nicky, here, is buying him coffee, rolls, shit like that. I'm telling Nicky the guy's stealing, I saw him lift a package right in front of me." Blaze looked up and stared at Nicky intently, his eyes focusing on him with great scrutiny.

"The bum shows one morning, Nicky was late coming in. Right, Nicky, you were late?" Nicky nodded slowly.

Blaze saying now, "The bum's running around driving everybody nuts. Finally he finds a place to squat behind some containers. It's my spot, I got this old chair back there, he knows it's my chair, he knew it was my chair, Nicky. Anyway, the bum sits in my chair and takes a piss. Right in his pants, right on my chair. I go off, I mean I lose it, I lit the fuck up."

Paulie glanced at Nicky. "You what?" he said.

Nicky said, "He burnt the old man, poured gasoline on him and tossed a match."

"He lived to piss himself another day," Blaze said. "It wasn't all that bad."

Paulie held his grin for a long moment, waiting. He said, "Jesus."

Blaze said, "I got in the wind. When the cops came they snapped Nicky up. Nicky just got there, right, Nicky? You walked in and the cops snapped you up. Held him for two days, Nicky never said a word. Stand-up guy, this Nicky."

Paulie said, "Je-sus Christ," shaking his head at Blaze. "You are one crazy sonofabitch, Blaze, I'll give you that, you're fucking nuts."

"You watch your mouth, fat man. I'll turn you into a candle, fat as you are you'll stay lit for a week."

"Honest to God," Paulie said, "I was kidding."

Nicky said, "*For God's sake, let us sit upon the ground and tell sad stories of the death of kings.*"

"There he goes," said Blaze, "the actor."

"Huh?" said Paulie.

"Shakespeare," Nicky said.

Paulie nodded.

"Nicky," Blaze said, "you should come around and give me a shout, I'm doing good. Need a job or something, come see me." Blaze winked and held Nicky's hand a long time, and Christ, Nicky felt goose bumps. Nicky saying, "A *nod is as good as a wink to a blind man. Dominus vobiscum.*"

"Fucking Nicky," said Blaze. "You are a kick."

Blaze and Paulie exchanged looks.

So far things had gone pretty much as Nicky thought they might. His easygoing style caught people off-guard, always helped him get up close. You didn't want to come into a joint like this screaming, jumping up and down. You act like that and no question people would get nervous, tense, and tight, ready for some action. You had to get them to smile a little, relax them. Then it was a matter of picking a target. Now he had one.

He had thought about it and decided it would be foolhardy to go at Blaze. The guy was a lunatic. One lunatic he could handle, but Blaze was not alone. It would be Paulie, Paulie knew Irma lived in his house, under his flag. Still, the fat man saw fit to abuse her. It would be necessary, Nicky thought, to teach a lesson here.

"I have to go back to work," Paulie said, giving Nicky a tight, thin smile. Nicky saw it turn before it disappeared.

Nicky was standing with his back to the wall, his right hand instinctively in his pocket gripping the switchblade.

In the next instant Nicky's left hand lashed out grabbing Paulie by the ear, Paulie went shoulder first into the wall then fell to his knees. Blaze took a step toward Nicky then stood there hesitating. The sharp sound of the blade opening echoed in the hallway. Nick straddled the fat man's back, he held the knife alongside Paulie's head.

"You shit, Paulie, I should take your ear."

"What's wrong with you? What did I do?"

"You know Irma's my cousin, you knew." Nicky twisted the ear, pulled it.

Blaze was grinning at him, a small demented grin. "Do it," he said. "Go ahead, let me see you cut him."

Nicky could feel Paulie trembling between his legs.

"Stop it, man," Paulie moaned, "c'mon, you gonna stop."

Nicky pulled and twisted the ear, stretched it, laid the knife in that crease between ear and head.

"Awright, I'm sorry," Paulie said. "Okay, okay, I'm sorry, tell Irma I'm sorry. Just don't cut my fucking ear."

"It's going, Paulie, your ear's going."

"No!"

"I'm taking it, ready, say bye." And very slowly, with a certain amount of care, Nicky twisted and stretched Paulie's ear, he touched the sharp blade to the skin in the crease.

Blaze was staring wide-eyed at the tiny drop of blood that appeared.

A cry came from Paulie's mouth, deafening and uneven, a child's cry.

Nicky closed the blade, playfully slapped the back of Paulie's head and dismounted saying, "You're a dumb bastard, Paulie, but even though you're a dumb bastard you should know that Irma's my family, Paulie. You knew that, she's my flesh and blood. Fuck with her again and I'll take your head."

Nicky winked at Blaze, then walked out the door.

On the top step now, outside in the morning air, the door closed behind him, Nicky could hear Blaze break out laughing. He had a wacky laugh and it lasted with hoots and howls and cursing. Nicky thinking, I made my point and that counts. Heading for home, walking along the street, Nicky experienced a curiously pleasant sensation.

Toward the end of the day Det. Jim Rice from the Safe and Loft Squad came by Nora's office. He handed her a set of keys, telling her he removed the lock from her apartment door and installed a new one with a dead bolt. Nora would have paid him some money, and started to write a check. Rice told her forget it, he had boxes of locks and keys. It was a few minutes before sunset and Detective Rice, who thought that New York City was the most beautiful city in the world, walked to Nora's office window and looked out at the light that was fading over the East River. He stood at the window a long time.

Nora asked the detective if he had traveled much.

"Upstate to hunt, a couple of summers out east on Long Island, that's about it," Rice said.

He was attractive, tall and fair. A German-Irish kid from Maspeth, an easygoing guy who spoke with a clear, clean Queens accent.

"I appreciate the favor," she told him. "Can I get you some coffee, a soda? I don't have too much here, but if you want something I'll get it."

"Nothing, thanks," he said after a moment, turning, looking around her office. Rice busied himself taking in the photos on her desk, the commendations on the wall. He seemed, to Nora, vaguely awkward, as though he were about to defend himself for being in the wrong office. "I should go," Rice told her, "my partner's waiting for me, we got something going down in the Bronx." The young detective turned the full light of his charm onto her with a great big grin. "A captain, huh? Wow."

Within an hour she left the office and took a taxi across town to a movie theater in the Village on Bleecker Street. The ticket taker was a small, thin man who was smoking a cigarette. His hair wasn't combed and he wore a kilt and a sweat shirt with cut-off sleeves. On his upper arm was the tattoo of a penis. Another dipshit.

Nora slouched down in her seat, crossed her arms over her chest and sighed as if it did not matter if she ever got home. During the trailers for upcoming movies, she was thinking how Max had set himself up to be humiliated. What an idiotic man. How could you marry such an idiotic man? You're the fool. When she went to use the rest room, she found the dipshit in his kilt smoking a joint near the candy stand. "That's illegal," she told him.

"There's a level, my lady, on which everything we do is illegal. Then there's a level on which nothing is," he told her.

Nora listened to him without answering, thinking the world's full of them, they're everywhere.

The film was Italian, subtitled and sad. A story about an older woman's obsession with a young man, her secret lover, how their passions built and then their lives unraveled. Nora thought the older woman a fool, and the young man reminded her of Detective Rice. During the love scenes, which were many and quite graphic, Nora found herself breaking into a slight sweat and squirming in her seat.

Around nine she stood in front of her apartment door nervously taking her keys from her shoulder bag. Not because she was afraid of bumping into Max, but because she wondered, had been wondering all night, if her will would remain strong. If Max walked up to her now and insisted on coming in she would . . . what? yell at him, chase him, carry on in the hallway. Nora wasn't sure, when it concerned Max, she was never sure. Her new key in hand, her hip pressed against the door, Nora unlocked the dead bolt. Once inside, the door closed behind her, she turned, closing it with her hand, making sure it was locked.

There were six messages on her answering machine, one from Sammy, all the rest from Max. Sammy called to remind her to report the loss of her gun, "Don't waste time," he said, "get it done." Max threatened and cursed her, used words she hadn't heard in quite a while. Words, just words.

Nora stood for a moment in front of the bathroom mirror giving her face the once-over. She had to wonder how people actually saw her, her reflection affording her a certain amount of comfort. Her look, as she called it, had changed little during the past ten years. A mirror's a wonderful thing, she thought, it never lies. You look young and unspoiled, lucky you. She smiled and pinched her cheek, with her index fingers she pushed at the corners of eyes. She looked Asian and Nora liked that. Her mother once told her that Nora's eyes were a caution, warning away the weak and unfit.

In the kitchen she took a glass and filled it with apple juice, walked into the bedroom and turned the radio on low. Listening to a sixties soft-rock song that she had liked. Suddenly she felt a crushing fatigue. Nora undressed, quickly tossing her clothes on his side of the bed.

She got into bed naked for the first time since she couldn't remember when. Her grandmother's great goose-down comforter felt like a lifesaver.

Nora and Max once owned a cat. A black, strong-willed, but skinny tomcat. She had named the cat Frankie Barnes after a famous Harlem drug dealer she'd arrested a few years back. The cat had died from a lung infection. She and Max had talked about getting another, but Max complained about the odors and torn upholstery. Stroking the soft edge of the pillowcase she decided that she'd look for a kitten, missed having something snake around her bed. As she tossed and turned, fighting to fall through the surface of sleep, Nora wondered who in the hell Blaze Longo was, and why did the chief have this Longo on the point of his nose. It was sometime around two, maybe as late as three, when the phone rang once.

''Well,'' Irma said, "it's been my experience that white guys are too controlled sexually, they never really let themselves go."

Nicky watched as Irma moved around the kitchen. Thinking any number of thoughts. That Irma was a helluva cook, a good housekeeper, the chicken soup was remarkable. And he thought momentarily that he ought to think about Blaze and Paulie, about how they would answer his performance at Paulie's club. And then he thought that you cannot undo what's been done, but you'd better be ready. The two clowns would not let it pass, they would not let him slide. And he believed that he had put himself in harm's way, Tino and Irma, too.

Nicky frowned at his soup. The casual way Irma talked about her sex life drove him up the wall.

"I've had one hell of a day," Nicky told her, "I'd rather not have to listen to you going on about your work."

"Who's talking work?"

"You," Nicky said. "I don't like that kind of conversation around Tino, he's twelve years old."

"Let her talk," Tino said. "Irma has interesting things to say. Black guys are what, Irma? More cool, right?"

Irma smiled. "I've never been hassled by a black guy, and that's the truth."

Nicky had called Irma when he returned home from Paulie's and asked her to come over and join them for dinner. At first he thought he'd talk sense to her, then decided, why bother, and just handed her the money. Irma quickly surmised that things went well at the club, that Nicky had handled Blaze and Paulie, exactly what she expected he'd do.

"Irma is an equal-opportunity trickster, Tino," Nicky said. "If you know what I mean."

Tino stretched his big black eyes wide and leaned his chin on his fist. "I don't," he said.

Irma picked up Nicky's plate, was walking to the sink when she spun around and said, "You want to talk johns, tricks, whatever. Okay, we'll do that." Holding the plate in her hand she moved it up and then down. "First of all, a man's color has nothing to do with sex. Anyway, what I do is not sex, it's business. And Nicky's right, this is no conversation for you, Tino."

"And why's that?" Tino said.

"Because you're still a boy," Nicky said. "No matter what you think, you're a kid, kiddo."

"What I know I bet would surprise you, Nicky, and you, too, Irma."

"Ooooh," Irma said looking Tino up and down. "Tino, there is nothing that is going to surprise me. I'm about ten years past surprises."

"What she saying, Nicky? She saying she did it ten years ago? Ten years ago Irma was my age. Irma," Tino said, "you hooked up with someone when you were twelve?"

"Thirteen," Irma said.

"Thirteen!" Tino shouted.

Nicky said, "Cousin Irma ran across Humbert Humbert, and he charmed her. Took our Lolita here and charmed himself right into her business. Another reason why I hate schoolteachers."

"I hope you kicked his ass," Tino said, "I hope you beat the shit out of Humbert Humbert."

"Oh, he did," Irma said, "he surely did," giving Nicky a vague smile.

"Good, Nicky, good," Tino said, "atta boy, that's my Nicky." Tino jumped up from the table, got into a fighter's pose, started dancing around the kitchen, jabbing the air, throwing lefts and rights. His black wavy hair and the gold chain Irma had bought him the previous Christmas flashed in the glow of the kitchen light. He danced around Nicky, weaving and bobbing, shoulders hunched, looking good, looking strong, looking nothing like the bewildered and whipped child Nicky had found five years before.

It was down near the Columbia Street overpass, right at Atlantic Avenue, about a block or two from the docks. Nicky had been making the rounds of a couple of Atlantic Avenue joints. Coming out of the Swedish Seamen's Lounge sometime around midnight, he walked past this old green Buick, windows busted out, tires gone. For some reason he still couldn't figure, he looked in the car. And man, oh, man, there was Tino, wrapped in an army fatigue jacket, asleep on the backseat. Nicky woke the kid up. Tino told him he was supposed to wait for his mother, had been waiting for a few days, a few nights. Then Nicky took Tino home, telling him he'd leave a note for his mother, figuring once he got home he'd call the cops. Nicky never called cops for any reason, thought he'd let the kid stay around for the weekend. Then after a few days he decided, what the hell.

Nicky and Tino returned to the car every day for a month, checking the note. For weeks Tino seemed to blame him for the loss of his mother, nothing direct, just a general despondency about the boy.

As the weeks piled up Nicky felt increasingly sure that Tino should stay with him. Better, far better, then being a ward of the state. The boy knew a phone number and nothing more. And that phone was in the Bronx and had been disconnected. And then for weeks Tino did not mention his mother at all, not even a word.

At times Nicky wondered if he was doing the right thing. The notion that he could raise the boy would not let go. One of the old Italian men from the club on Court Street sent him to Manhattan, to a club in Little Italy where for $1,500 he bought a birth certificate and a Social Security card. That September he registered Tino Ossman for school. Nicky not only shared his life with the boy, he also gave him his name.

Tino was about six years old at the time, and they'd been together now for six years. Tino had no father that he knew. Their present plan was that there was no plan, Tino and Nicky simply lived together. Nicky doing all that he could to be sure that neither poverty nor anything else would ever take them down.

"Someday soon," Nicky said, "cousin Irma is going to put this act of hers down. She's going to get a job, maybe go back to school," he said softly. "Someday," he said, "Irma will make us proud."

"I play the cards that were dealt me, Nicky," Irma said. "Like everyone else, I mean, I do what I can."

Nicky nodded, thinking, yeah, just like everyone else.

''What in the fuck is that smell?''

It was the end of one of those days that feel like satin. A gentle breeze in the early evening, the brilliant sun-filled day now fading into a sweet night and, what's this: a smell, a stink climbing out of the Jersey flatlands, blowing through Staten Island like rotten egg spiced with sulfur-neutron bomb. Jean-Paul Clement, the chief of New York's detectives, more bewildered than angry, closed the windows of his car and turned on the air conditioner. He was driving west through Staten Island, restless and antsy, heading for the Outerbridge Crossing and then into Jersey to Woodbridge, to a motel on Route 440. A motel whose rooms were knotty pine and exposed beams, giving you the impression you were in the Adirondacks, maybe up near Lake George. A place where you could pay for a room in cash and stay for an hour or two. It was the kind of motel where you brought another man's wife.

Jean-Paul had always liked the place, found it when he was a cop on patrol in South Beach. What he liked best were the dark parking lot and double king-sized beds.

Jean-Paul was feeling that particular anticipation now. He was in a bit of a daze, itchy, that delirious, grinning celebration of the exquisite sex to come putting a squirm in his seat.

He glanced at his wristwatch. In twenty minutes Roseann would be

all over him. And Jean-Paul Clement, Jean to his friends, Paul to Roseann, Chief to his subordinates, his underlings, was in a state of high
agitation.

Six-thirty P.M. Jean-Paul wanted to be out of his pants and into hers
by seven o'clock at least, since Roseann had to be home before nine. He
was not happy that she had to be home by nine, not her decision, not
his, someone else's. Her husband phoning from the federal can in Dan-
bury, keeping tabs on Roseann, fucking nerve of the guy. Half-ass gangster
connected to some low-level Mafia crew out of Bath Beach.

It was through the arrest of her husband Sal Palumbo that he'd met
Roseann. Five years ago, a windblown day in February at the federal
courthouse in Brooklyn. He was an assistant chief inspector then, working
a joint federal and city organized-crime task force out of the Eastern
District.

They brought down Sal and his crew, busted about twenty people.
One of those screaming headline cases that kept the media in a tizzy for
weeks and launched Jean-Paul right into the position of chief of
detectives.

The arraignment of Sal Palumbo and his cronies was a regular courthouse media event. Family, friends, journalists, and courthouse groupies
jammed the courtroom, the corridors, and the coffee shop.

He first bumped into Roseann coming out of the coffee shop and
Jean-Paul smiled at her: *Well, hello there.* Roseann stared at him, smartass
cop. And then again in the courtroom, he watched her shake her head,
giving him a killer look. It was a shame, gorgeous broad like that tied up
with a shitbird like Sal. He watched her sitting there, a real beauty, his
mind reeled and his cock swelled at her perfect tan and movie-star good
looks. She sat taking it all in, fingering a dress that must have cost more
than an airplane ticket to Europe. Major breasts, men walking by would
spot her and their heads would swivel. And a small lovemaking sound
would come from their throats like, mmmmm, geeze, mmmm.

Then later, in the corridor, Roseann stood there with the coyote fur
coat draped over her arm, watching him, finally smiling that smile at
him. When he asked her name she told him, when he gave her his card
she took it. He said, "If you ever need to talk to someone, give me a
call." Roseann said, "Don't hold your breath." Jean-Paul asked, "Maybe
we could go for a drink sometime?" Seeing her eyes get wide, giving him
the once-over, throwing out that chest of hers, nervous, but he could see
the excitement there, the interest.

Jean-Paul wasn't surprised to learn that Roseann had once been a dancer. She had a gorgeous body: long, strong legs, one of those high-riding asses, and the wildest laugh he'd ever heard.

He drove along holding his grin, remembering the day of the first phone call and then meeting Roseann later that night down in Sheeps-head Bay. It was the same day husband Sal left to set up housekeeping at the West Street Jail. Sal was a minor wiseguy but a major wifebeater. It served him right, fucked good and twice by the cops. Creep.

They passed that first night driving along the shore into Queens, to a quiet bar in Broad Channel owned by a retired homicide detective. That night she grabbed him in the car. Roseann was hungry, passionate, lonely.

"Why don't you find a place where we can be safe and comfortable tomorrow night," she said to him. "I'll bring dinner."

He knew just the place.

In the light traffic, Jean-Paul drove quickly, like a pro, as he did when he was a young cop right out of the academy. Back then he used the siren, lights every chance he had.

Twenty years since he'd been in uniform and shit how he missed it. He'd got laid all the time, could have got laid every day. Two, three times a tour and more if he wanted—he was a good-looking guy, sharp in his uniform with a sexual compulsion to rival Don Juan. Genes, whatever, he was one of those men that always had luck with women, women never a problem for Jean-Paul Clement. His wife, Bridget, told him he looked like a TV anchorman and she was not the only one. As a young cop starting out, he was the envy of all his friends, sexy with his gun and his cop-combat stories.

Now in his midforties, he was a bit wary because his face was well known around the city. Not like the mayor or police commissioner, but enough people recognized him that he had to be discreet, showing up as he did on TV news about once a week. A married man, father of twin boys, he had to be careful. Give the bastards a chance to nail you and you'd find yourself featured on Page Six, *New York Post*. Still, Jean-Paul was not comfortable unless he was playing in traffic.

Jean-Paul made a name for himself as a great administrator, great detective, and team player. He was politically astute and smart enough to stay away from money, never dirtied his hands like so many he knew. Women, just women, were his only weakness. And now, for five years just one in particular: Roseann Palumbo, Sophia Loren with a Brooklyn accent.

Jean-Paul located a spot behind the motel, pulled in, and parked. Walking toward the motel he found himself drifting again into a revved-up daydream, waiting to be touched, waiting to touch.

Roseann's white Caddy, with her statue of the baby Jesus propped on the dash, was parked near the rear entrance of the motel. He glanced around the lot, always careful, always on the lookout. Christ, he could run into anyone, a cop, some hotshot journalist, a lawyer, some jerkoff he busted years ago. Anyone.

Eight million people in this city and it was like a small town. A face like his, a job like his, they'd remember, bet your ass they'd remember.

Up the back stairs now, Jean-Paul loved the seconds before he saw her. That face, that body, that thick tongue, and those long fingers stroking his cheeks, the rising tension was making him nuts. Roseann loved him and he was crazy about her. Wild guinea broad, great woman, one of a kind, one of one of a kind, born to take care of a man, loving every minute of it. He took the motel's steps two at a time. Each time he came to the motel to see her, Roseann would have a basket of food. Cold chicken, sandwiches made with the best Italian bread he ever tasted. Veal cutlets, peppers and eggs, potatoes and eggs, the kind of sandwiches he wouldn't dream of eating anywhere else in the world. And wine, always a chilled bottle of wine.

He'd come through the door and they'd start right in. Roseann would be waiting in a blouse or a slip, nothing else. She'd grab him, Jean-Paul laughing happily as she pulled at his clothes, pausing only slightly, breathing quickly, and the smell of her, the heat from her would roll over him.

Jean-Paul knocked once on the door of room 240 saying, "Rose, Rosie, it's me."

"Bout fucking time, where the hell you been?"

The door opened and Jean-Paul's face suddenly broke into a grin. He wiggled with pleasure, his eyelids fluttered, and the tire iron in his trousers stood tall.

Roseann cursed him. Roseann Palumbo had a temper that could freeze a feeding lion. She stood there now, saying, "You lying son of a bitch, where's my father? You told me you'd find him. Where is he?"

"Rosie?"

"Get in here and don't Rosie me. Where's my father?"

"What?"

"My father? Three weeks, Paul. Jesus Christ, he's dead. They killed my dad. Christ."

Jean-Paul was thinking that seeing a woman, no matter how beautiful, delirious and frantic could give you an entirely different impression than seeing her calm and under control. Roseann was one of those women who had an expressive face, dramatic almost. When she was happy Roseann opened her eyes wide, stretched them to an incredible size. Same thing when she was angry, but they were changed, as though there was a fire there that nothing could extinguish.

Roseann backed away from the door. She was wearing a pair of black slacks and a red blouse. Her hair was piled high on her head, and her face was all distorted as if she were in some unbelievable pain. She turned away from Jean-Paul. Jean-Paul stood in the middle of the room, hands on his hips, patient. She went over to the table and poured herself a glass of wine.

"Calm down Rosie," he said, "calm down. Your father's running, you know he's gone, I know he's gone. He's running, he's not dead."

"Says you."

"Rosie, I have one of the department's best investigators tracking Blaze Longo, we'll nail him, put him away until the sun burns out. Then your father will come home. He's scared to death, he's running."

"The man's seventy years old, he never left Brooklyn in his life. Running? Where is he going to run?"

Roseann kicked off her shoes, sat down on the edge of the bed and pointed her glass of wine at him. "I trusted you." Jean-Paul said, "I'll take care of it." He sat in one of the chairs across from her. He found that he wanted a glass of wine very badly, but mostly he longed for her to ease up and calm down. "I'd like a glass of wine," he said.

"Help yourself."

Roseann puffed her cheeks and blew out some air the way you do when you don't know what else to do, and looked away. Jean-Paul glanced at his watch. It was already 7:00 P.M. He stood and went to the table, took a glass and poured some Frascati.

Roseann always talked about her father, adored the old cigar chomper from South Brooklyn. Jean-Paul had never met him, didn't know him, only his name, Alfred Nieri, Roseann's maiden name, Nieri. Her father was a small-time gambler, one of those neighborhood guys that never left the corner.

Suddenly he flashed on the old man wrapped in a blanket, tossed in a trunk, and buried in a garbage dump out in Mill Basin. He lifted the glass to his mouth and drank. Christ! He hoped the guy was all right. Who knew what Roseann would do if her father woke up dead. Temper like that. She had never come out and threatened him, but you could never tell. Sometimes she sounded like she would.

"You gave him the money," Jean-Paul said. "You gave it to him. Did he pay his debt, I don't think so. I think—"

Roseann cut him off. "What does that have to do with anything?" Jean-Paul said, "It tells me Alfred took the money and left town, scared to death, afraid to even call. That's what it tells me."

Roseann was silent.

Jean-Paul sat on the bed next to her, tried to think of things to say that would ease her down, make her comfortable, make her see that it was time for her to squirm out of those slacks. "Is Sal going to call tonight?" Softly, friendly, let her know it was getting late.

"He calls every night, he worries about me."

"And I don't?"

"You want to screw me, but I think it ends there."

"Rosie!" Shocked.

"So why are we here? Why do we always meet here or someplace where the only furniture is a bed? You know maybe we could go to a movie sometime, maybe even out to dinner. Surprise me, why don't you?"

"Maybe you're right." Jean-Paul thinking, oh, boy.

"Do you really think he's okay, Paul? Just scared and running?"

He nodded.

"My father hasn't called, hasn't sent word. That's not like him, he always calls me."

"Alfred is scared, maybe he thinks your phone is tapped."

"God, I hope you're right."

Jean-Paul had reached out and placed his hand on her cheek. Roseann smiled at him. That was encouraging; the old Rosie, sipping her wine now, saying it was a nightmare; telling him, as if he hadn't heard it a hundred times, that they disfigured her father, cut his thumb off. A seventy-year-old man. She was dropping the nasty tone.

"Try not to worry," he said, "I know it's hard, impossible maybe, but try."

She made a sad little-girl smile.

"Things work out," he said, "things usually work out. Christ, you know what, babe, it's been five years. Five years and we're still together, still doing our thing. Amazing." That got a nice reaction. Rosie with a big grin, "Our thing, whatever that is, I guess we're still doing it."

Jean-Paul thought awhile and said, "Hell, man, women never interested me until you came along. It was always the job, the job, the job, until you, until my Rosie."

One of his well-worn winner lines. Bingo, it hit a soft spot. Roseann reached over and squeezed his leg. Good. "And if not for those two innocent boys," lowering his head, a sad, sort of why-me wag. "Not for my sons, I'd have been divorced years ago."

"I know. You told me, been telling me for five years."

Jean-Paul believed that women like Roseann, in their thinking, respected men that hung on in marriage. He put his fingers in her hair, that beautiful thick glossy hair, not like any hair he'd ever touched before, so much of it. Thinking, shit, c'mon, what does it matter, what does anything matter, we're here, just the two of us; safe, hidden, and time is flying. "What do you say?" he said, "you want to get comfortable?" Softly, gently, no rush to his tone, a concerned guy who so very much wanted to make her comfortable, wanted to see Roseann get real cozy, out of those slacks, that blouse, that red push-up bra with matching red skimpy panties he hoped she was wearing.

Christ, the woman could be a *Playboy* model with that body. And when she was above him, astride him, that look of perfect pleasure on her face. He loved that, Rosie above him, the way she put her arms in the air, watching her hands open, close, holding those closed fists along her cheeks, jaw tightened until she let out a yelp. Rosie, a shouter.

The way she watched him now pushing the heel of his hand down across his cock. Jean-Paul was a little embarrassed. But, hey, he was about to bust thinking of the pleasure of it, the way he always tried to hold back, not being able to. What did she think he was made of, stone? Picturing Rosie dancing on him now, lap dancing on him, that curve of hip, then leaning over him, brushing those perfect breasts across his chest.

"C'mon," he said cautiously, "c'mon Rosie. I want you so bad I feel like my bones are burning."

"Forget it, handsome. My mind is elsewhere. And don't look so cheated, don't get me angry."

She was a beauty and an actress, but there was always the hint of violence there, something of the snarling avenger.

"You're going to stay dressed?" he asked softly.

"Yes. Do you think I could make love thinking that maybe my father is in pain right now? How could I do that, what kind of woman do you think I am?"

"Oh, shit," said Jean-Paul in spite of himself. "You're going to make me crazy."

She put on that smile again. Look at her, those great big black eyes, that mouth, people spend money, go through enormous pain and suffering to build lips like that. Look at her, saying now, "Paul, Paul, Paul, you'll never understand how I feel about my father. I grew up tough, hard, my mother died when I was a kid. No brothers or sisters, it was just me and my father."

He'd heard this story a hundred times. *Look at the time, look at the time.*

"Men came and went, but I only have one father, one."

"I don't understand that?" he told her. "Of course, I understand."

She wagged her head. "Anyway," she said, "I'm counting on you, if you can't help me . . ."

His heart was pounding at a terrific rate, the tire iron was about to tear a hole in his trousers, he was in agony.

Jean-Paul shook his head, with a blink of curiosity he thought of Capt. Nora Riter. Nora was in the street out after Blaze Longo, he wondered how she was doing.

Thinking, now that was another woman, his captain, Nora Riter, one terrific investigator and another gorgeous woman whose legs he would not pry open anytime soon.

In his mind Jean-Paul called Nora elbows, she was always pushing herself ahead. The thing was, her ambition never exceeded her ability.

"So, tell me," Roseann said, "this investigator you sent out after that shit, Blaze Longo, this woman, is she any good?"

"Believe me, having Captain Riter on your ass is like waking up on Christmas morning and finding a live cobra in a box under your tree. She comes beautifully wrapped, but man . . ."

"A good-looking woman?"

Jean-Paul nodded.

"More attractive than me?"

"Are you kidding? I said she was *attractive*. She is not in your league, honey."

Roseann lifted her eyes to him, vacant of all expression. With that thick tongue she licked her upper lip. "Take off those pants," she said.

The following evening, Nora arrived at her office a few minutes before seven. She had spent the day at Brooklyn South detective headquarters, going through their computer, talking with detectives, making herself familiar with what little information they had on Blaze Longo. The precinct detectives and the squad's commander would engage her from time to time in small talk about her assignment.

Nora was as artful at small talk as she was at many things. The precinct detectives made seemingly innocent probes, but clearly they were curious. She was sure to be polite and pleasant, making assurances that she was working a case and not on any inspection tour. Twice during the day she telephoned Sam at home but did not reach him. Before heading back to Manhattan she stopped at the front desk and picked up the summons report and arrest record on the character with the lamb, Nick Ossman.

Back at her office she kept running the last exchange with ADA Devlin over and over in her mind. The way Devlin sat looking at her, coolly, as though he had her number. Nora had to remind herself that she represented Chief Clement. If Devlin was skeptical of the chief's motivations, he certainly felt the same about her. Cops and DAs see conspiracy in a moonlit night.

Sitting at her desk going through Longo's rap sheet she felt tired and irritable. Max had her gun, but no bullets, she was certain. How tough would it be to get a box of .38s? About as complicated as buying the morning paper.

After a time Nora picked up the telephone, as she tapped out Sam's number she let loose a great sigh. The phone rang two, three times. When Sammy answered, she sat back in her chair and closed her eyes.

"Sam, it's me. I think I have a real problem."

"Yes, well, don't we all. That's how we get through this life, one problem after another." He sounded pleased to hear from her and she felt grateful.

"I've got to get the gun back."

"Yeah, right. And the jewelry, too. Maybe the dickhead is going to hold it all for ransom unless you let him back in."

"No chance."

"Listen, Nora, the guy's lights are out, but Max is not stupid, he knows he can jam you up."

"He got to the savings and checking. I can live with all that, even the jewelry. But the gun, my damn .38, that worries me."

"I'll go to the apartment in Queens. He's there, the jewelry's there, and your gun, too."

"You can't do that."

"Why not?"

"Because I won't let you. Listen, you're on terminal leave, in a couple of weeks you'll have your pension. I don't want you doing anything that will jeopardize that."

"I'll just talk to him."

"You can't do that."

"Why not?"

"Because he won't talk to you. He hates you. Come to think of it, Max hates every man I ever worked with."

"Are we working together now?" said Sam.

"No."

"Are we partners any longer?"

"C'mon, that doesn't matter."

"Does Max consider me a threat, you know what I mean, romantically speaking, does he see me . . . ?"

"No, no I don't think so."

He was quiet a moment, then Sam cleared his throat and said, "I rest my case."

71

"Let me think about it," she told him.

"Call your lawyer," Sam said, "and then let me know what you want to get done. You want to do something, right?"

"You bet. It's the 'what,' that's the problem."

"So that's why you called me? You want me to tell you what to do next."

"I know what I have to do. I should go to Queens myself, look him in the eye. Get my gun back."

"You put your finger on it. Get to him before he sells everything, hocks it, or whatever."

"I'd have to deal with the woman, him . . ." Nora stood up from her desk, took the phone, and walked to the window.

"Listen," she said, "I'm responsible for safeguarding my weapon. I did that, had it in a safe-deposit box."

"True," Sammy said. "Trouble is someone else had a key. There are people that would say that's not safeguarding, that's careless. Nora," Sammy said, "this husband of yours is a pain in the ass, he's out of his head, and he's dangerous."

"That's true."

"So, believing that . . ."

"What?"

"You can't just sit on your hands, you have to do something."

"Think about it, Sam. Help me make a decision here. Would you do that for me?"

There was a knock on her door. Patrolman Rogers, the night-duty man was standing there. Rogers held a message in the air, Nora nodded to him and as Rogers came into the office he handed it to her. Nora, asking Sam to hold on a minute, took the message, read it, and said, "Chief Clement is not coming back to work until Friday. That gives me what? including today, four days."

"Well, what do you want to do?"

"That's why I called you."

"Good enough, let me make a call or two. I'll call you at home later."

"What are you thinking?"

"Something, I'll let you know. Listen, you remember Jimmy Ceballos from narcotics?"

"Sure, he's bad news. What about him?"

"He owes me one."

"Yeah?"

"I'll let you know. Listen," he said, "speaking of nut cases, I picked up an intelligence folder on Blaze Longo for you."

"Terrific, where did you get it?"

"OCCB. Wait till you see this stuff. This guy's an out-and-out psycho. He kills people, Nora. This is one bad dude."

"Great."

"See? You think things can't get any worse."

Nora left the office a little after eight and went home and took a shower. She was thinking about what Sam had said about Jimmy Ceballos, about Blaze Longo. Sam coming through again and coming up with a good one. Ceballos a major hotshot and every kind of weird. Nora knew that in narcotics they talked about him as being a cop's cop. A real hardass. What could Sam be thinking? Last she heard, Ceballos was still in narcotics. She was amazed the guy was not in the can.

Nora stood naked in front of the mirror for a long time drying her hair, considering what clothes to lay out for the next day. She decided on her long jean skirt and silk blouse.

Nora had three silk blouses, red, green, and navy blue. She'd wear the green. The other two, she knew, were at the dry cleaners. She could use more blouses and more skirts. She thought of doing some shopping over the weekend.

When she tried on her blouse, her nipples tingled and ached, and she felt a twinge in her stomach, she thought that her period was late, again, as always.

Nora brushed out her hair then squirted some lotion on her palms and massaged it into her legs using both hands. Waxing hurts, it kills, Vera had told her. She thought about the photos of children on Vera's desk. Nora decided that chances were pretty good that she would never have a child. She realized that she'd been thinking a lot about that lately. It was not a good thought, the thought of being without a family. It frightened her, made her feel alone. But she had to admit the quality of life with Max was worse, far worse than being alone.

When Nora had come into her apartment she'd found a message from Max. Max using the cunt word again, a word that tightened her jaw, made her think that cops like Sam and Ceballos were good to have on one's side.

Nora took off her silk blouse and put on a T-shirt, her running shoes. Naked from the waist down she went to the telephone, checked the time, and called her sister in Rhode Island.

Nora stood leaning against the bedroom wall listening to her older sister Lilly complain about finding a decent job. Lilly told her what the president had said on TV about the job market growing, how prosperous the country was. "Unemployment was markedly down," Lilly said. "Well, you could have fooled me, the man's dreaming. The country's a mess and that beetle brain doesn't see it." Nora felt she was listening to her brother-in-law, Jed. It seemed that Lilly's ex-husband's spirit had come to inhabit her sister's brain and body. A wailing, complaining, lazy-shit caricature of a man, Jed never worked a day in his life. Lilly, her voice still heavy with distress, asked about the weather in New York City, mentioned that Wickford was already bracing for the coming tourist and summer-people season.

"Taxes have gone through the roof thanks to those fool New Yorkers. They come up and build these huge, ostentatious places sending real estate taxes sky-high."

"Max walked out," Nora said.

"Good for you, keep him out this time, will you? How the hell you ever hooked up with that loser is beyond me. He looked like death warmed-over at Thanksgiving. A filthy mouth. I wouldn't go near a man like him. Loser."

They talked about Lilly's daughter Maggie.

"Jed is still sending the money. I don't know where he gets it and I don't care. These WASPs got family money and Jed will pay through the nose to keep Maggie in private school. He's happy to keep on paying as long as she doesn't live with me. Max have any money?"

"Are you kidding?"

"A loser, that's all Max is. A loser. You know he told me this filthy joke. A mature man, talking about tits and pussy. He wanted to tell one in front of Maggie. I said, "Oh, no, you don't, my daughter will tell her father and then what will I do?"

"Max thinks of himself as a comedian, a joker," Nora said, wishing she had postponed this call. Lilly was making her tired.

"A joker! Maybe that's what you think. I don't. I think he's about as funny as cancer."

"Well I have a lawyer, a good one. I changed the locks, I'm not letting him back. *Fini* for Max. Listen, he cleaned out my safe-deposit box, got mom's jewelry. I might get it back, but I wouldn't count on it."

"The bastard. The rings and bracelets, that necklace with the pearls?"

"All of it."

"Well, serves you right."

"What do you mean by that, sister?"

"You never should have given him a key. A loser like that, a key to your treasures."

"He took my spare gun, too."

"Good, good, maybe the loser will shoot himself in his filthy penis."

Not filthy, Nora wanted to say, probably the best part of good ol Max. What she did say was, "C'mon. The guy's screwed up, a real mess."

"A l-o-s-e-r, I told you years ago. Remember?"

"How could I forget? Lilly, can you send me some money?"

"Sure, what do you need?"

"A couple thousand."

"I can send you fifteen hundred."

"Fine. Thanks, love you."

"You, too."

Not long after she hung up with Lilly, Sam called, it couldn't have been more than five minutes later.

"You have plans tonight?" Sam said.

"I'm going to bed. I've had a helluva day, I'm beat. Did I tell you that I pinched some character yesterday morning, busted this joker for stealing a lamb."

"Excuse me?"

"Right, a lamb from the wholesale meat market on Flatbush Avenue, he took the whole damn thing, hoofs and all."

"You busted him?"

"Gave him a summons, a desk-appearance ticket."

"Busy lady."

"That's me."

"I thought maybe we could get together with Ceballos, I set up a meet. Thought maybe you'd like to sit down with the guy."

"What for?"

"Talk with the man, see what he has in mind. Listen, maybe he can be of some help."

"I don't want anything to do with a guy like Jimmy Ceballos. What are you thinking?"

"How about I have Jimmy tell you?"

"You tell me."

"He works Queens Narcotics."

"I know that. So what?"

"All right, aright. Look, Max is shacked up in Queens getting some pink with his chippy, right?"

Getting some pink meaning sex. A phrase she had never heard Sam use before. She didn't like it.

Ten years in the police department working hookers, pimps, drug dealers, working with foul-mouthed cops, Nora had heard all there was to hear. It was not something she liked to hear, filthy language. And hearing it from Sam did not inspire her with too much patience, either.

"Sam!"

"Sorry. Anyway, your husband is laid up with this chick, he's got your jewelry, your gun, and you can bet he's got some coke."

"C'mon Sam, what the hell are you driving at? What do you have in mind?"

"Narcotics gets information that there is cocaine, a gun, and whatever at a location. What are they supposed to do? They watch, get a search warrant, and hit the place."

"Hold it."

"Listen, listen, Jimmy and his team hit the chick's apartment. Once inside they give us a call. We show up, you and me . . ."

Making Max, her own husband, the subject of a search warrant filled her heart with despair.

"I don't think so," Nora said. "I don't like that idea at all."

There was a knock at the door. Not a knock, really, you could hardly call it a knock, it was a bang! Then another, and another and another. Bang! A pause, then, bang! bang! bang!

Sam said, "The hell's that?"

"It has to be Max."

"Oh, Jesus," Sammy said, "don't let him in."

A long moment of silence then—Bang!

"What's the matter?" Sam asked. "Hey, do you have your service weapon?"

"Yes. Sam, c'mon it's only Max."

"Bang! Bang!—Bang, bang, bang.

"I'd better get the door, this is ridiculous. What the hell is he doing? Listen, I'll call you right back."

Then she hung up the phone. Sammy yelling, "No, no, what the hell *you* doing, keep the phone off the hook."

Bang! Bang!

"Okay," she called out, "I'll be right there."

Nora went to the dresser, opened the bottom drawer and took out a pair of running pants and quickly slid into them.

She drifted toward the apartment door, wondering what she should do. For a split second she considered taking her gun from the attaché case. She stared at the door, thinking a gun for Max, be serious. She knew Max well enough to know that such a thought was ridiculous.

Through the peephole she could see Max looking around the hallway as if he were preoccupied; with a curious little grin. For a moment it seemed to Nora that there was no sound anywhere in the building.

"Open the door, c'mon, please. I feel like a moron out here. Open up, will you? I can see you, you're there, I see you, open up. Don't leave me standing here like some . . ."

He stood there with his hands in his pockets, the lines of his mouth stretched into a pout. It was the look you saw on a child's face, a spoiled child. As she opened the door Max grunted.

"I've come for some of my things."

Finding herself calm, under control, Nora took three steps back into the kitchen, motioning with her hand for him to come in. She managed a small smile. "A helluva thing you pulled at the bank. I didn't think you would do that. How could you take my mother's things, all that was left of our money? Real lowlifes behave that way."

Max closed the door behind him then followed her into the kitchen. "I figured you'd say that, and know what, I don't give a shit."

"My mother's jewelry and my gun, I want you to give them to me."

"My mother's things, my gun," his voice got high, like a woman's. "I earned that money, that money is mine, it's what I charge to be tied to a castrating bitch. A bitch, I might add, who is thirty-four years old, and still does not know how to give a decent blow job."

"My gun, Max, I want my gun."

Max grabbed at his crotch. "Women like you, all women like you want is a man's balls," he shouted. "How much of my balls do you want?" Now he had two hands on his crotch. "This much? No, you want more, more, more . . ."

He removed one hand from his crotch and put it in his pocket, made the sign of the gun.

"Listen, Max," she said softly, "calm down. You're a smart man, one of the brightest men I've ever known. You know that things aren't right for you any more than they are for me."

"Shut up, you cunt!"

"Listen to yourself. Let me help you, I want to help you." She wanted to help him all right, she wanted to help him out the goddamn door, out of her goddamn life. Shit, she'd known the man almost seven years, married to him almost six. And not once in all those days, months, and years had he ever used language like that. Behaved like this. Grabbing at his balls like that, then his hand in his pocket, as though he would shoot her. All this off-the-wall behavior, it could be the drugs, it could be, but she doubted it, more like a symptom of madness. That's it, Max was breaking down.

Nora felt, in a very small way, that if things stayed relaxed and tranquil she could deal with him. "Hon," she told him, "listen to me. C'mon, now, please, calm down."

"I'm calm, I'm calm. Want to see what's it's like when I really lose it. Would you like to see that?"

Nora's heart was racing and cool tracks of sweat began to roll down her back. "Max," she said, "you have my gun. Let me have my gun." She tried her soothing, I'm on-your-side voice. And in truth she was usually very good at it. Max lost it.

"You want your gun, I'll give you your gun, bullets first, how's that?"

When she looked at him she saw craziness in his eyes, not even a hint of control. His pulse was beating in his neck. For the first time Nora began to be convinced that Max could truly be dangerous.

"Max . . ." She gestured with her hand for him to back off. Then she tried to pull away as he grabbed her by the arm.

"How's it feel, now it's your turn in the box. How's that feel? Change the locks on me, who the hell do you think you are?" Max's eyes going wide now, wild crazy eyes, screaming now, "For Christ's sweet sake, I deserve some consideration, just a tiny bit of understanding and pity. I thought you loved me . . ."

Nora pulled her arm away. "Let go of me," she said, "just keep your hands to yourself."

"What are you going to do, arrest me?"

"If you give me no choice."

"Try it and see what happens."

Nora said, "Okay, what do you want here? Whatever it is, take it. Take what you want and then get out."

"Get out!" he shouted. "*I* should get out!"

She could have tried to move toward the bedroom, made a stab at going for her attaché case on the bed, but he was coming at her now. And he was making an odd face, smiling, well, sort of smiling, as though this was all a gag, a prank, or something. Nora put her hands on her hips and stood her ground. "What in the hell do you think you're doing?" she said. Max hit her in the face, an open-handed slap, then pushed her with both hands. Nora stumbled backward, her knee gave way, and she fell against the stove.

"Now wait a minute . . ."

"You think I'm nuts, huh? You're wrong," he said quietly, his voice all of a sudden calm.

Nora decided that the best thing to do was to keep him talking, see how that went.

"You've got the money, that's ten thousand dollars. That's a whole lot of money."

"It's peanuts, it's nothing. And that other shit, the jewelry, most of it's costume."

"It is not."

She turned her head a split second, one of those silly-ass mistakes a rookie would make. Never, they told you, no matter what, ever take your eyes off the suspect. She did, and just like that, he had her.

Nora could see a perceptible pleasure rising into Max's face. Then a high, shrill laugh, a nutty laugh. He brought his hand back curling it into a fist, dropping his shoulder, he came up fast, driving his fist into her stomach. "Costume! Costume! Costume!" he yelled at the top of his lungs. "Not worth shit. Like you, just like you, phony!"

Nora went down, on her side, pulled in her knees, hunched up, chin tucked in, her arms covering her face and head. "Please, Max," she cried out, "you don't want to hurt me, I know you don't."

Evidently she was wrong since it seemed that Max was having the best time of his life.

When Max had taken hold of her there was a moment when she might have hit him, caught him in the throat, or on the jaw with an elbow. She nearly did. But Max was a lot stronger than she'd thought, and quicker. Max stunned her with his speed and strength.

Nora and Max stared at each other for a moment. He was a man consumed with righteous indignation, a kind of aggrieved fury. An executioner.

Max worked Nora over; even with his limp-wrist, open-handed jabs to the face he did damage. But the kicks really scored for him, to her shins, to her sides, the kidney with the heel of his boot, a left-footed kick to the face, a stomp that drew blood from her nose and mouth. Max flourished a cowboy boot in her face. Portraying precious little sympathy for her cries, eyes rolling back, he shouted, "I don't want to hurt you, but you make me hurt you, you force me to hurt you, you cunt."

She thought the kicks would kill her. Her body seemed so soft, even after all that running, all those days in the gym, judo training.

She would remember how she started to tremble all over, and how she began to blackout. When he shouted that he would kill her, she fainted.

When Sam arrived at her building and found the door to her apartment unlocked, when he went inside and found Nora curled on the kitchen floor, when he helped her up and took her into the bedroom and laid her on her mother's goose-down comforter, it seemed apparent that Nora was not going to die.

Sam thought she had a broken jaw and maybe a few broken or cracked ribs. But her teeth were solid and in place, and after a half hour or so her breathing became easy and regular. By the time she was able to walk and Sam got her to his car and drove her to the emergency room, there was no doubt that her wounds were superficial. Her face looked like hell, lips swollen, left eye half shut, and the skin on her cheek raw and scraped.

Six stitches in her lip and butterfly bandages for her eyebrow; a painful tetanus shot and some locals. A very attractive and very young resident telling her, "You're lucky, no ribs are broken or even cracked." The doctor giving Sam a look, Sam saying what the hell are you looking at?

Finally, back in her apartment, back in her own bed, Sam saying, "I told you."

Nora nodded.

"You shoulda shot the prick."

"Right, shoot Max. Perfect."

"I know how you feel. You should have shot him, anyway. But, no, you could handle him. He's really a decent guy gone a little batshit is all."

"Okay, Okay."

He rubbed her cheek gently, then ran his finger around her lips. Nora felt a curious shyness as he touched her.

"Bastard," he said. "Real hero."

"All right already."

"I'm not done, you have to stop fucking around with this guy. Leave it to me and Jimmy Ceballos, we'll set his hair on fire."

"I don't want to see his hair on fire, Sammy," Nora said and paused. "Though I've got to admit, it's an interesting idea." A searing pain as she tried to roll onto her side. Nora saying, "Sam, all I want is my gun, my jewelry, and a divorce. For better or worse, that's all I want."

Sam helped her along by the shoulder and hip. "Would you please let me handle it," he said.

"Geeze," she said, "I'm hurting. I suppose I underestimated Max a little."

"A little?"

"I want to meet with Ceballos myself," she told him.

"Yourself, yeah, okay. You don't want me with you?"

"Of course, I want you with me, I just want to be there when you talk to him."

After a moment Sam said, "I canceled tonight, we'll wait until you feel up to it."

"A day, maybe two, I'm not feeling too well."

"No kidding. I wonder why?"

''She's at the Roma," Tino said, referring to the Roma Cafe on Court Street. "Irma told me to tell you she'd meet you there." He spoke quietly as if confiding a great secret.

"C'mon, you're kidding me? I thought she was going to give it a rest."

Tino looked helplessly to Nicky, "Irma never rests. I am not kidding, Nicky, she had a busy day." Tino held up three fingers. He took a huge bite of pizza, grinned, and wagged his head. The boy was excited by it all, nervous, apprehensive.

They were in the kitchen of Nicky's apartment, Tino was seated in front of an open white box containing a pizza with extra cheese, onions, and mushrooms, one of Tino's favorite meals from Rizzo's. Rizzo's was this pizzeria around the corner owned by a Greek named Paul. Greek Paul had a kitchen where he made entire Italian meals that you could carry out. Now and then Rizzo's was Nicky's answer to the pressure of making dinner.

"Want a slice?" Tino said.

"No, thanks. Did you charge the pizza?"

"Irma gave me a twenty. She came in here, kissed me on the cheek, and gave me twenty dollars. Then she told me she was going to the Roma and you should meet her there." Tino was worried that Irma was careless and that she was working too hard. The way Tino put it, Irma was always running around, she never slowed down. "Man," Tino said, "she had three guys here today, Nicky, three."

"You saw them?"

"No, she told me. A triple-header, she told me. A three-bagger, is what she said, a hat trick."

"Geeze."

Tino followed Nicky through the apartment all the way to the bathroom. The boy was disturbed, really frightened, which wasn't like him.

"Have you finished your homework?" Nicky asked him.

"This is the last week of school, there's nothing going on, no homework, no nothing. Irma, Nicky," Tino said, "what about Irma?"

"You have books to read, plenty to do. I gave you the list."

"There's ten books on that list, I ain't reading ten books. Nicky, Irma looked scared."

" 'I ain't reading ten books,' " Nicky mimicked. "You have *The Legend Of Sleepy Hollow* and *White Fang*, finish those two and then we'll talk about the other eight. Irma," Nicky said, "always looks scared. It's part of her charm."

Tino was the kind of kid that walked around the neighborhood as if he were the coolest dude ever came down the pike, with baggy pants, the inseam hanging down to his knees, shirts way too big for even Nicky to wear, white high-tops and a Knicks hat that he pulled down around his ears, always walking with his head down giving people a funny look.

Tino looked like a street kid, a tough guy. The truth was the boy was shy, preferring to spend his time with his music and reading books and watching videos of old-time movies. W.C. Fields threw the boy into rolling fits of laughter with hoots and howls. He watched *My Little Chickadee* about nine times. Loved to do Nicky doing his Fields number, "Any man who hates small dogs and children can't be all bad." Tino once told Nicky that he thought there was a whole lot of Mae West in Irma. Nicky told Tino that Mae West was a genius.

Sometimes, when Tino read the books Nicky gave him, he'd sit still for hours, as though he were passing into a trance.

"Christ," Nicky said, "why does she want me to meet her at the Roma? She tell you? What in the hell is Irma up to now? Three," Nicky said, "Irma turned three tricks today?"

Tino held up three fingers one more time. Nicky noticed again that the boy was panicky. "You're going to go there, right?" Tino said. "You're going to the Roma."

"What the hell, Tino? What the hell is she doing? Why does she want me to meet her there?"

"I don't know why, Nicky. Irma didn't tell me, so I don't know." Tino was staring into the bathroom as Nicky washed his face, brushed his hair. "But you're going to go, right?"

Nicky made his way into his bedroom and changed his shirt. He took off his sneakers and jeans and put on a pair of slacks, socks, and loafers. He could hear Tino breathing through his nose. The kid was a nervous wreck.

When they returned to the kitchen, the boy began to spin like a top, hands on his hips. Tino couldn't stand it. "C'mon, Nicky, go. Go to the Roma, she needs you there."

"I'm going," Nicky said. "Listen, Tino, stop worrying about Irma." He nodded at the boy and headed for the door. Nicky took one step, turned around, and said, "I told you and told you, Irma's life is her life, not yours, not mine. We love her, fine, that's fine, she's family. But we can't live her life for her. Can't do it. If we try she'll make us both batty."

"Irma needs you, Nicky, she's waiting."

"Yeah, kid, I know."

It was seven o'clock when Nicky got to the Roma Cafe. He came through the door, waved to the bartender whose name was Jackie O.D., looked around, did not see Irma, and took a seat at the bar.

The place was quiet. People hadn't turned up in any real numbers yet, a few couples seated at the tables in the rear. Nicky sat alone at the bar. An unsmiling, short Hispanic man wearing a blue running suit, work boots, and a ponytail stood at the juke box, studying it. Nicky ordered a Coors Light, from the tap.

He'd had a tough couple of days, right from yesterday morning, that woman cop, and the lamb. What a circus. But to be honest about that he considered himself lucky. Sure, he had to spend the entire day and half of the night at the precinct listening to a bunch of cops bullshitting about this and that, but, man, it could have been worse. He could have spent a night in the slammer, maybe more than one, probably more than one.

Nicky put his elbow on the bar, rested his cheek in his hand, and glanced around the Roma with one eye. He was thinking about one of the cops' look of longing at that woman captain's ass when she'd walked by. The way her skirt clung to her. You know, he thought, a woman wears clothes like that, moves like that, she's got to know what men are thinking. He thought, as she closed the cuffs on his wrists, nice hands, soft and long fingers. He thought of some wonderful things he'd like to do with that body, imagined with equal and simultaneous joy the captain saying, "Okay, why not."

Nicky imagined himself a ladies' man with clear-cut talents and thus felt entitled to think such thoughts.

Yes, indeedy, getting to know that captain, her name off the summons, Nora Riter, had helped to make the day go easier. But then after she had left he had been forced to sit around while the cops took their goddamn time to give him a summons. What could he say? What could he do? The way Nicky saw it, he came away with a lucky break. Now, he wondered, what were his chances of running into her again? Nicky thinking, O Captain! my captain! you were one fine-looking woman. The thought of Nora Riter clung to his mind and would not let go. Even today, running around in Manhattan, trying to find some work, coming up dry, the picture of Nora Riter held fast to him.

"Jackie," he said, "have you seen Irma?"

"She's here, went into the ladies' right before you came in." Jackie's face was flushed and his lips were wet, Jackie dipping into the stock.

He saw her come out of the restroom, arms folded, walking quickly, head down. His eyes followed her across the room and then as she sat down next to him at the bar.

"What's going on?" he said.

Irma put a hand on his shoulder and kissed his cheek. "Blaze, that guy from Paulie's, he sent word to tell me to tell you to meet him here."

Nicky made a sour face, "Screw him," he said, "I'm out of here."

Then Blaze, all smiling and friendly, came through the door. The bartender Jackie O.D. whispered, "Shit."

"Nicky, Nicky the Hawk," Blaze said and sat down beside him. He removed a package of cigarettes from his shirt, looked up then down the bar and carefully removed one, offered Nicky the box. Nicky told him he just quit, which was not true. He had stopped smoking years ago and still sometimes felt the pain, especially in the morning with coffee. Someone once said to stop smoking was as painful as losing the love of your life, and Nicky believed it.

When Blaze sat down, Irma moved away from the bar.

Blaze said, "I'm glad you showed, I'm real happy." He smiled and waved at Irma, rolled his shoulders, and rapped his knuckles on the bar, saying, "Hey, O.D., a cranberry juice with top-shelf vodka for me. What'll you have, Nicky, name it."

Nicky lifted his glass of beer.

"Another beer for the Hawk here." Blaze lit his cigarette and went on. "One thing I was thinking is that we should hook up, me and you. I mean, I got zeros and zips under my employ, you hook up with me I make you the big kahuna, my main guy, I'll bury you in cash."

"The big what?"

"Kahuna, that's Hawaiian."

Blaze was a bad memory, some character from a horror movie Nicky had seen years ago. He tried not to think of the old man, the wino Blaze had burnt. He tried not to think at all. "Hawaiian," Nicky said, "thanks but no thanks. I got enough problems, more than I can handle." The trick was to appear uninterested and friendly, no easy task. A trick.

"Nicky, I want you to come and work for me."

"Doing what?"

"What I do."

"Which is?"

"Hang out, I'll give you a glimpse. It's no big thing, nothing too crazy. But you'll make cash, plenty. You won't be a souljah in Blaze's army, I'll make you one of my generals." He gave Nicky a spacey smile.

Nicky smiled and wagged his head. "Right," Nicky said. And he thought, Right after I finish eating this box of snails.

Jackie O.D. brought their drinks and laid them out.

"Blaze," Nicky said, "you know me, I do my best to stay away from your part of the world. You do your thing, I respect that, that's fine, I do mine." Nicky turned his head as far as he could trying to keep an eye on Irma. Irma stood whispering and grinning to the little guy in the running suit. Irma on the hustle, going for four.

"Nicky," Blaze said, "you know the other day, I stood up for you. Let you slide. Anybody else turn one of my people into a stumblebum I take their head off."

Nicky didn't say anything, so Blaze said, "You know that's true, buddy, people lose respect, lose the fear, they weaken you. I can't have that."

Nicky knew that he had to sit and listen to this nutjob for a while. Fair enough, he thought, I'll give him ten minutes, then I'm out of here.

"So," Blaze said, "what are you gonna do, spend your life being a bust-out jerkoff? An actor, some silly shit, what's with that?"

"I do other things, too. I live my life, I get by."

"Taking little bullshit jobs here and there, watching out for Irma, being a pimp like some *nigga*."

"Don't say pimp, Blaze, don't say that."

Blaze put his hand on his shoulder and spoke softly, "Nicky, I do and say what the fuck I want."

"I know who you are, Blaze. What do you want from me?"

"Hang with me, brother, I'll show you where it's at. I'm gonna be famous."

"You're already famous, bouncing people around and shit like that. I'm not interested in that. I'm no hard guy."

"Nothing, nothing, that's nothing. And, don't tell me you're no hard guy, I've seen you in action, man. You're a crazy bastard just like me."

"Not like you, Blaze, there's nobody like you. You are one of a kind." He tried not to remember the stink that day at Pier 1. The sour smell of the harbor, gasoline, smoke, burnt upholstery, burnt flesh. His face going pale remembering.

Blaze smiled and nodded and sipped his drink, saying, "Let me tell ya, there's all kinds of money out there in these streets. All we gotta do is go and take some."

He sat there listening to Blaze talk and didn't know why he didn't just get up and leave. The guy was smiling to himself about something, hearing voices maybe, maybe Blaze heard voices. The man was like some bad actor that you sat and watched and listened to because you couldn't figure out how to get up and go. Like you had to sit and suffer through his one-man dingdong show. White man affecting his black man rap, a nut factory.

"C'mon," Blaze said, dropping a twenty on the bar, "let's me and you take a walk. I don't like talking in here."

Nicky could feel Blaze's eyes on him, he turned away and drummed on the bar, thinking, times in your life you know just what to do, other times . . .

"What's the matter, you too busy?" Blaze said.

"No, no. I had a bitch of a day," Nicky told him, "I'd like to get home and grab some sleep."

"It's not even eight o'clock."

"Yeah, I know. I'm beat."

"C'mon, we'll only be a minute." Blaze took Nicky by the arm. "Let's go, we'll walk and talk, like the old days. Man," Blaze said, "how come that seems like such a long time ago?"

Nicky shrugged and raised his hands, he turned away from Blaze's nutty, happy smile. "Because it *was* Blaze, it was. Irma," he said, "I'm going to take a walk with Blaze, here, then I'm heading home."

Irma put her hand to her mouth and blew him a kiss, the short guy in the running suit and work boots was smiling.

Out on Court Street neither of them spoke for a few minutes until Blaze said, "Like I said, we gotta hook up. I love the way you scared the shit out of Paulie yesterday."

Nicky laughed. "I wasn't serious, Blaze. I was playing with him."

"Maybe," Blaze said, touching his arm to make his point. "Don't matter, bro. You were the man, you ruled."

They walked along Court Street. Half a block from the Roma a sanitation truck with a man hanging from its rear end rushed by. Two teenage boys came out of the video store on the corner whooping and hollering. Blaze turned to the noise. "Working stiffs and assholes. We're better than that, Nicky, me and you, we're better."

"I don't see myself better than anyone, Blaze. I'm a realist, I know who I am, what I'm about. See, that's what you got to understand. I'm a realist, a man that understands his place in this world."

Blaze took hold of Nicky's arm by the elbow and squeezed. "C'mere," he said, "come over here, I want to show you something."

He led Nicky into the hallway of an abandoned building, Nicky wondering what in the hell the guy was up to, he found out soon enough. Blaze removed a leather string pouch from the back pocket of his trousers, loosened the top, shook the contents a bit, and said, "Look at this."

Nicky took a peek and said, "Shit, what the hell are they?"

"Ears."

"Excuse me?"

"Whadaya deaf?" Blaze was laughing now, a wacky, no-brain kind of laugh. "Get it, what are you deaf?"

"Whose ears?"

"Assholes, I got a bag full of assholes' ears."

"Jesus, Blaze. Jesus."

"C'mon, what's the big deal, you were ready to take Paulie's the other morning. I saw you, Nicky, I was there. That's when I knew I had to have you with me."

Nicky straightened. "How many?"

"I dunno, wanna count em?"

"No, thanks. Listen, Blaze," Nicky said, "Maybe you should consider attending an anger workshop, maybe get a little electroshock therapy."

Blaze said, "Shit," and walked back out onto the sidewalk, saying, "C'mon, c'mon."

On the sidewalk now, Nicky thinking, a net, someone had better drop a net on this character. Thinking, this is one evil, mean, crazy sonofabitch.

A blue-colored Buick pulled into the block and stopped ahead of them. Fat Paulie got out along with two other men Nicky had not seen before. Paulie said something to the other two and they stood back leaning against the car.

Blaze put away whatever smile played on his face, looking at Nicky now as if he'd ambushed him. "Okay, mister realist," Blaze said, "I'll tell ya what's real. You listen to me now and I'll tell ya."

Nicky reached out and delicately took hold of Blaze's shirt. "Silk," Nicky said. "A nice shirt, you're doing good. Don't waste your time with me, you got more important things to do."

Blaze seemed to like that. He smiled. "I want you to think about my offer, Nicky. Think hard."

"Hey, Blaze, c'mon, be serious. You know me, this bad guy nutty shit is not for me."

"You afraid of going to the can, right? I know you, you were always scared of the joint."

"Blaze . . ." weariness edging into his voice.

"I'm hooked up, Nicky," Blaze said. "You'd be amazed how hooked up I am. With me you'd be counting money, never days in jail. I'm hooked up, Nicky. I'll amaze you."

"Nothing about you amazes me, Blaze. Nothing."

Blaze shrugged as if it didn't matter. "Right now I'm the master of your destiny," Blaze told him. "I unleash those three, you're chop meat."

Nicky glanced at Paulie, saw him smiling at something one of the other two said.

"The way I see it," Blaze said, "you're either with me or I gotta teach a lesson here. You understand?"

Nicky shrugged and looked up then down the street. Everything along the avenue appeared to have stopped. Or at least to Nicky it seemed that way. "Pilgrim," he said, "a man's got to do, what a man's got to do." Giving Blaze a little of John Wayne, see if the Duke could ease some of the tension here.

It seemed a long time before Blaze answered him.

"Then you're on your own. I'm washing my hands of you."

And Blaze did just that, a kind of wiping of his hands in the air, a signal.

Fat Paulie and the two other men moved away from the Buick and began to walk toward him. Blaze cocked his head and looked at Nicky in a curious way, as if trying to figure what could not be figured.

Nicky was smiling and Nicky knew that it was the wrong time to smile. He could see Blaze the nutjob looking at him from his spot in a parallel universe. It was right about then that Nicky heard voices and when he turned, he thought, what the hell?

Tino was coming along the street, his head up, his shoulders moving like a dancer. In his right hand Tino was carrying a baseball bat. Trying to close the distance behind him, but unable to, was Irma. Cousin Irma not able to keep up, unable to move nearly as fast as Tino, in her high-heeled shoes.

What Nicky heard was Tino and Irma both calling his name. When the boy got to the intersection Tino hesitated, looking down Sackett, the crossing street. Nicky turned away, frightened now, and looked to see what Blaze and Paulie and the two men were doing.

The baseball bat was black and Tino was holding it in the air now, pointing with it, pointing at Nicky. "Hey," he said. "Hey, you guys, maybe you could use this, huh? Play a little ball with me." Tino standing next to Nicky now, doing a little something with his shoulders and his lips, putting on a tough-guy look. Tapping Nicky with the bat, handing it to him.

Blaze stood still, throwing Nicky a grim, confused look, saying, "Who the hell is this street rat? You don't mind my asking?"

Fat Paulie and his two pals took a step toward them then hesitated. Nicky pointed the bat at Blaze and said, "They come near me I'm going to drive your head to Flatbush Avenue," doing a little of Stallone, doing *Rocky* 3, when he was cocky, the heavyweight champ. Blaze stuck his arm, his hand out, like a traffic cop, telling Fat Paulie and his pals to stay put. Nicky walked toward Blaze, about a bat's length away.

Blaze turned sideways, keeping an eye on Nicky, glancing at Paulie. He appeared unsure of himself, his mind wandering, weighing things.

"So who's the punk?"

"Excuse me?" Nicky said.

"The kid, who's the kid?"

"His name is Tino, Blaze. He's my son."

Blaze didn't answer, he gave a long hard look at the boy then turned and walked to the Buick. Blaze motioned with his head for Paulie and the pals to get in. They got in the car, Paulie behind the wheel, Nicky saying, "See you around." Paulie saying, "Yeah, and when you do you better hope you have a bulletproof ass."

They drove off, south, down Court Street. Nicky stood perfectly still watching as they pulled away, slapping the bat in the palm of his hand, watching until they made a right into Third Street.

Nicky would remember the look on Tino's face, that grin spreading, wide, wider, the eyebrows dancing. "Whew," Tino said, "that was a close one, eh, Nicky?"

"That it was," Nicky said.

Irma walked forward placing her hands on Tino's shoulders. She looked deadly serious, saying, "I don't know if that Blaze is dumb or just stupid. But he scares me Nicky, he scares me a lot."

They stood there, the three of them catching these strange looks from passersby, while Nicky told them that it was smart to be scared of crazy, dumb people.

"You told him I was your son," Tino said.

"I did, didn't I."

"I like that."

Nora called into headquarters the following morning and reported herself sick at home. Her clerical man, Officer Howard, said maybe I should notify the chief?

I'll call him, Nora told Howard. Officer Howard saying now that the chief was out of town, at an OC, an organized crime conference in Philadelphia. Howard said it was a problem, had always been a problem when the chief was out of town. People called, all kinds of people called, media people, other agencies, they wanted to reach him, but the chief left word to phone him only in case of an emergency. Saying this to Nora who was his superior officer.

"I understand. But you can give me his number," Nora said and waited. There was a moment, some hesitation. Nora said, "Officer Howard, give me the phone number where Chief Clement can be reached."

"I'm in a bad spot here, Captain. The chief left word . . ."

Nora's head was splitting, she brought her fingers to her forehead and held them there, saying, "Let me have Chief Clement's number." With that infuriating feeling that she'd had enough of this Patrolman Howard's prissy bullshit.

"Well, Captain . . ."

Nora spoke softly, carefully. "Howard," she said, "have you ever been to Far Rockaway? A nice beach community, they tell me. Or maybe you'd prefer Staten Island? What's the toll on the Verrazano nowadays, five, six dollars? I'm going to count to three. One . . .''

Sam came by in the afternoon, he brought her some food from T.G.I. Friday's and hung around an hour or two. They considered calling the chief in Philadelphia, telling him about Max, her gun. The department rule was clear enough, you lose your gun, you inform your superior officer. And that was just for starters.

Nora was unsure what to do. Sam convinced her to wait, give it a day or two, see what happens.

The third day, that Wednesday, her wounds healing well, she told Sam to reach out for detective Jimmy Ceballos. Sam phoned the narcotics detective at home telling him that Captain Riter would like to meet with him. Ceballos said, "Just tell me where and when."

That Thursday they all met a few blocks from the Queens Narcotics Division headquarters, at a coffee shop on Hillside Avenue. It was early in the evening, sometime around seven. Nora was wearing a kerchief and sunglasses, but she couldn't hide her mouth, her torn lips.

Jimmy Ceballos was tall, well over six feet, and very thin, you could say frail, with a long narrow face, and extraordinary eyes that put Nora in mind of a hyena. As best she could Nora explained the situation to the narcotics detective. Ceballos listened carefully and stared at her in a way she found vaguely irritating.

Listening to Nora, nodding his head, serious, no problem, he'd find the gun, snatch it, and then return it to her. No one would know she'd ever lost it.

Ceballos was as calm as Nora was nervous. She knew that there were violations of the Rules and Procedures here. She knew it, Sam knew it, and Ceballos knew it, too. Nora also understood that once done she would owe this guy big time. Detective Ceballos would have a captain in his hip pocket.

Yet, in that very moment she felt somehow reassured. Nora was forming an unholy alliance, of that she had no doubt. Down the road this narcotics detective would come to call in his chips. Guys like Ceballos always did. Nevertheless, she had thought it through and didn't see any options.

Nora sat silently listening as Jimmy Ceballos spoke in that quiet comforting way cops do and she paid silent homage to that most-sacred commitment of the police: the blue wall of support and silence. The narcotics detective talked about how something petty and trifling could blow you out of the water, screw you over, and ruin a good career.

He was close to being right and Nora said as much to Detective Ceballos. Ceballos shrugged gently, to overemphasize the fact that they understood each other.

Earlier she had felt defiant and angry, convinced she had every right to protect herself. Why shouldn't she? Nora telling herself over and over, if you were a man, would you sit still for this crap? Getting banged around and abused like that by a guy like Max? Bullshit on that, baby, *bullshit*. You are nobody's victim, nobody's punching bag. You allow yourself to roll over and you'll get crushed. It was a matter of survival.

But sitting there in the coffee shop, looking at Sam, listening to Jimmy Ceballos, her defiant mood passed and suddenly she felt a little lost and depressed.

Look at you, you're a captain in the chief of detectives' office sitting in a coffee shop asking a dark favor from the kind of detective who had a reputation for being serious bad news. And for what? To protect your career? Assuming your career was worth protecting, is this worth it? Hunkering down like this, plotting and planning to save your hide, scheming like some mobster?

Absolutely.

Still, as she sat looking at Ceballos she wished she could think of something else to do instead of what she was doing. Nora did not like being part of the conversation, had never been a part of a conversation of this kind before, as though she were a criminal. She hated the thought and feel of it. As if she had crossed an invisible boundary. What she was asking wasn't illegal but it was close. All because pathetic Max lost his mind and disappeared off the radar.

"Don't think me impolite," Ceballos said. "But I'm curious, you're not going to have a problem if we have to collar this guy? Your husband, we may have to bust him."

"I don't know," Nora said. "I'm not sure." She folded her arms and looked around the coffee shop. The thought of having Max arrested did not please her. At the same time, things were being set in motion here, things that certainly could lead to Max being dragged off in chains.

Like Sam, Ceballos was an old-time cop, saw the world through those eyes, us and them. And according to the mysterious rules of cops Max was a *them*. It was the accepted wisdom, you pick up your hands and hit a cop—you're one of *them* in spades.

"I could talk to him," Ceballos said. "You know, come at him both ways. Reason with him, and if that don't work, threaten. I can threaten, man, it is what I do best. Scare the shit out of people."

"Maybe." Nora said, "I suppose it's worth a try. I can't be in any worse shape than I am already."

In the end they decided Ceballos would play it by ear, see what he found, see how it went.

Once satisfied that Ceballos seemed to understand her position, Nora felt more composed. Everyone started relaxing, recalling their days working the Narcotics Division together.

Ceballos smiled and turned to Nora saying, "I heard you're being groomed for big things."

Nora laughed, thinking, right, just like a horse, a claimer.

They spent the rest of the evening talking options. Ceballos agreed with Sam, he would squat on the schoolteacher's apartment for a day or two, then get a search warrant. Did he need a hand? Sam asked. He'd help. Just ask, he had nothing but time. He'd sit on the apartment building. He thought maybe he'd better do that. He knew Max and the woman, too. He'd make the observations. He wanted to. Ceballos shouldn't be afraid to ask for help if he needed it, he said.

"Thanks, anyway," Ceballos told him. "We'll handle it, you know, me and my partner. No big thing."

When they broke up, Ceballos told Nora not to let this get her down, it happened in the best of cop families. It'll all work out, you'll see. We'll handle it for you.

Nora nodded.

"I was you," Ceballos said, "I wouldn't make any plans for Saturday night. Stay near a phone on Saturday."

She nodded again, thinking, show me someone who sits back while others handle their problems, I'll show you someone in deep shit. Oh, boy . . .

Around lunchtime the following day, Nora telephoned the hotel where Chief Clement was attending an FBI organized crime seminar in Philadelphia. The agent with whom she spoke was polite but cautious in the extreme. It was peculiar. The agent told her he would get her message to Chief Clement. The chief was not registered at the hotel and there didn't seem to be any other way to reach him.

As things turned out, Nora didn't hear from the chief until late on Saturday morning. He told her his trip to Philadelphia was a waste of time, boring, four days of meetings and seminars given by people who walked around with their tongues out in the rain. He asked why she had called.

"I was out most of the week," she told him. "I'm not feeling very well. I thought I'd let you know that I was not at the office."

"Nothing serious, I hope."

"No, a virus, a stomach virus. And I slipped coming up the stairs to my apartment, banged my face a bit."

There was a long moment of silence. "Your face, huh?"

"Yes, I got a few stitches. I'm fine, but I look terrible."

"You're fine?"

"Yes, yes, I'm okay."

"And that's it?"

"All there is."

Another moment of silence. "You'll be in on Monday?"

"Sure."

"Fell going up the stairs, huh?"

"Embarrassing."

"What's to be embarrassed about? It could happen to anyone. Don't be so hard on yourself."

"Clumsy," she said.

"Who are we talking about? Not you, you're anything but clumsy."

"You haven't caught my act lately," she told him. Nora was thinking that Jean-Paul, in certain circumstances, could be a perfect gentleman.

"Listen," he told her, "even though you may think otherwise, you're not perfect. By the way, were you able to speak to ADA Devlin in Brooklyn?"

Nora sat still for a moment, the receiver in her hand. The stitches around her eye felt as if they were pulling, pinching her. And her lips, forget the lips.

"Nora?"

"I spoke to Devlin."

"Have you started the Longo case?"

"Started? Yes, I guess you could say I got started. Then I fell and, you know . . ."

"All right, take care of yourself but get this Longo case going. You need any help, ask for it."

"Honestly, Paul, I don't know what I have here," she told him. "People ask why our office is interested in this character, and the truth is, I don't know what to answer."

"Who asked?"

"Devlin, for one."

"Devlin wouldn't know a case if it came up and bit him on the neck. Look, I've been at this awhile, I know a big-time sleeper when I see one. Some dunce sees himself ready to break out. Make a name for himself, the next John Gotti, that kind of thing."

Nora said, "All right."

"This guy Longo is a new one, one of the young Turks ready to be a major player. I'll get you the FBI file, you'll see."

"A major player?"

Jean-Paul explained that these characters, Longo and his crew, were an underground credit union for people who were unable to get legitimate loans. Small-business people, bar owners, restaurants, gas stations, junkyards, street people, all sorts of criminals, burglars, thieves, hijackers, small-time drug dealers, and gamblers that wanted to expand their business went to them for loans. That was their game. They crawled on these people like flies on a corpse. Longo put money in the street and got huge returns coming back on a regular basis. "What I think you're going to need to do is find someone they trust, someone that can go to them and get a loan. The Organized Crime Control Bureau tried sending undercovers in, but Longo's not stupid. Look, they only deal with people they know. You know why?" The chief was silent a moment, as if overwhelmed by the very thought. "They need to know just where to find you. Why? Because if you don't pay, they chop you up. I mean, chop, chop, chop, literally chop you up."

"What are you saying?"

"Nora, I've seen an intelligence report that detailed the search of a car Longo had reported stolen. In the trunk detectives found boning knives, orange butcher coats, rubber gloves, garbage bags, and rope. Longo was a butcher," Jean-Paul said. "The dunce told the investigating detective that he carries around the tools of his trade."

Nora listened, nodding to herself, telling herself, you need this like stomach cramps.

"If you can find an informant with the smarts to get to Longo, you'll have a helluva case. I know what you're probably thinking: Is Longo mob connected?"

Nora didn't answer. She wasn't thinking at all.

"Not that anyone can tell. He's a psycho killer. Mob guys stay away from him, he's totally nuts. Look," he told her, "It's a helluva case. But you can handle it. I'm counting on you."

Nora exhaled a long breath of air, almost a sigh. Jean-Paul was a slick piece of work, stagey-serious when he wanted something done. And it worked most times, most times she'd get the urge to get it done. Except this time Max was on her mind. Max, Ceballos, and Sammy were enough to handle.

Nora said, "I'll get right to it. Give me a few days, I'll feel better in a day or two. Then I'll get right to it." Her voice sounding as though she meant what she said.

Sometime around three in the afternoon, the telephone rang again. Sam was on the line.

"Jimmy called me, he's going to hit the apartment tonight. He figures, seven or eight o'clock."

"Where should I meet you?" she asked.

"The Queens coffee shop, how's that? We'll take my car."

That night, Nora sat with Sam in his blue Toyota on a dark street in Forest Hills. She sat across the street and up the block from a woman's apartment building, a woman who was a New York City schoolteacher and apparently gave her husband memorable blow jobs.

Jimmy Ceballos stood alongside the car going over things. His tough, soft-spoken reassurances reminded her of what an unmerciful hard-ass Jimmy Ceballos was. He handed Nora a radio tuned to the Narcotics Division frequency.

A half hour later, Nora was sitting back relaxing to the sound of one of Sam's 100 Sinatra tapes when she saw Ceballos and his partner get out of a department car.

Ceballos threw her a thumbs-up sign and headed for the apartment building. Sam turned the volume down on his cassette player. "There they go," he said.

Nora nodded her head.

Sam said, "Knowing Jimmy Ceballos, Max had better be on his best behavior."

"I hope Ceballos behaves himself," she said. Unable to keep from saying it. "I hope this goes nice and easy."

Sam seemed to think she was joking.

"It's all up to Max. You know that. You've been there."

She had to admit Sam was right. Cops executing a search warrant did their best to avoid problems. All normal cops wanted things to go down nice, nice. On the other hand, Jimmy Ceballos was no normal cop.

A tiny groan escaped her and Nora felt a wave of panic take hold. Sitting there, watching the detectives move with their tough-guy strut toward the apartment building, she realized that there would always be a part of her that would remain Max's caretaker.

"It's just that Max is so loony nowadays, Sammy. And he has my gun. I don't want to see anybody get hurt here." Meaning it.

"Jimmy and his partner are pros. They won't take any chances."

Nora wrinkled her nose. "You're right, of course, you're right. Only I wasn't thinking of Ceballos, I was thinking of Max. The guy is such an amateur. I hope he doesn't panic."

No answer from Sam, just a quick nod.

"Listen to me," Nora said, "after all the man has put me through, I still can't help but worry about the guy."

"Listen to you, is right." Sam squinted, half smiling. "Screw Max, screw him twice."

The apartment house where Max hung his hat was on Sixty-seventh Road off Austin Street, right across from a baseball field and two tennis courts, and just about ten blocks from the Queens County Criminal Courts building. It was a middle-class neighborhood with modest one-family homes set among a series of apartment buildings with cars parked along the street.

Detective Ceballos and his partner Frank Rawlings walked toward the building, Ceballos scanning the second-floor windows then looking back toward Sam's car. A vicious wave of excitement ran through him. Let's do it and get it done, he thought.

A teenage Asian girl wearing headphones entered the building with the two detectives and stood along the wall by the door bells. She was an attractive kid, serious-looking. She stood, arms folded, not using her key, or pushing a bell, waiting. Jimmy figured she was waiting to see where the two strange men were going. Jimmy studied the girl leisurely. She in turn studied him.

"The super's 1-G," Jimmy said.

Frank nodded and pushed the bell.

The door buzzed and Jimmy opened it, holding it open for Frank who passed on through. The girl didn't move, just stood there, arms folded, her key hanging on a string in her hand.

"You coming in?" Jimmy said.

She didn't answer, just stood still and wagged her head. Jimmy motioned for her to come ahead. "You live here, right?"

The girl hesitated then nodded her head.

"Well, come on in."

"It's okay," she said. "I can wait."

"What's the matter," Frank said, "you afraid or something?"

"Why should I be afraid?"

"I'm not going to hold the door open all night," Jimmy said. "For shit's sake, you coming in or what?"

Down the hall the door to the super's apartment opened and Felix Ramirez stood there, hands on his hips, a spacey half smile on his face. He wore a cutoff red sweat shirt, blue jeans, and white tennis shoes with the laces undone.

Jimmy Ceballos and the super exchanged a quick embarrassed look. The super squinted at the girl, then turned to Jimmy. "Wha joo doin, man?" he said.

"Holding the door for Miss Saigon here," Jimmy said.

"Es okay, Kim, they won't hurt you, honey. Come in, baby, come in."

The girl looked up at Jimmy in surprise then scooted through the door and ran up the stairs.

"Thees girl, man, thees kid she have problems, man, joo shouldn't scare her like dat."

"The fuck you talking about?" Jimmy said, "We didn't do anything."

Now that both of them were standing in front of the super's apartment, more or less face-to-face, Jimmy whispered, "What's with the kid?"

The super saying, "She's a good kid, man, a nice girl, nice family. A year ago these two guys, a couple of *cabrones*, follow her home from school, push in the door to her apartment and, man, they rob the apartment. Then they, joo know, they rape her, something like that, beat her up. This is the first time in a year I see her alone. De family from Korea, close family, Koreans. I never see her without her brother or father. She's scared all the time now, poor kid."

Jimmy spoke in a confidential murmur. "You want to know what I think? I think she's a fucking nutty gook, is what she is. The hell she scared of us for?"

The super went up on tiptoe to poke his finger in Jimmy's chest, "The bums," he said, "they were white guys, American guys, they look like you and your friend."

"Whaddaya mean like us?"

"Like you, big white guys. Maybe they were cops, too."

Jimmy shot him his best obnoxious look, then he took two polite steps back. Jimmy smiling, thinking, I love it. "Felix," he said, "we're ready to go. You check the apartment for me?"

"Five minutes ago they were watching television. I went upstairs, stood by the door. They were there, the TV was on."

Frank Rawlings, who had listened carefully, nodded at Jimmy.

"Got the key?" Jimmy asked the super.

Felix handed him the key to 2-G and Jimmy took a fifty-dollar bill, folded it carefully, and put it in Felix's hand.

The super stepped back into his apartment, twisting his head up to the cops standing in front of him. "So, *amigos*," he said, "I go down now to the basement and shut the power. Take me minute. Throw the main, and then pop. Lights out, everything black."

"That's what we need," Jimmy said. "Listen, leave them off until we tell you to turn them back on," Jimmy told him.

By way of introduction, the night before Jimmy had brought a bottle of dark rum to Felix. The two men had sat in the super's kitchen drinking the rum neat, with *café con leche*, eating fried shrimp, and chicken with rice, discussing their mutual Cuban heritage and their shared view of the world.

Felix loved cops with the same passion that he hated Fidel Castro. Of course he would help Jimmy, it was something real he could do. Flags in the wind. A good citizen doing a good turn for a compadre.

"They should come out shouting when that electricity goes off," Jimmy told him now. "They don't come out, then we'll use the key."

"Oh, they'll come out," Felix said. "It happens, sometimes the power goes off, and, man, they come running to me like I'm de Con Edison company."

"Good," Jimmy told him, "that's good."

What Jimmy Ceballos knew best were people. People that used and sold dope, people in the sporting life, how to handle them. It didn't matter that he'd never met this guy Max, or the broad he was shacked up with in 2-G. He knew them. Oh, yeah, he knew the two of them, the types. He knew just what made their day, or, for that matter, what terrified them. Mostly he knew how to take people down, turn them around, and use them against one another.

Starting out in narcotics Jimmy had spent a lot of time hating drug addicts and dealers.

That ended years ago.

Nowadays, the fact that so many people sucked Bolivian dancing powder up their noses, or spent their last nickel for a ten-minute crack high, or shoved a heroin needle into collapsed veins running HIV-infected blood, was all beside the point. Jimmy Ceballos was hardly the type to judge people on their vices.

The way he saw it, for reasons beyond his control, this drug epidemic was a big money game; and he figured that fate and good fortune had chosen him to be a player.

For a man like Jimmy, a cop like him, working drugs was a crazy kind of turn on. Others might think that assignment anywhere in the detective division was preferable to kicking in doors, chasing junkies and dealers over rooftops and through basements. But Jimmy loved it. He was one of those guys who were convinced that someday he'd luck into a trailer load of cash. Kick the right door and, bingo.

Cops that knew him well, said of Jimmy, the guy would take a hot stove and go back for the smoke. The man was a born thief.

Jimmy and Frank made their way to the second floor. Frank said, "That half a yard you gave the super is out of your pocket, buddy." Jimmy said, "Money in the bank, brother. Better than a 401-K, an investment in the future."

Frank saying, "This is total bullshit, we got all kinds of shit to do and here we are chasing a couple of deadbeat junkies."

Moving along the hallway Jimmy whispering, "A favor brother, a big-time favor. Do you know who this captain is? C'mon, use your head."

"I know, I know. It's just that we got plenty of our own work."

"Brother, we can chase Dominicans and niggers every night of the week. How often does the chief of detectives' top captain ask for a favor? C'mon," Jimmy said, "use some of that insight of yours. Put on your thinking cap, consider the long term. We're gonna make a powerful friend."

The hallway was narrow and airless with its walls painted a mellow shade of green; there was a light in the ceiling and it was dim. The tattered hall carpet muffled the detectives' soft steps as they moved along.

The apartment stood before them. And the two detectives, guns and flashlights in hands, took up positions on either side of the door. Jimmy gently leaned his forehead against the door; he could hear voices from inside the apartment, the sound of laughter, a TV, some music.

The overhead hallway light flashed off, then on, then off again. Jimmy and Frank backed away. Then a male voice from inside the apartment, "The hell happened?" Then a woman's voice, "Everything's off." The man saying, "I'll go check." The woman answering, "No, sit still, I'll go."

Inside, footsteps along a hallway, coming closer. "I'm getting the mother of all hard-ons," Frank whispered. "Shhhh," Jimmy said. "Okay. Ready. Let's be bad motherfuckers."

Jimmy heard the latch.

Jimmy Ceballos's whispered voice came over the radio, saying, "We're in Josephine Rio's apartment." Nora hit the volume knob and Sam shot upright, looking around the street. There was shouting. From the radio came the sound of accusations, of what sounded like furniture being tossed about, a woman screamed denials, a plea, the sound of a slap.

Nora sat still, her hand firmly clapped over her mouth.

"Miss Rio," Jimmy said, "has a male visitor who, at the present time, refuses to identify himself."

Sam murmured something into his shoulder then took the radio from Nora's hand. "Listen," he said, "you find anything?"

"Approximately an ounce, an ounce and a half of cocaine and some U.S. currency. About five thousand dollars."

"Weapons? You find any weapons?"

"No weapons, but we're not done looking."

Nora could make out a woman's voice, the same woman, she supposed, who had shared the joys and sorrows of dear ol Max for the past six months. The woman saying, "You're upsetting me, I don't want to be upset anymore." Then she heard Max's voice. Ceballos holding his radio so that everyone got air time. Some game, some trick, Max saying, "That's mine, that's my stuff, leave her out of it." Nora had always believed Max

109

a much underestimated man. His voice was harsh and alert but it called out fear.

Sam said, "Christ, I wish I could go up there."

"Sure," Nora said, "That's just what we need. I'm sure Max would love to see you." Nora was sitting hunched over, elbows on her knees, eyes on the floor. "Let me think," she said. "First question, how did Max go through five thousand dollars in less than a week?"

"It's possible," Sam told her. "You know it's possible. That shit is expensive."

"Maybe. Okay, next question. What the hell could Max have done with my off-duty gun?"

Sam gave it a long silence, his face inches from Nora's shoulder. "You see, you think everything is going to fall into place and then shit happens. You want my guess, based on what I know about this guy, the man put the gun in the street. Say, he sold it or gave it away to some a-hole. The gun shows up at a crime scene, you're in deep shit. Either way, your gun's missing, and good old Max is getting busted. Can't see how we can avoid it. An ounce and a half of cocaine, that's a whole lot of dope. Right?"

Nora didn't say anything.

Over the following week, Nora got used to frequent phone calls from Max. At her office, at home, early morning, in the middle of the night. His voice was nervous, coy, then angry, he whooped and whimpered. At first Nora waved him off, hung up the phone, castigating herself: Change the damn number, forget this jerk.

Now, it was before six A.M., the phone started to ring on the nightstand. Nora let it go, waiting for her machine to kick in.

"Please," Max said.

Staring at the ceiling, Nora reached for the phone. "Max, will you get a life," she said in a distracted monotone. "How many times do I have to tell you to stop calling me? Aren't you in enough trouble? Christ, you've done your best to ruin both our lives. Enough, Max, enough."

But Max as usual was not listening, going on and on, lashing out, then crying. Crying. "Please hear me out." Max's voice, his tone, the bewildered child touched her. "Max," she said softly, "get yourself together. Get some help. And get it through your head that I never want to see you again. I'd better not see you again." Max saying, "My God, you're so unfeeling, I can't believe what I'm hearing. I'm sorry, you know how sorry I am."

"Max, it's time you grew up. Be a man, for chrissake."

"I'm living in hell," he told her. "I've nowhere to go."

"Why don't you go to Queens, to your sweetheart Josephine?" Nora taking a certain pleasure in the sarcasm.

"She won't talk to me."

"Poor Max," she said. "Poor deserted Max."

"They beat me up, you know that, your fucking cops beat the shit out of me."

"Strange, you sound fine."

"They beat me! And Josephine Rio is a decent woman, ten years a schoolteacher. Those cops made sure that she'll lose her job."

Nora saying in a faint sardonic voice, "You're breaking my heart."

"I've had a brush with death, Nora. Now I know what that feels like."

"You beat me, you bastard. You should see my face."

"I am sorry. You know me, I'm not well."

Nora didn't bother to answer.

"I have nowhere to go. Let me come home. I'm living in my car, for chrissake. Nora," he said, "I have no money. The cops took my money, they took all of it."

"Confiscated Max, they confiscated the money. And what do you mean, your money? You mean our money, don't you?"

Max cut her off. "I'm coming home. I have some rights, too," he said, trying to sound as though he knew what he was talking about.

"This is not your home, Max," she told him. "This is my home. I have a writ of protection. Do not, I repeat, do not push your luck. Go to your parents. They did one hell of a job raising you, go back to them."

"Please don't start attacking my parents. They put up the money to bail me out. Not for them I'd still be in jail."

"Then go home, that's your home, go there."

"I'm begging you. That's where I'm at now, I'm begging. Give me one more chance. I'll make things right between us. C'mon, hon, you said you loved me, think about it, think about us."

Nora would tell you that she thought that real love was nothing less than spiritual love. She'd say she spent six years in a marriage before she knew just who it was she was married to. She'd say she still looked back on several of those years as the best years of her life. She'd say that maybe, maybe, various hungers had combined to make poor Max wacky. But then she'd also tell you, you'd have to have a hole in your head not to know when enough is enough is enough.

"This love of ours," Nora said, "if love was what it was, is dead. You killed it, Max."

112

"You have any idea what this noise in my head is like? You're killing me."

"You need help, Max. Do us all a favor and get some."

Max said, "Fuck it, fuck it, fuck it," then he said, "Listen you want your gun back?"

Nora was listening, sitting up now. Thinking, Hey, what is this?

"You told me last week that you threw it into the river. That's what you said, Max, you said you went down to the river and threw my gun in. What are you trying to pull here?"

Max laughed hard and short. Then he said in that sudden-afterthought way of his, "That's all you're worrying about. Right? Your damn gun. Well, I didn't throw it away, I have it."

"You bastard."

Nora thinking of Chief Clement, pictured how he sat in his office, his head in his hands, the way he opened his mouth and exhaled as if the weight of the world had landed on his back. Nora explaining, or trying to explain Max's arrest, the loss of her gun, figuring that she'd just get it out, tell it straight out, just the way it happened. Hoping for the best. The way the chief then leaned forward, putting his elbows on his desk and his face in his hands saying, "Oh, God, we don't need this, this is the last thing we need." Saying, "Are you sure he threw it away? Can you be sure it won't turn up?" Then trying again to explain the inscrutable Max. Nora now touching the scar that ran in her eyebrow, the scar that pulled in the skin on the right side of her head. The scar that looked to her like a tiny snake beneath the skin. The scar the doctor promised would disappear in a few months, a year at most.

"You know," she said, "I'm lying here, it's six o'clock in the morning, and I'm thinking I'd like to see you dead. You have my gun? Good. Keep it. Better yet, do something worthwhile with it, shoot yourself."

"Funny thing is," Max said, "I know you, I know you don't mean what you say."

"I'm going to hang up, Max. You call me again, bother me again, I'm telling you that it's within my rights to have you arrested. Do it, and see if I don't mean what I say."

"The gun, you want the gun?"

Nora switched on the night-table lamp. She looked around the bedroom trying to get her bearings. "Dammit," she said, "do you have it?"

"Sure."

"Well, get it to me."

113

"Say please."

"Bye, Max."

Nora hung up the receiver, hard, hard enough to make herself jump. Leaving her wondering, nervously thinking, What next? As she reached for the switch to turn off the lamp, Nora swore to herself that she would never talk to Max again.

On a chair in his kitchen Sam Morelli sat drinking coffee and browsing through a book of Pulitzer Prize–winning war photos. Photographs portraying man's unceasing ability to deliver violence and death.

First thing that morning Nora had called to tell him of her most recent conversation with Max. Solid citizen Max, it turned out, still had her gun, at least he said he still had it. The half a hump phoning Nora trying to see what mercy and sympathy could buy.

Sam had come to realize that he'd have to take this mess into his own hands. Straighten Max out once and for all, he thought, start today.

Now he sat looking at the book, thinking of Nora, Max, and Jimmy Ceballos. The book was titled *Requiem* and had been put together by photographer Horst Faas.

Years earlier, one photo in particular had greatly disturbed him. Sam remembered being mesmerized while reading a copy of *Newsweek* or *Time*, he couldn't remember which. Something which involved seeing the face of one's own death.

The scene was in Bangladesh, there was a circle of soldiers watching in sober silence as two of their comrades executed three captives with bayonets. One of the executioners wore a sporty Panama hat. The marked man lay with his back on the ground gripping the shaft of the bayonet while the executioner, in his Panama, sent the blade home.

Sam actually thought that it was easy to get away with murder if you were on the side that made the rules. He believed it.

Looking at the photo he told himself that he would never lie still and take it. That he would do something, anything to change the look of quiet satisfaction on the face of the weasel with the bayonet. That, too, he believed.

Sam was suddenly struck by the notion that only a fool or a coward is taken by surprise. Know your enemy, that was the trick, that was the answer. For reasons he could not name, the photograph made him very angry. About as angry as Nora telling him, "Look, the way I see it, I'm going to have to do some penance and endure some torture on account of some fundamental error I made earlier in life. It's not unusual, it happens to people. I'm the one that married Max, I'm the dingaling."

Hey, he wanted to say to her in that good-partner, good-friend style of his, I love you. And you know me, I could never love a dingaling. But, boy, do I love you.

Sam Morelli was deeply in love with Nora and believed with all his heart and soul that he alone had the power to care for her. This desire ate at him like some terminal disease and had always made Sam feel foolish and silly.

During all the years he'd known Nora, Sam could never bring himself to tell her, to say to her, guess what, I'm in love. There were times when he felt sure of himself and wanted to open up to her. But those times were few and they always passed. There had been a time or two when he came very close. Almost there, almost letting his secret out, the secret that he loved Nora.

Sam understood that Nora had none of these feelings for him. Sure, she liked him, often said that she loved him. But Sam knew that the way Nora loved him was the way cops loved their partners. That wasn't love, that had nothing to do with love, love.

Sam had worked with Nora for ten years. And in that time he could have arranged to have himself transferred. Put himself in a position of not having to see her day in, day out.

Split, he'd tell himself, take a hike, do the paperwork, talk about stress, too much travel, kiss some ass, anything to get a transfer. Do something.

But to his dismay Sam could never find the strength. Pussy-whipped and loved-starved is what they call people like you, he'd tell himself. Sam would argue that Nora needed him. Without me around to guide and protect her the pricks would land on Nora like wolves on a wounded deer.

Being around Nora everyday was like living in purgatory. But life without her would be hell, a suicide mission. All these excuses for standing pat he believed to be true. So he had endured the alternative, and the alternative was to be near Nora and simply go on loving her, knowing and understanding that his love was a one-way street.

Now that was all coming to an end. Retirement, time to pack it in. Twenty years was one hell of a long time, count your blessings, he told himself, kept telling himself, get out.

Lately he would lie in bed at night next to his wife, Julie, eyes wide open, unable to sleep. Thinking about retirement, considering life without Nora.

"You know what I think?" Sam had told Nora that morning. "I think that gun of yours makes Max feel important. Think about it, half a pound of steel is all the man has left." Nora said then that she would have to find another way to handle this guy. Because if there ever was an example of her plans and schemes not working, what she'd done up till now surely was it.

"Twenty-twenty hindsight makes fools or geniuses of us all," he told her.

"I know that. Sure. Anyway, Max really did a job on me. I've had all I'm going to take. I won't see or talk to him again. I don't have to. My lawyer will. So he has my gun, he can keep it."

"You're talking nonsense."

Nora saying, "What if I told you that everything up until now has been nonsense."

"Well," Sam had said, "you do the best you can do. Give yourself a break, will you?"

"My fear is that he sells my gun. It would kill me if my gun ends up in the hands of some lunatic, and an innocent person dies because I didn't safeguard my damn weapon."

Sam had explained to Nora that she had better stop making herself nuts. She'd made herself and him nuts enough over the past few weeks. "Right now," he'd said, "it's time for a major housecleaning. Tidy up your life. You got things to do, a case to work. Figure how to get into this Blaze Longo. Forget Max, he's history."

"What I need is a vacation," Nora said. "Some time away."

Early in the afternoon Sam telephoned Jimmy Ceballos at the Narcotics Division office. Sam pointed out to Jimmy, made a point to explain to the narcotics detective, that he needed his help. That he wanted to get word to Max Riter. Maybe through Josephine Rio, or the super of the building, whatever way Jimmy could figure.

"Listen, Jimmy," he said, "this is important, give me a hand here. I want to reach out for Max Riter. I want to set up a meet with the guy." Jimmy said, "Hey, no problem."

More and more frequently as he paced his kitchen, the thought of how he would deal with Max came to him. The fact was that he could work the whole thing through Jimmy Ceballos. Jimmy would do whatever he asked, there was no question about that. Sam was thinking he would promise Max that he'd walk away from his case. Give me the fucking gun and I'll see to it you're cut loose. Try that out, see if Max went for it.

Sam walked in and out the rooms of his apartment, thinking, It's what you need to do. Stop tormenting yourself. Get it done.

His determination rose and fell irrationally. He became angrier. Shortly before four o'clock Ceballos phoned—where would he like to meet with Max? Name the place and Max would be there.

On the boardwalk at 110th Street in Rockaway Beach, he told Jimmy. Five o'clock would be good.

"Consider it done," Jimmy said. "I hear Max can't wait to meet with you."

"Yeah, and who told you that?"

"My man, Felix the super," Jimmy said. "Listen," he told him, "the only part I don't like is that I busted this character, and let me tell you the guy's a snake. You think it's smart to meet him alone? I'm there you need me, buddy. Just ask."

Sam didn't like to ask favors, but he didn't mind asking Jimmy. Jimmy Ceballos was a slick, knock-around, old-time cop. The type who expected to be asked favors. Fact was, Sam was pretty sure that doing favors and sticking his nose in other people's problems was the kind of thing Jimmy Ceballos loved to do. Because that would mean Jimmy could call in a favor if he ever needed to. And the way Jimmy did his job, chances were he'd be calling for help sooner or later. And, he'd get it. It was done that way.

I can handle a roomful of Max Riters one hand tied behind my back, Sam had told him. And Jimmy had said, "Both hands tied behind your back."

Sam stood in his kitchen, wondering if he could pull this off. Straighten out the confusion once and for all. If Max were some ordinary mutt off the street, no problem, but he wasn't. Still, Sam believed that if he had summoned the presence of mind to make this move earlier Nora would have had her weapon back by now. He realized, too, that there could be consequences, maybe bad consequences.

Sam left a note for his wife on the kitchen table. It was almost four o'clock.

Forty-five minutes later, Sam was leaning on a boardwalk railing and looking out at the Atlantic Ocean. The early evening was breezy with the sun still surprisingly strong. Sam narrowed his eyes against the bright reflection of the water. Overhead, the wind was moving clouds in from the sea toward New York City, and around him sea gulls glided, hungry eyes searching the shoreline. Offshore two trawlers were moving east trying to wrest a living from the sea. Far out, huge waves were forming, sucking up water, heading for the shore in a greenish, blue-white surge. Sam was thinking, forty-five minutes from Times Square to the very edge of nowhere.

Standing there, breathing deep, taking in the salt air, barely thinking, Sam felt completely still in time.

What he thought next was how quickly life moved you on, twenty years in the PD, from beginning to end a flash in time, a little dot, a point of light, then over.

He had been young, he could feel now how young he was then and how little he knew of life. His past felt real and tangible, and whatever his future held was as foggy and as far off as the horizon.

Sam was wearing his zippered tan windbreaker. On his hip he carried a snub-nose .38 detective special. It wasn't one of the new automatics so many carried nowadays, but it was good enough. He took the gun from his holster and slid it into his jacket pocket.

Just as he did that he felt a chill spin in on him so that he was pinned to the rail with panic. He stepped back and looked up then down the boardwalk and then down again at the beach. He patted his jacket pocket where the gun was.

The unusually warm evening had brought out an elderly couple who were walking the beach with their dog. The couple wore matching navy blue running suits. They walked along arm in arm and even from his spot on the boardwalk it was apparent to Sam that these two were still lovers. Every so often the man pulled the woman in close to him, she in turn would nuzzle her head on his shoulder. Off to Sam's right empty Kentucky Fried Chicken boxes lay atop an open trash barrel and creaked in the gentle wind. The sound, like the elderly lovers, made him uneasy.

"Hey, Sam," he heard and turned around seeing Max walking toward him, his head back, a big smile on his face, and right away Sam could see a difference in the guy. The hat, Sam thought, it's the hat. Max was wearing a cowboy hat.

They exchanged looks. Sam couldn't believe it. He had expected to see some sadness, a little pensive contrition, some sorrow. Sam stood staring at Max Riter, frowning because he couldn't figure it, couldn't figure it at all. The guy seemed lighthearted and cheerful, a kind of how-the-hell-you-been, smile on his face. "Sam," he said, "Sam Morelli, world-class cop, world-class tough guy. How the hell are you?"

"Fine, I'm fine."

Max was looking around the boardwalk; the guy all jazzed up in his jeans, leather jacket, his cowboy hat, and boots. Max waved to the couple with the dog. "Nice dog," he called out. Continued to look around then turned back to Sam. "Nora know you're here? I bet she don't. I'd lay some money on it. If I had any money to lay on it, I'd bet you never told her you were going to meet me."

"You'd be right."

Max still looking around, now it seemed to Sam the guy was a bit fidgety, a little goosey. Sam waited until Max's eyes were on him. He said, "You give me Nora's gun and I can guarantee you walk away from your case. I can fix it, I can do that, and I will."

"And, I believe you. You fixed it so that I got into this jam, so you can unfix it. I believe that."

"Are we going to do business?"

"Sure."

"You have the gun with you?"

"Naw."

"Christ." Sam sounded depressed and drained.

"C'mon," Max said. "What the hell do you think I am, some cocksuckin eunuch, a gelding?" His expression changing, his eyes opening wide. "You think you low-rent, schmuck cops can go on intimidating me and there won't be any payback. You must be crazy if that's what you think."

Nothing from Sam.

"Well, what do you have to say?"

"Free as the breeze, Max. You can walk away from your case, free as the breeze."

"You said that. I heard you, I'm not stupid. But, say if I do that, be a nice guy and all, then Nora's off the hook. I don't think I want to do that, take Nora off the hook she's on. I kind of like the idea of her squirming. You know what I mean?"

"You know Max, what you're doing is unfair. Think about it."

"Oh, man, the *world*'s unfair. Look around you, there is terrible misery everywhere, not my fault. None of it is my fault. I minded my own business until you cops came along. You ruined my life, Sam, that's what you did, you know. Threw my life in the sewer."

He could kick Max's ass, knock his ass from one end of this beach to the other, Sam was thinking. But where would that get him?

"I'm the victim here," Max said. "I've been victimized by this bitch I married, this bitch I know you've been fucking. Nobody has to tell me, I know. I'm smart enough to figure that a woman looks like Nora, loves sex like Nora, a woman like that has got to be fucking somebody. She sure as hell hasn't slept with me in a month of Sundays."

"I don't sleep with your wife," Sam told him.

"Maybe not, but you want to and that's the same thing."

Sam nodded. This character Max was a lost cause. What he should do was reach out and grab this motherfucker and break him in half, but the truth was, he felt sorry for the guy.

Sam looking at him now, two, three steps away, trying to understand the guy who had stomped and kicked and beat Nora senseless. "Sad," Sam said, "you're a sad man, screwed up and sad."

Max placed his hands on his hips and turned his head toward the sky. White puffy clouds were moving in from the sea. Suddenly he started screaming. "H'lo! Who you looking at? Looking at me like that? Who the hell do you think you are, with your guilt-tripping, sanctimonious bullshit? You're nobody, nothing but a nickel-and-dime cop."

Sam speaking softly now, "You're an asshole, Max. A coward and an asshole."

From his waistband Max took a pistol. He held the gun in his hand as though he knew what he was doing. He pointed it at Sam. It was a heavy-barrel Smith and Wesson, Nora's old service weapon, a big-ass gun. Sam was stunned.

Sam leaned back against the railing. "You told me you didn't have Nora's gun," he said flatly.

"I lied. That's me, the liar."

"Okay, what do you plan to do with it?"

Max mumbled something that Sam was unable to hear, but it didn't matter. He saw the scene in Bangladesh, and he and Max were in it. Know the face of your enemy, he thought, use your head. God, this was something he never figured, never thought this Max, a man full of fear and trembling, had the heart to pull a gun on him. Max was now gasping for breath and his eyes went wide and were full of pain.

"Max," he said, "you're a mess." Sam's voice, however, quivered just slightly, spoiling the suggestion that he, the man without a gun, was in charge.

Sam steadied himself against the railing and slid his hand into his jacket pocket. Felt his gun waiting there and put his finger on the trigger. Max did not seem to notice. The elderly couple with their dog had moved a good distance down the beach.

Max went blank and nodded. "A mess, you're right, I am a mess. But now that's finished, everything is finished. It's all a joke anyway. Trouble is, I never got it. Whatever the joke is, I never got it."

Sam smiled, desperate to get Max to relax. He said softly, "Hey, c'mon. What are you going to do? Don't be silly."

"It's finished!" Max shouted at him.

"Listen," Sam said, "put the gun down. Let's talk." He was amazed that no one was on the boardwalk, a nice evening like this, more people should have been out and about. The only sound he heard was the kew, kew, kew, of the gulls and the waves breaking along the beach.

"I'm tired," Max said, smiling sadly. "I have nothing, nothing. No Nora, no money, no dreams."

"You can fix all that. I can help you."

"Fuck you. Who you kidding?"

Sam felt no fear. He did not see Max as a serious threat. The fucking guy was from Scarsdale, for chrissake. Besides, in his jacket pocket, he had his hand on his own gun, the barrel pointed at Max's chest.

Sam watched with fascination as tears ran down Max's cheeks. He stepped toward him saying, "C'mon Max, give me the gun. You don't want to hurt me, you don't want to hurt anybody."

"Back off!"

Max waved the gun in the air with a flourish, he was losing it now, the guy getting crazed and out of control.

Sam thinking, What do I do? I can't shoot him, how can I shoot this man. This is not the face of my enemy, this poor lost wacko. The idea that Max was sick and weak took the pressure off. Max raised the pistol and fired a shot out at the ocean. It was loud, exploding over the quiet beach.

"The hell you doing?"

"I don't know."

"Okay. Listen. You've gone through a whole lot lately. It's been tough. But now it's over, you can straighten it all out and start fresh," Sam told him and meant it. "Give me the gun."

"The gun," Max said, "the gun."

Sam stepped close to him. He reached out his hand to take the gun, and said again, "It's okay, it's over."

"Over," Max said, and pulled the trigger.

The bullet hit Sam in the chest, shoulder high and knocked him back, but he didn't go down. Sam held his shoulder with one hand and reached out with the other.

"Give it to me!" he shouted.

"You didn't say please," Max said, in a kind of high silly shriek. "No one says please or thank you anymore."

His face assumed a composed look, an effort at dignity.

"Please give it to me," Sam said clearly as though speaking to a young child.

Max smiled, saying, "See, see how easy that was."

He opened his mouth, put the barrel of Nora's gun in and pulled the trigger.

Nicky stood in the center of a tiny kitchen looking down at Irma who was sitting at the table in the shortest, tightest, leather miniskirt he'd ever seen. Irma sat in her padded demibra doing her nails.

"Check this out." Irma extended a Victoria's Secret catalogue to Nicky. "Is that hot or what?"

Nicky scanned a photo of a small, thin blond model who looked extraordinarily like Irma. The catalogue described the model wearing a stretch-lace bralette, camisole, and boy-leg matching briefs.

"Well?"

Nicky glanced at the opposite page: a full-length, purple-mist gown in stretch lace. His heart skipped a beat. Nicky feeling a buzz and tingle right then, thinking that he'd been bewitched by that cop. Those legs, that ass, all that hair. Flashing on Nora, seeing her in that stretch purple-mist gown. Tripping out a bit like some horny high school kid, saying, "Humm, this one, this one is gorgeous."

"I'm too short to wear that."

"Too short?"

"I am short, Nicky. Petite."

"I think it's you."

"Me all the way, if I was three inches taller," she said. Irma gave him her crafty smirk.

"Irma," Nicky said, "I want you to listen to me, okay?" He kissed the top of Irma's head then took a seat across from her at the table. Irma saying now, "Nicky, if you weren't my cousin I'd eat you up like an ice cream cone. By the way, is a cousin incest? I don't think so, Nicky, I don't think a cousin is incest."

"C'mon, girl," he said, "for Christ's sake."

"Kidding, I'm kidding. Go on, speak, I'm listening."

"You listen, but do you hear me?"

"G'wan."

"Irma?"

"Whatsamatter, Nicky?

"I don't want you leaving here," he said. "I don't want you going anywhere, seeing anybody, turning any tricks until I say you can."

Irma shrugged and tried to smile. "You're telling me I'm in jail here? That's what you're telling me?"

"This is your home, Irma, not jail. Make yourself comfortable, watch a little TV, and keep an eye on Tino. I don't think that's asking too much."

"Like I said, you're putting me in jail."

"Are you going to do what I tell you, or are you going to give me an argument?"

"Sure, sure. Whatever you say."

"I'm not kidding."

Irma nodded and looked away.

"I rented two videos. You and Tino kick back, watch the films, and stay put until you hear from me. Do what I tell you. Do not screw around, Irma. I'm serious."

Irma was watching Nicky without any happiness in her face. "Why are we doing this? Are you going to tell me what's going on?" She sounded like she was twelve.

"We got some enemies in the street. Bad people, Irma, lunatics. I need to see if I can reach out, square this away. We don't need problems like this. We don't need Blaze and Fat Paulie stalking us. It's bad shit. Dangerous, is what it is."

"I won't move until you say it's okay."

"Atta girl."

"Nice, nice, very nice. This is all my fault," she told him.

Nicky shrugged. "It's nobody's fault. It's everybody's fault. That don't matter, it's a problem, but I'll fix it."

"Since we were kids you've been picking up after me. I'm sorry, I don't know what's the matter with me." She looked embarrassed.

"There's nothing the matter with you. You are, well, Irma, you are you, and there you have it. Anyway, this problem with Blaze has more to do with me than it does with anyone else."

Irma cleared her throat. "Did you talk to Tino?"

"Yes, he's fine. He understands. I worry less about him than I do you."

"Such a good kid, Nicky. Ouuuu, the other day with that bat, was that cute or what?"

"Tino is smart, he'll listen to me and do what I say. You, on the other hand, are liable to get an itch to hit the street. Promise me you'll stay home. That's all I'm asking, you stay home with Tino until I get back."

"One thing," Irma said. "I don't have anything to eat here. We're gonna need to get some lunch, dinner. Nicky," she said, "I am thin enough, I don't need to lose anymore weight. And Tino needs to eat."

"I'm not going to Europe. I'll be back in three, four hours. I'll stop at the Roma, have O.D. make up a something nice."

"Get us that baked macaroni with eggplant. I like that, Tino likes that, too."

"Whatever," Nicky said.

"What movies you get?"

"Good ones, you'll like them."

"Which ones?"

"*North by Northwest* and *Breaking Away*, good films."

"Never heard of them."

"You'll like them. Trust me."

"You know what, Nicky," she said suddenly, "you know what I heard?"

Nicky shrugged good-humoredly and smiled.

"This is going to shock you. I'm telling you, this is a shocker. Smart as you are, I bet you didn't know this."

No response from Nicky.

"You know that Mae West is buried in Brooklyn?"

"I knew that."

"Really? Wow. Yeah, did you know that we don't live in Red Hook? All these years people ask me, where do you live? I tell 'em Red Hook. An' you know what? We don't live there."

"They changed the name of our neighborhood years ago, sweetie."

"Who did?"

"They did. They got it wrong but they did it anyway. Changed the name of our neighborhood to Carroll Gardens."

Irma looked amazed, her mouth forming a small, silent o.

"For me and you it will always be Red Hook," he told her then.

"You got that right."

Early in the afternoon, sitting in her office, when she couldn't work, couldn't get a thing done, because she kept going over and over the phone call, the disjointed conversation with Max, Nora decided that what she really needed was a break. Some time off to regroup, a few days, maybe even a week in the country. That sudden oncoming of emptiness and sadness and fatigue washing over her. Max.

Coming around the corner and into Chief Clement's office, Nora saw Jean-Paul standing at his window, his back to the door. Nora saying, "Paul, I'm out of here, I need some time off. I have to get out of this city, I'm going nuts. Chief," she said, "I have enough lost time to take six months off, I'll take ten days, that's all I need, ten days in the country."

Jean-Paul stood by his window, wearing a New York Mets cap, tossing a baseball in the air, going from hand to hand, having a conversation with himself. "Seaver, Koosman, Matlack, man we had some pitching staff. And out of the bullpen, 'You gotta believe.' What was that kid's name? A left-hander, had the heart of a lion and I can't even remember his name."

"Chief?"

"Tug McGraw, Nora, his name was Tug McGraw."

"Chief?"

"Our front-line pitchers today are people I never heard of. Who are these guys? I think we'll probably lose a hundred games."

She thought about going over to Jean-Paul and ripping the cap from his head. But she didn't.

The chief turned to look at her. "What were you saying? You want some time off? This business with Max, a nightmare. Sure, I understand. Sure, take whatever time you need. Take two weeks, a month. Hey, take all your lost time. You've earned it. Put in a 28, I'll sign it. But first, you slam-dunk this Blaze Longo; get that done and you can have all the time you need."

Nora was tongue-tied for a moment.

"You are turning down my request, you mean?"

"That's precisely what I mean."

"It's not fair."

"Not fair? Let me tell you about fair. This sonofabitch Blaze Longo is taking tokens. And not an article of clothing, nothing like that. His souvenirs are fingers and ears."

Jean-Paul went on, and as he went on, Nora stopped listening, thinking, Dearie, somewhere along the line you missed the boat. You could have gone on to graduate school, maybe taught in some quiet New England college. Maybe, something on Wall Street. Could have gone to law school, or been a hooker. Or, could have gone to law school *and* been a hooker.

Jean-Paul took off his cap and put the baseball in his desk drawer. When he spoke, he spoke softly and avoided her eyes.

"Longo's a street slug, he's not going anywhere," she said.

"Not going anywhere?" Jean-Paul said, chewing on the phrase for a moment. "Nora, how do I say this? Look, I have a personal interest in Longo. He disfigured an old friend of mine. He cut the man's thumb off. The next time Longo sees him, he's promised to cut off his head. I want this bastard, and I'm counting on you to nail him."

Looking at him, watching the chief, she couldn't tell if the story was true. He seemed sincere. Nevertheless, there was something bizarre in all this. The chief was making her very uneasy.

"When did it happen?"

"A few weeks ago."

"Can I talk to him? I'd really like to talk to him."

"Not right now, but there's a lieutenant you can talk to from Brooklyn

South Homicide. I call him Big Time, he's one helluva detective, and he has a thing or two on Longo. Talk to him."

"Okay, all right, if it's all that important to you . . ."

"I've been telling you right along how important this is to me. How many times do I have to spell it out? This bastard Longo can hurt me."

Momentarily perplexed by his frankness, Nora changed her tone. Thinking, *hurt you?*

"All right, chief, I understand. You can count on me, I'll take care of it."

Nora stared at him, and he met her eyes with a resolute steadiness. "Please," he said.

Nora left the chief's office thinking, now she'd have to go and hunt down this dipshit. No problem, only something else was going on here, but she couldn't get to it. At least not yet. Thinking, Jean-Paul said, Hurt me, Blaze Longo can *hurt me*. What's with that? Nora had always hated the feeling of being used, a feeling that choked her, made her stomach whirl. The same feeling she'd felt day in, day out, lately living with screwball Max.

It was near two o'clock when Nora left One Police Plaza to go and meet the detective Jean-Paul called Big Time. He was assigned to Brooklyn Homicide but more times than not he was on special assignment with the Major Case Squad, the chief said. The detective's name was Clarence Taylor. He would be waiting for her at Brooklyn South detectives headquarters, on the second floor of the 76th Precinct.

When Nora arrived for her appointment she found the precinct a howling zoo. Narcotics detectives from all over the city had conducted a series of raids on Dominican-run *bodegas*. Nora was having a hell of a time trying to figure out who was who, cops and bad guys, all the inmates, lots of red-and-green T-shirts. There were enough people running around, shouting, cursing, to make Nora feel as if a riot were about to shape up at any minute.

Nora identified herself and was pointed toward the detectives' office. Clarence Taylor was an attractive black man in a pearl-gray suit, black shirt, and silver tie, one of those ties big rollers wear. Silk, it had to be silk. He looked like a Motown hit man. He came to the doorway of his office to greet her. A set of golf clubs was propped against his desk. On the wall were framed and signed photos of local politicians, of Dr. Martin Luther King Jr., and the Kennedy brothers, Jack and Robert. And there was one of the heavyweight champion, Evander Holyfield (TO BIG TIME, THE BEST DETECTIVE IN THE WORLD).

"Hey, Captain Riter," he said, "C'mon in and take a seat."

His office had three huge windows that were covered in steel mesh and looked out over the street. A chocolate-brown refrigerator and a table with a coffee machine lined one wall. There was a gray metal desk and two swivel chairs on wheels. Just as they settled down to talk, Clarence Taylor reached beneath his jacket, removed a small beeper, and made out the number on it. He smiled, wagged his head, clicked off the beeper, and put it into the top drawer of his desk.

Any authority Nora might have had as a captain in the chief of detectives' office didn't mean shit to Big Time. This was his office, his command, his things; his stuff was everywhere and he made sure she knew it.

"A busy day," he said pointing toward the muster room on the first floor. "You want something, a coffee, something to drink?"

Nora wagged her head. "No, thanks."

"How do you like working for Clement?" he asked her.

"Just fine. He's a good guy." She was feeling subdued by this man and it made her uncomfortable.

"Is that what you always say? When people ask about the chief, you always say he's a good guy?"

"He *is* a good guy."

Clarence smiled. "Yeah, he's just peachy."

"He's a five-star super chief, that makes him peachy."

Clarence winked at her. "You got it, Captain."

Nora could smell his cologne and she thought suddenly of Max who used only after-shave. And it was light, nothing like the severe, sweet smell that came off Detective Lieutenant Taylor.

"You think you'll like working Brooklyn?" he asked.

"I doubt it," said Nora.

"Sure you don't want a coffee?"

She declined the coffee and after a moment he was talking about his years working in Brooklyn South, the docks, organized crime. He had worked several joint-task-force cases with the Eastern District, Gotti and Gravano, loved to work wise-guy cases. Nora explained that she lived in Manhattan, preferred to work there.

"I came across this Blaze Longo a few months back," Taylor told her. "Then they sent me to the Eastern District and I lost track of the guy."

"He lives here in Brooklyn?"

He shrugged.

"What can you tell me about him?"

"Blaze put a crew of real tough guys together, they were doing ripoffs of drug dealers, money men, stuff like that. They killed a few people."

"I thought this guy was a street gorilla, a nobody?"

Clarence opened his desk drawer and removed a small yellow pad. He began to draw circles. "You're right. Listen," he said, "I have this stool, this broad's been my informant for years. Anyway, she works at this Cuban club out near La Guardia. She told me that Blaze and a couple of guys snatched the owner. I know the guy, the guy's a big-time fence. Major player, did business for years with a crew from the Gambino family."

"Can I talk to her?"

"Who?"

"The stool, your informant." Nora wondered if Clarence went in for fucking his informants. She wouldn't be surprised.

"Forget it. She's my stool, mine, won't talk to anyone else. I trained her good."

"How about the Cuban?"

"I just told you the guy's connected. No way. The thing is, Blaze and his boys, they took this guy's ear. Cut his fucking ear off. Can you believe that?"

"I'm a New York City police detective. By temperament, I tend to believe anything."

"Really," he said. "You know what I believe, I believe that sometimes, some things just click. People, too. Sometimes you just know."

Nora smiled. This was familiar ground, she'd been down this road a few times.

"Would you believe," Clarence told her, "that on this lovely spring evening, I don't have a date for dinner?"

"I'll tell you what I believe, Lieutenant. I figure that if you'll return that call from your beeper, you'll be able to fix that." A great big grin.

"Man," he said, "you are good."

"Average, I've been told. Kind of run-of-the-mill."

Clarence hesitated. "Whoever told you that should get his head checked. Look," he told her, "I put a little file together on Blaze. Associates, some background. Here, take it. Make a copy of whatever you want."

"Thanks, I would like to go through some of this, and I need to make a few calls."

"Captain Rizzo is on a day off, you're welcome to use his office. It's right next door."

She stood and offered her hand. "Nice meeting you."

"Sheepshead Bay, lobsters."

Nora started toward his office door, stopped to look back over her shoulder. "Be a good guy and call your wife. I bet she just loves lobster."

"Hates em." A small grin.

Outside there was a Red Hook taste to the afternoon air. The day was clear and warm with a stiff breeze coming in off the harbor. Nicky stopped when he reached the corner of Court and Fourth Place and looked over his shoulder. He saw no sign of Fat Paulie's blue Buick and the people he had passed, all those that he knew, smiled a hello. No one, it seemed, was concerned that he might be a target.

Nicky walked in the direction of the harbor and stopped in front of Andrew Joey's butcher shop. AJ behind the counter waved a quick greeting, a big smile on the butcher's face. AJ's smile, the clear bright day, the peaceful, orderly quality of his neighborhood, led him toward a certain confidence. It was possible that Fat Paulie's threat was nothing more than the fat man making noise. Nicky allowed himself to imagine that Paulie and Blaze were simply strutting their stuff, trying to give him the cold creeps. He walked along thinking that it was possible the two shitbirds would move on and leave him and his life in peace. It was possible.

After a while he became tired of walking. Nicky picked up a container of coffee and went to the park on Verandah Place and Congress Street and sat on a bench. He sat fingering the container, considering options. What he had to do was tell himself, keep telling himself, that Blaze and Fat Paulie were a pair of wackos. But wackos were dangerous. He had to take some time and think this through, because when wackos get it in their heads to do some damage you'd better be prepared. It was risky to sit back and wait. What if they went after Irma? What if they went after Tino? What if Nicky thought of the boy standing tall, threatening to brain Blaze with the black baseball bat? He's my son.

Think about it. Think about it. Nicky felt himself floating off, he couldn't come up with anything he could do. He thought again about Blaze and the wino, the way Blaze had put flame to the old man. He finished his coffee, walked over to a trash barrel and threw the container in. Nicky was beginning to feel himself panic, thinking of Blaze, that nutty laugh of his.

Blaze and Paulie were putting him in a corner. Guys like that put you in a corner, you'd better be ready to break out. These two were the kind of sick bastards that would fool with a kid and—

"Hey, Nicky," the voice coming from behind him so suddenly that Nicky jumped and twisted and made a nitwit kind of sound like, "Whaaa, woo, yeah?"

"Nicky, I've been looking all over for you."

Ba-Bing Billy, ol canvas-back Billy, the onetime almost champ of New York's Golden Gloves welterweight division, walked toward him, stopped and pointed a finger. "I knew I'd find you here," he said.

Billy walked into the park in his white-hooded sweat shirt and black sweat pants. Billy announcing to Nicky, saying, "Man, if I were you I'd be in the wind." Nicky heard something in Billy's voice to let him know the guy was panicky.

Nicky had known Billy for years, back since high school hangout days. Back when he was sixteen years old, a junior at Madison High, and ran the streets with Billy and some other kids who were now either dead or in jail or cops.

Looking at Billy's face, Nicky saw his skin was ashy and doughy from years of playing with the heroin lady. Still he couldn't help but feel a certain affinity for the guy, a kinship that went back over the years to when they were all boys bound together by language and the music they loved and the foods they ate and the cars they hoped to own. In those days it seemed they were always talking about cars. Find a spot to park and hide, jump in the backseat, the place where you could charm girls and get their legs open and feet up while you listened to, *"Baby love, my baby love."*

Their spot was a candy store on Union Street that had a juke box and a basement room, clubhouse for the Union Street Boys. Tough kids but nothing serious—except for one Friday night, coming home from a party, down near Hicks and Henry Streets. Nicky, Billy, and two other kids were jumped by a gang of about ten Puerto Ricans. The typical juvenile gang crap.

As the Puerto Ricans began to circle, Billy announced that he'd fair it with any two of them.

Suddenly there was a ring of kids and Billy was in it with two Puerto Ricans that he punched so fast and hard that they went down in about three seconds without a clue as to what happened.

The Puerto Ricans were impressed with Billy and Nicky, too. The Union Street Boys made an alliance that night with the Puerto Ricans, Nicky handling the negotiations.

Nicky found out the next day that Billy had dropped two of the toughest kids from Columbia Street. In the neighborhood they still talked about Billy and the circle of Puerto Ricans. The guy was a legend.

People would say, "Billy hit this kid with a murderous right, ba-bing. The kid dropped. Then Billy popped the other one, ba-bing. And that kid dropped, too."

Ba-Bing Billy.

For a year or two the Union Street Boys ran with the Puerto Ricans. They went to parties, learned to cha-cha and mambo, and had some wild brawls with cruising gangs from outside the Hook.

Of course, Billy decided to become a professional fighter. Billy never went anywhere. Never did a thing with his God-given talent to punch shit out of people. He never went to the gym, never trained, never put in the work. Nicky knew that to be hardass tough in the street had nothing to do with being a winner in a professional ring. In no time at all, Ba-Bing Billy became Canvas-Back Billy with an outrageous heroin habit to boot.

Nicky waved to him in greeting, saying, "What's up, Billy?" Ba-Bing standing in front of him now, his shaved head showing all the scars, his voice shaking as he went on. "They are looking for you, man, they're stalking you."

"The hell you talking about?"

"Such a mean motherfucker. Blaze gave me this. See? He gave me this scar." He pointed to his cheek, where a long thin scar ran from the corner of his eye to the edge of his mouth. "I was so worried about you when I heard," he said, choking and sniffing, running the back of his hand across his nose.

"The punk rip-off artist Vinny Shay was driving Fat Paulie's car, and Blaze, like king shit, was in the backseat playing with that fucking knife of his. Blaze asked me if I'd seen you around? I told him, I said, me? No, no way. I don't see Nicky the Hawk. I told them, Nicky, the last I heard the Hawk was in the wind heading south. That's what I told em. That's just what I said, you were heading south."

Nicky nodded. He could feel his heart beating.

"Man, I was worried for little Tino," Billy said. "I was thinking, something happens to my man, the Hawk, little Tino's screwed. And you know how much I like Tino."

"Blaze, Fat Paulie, and Shay, huh?"

"Yeah, I was doing my run and they pulled up and called me over. Soon as I could, I made it over to your place. I rang the bell, no one answered. So I rang up to Irma. She told me you were out in the streets. I've been looking for you."

"Irma buzzed you in?"

Billy mumbled something about Irma not thinking, then he tilted his head and grinned at Nicky. "Sometimes," he said, "Irma doesn't think right." Billy nodded reasonably.

Nicky explained that he had had a little misunderstanding with Blaze, that's all. No big thing. Telling Billy that he and Blaze went way back. "We need to talk, is all."

"I was at my mother's the other day," Billy said. "And there you were on the TV in that car commercial. You looked so fucking cool. My man, the Hawk, a TV star."

"It was a five-second spot, Billy, just about five seconds." Nicky stood up from his seat, put his hands on his hips and looked around.

"Anyway, you were good," Billy said and clutched him in a bear hug. "You can't talk to Blaze," Billy told him. "Don't try. How do you talk to a clown like him?"

A grumbling, whirring feeling had started up in Nicky's stomach, prompted by Billy's story and the look of cold fear on the fighter's face. "I have to sit down with these guys," Nicky said. "I've got to straighten this out."

Billy told him to forget talking to those two hard-ons.

"Go over to the club," he said, "go and talk to Charlie Chan."

Nicky said, "Charlie, why didn't I think of Charlie?"

Billy said, "The man thinks the sun shines on your ass. Me he would chase, but you, Nicky, Charlie's a fan, brother, always has been. I was you I'd a been there by now. What are you thinking? Charlie decides to step in, your problems are over. Even a nut case like Blaze would back off Charlie told him."

Nicky listened, amazed that he hadn't thought of the Chan from the get go.

Billy said, "Everyone says Charlie's power ain't what it used to be, 'cause most of those guys are doing time and all. But man, Charlie is Charlie. Charlie is the Chan."

Suddenly everything was different.

"All you got to do is ask," Billy said. "What you got to lose, is what I'm saying to you."

It was all Nicky could do to keep from smiling. He'd found a way out. He always found a way out.

Nicky the Hawk.

Nicky was silent. It was starting to come in on him, the guilt, shaming him into thinking of the ways he'd been able to glide by and get through this life. Things unconnected to Blaze and Paulie, forcing him now to consider who he was and what his life was about. A faint smile crept across Billy's face.

"You'd better do something, my man," Billy said then. "You lay still, those two creeps are liable to sneak up and whack you in the back of the head."

Ba-Bing was pale. His face framed in the folds of the sweat shirt was bloodless, his eyes were dull and his hands were colorless, too, except for the places behind his hands and below his fingers that had purple, lump tracks. Billy had been a junkie a long, long time.

"I have to make a move of some kind," Nicky said placidly.

Billy didn't answer him.

"Maybe it's all in my head," Nicky said then. "Maybe there is no real problem here?"

Billy laughed weakly. "You made fools of them. Showed them up to be clowns. It's really funny, but these guys are morons, they got no sense of humor."

Nicky began to laugh.

Billy grinned happily. "In this neighborhood word gets around. Nicky the Hawk humiliated Blaze and his boys. They can't live with that, they'll come for you. Bet on it."

Suddenly Nicky was tired. Billy was wearing a kind of familiar grin, mocking, like, "You're in deep shit, whadaya do now?"

Two young mothers pushing baby carriages came walking into the park. They glanced at Billy and Billy made this clicking sound like urging a horse. "A couple of snappers," Billy said. "Whadaya say we go over and say hello."

"What for?"

"Maybe we get lucky. Ya know, grab some snapperoos, young mammas in the afternoon." Billy was being very uncool, puckering his lips in the young mothers' direction.

"You keep staring at them like that and they're liable to call the cops," Nicky told him.

"Man, I bet they'd love to drop off those kids, maybe smoke some dope and take a walk on the wild side. Put a little adventure in their lives."

"Yeah," Nicky said, "I bet that's just what they're looking for." Look at the two of them, Nicky thought. Each with their pulled-back-and-tied blond hair. Their turtleneck sweaters and jeans, two-hundred-dollar tennis shoes, leaning forward into their baby carriages. You can see it in their faces, hot-shit broads, chins thrust out, silly-ass grins, got life by the short hairs.

Nicky felt a queasy shame stealing over him like the oil and muck in the Gowanus Canal.

The women started toward one of the antique-style benches near the kiddie play area. "Nice day, ladies," Billy singsonged, pleased with himself. Billy making these limp-wristed little waves. Ba-Bing's idea of seduction. Ba-Bing saying, "Hey-hey ladies, whadaya say." The women half smiling, anxious, glancing at Ba-Bing with such apprehension that Billy might have been the Son of Sam himself.

Nicky imagined that the two women could see the danger in Billy, or at least could sense it. Nicky thinking this is it, I'm wasting time. It annoyed him to see the smile on Billy's face.

The two women, eyebrows raised, glanced around the park; when their eyes met Nicky's he smiled at them and they nodded their heads in greeting. Kept nodding their heads, nodding, nodding, nodding.

The neighborhood had changed dramatically during the past several years. Yuppified. Law-abiding, mainstream, conservative types running from the outrageous rents and hustle of Manhattan, moving into a neighborhood once called Red Hook, and now known as Carroll Gardens. People so neat, so winning and, above all, innocent.

It was apparent to Nicky that the two women were good and scared.

And at the heart of their fear was the threat of the unfamiliar, the unknown. Ba-Bing, with his grins and funny sounds, witless gestures, some creature come to hassle them from another solar system.

"Ladies," Billy called out, "nice day, huh?"

Neither of them answered, although Nicky caught the eye of one who threw him a wary look.

"I'm out of here, Billy, see ya around."

"You gonna go talk to the Chan?"

"Yeah, I might."

"Do it, man, do it. Do it before Blaze kills your good-lookin ass."

Walking quickly Nicky passed the two women, wanting to apologize for Billy. But what to say? Standing straight, hands in the pockets of his windbreaker, what he said was, "Ladies, take my word for it, that guy is harmless."

The women turned away oblivious and only Ba-Bing Billy looked at Nicky, squinting and then smiling, nodding his head.

Nicky walked to the Society of the Sons of Calabria club in only fifteen minutes. Moving quickly through his hometown neighborhood, thinking, What the hell am I going to say?

That's the thing with a guy like Charlie, he asks you to drop by, and you say, sure, sure, knowing goddamn well there ain't no way in hell you're going to stop by.

What had it been? A year, a year and a half? More, Nicky believed it was close to two years.

Remembering Fat Paulie and Blaze, feeling in turn, angry, frightened, and then self-conscious, trying to come up with a way to put it to Charlie Chan. I've been meaning to come by, but you know, life gets away from you and before you know it, a day, a week, a month, a year. Proof, time flies.

Anyway, there's this guy Blaze from out on the Hook, this deranged son of a bitch is looking to drop the hammer on me. Whadaya say, Charlie, can you give me a hand here?

Right.

Nicky doing what he could to convince himself that time was precious, he had a busy life, no time to drop in on the Chan. But that was a pile of crap.

Nicky wanted to believe that Charlie Chan had figured a long time ago that Nicky was a solitary sort. That he lived his life like someone in the witness protection program, staying away from spots and people that drew attention and trouble. But he'd always avoided being pulled along by the surge of things. He could not bring himself to believe that he alone had put himself in this jam. All the while he was talking to Ba-Bing Billy the feeling pressing in on him that things were spinning beyond his control.

So now, he would need help, the hand of someone powerful who had neighborhood respect in an impressive way. He needed the Chan.

Respect. It never ceased to amaze Nicky how these old-time guys with their serious faces and missing teeth used that word, given how they lived their lives. What a bunch of phony bullshit.

Anyway, the truth of it was he'd never had the patience to hang out with those bust-out hard-ons from the Chan's club who stood around like a pack of CO_2 inspectors saying, "Fuhgedabout this, fuhgedabout that," nothing going on in their motley little lives except hanging out, waiting for the score that never showed up.

But, the Chan was different.

It was the kind of warm and sunny day that brought the old people and young mothers and toddlers out in their beach chairs, chitchatting, joyful, and laughing, the kids running and playing, doing somersaults, some running into the street, some just thinking about running into the street, all of them celebrating the gift of a bright and warm spring day.

Nicky was walking more quickly now, and he knew that the Chan would be pleased to see him.

The Chan, always a big fan.

He turned the corner and stepped on Court Street, his gaze trained on Charlie at the curb polishing his car.

But for Charlie Chan, Nicky would have been in a real predicament with Tino. It was Charlie who had sent him with his fifteen-hundred dollars into Little Italy to get a birth certificate and Social Security card. It was Charlie who made all the arrangements. Charlie not asking for anything in return except a little respect. Respect in a recognizable manner. Charlie always asking Nicky to take some time out of his day to come around. The Chan loved to talk current events, politics, and show business. "I need a little normal conversation," Charlie would say. "Some talk with someone that reads a book, discussion with someone that can fucking read."

And even though he knew that Charlie understood, even though

Charlie had told him, "Don't worry about it, come by when you can. I know you're busy." Even though Nicky understood all that, he stood frozen now, thoughts fading and returning, seeing Charlie with a rag working over that gleaming black Oldsmobile of his, all this guilt, the guilt of never coming by, his failure to say thank you, thank you, time and again; all this guilt collapsing down on him, making him feel like the cheating husband, returning home after a night on the town covered with the stink of betrayal.

Wearing a self-conscious smile, Nicky walked up to the car, saying, "Hey, Charlie, how you been? Remember me?"

Many of the old Italian men from the Society of the Sons of Calabria had gone. Some to the cemetery, some to jail. Others had moved, with their loyal and long-suffering wives, to Naples, Florida, leaving behind stacks of unpaid legal fees, restaurant bills, and weary and worn-out mistresses. They all took with them their memories of bygone days, the time when they were exalted masters of the city and controlled the streets.

Charlie Chan Conti stayed put.

Even though Charlie knew that his club and his Cosa Nostra had gone to havoc and ruin, he stayed put. So linked was his life to Red Hook it was clear to everyone that Charlie Chan would leave his neighborhood only in a box.

"How've you been, kid?" Charlie said.

"Maybe you don't want to know."

"That good, huh?"

"Can I talk to you?"

"Sure, give me a minute. Let me finish up here."

Charlie rubbed his car with a salmon-colored cotton towel and every so often he'd peek at Nicky, wag his head and smile.

Once, at the Sing Sing reception center Charlie had been given an IQ test. He scored 150. Charlie was a genius, a man capable of serious thought, a remarkable mind full of light and curiosity.

The Chan said to Nicky, "You in a hurry or do you have some time?"

"I need to talk to you."

Charlie regarded him, smiling. "Yeah?" he said. The Chan gave a short laugh and returned to his work.

Nicky watched as Charlie polished his car in a devoted and melancholy and systematic manner. And Nicky said to the Chan, "No, no rush. I've come to ask a favor."

The Chan was going a little paunchy, but there remained the framework of the longshoreman in his shoulders and arms, and in his face that looked like a battered dock piling all creased and hard and tide-worn. He wore a shapeless running suit the same shade of black as his Oldsmobile.

Nicky knew that the Chan loved his life, but to Nicky it was a place of loneliness, violence, and uncertainty. Nicky asked himself, could you do it? Could you live Charlie's life? Could you come to the corner day in, day out, every day dealing with treachery and slyness? A world of people plotting to kill you or put you in jail. Could you live like that and not go totally nuts?

Charlie glanced through the window of the car, looking at the *New York Post* that rested on the front seat, the headline ablaze in blocked red ink.

HEAD OF NEW JERSEY CRIME FAMILY TO TESTIFY FOR FEDS

"Did you read today's paper?" Charlie said.

"No, no, not yet. Anything good?"

Charlie shrugged with a mournful smile. "There's been some virus in the air a long, long time," he said. "And the bitch of it is, it looks like it's contagious."

Nicky glanced at the headline saying, "Bad, huh?"

Charlie smiled. "What do you think?"

"It don't look good."

"Give the man a cigar."

Charlie Chan Conti talked a lot. For a man in his line of work he talked a lot. That's not to say that Charlie Chan talked more than the average person, he simply talked more than the average wiseguy. And he had strong opinions about everything. Charlie loved discussion and interaction, but most of all he treasured his neighborhood life. In Red Hook, Charlie was a celebrity of gigantic proportions.

Friends and friends of friends would go to Charlie for a wide assortment of favors. Union jobs for their kids, a recommendation to a lawyer, advice about children that they were losing to drugs. The Chan could take care of it all. The man could transform someone from a nobody, to a person with a powerful patron, into someone to be feared.

Charlie gave Nicky an appraising look. And Nicky wondered what he saw. He felt there was something he ought to explain about the past couple of years. Nicky had that terrible feeling you get when someone studies you, and you both know that you have done a serious wrong, a wrong for which you haven't expressed regret.

Charlie said, "You're doing good? You look like you're doing good."

Nicky shrugged. Charlie asked about Tino, all the while staring in a certain way at Nicky, and there was something in his voice that made Nicky nervous. Some guy built like a lighthouse came out of the club bringing Charlie a message and Charlie introduced Nicky to him.

"Sonny," he said, "this here is a friend of mine, Nicky Ossman. Some day he'll be a famous actor. Say hello."

Sonny said, "My pleasure." Biting his lip, Sonny nodded and walked back to the club's front door where he stood, his head on a swivel, checking the street.

Charlie turned to Nicky again.

"So, the kid's okay?"

"Fine. Doing well. Going to school. Gets good grades, better, way better than I ever did."

"Keep an eye on him, keep him out of trouble. I see him once in a while walking the streets. You should tell him to stop by and say hello."

"Tino's into a million things," Nicky explained.

"My daughters moved to Florida, can you believe that? I have three grandkids, I want to see them, I have to take that hike."

"Florida's nice," Nicky told him.

"It sucks. What you should do, Nicky, is move to L.A. so you can rub shoulders with all those producers. Show your face, get yourself known."

"I don't want to live in L.A.," Nicky told him. "It's a place where they shoot too many shitty movies and not enough lunatics."

"You know, you're right. I saw this piece on 60 Minutes, drive-by shootings, everybody got guns. Crazy."

When Charlie finished with the car, he unlocked the trunk, tossed in the rag, then stood with his hands on the car's roof. Charlie puckered his lips and pointed with his chin at the window. A simple action that he surrounded with explicit ritual.

"See this guy in the paper, Nicky, this guy here testifying for the feds? I know this guy, and let me tell you, this rat's life had more violent scenes than the Old Testament. This bum killed ten, fifteen people and the government makes him a hero. You figure it."

"I can't figure the government," Nicky said softly. "I can't make sense of my own life, forget the government."

Charlie stood for a long time looking through the car's window at the newspaper. "Do you believe in original sin?" he said.

"I'm not too religious," Nicky told him.

"No kidding? I'm surprised, I figured you for a spiritual sort of guy, Nicky."

"When I was a kid they crammed me full of all that jazz, wore me out."

Charlie nodded solemnly, "Interesting," he said. "Anyway, I don't believe sin is original but cumulative. Life is filled with compromises and concessions. If you think you can do right in a world where everyone is willing to do wrong, think again. You know what I mean?"

"Sure."

Nicky didn't tell him that the last thing he wanted to talk about was religion. Instead he told him about the afternoon at Paulie's afterhours club. And Nicky let Charlie tell him what dangerous loonies Fat Paulie and Blaze were, something that Nicky already knew.

Charlie said, "A few months back, Paulie came to see me accompanied by this Blaze and two other guys. All of them strung out on I don't know what. All of them trying to convince me that they were seriously bad. They tried very hard to appear dangerous. It worked. I chased them. Lunatics, I don't need more lunatics around me."

"I'm sorry I haven't come by, Charlie. I'm embarrassed, I don't know what to say."

"I missed seeing you. I know how you feel, at least I think I know how you feel. But it can't hurt, come by, say hi. It's the right thing to do."

"I will."

"Sometimes it's wise to schmooze a little with the purveyors of crime. You gain insight. Makes you a better actor."

"I'll come by, Charlie."

"Good. So what's the deal? You got a problem, huh?"

"I'd say. This Fat Paulie and that guy, Blaze, they're gunning for me."

"For you?"

"It's for real."

"You're worried? You're really worried. Stop worrying."

"Just like that?" He was hoping Charlie would say something specific. "These guys scare me."

"What did I say?"

"You said I should stop worrying."

"So stop."

"Okay . . ." Nicky felt as if he were ten years old.

"Look, Nicky, you're smart to be scared. These two guys dance between the lines of evil and the demented. They're doing all sorts of things out here. Pushing it. A couple of bust-out jerkoffs who suddenly got boxes of money to put in the street. It's amazing."

"So I hear."

"No, it's really amazing. Do you know how much money they have in the street? Plenty, they're lending plenty of money. A couple of hammerheads."

"Now that you mention it, I know Blaze from way back. He never had the brains of a rock. How does a nobody like this come up with big money?"

"I'm thinking that Paulie and Blaze are not out here on their own. Somebody is aiming them. Somebody's got a treasure map and, whoever it is, he's showing Blaze and Paulie where the gold is. Someone is pushing his button."

"And he collects ears."

"What's that?"

"I saw them, he carries around a bag of ears."

Charlie Chan had to think about that a second. "C'mon!"

Nicky said, "In his back pocket, a little pouch of ears."

"Some guys dream of making their mark; some guys want to show they got what it takes. I can just see this guy Blaze going into his room at night, closing the door and taking out his little bag of ears. We're talking a sick bastard here," Charlie said. Then his eyes wandered away from Nicky and an expression of singular, cold hardness came over his rugged features. "I heard it was fingers, I heard they like to make people's fingers move away from their hands. It's the kind of thing they do."

Nicky filled his cheeks and blew out some air.

Charlie saying, "They leaned hard on one friend of mine already. Let me tell you, I can't help it, I have a violent nature. Blaze and Paulie keep this shit up, I'll see to it that their heads move away from their hats. A couple of tough guys, huh? We'll see how tough they are." Charlie stretched his arms; king of the jungle.

Nicky thinking that Charlie could take ten years off your life with a look. Charlie Chan, Nicky considered, would make one helluvan actor.

Charlie pointed with his chin across the street. "That's your cousin, right?" he said.

Nicky followed his gaze to the doorway of the Roma Cafe. Irma standing hesitantly on the sidewalk in front of the restaurant, one hand raised in a timid greeting.

Nicky thinking, Jesus. "That's her," he said, grinning, then stopped smiling as that strange-looking character, the guy with the ponytail and work boots, that little weird fucker who had been talking to Irma near the juke box in the Roma the other day, came waltzing out of the restaurant to join her on the sidewalk. Charlie saying:

"You should tell your cousin to find a new line of work."

"I've told her. She won't listen to me."

"What do you mean, won't listen to you? Make her listen to you, convince her. Hey," he said, "be a man."

Walking now, Irma held on to the guy's arm, guided him down the street toward home with a playful step.

"So who is the little dude in the ponytail?" Charlie said.

Nicky shrugged.

"We don't know that guy, Nicky. Who is he?"

"Some guy from the Roma." Nicky felt as if he were testifying in court.

"Some guy. Who?"

"A trick." He almost said. "I've seen him around."

"Yeah, well, you should talk to Irma, convince her to change her ways."

"Right."

Charlie shrugged apologetically. "It's your business, yours and Irma's. I just think about the kid, the boy should not be around that."

"Uh-huh." Nicky started to walk after Irma.

Charlie was momentarily distracted by Sonny, who called out that there was a telephone call for him. "Take the message." He pointed at Nicky saying, "The boy Tino should not have to see that."

"I'll see ya, Charlie," Nicky said.

"Yeah, I'll see ya when I see ya. Hey, Nicky," he called out, "keep your head up and your hands over your ears." Charlie laughed kind of a crazy laugh, not unlike Blaze's nutty howl.

Nicky walked after the couple who were a good two blocks ahead of him now. What the hell was she thinking? Irma was killing him, making him nuts. Talk to her, convince her to change her ways. And then if she doesn't . . . Be a man.

Nicky walked faster now, talking to himself, looking around the street, his hands curled into fists in his jacket pocket, people moving aside as he went past, really angry now, showing his anger, Goddamn Irma.

Nicky felt like some sort of homicidal maniac right on the edge of blowing his stack. He imagined Tino at home, wondering where Irma was, where he was. Nicky tried to calm himself down, hearing Charlie now, Be a man.

He couldn't tell the Chan how hopeless it all was, dealing with Irma. He remembered explaining to Tino—You see there are these two guys, you and Irma have to stay put. Then added almost as an afterthought, Irma will look out for you.

Now there she was cruising down the street, her hooker's grin in place, with a stranger on her arm. Irma, Nicky considered, was a king-sized pain in the ass.

For years Nicky had preached to Irma to find a real life for herself. Do something worthwhile, he'd tell her. Irma would come at him talking trash, "What?" she'd say, "What the hell am I going to do? Work as a waitress, a barmaid, maybe drive a cab? C'mon, Nicky, c'mon." Irma could make Nicky heartsick with disappointment.

He'd been so desperate to make this life work for him and Tino that he'd been blind to Irma's problems, had no time for her. And Irma, she had fallen right into the gutter. And then disappointment became tacit approval, and Nicky made excuses for himself and for Irma, too. He shook his head laughing at himself. Putting himself between Irma, Fat Paulie, and Blaze. What a joke. Making himself a target. Furious at himself, sorry now that he ever took that walk over to Paulie's.

A new Nicky, he thought, reborn with a sound understanding of what the hell he was doing. He considered the new Nicky: A guy who was going to wash his hands of Irma. A guy who would put his life in order, maybe find a real day job. A guy who was going to get on his agent to find some work.

Why not?

Well, he told himself, it's up to you. If you really want it that way, that's the way it will be.

Now, he asked himself in his new Nicky voice, where in the hell did Irma go?

It was sometime near three o'clock when Irma woke from a nap, hungry, bored to death, and needing a smoke. She had tried watching the video Nicky had left, but it was silly shit about some kids and bicycles and sent her right off to dreamland.

"Oh, man," she thought, and began searching the apartment for cigarettes. In her first minute of waking consciousness the nicotine fit hit, now five minutes later, she was bonkers. And, she was hungry.

"Screw this," Irma said, combing out her hair, feeling that feeling she could only describe as the thrill of hitting the set, hitting the street. The feeling was hard to fight, impossible to resist, the pure joy of being out there.

It was a sunny day, not a cloud in a sky as blue as a sapphire. She wanted out of her apartment, out into the sunlight, catch some of those rays. Screw Blaze and Paulie, the fat bastard. It was already afternoon, heading toward night, she needed to be out there.

Already dressed in her leather skirt, Irma put on a red blouse she had bought two days before at Regina's, on Montague Street, then she walked across the hall to see Tino.

Tino kept his head down and his eyes up, the boy getting nervous eyes that he couldn't mask, watching her as she came in. "Uh-oh, where you going?"

"To get us something to eat."

"Nicky said to stay put. I'm not hungry."

"Yes. Well, okay, I know that. I'll only be a minute. What should I get you? You must be hungry, I'm starved."

"Stay put, Irma, means stay put."

"You won't even know I'm gone," she told him, then she went out the apartment door, into the hall, down the two flights of steps, and into the street. She kept her eyes down, not thinking at all, humming a little k.d. lang, her leather bag slung over her shoulder, and went up to Court Street and into the Roma Cafe. It wouldn't be too long before she headed back home, she thought, it should only take a few minutes to pick up something to eat, get some smokes.

In the cafe she bought a package of Camels from Jackie O.D., and ordered two sausage-and-pepper sandwiches. She took a seat at the end of the bar where she could observe the street, see any trouble coming. Be on the lookout, she told herself, be ready to scoot.

Irma loved the Roma Cafe. She felt at home there, great bar stools, soft upholstered backs you could get comfortable against, the plush carpet. And every so often O.D. would drop a cherry and an umbrella in her drink. Homey.

Irma stretched, closed her eyes, and arched her back. When she opened her eyes again she looked out the window and, wow, there was Nicky across the street talking with Charlie Chan. Wow.

What she had not considered until she got to the Roma and spotted Nicky talking with that chinky-eyed mobster, what she hadn't thought about at all, was that she might run into Nicky. So she was not prepared, even though she should have been, when, sitting on the comfortable bar stool, staring at Nicky and Charlie, this guy tapped her on the shoulder. She about jumped through her skin.

"Hey, babe, where've you been?" he asked.

She turned and looked into big brown eyes that he was moving up then down like some kind of puppet.

"Around," she said with a smile.

"I've been looking for *you*," he said mildly. And, he had an accent, the tiniest trace but an accent for sure.

He said the word *you*, as though he was in love or angry.

One of the prerequisites of being a hooker and surviving without getting messed up, Nicky had told her, was that you stayed clear of strangers.

Hookers, Nicky had said, must be like the Masai with their cattle, constantly attentive.

He smiled at her, turning the full light of his charm on her, a charm she had instinctively recognized in two seconds the last time they spoke. The guy was a trick. She asked the strange trick to come home with her.

Irma forgot all of Nicky's warnings, if only for the time it took to pick up the sandwiches and walk out into the street.

Nicky stood shoulder to shoulder with Charlie Chan, returned her wave of greeting. As they walked, Irma and the stranger, she was scolded for wearing such a short, tight leather skirt. "The skirt," he said, "makes me so hawney, I could fuck you right here on the sidewalk."

"Cost you another hundred," she told him with a smile.

Inside her apartment the trick saying he wanted to have his prick professionally sucked, and Irma doing some of her best work on the stool in the kitchen, Tino across the hall, sitting on his sofa, watching the last act of *North by Northwest*. The trick, accepting all that he asked for, didn't speak recognizable words during those first few minutes, he did make little yelping and moaning noises. And then afterward, after he was done and he was done very quickly, the trick showing his appreciation by laying a badge on Irma, a badge instead of money, which led first to a God-awful scream from Irma, then her attempt to claw the strange trick's eyes from his head.

"Tino!" Irma screamed.

Tino ran into her apartment and found Irma and the trick rolling around on the kitchen floor like a circus act. Then Nicky, huffing and puffing, after charging up two flights of stairs, exploded through the open door, yelling "Tino, Tino get the hell out of here." Irma screaming, "I sucked his prick and he won't pay me."

The trick saying, "Jesus Christ, I'm a cop, I'm a cop, get off me." Of course Nicky didn't believe him, the strange trick was short and had a gold tooth, he resembled Danny DeVito in a ponytail. And, as far as Nicky knew, vice cops in their crusade against whores didn't get blow jobs before they showed their badge.

Nicky pulled the trick to his feet, putting a full nelson on the guy. Tino kicked him in the shins. Irma snapped her arms around the guy's leg like a bear trap and yanked. They all collapsed to the floor. "Jesus, I'm a cop," the trick kept saying. Nicky shouting, "Tino, beat it, boogie, get out of here." Tino headed for the door saying, "Irma, I told you to stay put. I told her, Nicky, but nooooo, not Irma."

Nicky hit the trick in the stomach and the guy vomited, first on the floor then on Irma, sending both Nicky and Irma scrambling, groping back out of his way. Then the trick managed to get to his ankle holster and pull his gun. It was at that moment that Nicky decided that this trick had cop written all over him.

The patrol cars arrived, and the cops grabbed Nicky and Irma, beating on Nicky, shouting, "You wanna hit a cop, you wanna fight, tough guy?" The trick shouting, "A kid, there's a kid around here, the little bastard kicked me." The cops urged them down the apartment house stairs, out onto the street. People were lined up on the sidewalk and around the police cars, shouting Nicky's name. Nicky looked around for Tino, not seeing the boy anywhere. More cops bore down on him and dragged him to the police car.

Shanghaied by the cops, Nicky thought he'd give them a little Nicholson in One Flew Over the Cuckoo's Nest. He rolled his eyes playfully and shouted, "There is anger everywhere. The world is going insane." Psychotic, non compos, crackers, loony, and lost, but charming, always charming. Not guilty by reason of insanity.

For two hours Nora had been sitting in the glow of a desk lamp, going through file folders. She was supposed to be in Captain Rizzo's office familiarizing herself with DD5s and 61s, police reports that mentioned Blaze Longo. She was in the office, all right, glancing at the files, but she was doing all this in a cold sweat, unable to concentrate. Nora would read a page here and there, glance at a mug shot, then she'd make a telephone call.

She called Sammy's beeper three times and left messages for her lawyer Vera Ryan, twice. For a hot minute she considered dropping everything to go out in the street and track down Max and her gun. Where Max was concerned, she was more baffled now then she'd ever been.

The man clung to her like a hunger, with his conspicuous display of need, some kind of an addiction, a craving to keep her walled up inside his insane life. What drove this man on she could not imagine, but she was drained of pity, finally leaving only frustration and anger.

It was five o'clock.

Nora sat, trying to focus on an old copy of a 61, a complaint report, going back five years. It contained only one charge, Felonious Assault, Maiming. The place of occurrence was Pier 1, Grand Colombian lines. Fredrick Walker, male, black, 64 yrs, address unknown, assaulted with gasoline and fire. The 61 consisted of a perfunctory paragraph about

Walker, apparently homeless, receiving severe burns, and treated at St. Anthony's Hospital. A copy of the Aided Card was attached.

The investigating detective was unable to get a statement from Walker, unable to get a positive ID on the perpetrator. The DD5s described two attempts to interview the victim at the hospital without results. Then, upon Fredrick Walker's release from St. Anthony's, the detective's inability to locate him for further interviews. The 61 was filed two months later: Unable to substantiate, unable to close with arrest. The classic stamped, closed case. Meaning, the investigating detective, weighed down with a ton of open cases, had spent as much time as he could investigating a crime against someone who refused to make a statement. Other than his name the victim was anonymous.

Nora sat back, opening then closing her hands, wondering if Max did in truth have her gun, then thinking, c'mon, c'mon, get to work. Forget Max and all his off-the-wall, crazy head games. Read the DD5.

Suddenly she was filled with overdue energy, a giddy complete surprise. Longo had been in the company of one Nick Ossman. "Whoa," Nora grunted, envisioning the character with the lamb. That good-looking dipshit from the week before.

Not long after the incident had occurred, Ossman had been picked up by responding uniform cops and brought into the precinct for questioning. Nora paused, savoring the paragraph. She fought off a surge of optimism, and read on, trying to collect her thoughts. Ossman knew Longo, here was a way in.

Nora was still trying to figure out her next step, when she heard them—barking like a pack of junkyard dogs—officers coming up the stairs with a prisoner, maybe more than one. She could hear the shouts coming from the detectives' squad room down the hall, the cops and the prisoner, a voice so familiar.

Nora eased herself out from behind the desk, walked slowly down the hallway, and looked into the squad room. And, sure enough, back there in a cage stood a figure. And he was indeed that good-looking guy with the lamb or sheep or whatever the hell it was. The preposterous Nicky Ossman. This could be, Nora considered, her lucky day.

It was five-fifteen.

So what if it had been five years ago? He knew Longo. Nora blinked hard, thinking, a combination of luck and a little work, being in the right place at the right time. Bingo, she thought. The story of my life.

Nora stayed out of sight, listening, looking right through the arresting officers, right through Nicky Ossman, her mind playing with the image of this character running with a lamb over his shoulder.

A pair of uniformed officers took him out of the cage handcuffed. She watched a Puerto Rican detective with a goatee remove the manacles and bring him to the fingerprint board. Nicky appeared to be in shock, as though he couldn't believe what was happening. She heard him say, "Who would ever make a fat little guy like him a cop? The bum was beating up on my cousin. What would you do?"

The detective in the goatee saying, "Bum? Bum? The man's a police officer, you asshole. Procuring. Okay? That's for a start, then assault on a cop. You'll get time for this. Oh, yeah, you'll be decorating a bunk in a cell, playing with your weewee for the next couple of years."

"Jail, oh, no-o-o-o, that's not me. What we got here, fellas, is a simple misunderstanding, a failure to communicate." Sounding like Newman in *Cool Hand Luke,* the guy was a bag of tricks.

Nora stepped into the room, Nicky looked to her with helpless dismay, Nora saying, "Gotcha."

Nora glanced at the Puerto Rican detective sheepishly then nodded to Nicky. "What do you have?" she said.

"Procuring and assault on an officer, Captain."

"How's the officer?"

"Nothing serious. He's downstairs with a policewoman, they're doing a body search on the female prisoner."

"Would you mind if I spoke to this guy in private?"

"No problem, Captain," the detective told her, smiling. "Just give me a second to cuff him."

For Nora, sitting in Captain Rizzo's office with Nicky Ossman was like being trapped in some hellish, two-bit, off-off-off Broadway show listening to horrible comedy riffs, a symphony of stories and excuses and give-me-a-break looks. Nicky saying, man, you must be exhausted, considering the way you've been running around in my head for the past couple of weeks, you must be plumb worn out. "By the way," he said, "you look like you've been in a hammer fight without a hammer. What the hell happened to your face?"

"I'll tell you what," Nora said, "you stop trying to be cute. What happened to my face is my business. Cut the jokes."

"Sorry. Look, I happen to be a man that appreciates a beautiful woman. You are a beautiful woman, Captain, and it irks me that somehow . . ."

"Shut up!"

"You say that a lot."

"What?"

"Shut up."

"Hmmmmm. Maybe you're right."

"I am."

"Could you try to be quiet for just a minute?"

"Certainly."

"All right, look, snatching some meat is one thing, beating on a cop is a whole other story."

Nicky held up his cuffed hands and nodded toward the door. "What those cops are saying in there is not half true." Sitting facing each other across a desk, Nicky giving it all he had with that grin of his, figuring maybe I got a shot here. "I'm coming home, coming up the stairs to my apartment, listen to this . . ."

Nora, behind the desk, her head down, reading the 61, said, "You and an Irma Tucci assaulted a police officer in the performance of his duty. Ms. Tucci came on to the officer at the Roma Cafe, offering oral sodomy, offering oral sodomy for one hundred dollars. Not cheap, she must be good. A hundred bucks for a blow job, geeze."

"Irma's my cousin. A bit promiscuous, but no whore. She's at the Roma picking up sandwiches and bumps into this guy, they chat, they know each other, seen each other before. The guy, listen to this, the guy is romancing her, she goes for it and takes him home. It happens, happens everyday. They have sex, they did the dirty and the guy says, 'Irma I'm a cop, you're busted.' He's serious. Irma goes, 'You're kidding me? I didn't do anything but suck your dick.' The guy takes out a badge, starts to get rough, tries to grab her, she screams. I'm coming up the stairs, hear the shouts. I think, hey, hey, my dear cousin Irma is getting raped."

Nora told him, "That's not what the cop says, this is serious, procuring and assault."

"C'mon, Captain, they had sex. You can check that out. Take a swab of her mouth, semen stains, run a DNA test. I watched the O.J. case. You can do that, I know you can do that."

Nora said, "Shut up."

"Okay."

Nora took a moment. Heard, from the detectives' office down the hall, laughter, conversation, a woman's voice, this Irma, Nicky's cousin. Nora said to Nicky, "I might be able to help you." Nicky nodded his head, he said he could use whatever help she could give. She stared at Nicky a minute, watched him turning his head, looking around, trying to be cool. A big sigh, like, what am I doing here? Looking, or trying to look sad and vulnerable, the poor guy caught up in something he didn't understand. He dropped his head into his hands.

Nora said, "I don't want to see you arrested, hell, the jails are full up already. And this charge, this assault and whatever, they can work that out right there in the stationhouse. That is, if the arresting officer goes along, which, I'm confident I can convince him to do."

Nicky said, "I've been thinking about you a whole lot lately. I have."

He gave Nora a smile. Nora watched, fascinated, as Nicky tried to get an expression of sincerity in his eyes.

Nora said, "Hear me out, listen to me, and I'll save you a couple of years of prison time."

A great big grin from Nicky.

The two of them sat like two sweethearts in a quiet room with Nicky sitting still, hunched slightly forward, listening, eyeing Nora. Nicky was trying to lay it on thick, frightened more for Tino than he was for himself, giving this woman, this cop, his very best help-me plea and trademark smile as she tried to cut him a deal.

Nora told him she'd justify it to the DA and spell it out to the cop, but Nicky would have to submit himself to her. She spoke in code, hinting at this and that, sort of explained the ins and outs, and Nicky listened. Finally Nora stared at him a moment and said, "What do you know about a creep bastard named Blaze Longo?"

Oh, boy.

Nicky looked at Nora and sagged. He knew Blaze, sure he knew him, he told her. To most people in the neighborhood Blaze was a shadowy, almost mythic figure. But not to him, he'd known the guy for years. Nicky thinking, screw Blaze.

"Can you get to him?" Nora asked. Nicky looked around the room, then at the cuffs on his wrists, and said, "I've known Blaze since we were kids. We don't like each other."

"Could you get to him for me?"

Nicky pressed his splayed hands together in prayer. "Can you keep me and my cousin out of jail?"

"Of course."

Nicky grinned, his head frozen at that chin-cocked, head shot-picture angle. "Blaze is serious bad news. He makes his living scaring people to death, because death is what he can deliver."

Nora nodded her head. "I've heard," she told him.

Nicky asked her what she knew about Blaze and Nora told him, not much, just a little. That's when he said, you ever see the movie *Cape Fear?* Not the old one with Robert Mitchum, but the new one with De Niro, Nolte, and Lange? Nora told him she liked the movie. Nicky saying, that character, the De Niro character, the psycho that brought a plague of terror, misery, and mayhem into the lives of Nolte's family, that guy was a ray of sunshine compared to Blaze Longo. Blaze is no ordinary street wanderer, he told her, the guy is completely immersed in craziness. He'd come after you as easily as he would me. You ready for that? Ready to take on an absolute nutjob?

"I've been doing this job a long time, Nicky," Nora told him, "the likes of Blaze Longo don't frighten me."

"Captain, I have a feeling that you don't know just how bad this world around here can get, even by a guess."

"Work with me or go to jail," Nora told him. "Your choice."

He stuck his tongue out at her and made a face.

Nicky said, "The world is full of people doing their thing, getting by, and getting along. And here you are trying to get me killed. A siren, a temptress to destruction."

"It's your choice."

Nicky was smiling at her in a way a man smiles when he has hopes and plans. "You'll spring me and dear cousin Irma?"

"Yes, of course. You and dear cousin Irma," she smiled at him. Nicky thinking, this woman had the ability to rope you in, speak to you with that look in her eyes that made you believe her, made you want to believe her because suddenly you felt it was important to be her friend, more than a friend maybe, yes, maybe, who knows? stranger things have happened.

Nicky gave her the five-minute version of his life. A struggling actor, not a bad guy, no street guy. Sure he was born and raised in the Hook, knew plenty of people, some bad guys, sure. You grow up around here, can't help but know a few. But he stayed away, far as he could get from the likes of Blaze Longo.

Nora listened, nodding, engrossed and overwhelmed; the guy was a natural. She saw the smile and couldn't help herself. There was something rivetingly attractive about this hotshot, rustler, bodyguard for a prostitute, this actor with his bedroom eyes. He dripped with sex. It oozed from his every pore, his expressions always turned unmistakably sensual. Not that she would ever be interested in a character like him for a sexual partner.

He was a street guy. An articulate and smart street guy, but a street guy nonetheless. She could see that he was appraising her, wondering what she'd be like in the sack. So much the better. Nora knew how to use sexual tension, it was one of the things she did best, get the undercurrent going, put the electricity into the air. When she left the room to get them both coffee she wiggled like a streetwalker. Let him get his hopes up, let him get whatever he wanted up. It was a healthy outlet for anxiety and this guy Nicky was scared to death, she could see it, no way was he going to jail if he could help it. She had him just where she wanted, at least she thought she did. Then again, where men were concerned, Nora had always lacked normal attributes known as common sense and caution. It never would have occurred to Nicky that he was part of a pattern.

"Give me your word you'll help with Longo, I'll get you and cousin Irma both cut loose."

Nicky stared at her a moment then leaned in close to her, "You know," he said, "trying to jam up Blaze Longo could get us both killed. See this face, this face is the kind of face tough guys want to ruin, especially guys like Blaze Longo. But if jamming him up is what it takes to get me and Irma out of here, then I'm your man."

It was just about then, right around five-thirty, when the detective with the goatee knocked once and then came into the room. The detective started to smile. "Captain," he said, "there's a call for you from the chief of detectives' office. I could have them switch it in here, if you'd like?"

After a second Nora said, "Sure, have them put the call through here." Something stirred inside her. After a moment the phone rang and Nicky looked away then turned back to her.

"Captain Riter," she said.

"Nora," The chief said, his voice seemed unfocused, almost distorted and cramped. "I've got to tell you something. I don't know how to begin."

"What happened?"

"It's Max."

"Paul, what happened?"

"He shot himself, killed himself."

"God."

"There's more, he shot Sam Morelli. Sam's in critical condition at Peninsula Hospital."

Nora turned and looked into Nicky's eyes, locking on; and in that instant something important seemed to pass between them.

Jean-Paul said, "About ten minutes ago, a sector car from the 100th Precinct responded to a call of shots fired. They found Max and Sam on the boardwalk. That's all anybody knows."

"Jesus."

"Look, have someone drive you, but get right in here. Nora," he said. "I hope Max didn't use your gun."

"Of course, he used my gun, what else would he use? Chief," she told him, "I'm going to the hospital."

"I'm not sure that's . . ."

"I'm going to the hospital."

They spoke for another minute or so, mostly questions and answers, Nora trying to keep her voice down. She would go to the hospital and then come into the office. She hung up the telephone using both hands.

Nicky said, "Are you all right, Captain?"

Nora shook her head.

Nicky offered a small nervous smile. "Can I help?"

Nora shook her head again. He looked at her curiously. Nora said, "I don't know how to say this."

"Just say it."

"My husband shot my best friend and then he killed himself."

Silence from Nicky.

"It just happened, I don't know, fifteen, twenty minutes ago."

Nora sat back in her chair, folded her arms across her chest, sitting still, keeping her eyes straight ahead.

Nicky shifted uncomfortably in his seat, toying with his handcuffs.

"I'd better go," she told him.

Nicky looked down at his hands.

"Look," she said, "I can't . . ." Nora's mouth went dry, she could feel her legs weakening.

"Don't worry about me," he told her. "Me and Irma, we'll be okay."

She watched him closely for a few seconds. Cops were coming up the stairs, there was noise, people shouting.

"You've enough to worry about," Nicky said.

"I just . . ."

"It's okay."

"Oh, Sam," she said.

"Your husband?"

"No, my friend. My former partner."

Nicky dropped his head thinking, your husband, your partner. Sounds like a dangerous mix. "Will he be all right?" Nicky said.

Nora shrugged. "I don't know."

They looked at each other.

"Are you sure you'll be all right?"

Nora nodded once, letting out a huge sigh.

Nicky saying now, "You really shouldn't drive. Have one of these jokers here drive you."

Nora stood and gathered her papers. "I can drive," she told him. "Look," she said, "maybe you've fooled me, maybe you're trying to act nice and concerned, saying all the right things. Which is okay, I guess, considering the circumstances, it's the way things are. I got to admit though, I have this feeling that you're not such a bad guy." A small smile from Nora.

"Me, a bad guy? Naw. I'm an actor. Nicky the Hawk, that's me. If you let me, I'll be your savior."

"I'm going to be busy, but I'll get you out of here," she said. "It may take a day or two, but I'll get you out. My savior, huh?"

"You'll see. Hey, I'm the guy you're going to want on speed dial when things get tense." Nora's smile faded. And Nicky glanced at the file folders in her hand and then at Nora's face. He held up his cuffed hands, tried a little grin.

Slowly, with a certain amount of ceremony, Nora put the files in her shoulder bag. Then she started toward the office door and when she turned back he was sitting there watching her. Down the hall, from the locker room, Garth Brooks was singing out "Friends in Low Places," the music mixing with the sounds of laughter and horseplay. The 6:00 P.M. to 2:00 A.M. shift making ready for their night. A fire raged in Nora's stomach and brain, and her legs felt unsteady.

"Nicky the Hawk, my savior," she said slowly.

"What I'm saying, what I'm telling you, is that you can count on me."

"If you were half as sure of yourself as you pretend, I'd feel better. But you're not, so I don't." A small smile.

Nicky knew little about the pain this woman was experiencing, but he believed he knew plenty about fear and anxiety. How it ate at you, turned you around, and froze your heart. How some people smiled when they were scared. She was smiling at him now, a sad smile but a smile nevertheless. And he wondered what that smile meant. Maybe he should jump up from the chair and tell her to take him along, have him accompany her, he'd help her get through this night. What he wanted, he realized, was to be with her. Simply that, to be with this woman, this police captain.

The realization made him depressed. Nicky believed that the chances of his getting close to a woman like this were nonexistent and such dumb flights of fantasy were peculiar to him and this life of his. They touched his sense of self, these thoughts bringing him down.

"Well," he told her, "if you need me, you know where to find me."

Nora stood by the office door a moment, then she opened the door, turning back to Nicky, saying to him slow and easy. "You're a good guy, Nicky the Hawk. You've got a good heart, and that counts. For me, that counts big time."

Hearing her say it, the way she said it, was a wonderful thing for Nicky.

"Here," she told him, "take this." She returned to him and handed him her business card. "You may not reach me there, but you can leave a message and I'll get back to you."

"No home number," Nicky said.

"Nicky the Hawk, don't push it."

Nicky only nodded his head.

In the hallway leading to the stairs Nora caught the arresting officer's eye and gave him a beckoning wave: Straighten this character out.

"Are you going to be the officer of record on this collar?" Nora frowned down at the fingerprint cards in the officer's hand.

"I guess so," the officer said, looking curious but in charge. He had walked to her, slapping the fingerprint cards in his hand, a smile on his face as if he had just collared John Gotti.

"At the arraignment," she told him, "I want you to ask for low bail, or no bail at all. Okay?"

"Excuse me?"

"Excuse me. You had sex with your prisoner. Do what I ask, if anyone gives you a hard time, have them contact me at the chief of detectives' office. Okay?"

The officer turned away, a small grin on his face.

"What's so funny?"

"Captain, I didn't have sex with her," the officer said slapping the print cards off his knee.

"Really? What if I have that woman's mouth swabbed and we do a little DNA test? How do you think that would go?"

The officer stared.

"Do what I ask, don't break my balls."

"Sure, Captain, you're the boss."

Walking down the stationhouse steps Nora looked at the sun going down behind the rooftops of Brooklyn and felt her mind wandering, thinking of Max, and Sam, and this character Nicky the Hawk. He was a very self-confident young man, very assured, arrogant—not easy to like. But for some reason he had touched a spot in her. It might be that there was a hint in this Nicky of someone she once knew, she thought.

When she got to her car the weight of things came down on her. Max was gone, Sam was in critical condition, her own gun responsible for all the horror. She felt nauseated and a little desperate. Nora put her shoulder bag on the roof of the car. There was something falling inside her, something between her heart and stomach, a hard, hot thing like a lead ball of fire. Nora bent over and folded her arms across her stomach feeling as she had felt sometimes as a young woman, frightened, and above all, ashamed. Still, she found now, as she had found then, that she was unable to cry.

Heartless bitch was what Max had called her.

In that moment Nora felt more alone than she had ever been.

PART TWO

On a sunny and warm spring morning, Blaze Longo awoke to the sound of a ringing phone. Several hours past midnight he had fallen naked into bed. Seven hours later, he was lying spread-eagled with a mighty erection catching the last act of his dream. He had dreamed of a green Caribbean island, of blue and yellow birds, white crystal dope, and of one particular adobe house with its red door. Behind that door were brown child whores, Indian-faced little girls who opened their shawls and displayed tiny breasts saying, "Here, here is a treat for you."

Blaze had never been to a Caribbean island, but the past February he had spent five days in San Antonio and two nights in Mexico, and was amazed at what he saw at a whorehouse called Boy's Town. More amazed that the things he saw didn't surprise other people. The ringing phone brought him back.

He struggled out of bed and got to the telephone.

"Yeah?"

"Ten minutes," said the Wizard in his hear-me tone.

Without a word, Blaze hung up the phone and returned to his bed. Sitting, he pulled on underwear, pants, socks, and steel-toed boots. Standing, he admired himself in the bedroom mirror that hung above the dresser. He stretched then fell into his weight lifter's pose. Blaze was dark-skinned and black-haired. His head was shaved along the sides back up toward the crown where the hair was longer, giving him a modified Mohawk. On this morning he felt drowsy, a bit hungover but good.

Feeling good to Blaze meant that his life had met some definite standards. He was on the rise, coming into his own, a tough guy with a serious reputation and important connections. He particularly liked that at last he was linked to a source of power. Puckering his lips and nodding, he stood admiring his muscular and supple body. Blaze delighted in the cut of his biceps, triceps, pecs, stomach muscles. He cupped his hand and held his balls, gave himself a little lift.

Seven minutes later he was on the corner of Van Brunt and Clinton Streets standing by a pay phone, arms crossed, blowing powerful clouds of cigarette smoke skyward.

Blaze had been receiving telephone calls from the Wizard for about a year now. It was a year more or less since that moment of great fortune had arrived in Blaze Longo's life. A rainy Saturday night, after one of those long days, a run of bad luck, one thing after the other, snake eyes from sunup to sundown, grinning at him as if they were buddies, then up popped the Wizard.

He remembered thinking at first that the voice on the phone was some sly, shifty, sneaky, miserable cop bastard and he was being set up. Or maybe some kind of vengeance deal. One of the neighborhood ninnies he'd leaned on, out to make him a target, trying to come up with a new way to turn him around. The slow talker, no name on the other end of the line, offering him a highway to fortune. The Wizard laying a name on him, an address, the crib of a Dominican who ran a high-roller crap game and walked around with bags of cash.

Now, close to a year later, Blaze was still marveling at his singular stroke of luck. It turned out that the Wizard would get 50 percent of the take. Giving Blaze an address in upstate New York, and a post office box number. Telling him that if he didn't fuck up, there was a whole lot more where that came from. Bingo. Lottery time.

Blaze had lived in the Hook all his life. Knew everyone who was anyone, and everyone was nice to him because everyone was afraid of him. Only the voice on the phone was a voice he hadn't heard before. The slow talker's sound the opposite of afraid. So Blaze and the man he called the Wizard worked out the details and from then on things began to move.

Blaze and Fat Paulie took off the Dominican early one Sunday morning in gorilla masks, a slap to the face, a kick in the nuts, and Paulie doing a soft-shoe on the Dominican's chest. They took him off good and proper. Thirty Gs in a leather bag, tossing the man into his own car, taping his hands to the steering wheel. Blaze remembered the scene quite clearly, the terrified man in his car trying to twist himself free, pleading when Blaze showed him the razor. Fat Paulie standing, arms crossed, laughing at him. Blaze using his razor to remove an ear, a trophy, a symbol. It still surprised him that it all worked out so easily.

Fat Paulie knew Blaze had something going, always talking about the next hot score, but he would wait before telling Paulie about the Wizard.

The street phone rang and Blaze grabbed it, the Wizard saying, "Get your posse together, brother. Swear to God this is the best score I ever gave you. This, brother, is some serious cash."

"I'm here and I'm ready."

Red Hook Ronnie, a toothless street wanderer, who was the most articulate wino in South Brooklyn and therefore regarded as a sort of neighborhood idiot savant, walked up to Blaze throwing him a look like, whadaya say, I need the phone. Ronnie was wearing a New York Yankees baseball cap and red sweat shirt. Blaze smiling his go-and-fucking-die look at the guy.

The Wizard said, "You'll need help with this." The man breathing so hard with pure excitement that Blaze thought the phone was on the fritz.

"I have it."

"You'll have to get the little things right. The score is a legit doctor, a Cuban physician who thinks he's a voodoo priest."

"Whadidyacall him?"

"Vooooo-do priest."

"Uh-huh." Blaze shook his head, the Wizard sounded a bit flighty and a little stoned.

"I want you to move on this, Blaze. This guy is not going to be around forever. People are looking at him, important people. The man's a bank, his house is a vault for major players, drug dealers, and alike." The Wizard saying now, "You want to know why they trust him with the cash? They trust him because they believe he's touched by the spirits. They call him Godfather. He's a Santero. You know what that is?" The Wizard didn't wait for an answer, telling Blaze a Santero was a Santería priest, some kind of Cuban, voodoo, weird shit that came out of Africa. The priests dress all in white. Head to toe, underwear and all, white. "Have you ever seen a Santero, Blaze?"

"Sure. They're everywhere," Blaze said. "Tell you the truth, no."

The Wizard offered advice on how Blaze should go about ripping off the voodoo doctor. He gave Blaze the man's name, his address in Bay Ridge. Blaze listened with his eyes closed to remember the address because he'd forgotten to bring pad or pen.

After Blaze had hung up the phone he stood for a long moment, his head down and his arms folded, repeating the doctor's name and address. When he looked up he spotted Red Hook Ronnie standing a few feet away, checking him out, eyeing the telephone. "The fuck you still doin here?" Blaze looked at his watch, ten-thirty. "Ronnie, are you gonna get outta my face, or do I have to take out my razor?"

Ronnie looked at Blaze with eyes that hadn't registered surprise in decades. "I simply want to make use of the telephone," he said.

Crazy-looking people made Blaze uneasy and a little frightened. He didn't understand it, but the likes of Ronnie made his head go bad.

"When I'm done you can use the phone. When I have finished my business," he told him.

Ronnie half turned and said, "Looks to me like you're through. It appears that you have hung up and completed your business." Then he said the same thing about six more times and did some thrashing about, showing Blaze some t'ai chi.

Blaze spun on his heel. "You crazy bastard, I should kick your ass all over this street. I should fuck you up, is what I should do." Blaze was trembling with barely controlled fury. "I should ignite your ass, Ronnie, I should burn you."

"You might cut and burn me, Blaze, but you'll never snuff out the truth. And the truth is, this is a free country and I have a right to that telephone, sir."

"Oh, man," Blaze said and tried to walk around him, but Ronnie moved in his way. "It's reality," he said.

"I'll kill you," Blaze screamed. "You're pushing me," and Ronnie let him pass looking at him with loathing. Ronnie looked at everyone that way.

As he maneuvered around Red Hook Ronnie, Blaze heard his name called.

''Hey, Blaze, I figured the guys in long white coats and butterfly nets would have come to take you away by now."

"Nicky," Blaze said, "look what fell out of the sky like bird shit and landed on my head, Nicky the Hawk."

He gave Nicky his good-guy, happy-to-see-you-grin. Blaze saying now, "I heard you were busted. That's what I heard, you and Irma got pinched by the cops. I figured you'd be at the Tombs by now, setting up housekeeping, some big ol nigga tickling your prostate with a spoon."

When he had turned the corner, Nicky looked down the street and there were Blaze and Ronnie doing their sidewalk jig. For a moment he experienced a dreadful anxiety, telling himself, whoa, slow down, wait a minute, do you really want to do this? But that moment passed and Nicky the Hawk fell into the role of his life. Nicky came onstage, a little Red Hook repertory, think Stella Adler, he told himself, the Stanislavsky method.

"Me and the cops did have a sort of misunderstanding, but now we're friends, everyone friendly. Things worked out."

"Worked out?" Blaze said, glancing at Nicky as though he had him. "Worked out? How do you work things out with the cops? You become a special deputy or something, some kind of rat? You know: *rat*."

Then Blaze waited, standing head cocked, arms folded, his eyes darting around the street like bees. Nicky thinking, wack job, nut factory.

177

"You know me, Blaze, I make friends with everyone, easygoing, that's me. But I'm no rat, and maybe you should think a little before you say that again."

Blaze had turned to watch Ronnie prancing off. "You do have a way about you, Nicky," he said. "Nicky's way. Romance lowlives, make everyone your fan." The expression on Blaze's face looked like a smile, but it wasn't. "Even Charlie Chan's your friend."

Nicky smiled, gave a little shrug.

"Your fan Charlie sent a couple of people to pull my coat, telling me to back off you. But I guess you know that."

Nicky had the clear sense that Blaze had been both talked to and warned, and had got the message. Good ol Charlie.

"Misunderstandings, Blaze, a failure to communicate will jam you up every time. I just want to make sure there is none between you and me, no misunderstanding."

"Forgotten, it's done, a dead issue, water under the bridge."

"What is?"

"Our misunderstanding, that's what."

"In that case, buddy," Nicky said, "I'm prepared to buy you some breakfast, and maybe have a little chitchat. You know me pretty well, I'm always ready to start fresh."

"The fuck you talking about?"

"Blaze, there are times when you're a funny dude. You were about ready to put a match to ol Ronnie there, weren't you?"

"Guys like you and Ronnie bring out the comedian in me, Nicky. Which is really weird because I don't have a sense of humor. You asking me could I do it, burn that old worn-out wino bastard? I could do it, if he kept pushing me, I could and I would. So, what are you talking about, start fresh?"

They stood in silence for a moment. A few feet away Red Hook Ronnie screamed to the sky something about losing his medication.

They turned and began to walk down Clinton Street toward President. On the first corner they came to Blaze halted, turned to Nicky, saying, "So what are you doing down here?"

"Came by to see if I could run into you. I was just standing around when I caught your act with Ronnie. New day, same shit, same ol Blaze."

As they walked on, Blaze offered Nicky a cigarette and Nicky refused with a small wave of the hand.

"So you did," Blaze told him, "you ran into me, now what?"

"I've been thinking about some of the things you said. And the truth is, some of the things you said make sense."

"What else did you think?"

"I thought, Nicky you're broke, you stay broke. It's not manly. Maybe with you I could earn a little, you know." Nicky smiled.

"What are you up to? You trying to run some game on me, Nicky? Because let me tell you, if it's a game you're running, Charlie or no Charlie, I'll hurt you."

Nicky Ossman figured that probably there was a real discrepancy between Blaze's reputation and his talent. He also knew that it made no sense to push the guy. This was, after all, just the first scene of the first act of his new role. You may not like any of this, he thought, hanging with the likes of Blaze and Fat Paulie, but you've been set free from four walls and bars, and that woman did that for you. She came through for you, and Irma and Tino, too. Never before had he had such a powerful sense of being in someone's debt. He said this to himself in his new, take-charge voice. You and Irma would be slipping and sliding at Rikers Island prison at this moment, if it weren't for Nora Riter. Tino would be running the streets, not at home. They were like he was; their lives were in her debt, too.

"Fuck with me once, Nicky, and luck can bring you through. Fuck with me twice . . ."

"I may do dumb things from time to time, Blaze, but I'm not certifiably crazy."

Blaze said nothing.

"I saw Fat Paulie and that other mook he runs with down by Court Street last night," Nicky said. "He may be your guy, but I don't see anything there. The man's got nothing upstairs."

"Sez you."

"Sez me, that's right."

"Maybe I agree with you," Blaze said after a moment. "Sure Fat Paulie's a dunce and Vinny's not half as slick as he is. They both blow too much coke, drink, and get fucked up. Talk too much when they're high, that's always been Paulie's problem. You do have a point, Paulie never comes up with anything on his own, for me or himself, or anybody else, for that matter. But to tell you the truth, I don't care. Paulie listens to me, he's a warrior, cannon fodder, a spear carrier. I keep him with me because I need him. He does what I tell him because he's a believer. He believes I'll burn his ass he fucks up. I need that, I need believers."

"Okay," Nicky said, "I'm a believer. So, now what?"

"I don't know about you," Blaze said. "I have my doubts."

"Don't. I'm ready, look at me, I'm here, ain't I?"

"That's the trouble, you're here and it don't feel right. Why don't it feel right, Nicky? Tell me, why don't it?"

"Sure it does," Nicky told him. "It would feel right if you'd let it. But you won't let it, Blaze, you don't trust anyone, that's *your* problem. Always figuring your left hand is scheming against your right. I hate to say this, but it's a game you play, a crazy game."

"Don't say crazy Nicky, don't say that. And it's you that plays games with this acting bullshit, shit like that. Not me, I don't play games. I'm for real."

"Okay, I may play games, like being an actor. But I give it all I got. I like doing it, and I do it. I don't have any dreams of being big time, big bucks, nothing like that. I'll take what they give me. I never fought it, I figured, what's the use. But now I'm up against it, I need to turn a score. I need some money."

"Why's that?"

"I want to move to L.A., start over. Give myself a shot, I got no shot living around here. And, moving to L.A., starting over, is gonna take some serious cash."

"You know what you got, Nicky? You got a fantasy life, fucking make-believe. You scare me, brother, with your make-believe. I don't know how you figure to do the things you do, but I'll bet you don't pull it off."

"I'll take that bet," Nicky said. He didn't say what forms his fantasy had taken lately; anything about a woman with long black hair, a great ass, a perfect smile, a woman who had Blaze right in her crosshairs.

Nicky and Blaze walked through the neighborhood; an aimless stroll. When they came to Tiffany Place, Nicky could see a parking lot behind trees and a chain-link fence ahead of them. The street was strangely quiet. Halfway to the corner they passed a policeman with a little boy; the pair of them stood on the sidewalk facing the parking lot. The policeman was twirling his stick.

"Another one of your friends?" Blaze said.

"C'mon," Nicky told him, "don't be silly."

"Why'd they cut you loose?"

"Not cut loose, I made five-thousand bail for me and Irma."

"That's five-hundred bucks. And now you got a case, what is it, any-way, how'd they charge you?"

"They charged Irma with prostitution and me with assault."

Blaze stared at him. Nicky saying, "It'll be all right, a misunderstanding. I have no sheet, no record. Some kid shit, nothing to worry about."

"Are you going to keep saying it was a misunderstanding?" Blaze asked him. "Because if that's what you keep telling them, you could end up with time."

"I don't think so."

They walked across the street to the parking lot and Nicky watched Blaze go to Fat Paulie's car and take out a pad. He wrote something and then tossed the pad back into the car and locked the door.

When he came back to where Nicky was standing, Blaze stopped for a moment and looked at him.

"What?" Nicky asked.

Blaze smoked thoughtfully. "Nothing," he said. "I was trying to remember what you told me once about jail time. Something about you'd never do any."

"Listen, Blaze, we all do what we got to do. I don't plan on doing any time, at least not for this bullshit. This, this cop that busted Irma never identified himself. He . . ."

"Yeah, yeah, yeah. I know, but cops lie. If that's your out, the guy didn't identify himself, you're screwed."

"No, I'm not," he protested mildly. "Look," Nicky said, "I came by to see if we could maybe do something together. If we can, fine, let's do it. If not, I'll figure a way to get by. Blaze," he told him, "I'm prepared to take some chances at this point."

"Let me think about it," Blaze said. "Probably it's too late for me and you, but you never know. I'll call you at the house?"

"You got my number?"

"Oh, I got your number, Nicky, and that's what worries me."

"You don't know me, Blaze, not really. I got shit going on in my head. Serious shit. I've got ideas."

Did I say that? he thought. Yes, his new voice said, you did. You said it, and it came out pretty good. Convincing, it was real.

Blaze turned and looked up the street, then half lifted his hand, wagged his hand back and forth, a quick gesture taking in both sides of the street meant to include the people walking, doing business in the shops, everyone. A look came into his eyes, his look of directed enjoyment, his, I-don't-give-a-shit look. "These are all assholes out here, Nicky," he said. "All of them victims. I'm nobody's victim, I make victims, do not fuck with me."

"It's on you, Blaze," Nicky said. "It's up to you to trust me or not. What can I say, what can I do? It's all up to you."

They strolled back toward Clinton Street. Nicky didn't say anything and Blaze didn't either. They began walking faster, Blaze speed-rapping now, asking questions about the arrest, specific questions. He made no accusations, listening again to Nicky's explanation. And to Nicky, his lies seemed better, more and more like the truth.

At the corner of Clinton and President Streets they halted. "Give me a day or two," Blaze told him. "Let me think about it. I'll call you."

"Good," Nicky said. "But let me know, I got things to figure. The thing is, Blaze, I need serious cash. Gotta stop wasting my time."

Blaze looked at Nicky in a peculiar way, or Nicky supposed he did, because Nicky had turned away from him.

Blaze said, "You going to be around the house, the next day or two, you going to be home?"

"I'd say so," Nicky said. "I may be in and out though. Keep trying until you get me."

"What I'm curious about, guy turns you down flat, wants no part of you, grabs hold of a baseball bat to let you know he wants no part of you. Then that same guy, the guy with the baseball bat, gets himself busted then comes around looking for the same job he turned down, you gotta be a little curious, don't you?"

"See, what you got to remember is that things change. Circumstances."

"I can see that."

"It was only like a week ago I thought I was well off. Now, look at me, I'm broke and I'm pissed off. Things change."

"I gotta think about it. Christ, I gotta think this through . . . You want to go for breakfast? I'm getting hungry."

"No. I'd better get going."

"You were gonna buy me breakfast. That's what you said, Nicky, you'd buy me breakfast."

"See, see what I told you. You see how fast things change?"

"Yeah, things change all right . . . You know, I was thinking, I could get rid of Vinny, one or two of the other jerkoffs Paulie runs with, pay you half their share. What would you say to that?"

"Well, think about it and call me," Nicky told him. Talking softly, a secure, confident look on his face, doing De Niro, doing Ace Rothstein in *Casino*.

Walking away, heading for home, Nicky thinking, So there, that's the way it's done. He had confronted his role and mastered it. He could play undercover spy as well as anyone.

But there was something eating at him, taking the strut from his step, slowing him down. Listening to his new voice speaking in a slow, calculated monotone, This Blaze is a total lunatic, he collects ears, for chrissake, and you're going to throw in with him? Clear thought was extremely important to Nicky, intelligent thought was how he survived. This is crazy, he told himself, this is nuts.

\

Chief of Detectives Jean-Paul Clement, tall, elegant, charming, stood waiting for Nora at the bar of the River Café. He was surrounded by four business executives from Osaka wearing gray suits, pale blue shirts, and navy blue ties. When Nora caught Clement's eye, he smiled and waved with both hands then pushed his way through the crowd to her side.

The four men from Osaka looked at her without expression. The bartender said something and one of the men laughed, then they all turned back to the bar.

"You are one beautiful woman," he beamed, "you look great. Last week you looked like death, today, Captain, you look like your old self."

He had been gorging himself on free pizza canapés from the bar and a tiny string of mozzarella hung from his chin. With the nail of her index finger, Nora flicked it off.

"What?" he said.

"You had cheese on your chin."

Jean-Paul drew himself up, he seemed somber and concerned. "Nora, you believe that a steak dinner for a party of four in Tokyo sets you back about a thousand dollars. A *thousand*."

She watched him, wondering if he had been drinking. It was difficult to tell with the chief. Rumor had it that he had quit drinking, but not

184

today apparently. And frankly, lately, the guy seemed a bit at loose ends, preoccupied, in the midst of some kind of struggle. The chief was a trip.

"Really?" she said.

On the way to a table, bringing her along by the arm, Jean-Paul briefed her on the week she had missed. "Sam is doing fine." She said, "I know that." He said, "No, I mean he's doing real well. Man, his wife, Julie is there every minute. She really loves the guy."

"And . . . ?" Nora couldn't help asking.

"And nothing," Jean-Paul said. But it *wasn't* nothing. The way he said it suggested a troubling . . . something. Did Sam's wife complain to the chief? Let's suppose she did. Could be trouble. It was not beyond the realm of possibility. During the past week, when Nora had visited Sam at the hospital, Julie Morelli did not seem at all happy to see her.

Nora figured that she and Sam and Ceballos had violated at least four department rules and regulations. And maybe a couple of statutes of the criminal law. Christ, what had she been thinking?

Nora was certain that Sam hadn't said anything. She'd spoken to Sam and even in his pain-killer drug fog, even after Sam had whispered that he'd loved her, had always loved her, right from the start, they had got their stories straight. Maybe Julie told the chief that Nora had asked her husband to lean on Max? Or maybe she mentioned Sam's involvement with Jimmy Ceballos's raid on Josephine Rio's apartment. And even though Julie Morelli was in the corridor when Sam shocked Nora out of her shoes, telling her how much he'd loved her, Nora had noticed Julie looking at her, alert, guarded, and blank. If Julie told all this to Jean-Paul, wouldn't the chief say so? No, maybe not.

The chief saying, "His wife, what's her name, Julie, right? Anyway, she gives everyone coming to visit a hard time." Jean-Paul explaining that he had been to the hospital three times and had talked with Sam. It had been amiable enough, but the wife, this Julie, kept after him, making him feel uncomfortable, not wanted. "The thing is, you have to wonder why she's so pissed."

"I couldn't imagine," Nora said. "On the one hand her husband is on terminal leave, days from total retirement and on the other, he is shot, nearly killed on a boardwalk in Queens. Things like that tend to . . ."

"You're right, of course, you're right. But she really has a short temper, doesn't she? Anyway, Sam did seem happy to see me, and the happiness seemed genuine. But the wife, with that cold, mean, hard-hearted grin of hers, sure does get your attention."

Nora smiled at that. "Julie's a no-nonsense woman and probably a bit confused."

"I know."

"I'm glad you made an appearance and had a chance to talk to him. . . . Chief to detective, I mean."

Jean-Paul called a waitress and Nora told him to order her a Pellegrino with a twist of lemon. For himself a very, very dry Absolut vodka martini, no olive, in a short glass over ice.

Amid the steady din of soft conversation and Vivaldi's *Four Seasons*, coming from a hidden stereo somewhere, Nora was dying for a real drink. Something to ease her ruptured nerves. Something to help clear her head of all the crap that had been ricocheting through her mind for the past few days. But she never drank with Jean-Paul, never wanted to lose the cold sobriety she needed when dealing with the chief.

"Anyway, I'm glad I had a chance to speak to Sam," he told her. "Nora?"

"Uh-huh?"

"Is there anything about Max's suicide that I should know? I mean, is there anything that I don't already know that I should know? Because I'd hate to have something blindside me."

"No," Nora said. "Why would there be?"

The chief nodded coolly and Nora took a sip of her drink. They sat for a long time making small talk, tiny talk, really. The weather, the fabulous restaurant. "Too upscale and New York-spiffy for my taste," she told him.

Jean-Paul said, "Captain Greta Hartmann, you know her?" Sounding suspicious.

"A flower in the garden of assholes. Sure, I know her. Greta the Hun's been with internal affairs for years. She's no fan of mine. What about her?"

"She has the case." His voice very quiet.

"Chief, what case?"

She could hear the sound of a helicopter low over the river. The stereo went off and a young, sensitive-looking male in a ponytail sat at the piano. He started in with, "Music of the Night."

"Max's suicide. There's been a letter, something like that. I'm not sure, but I know IAD is opening a case and Hartmann has it."

Nora kept quiet.

"Look, Sam Morelli was still on the job when he was shot with *your* gun. And your husband killed himself with *your* gun. You had to expect an investigation."

He was telling her that she'd better be prepared. It was okay, she was. The whole thing made Nora's head hurt. She couldn't imagine having to deal with Greta the Hun, and certainly not in a situation where her neck was out this far.

Nora knew that there were certain cops that were naturals for IAD, tight asses usually. Greta Hartmann was a classic, the woman never worked a day in the street and had been an internal affairs investigator for years. One of those anticop cops filled with paranoia and bitterness.

"You never reported the gun missing because you didn't know it was missing. That's the way it went, right?"

He was saying, you're smart, you know the questions, just get the answers right.

Nora nodded.

"Someone has to open the case so they can close it. Open and shut, filed, end of story. Well, you know what I mean."

Yeah, all right, Nora thought. "Why the Internal Affairs Division? Max was a civilian."

Jean-Paul shrugged, finished his drink then ordered another.

The worst part was that Greta the Hun had never even tried to be subtle about her feelings for Nora. With that short blond hair parted on the side, those squinty, pig eyes and no lips, and four inches of fat around her gut. The captain let it be known that she had it in for Nora. Said she figured that Nora was sleeping with the chief. Had to be, the way he took care of her, no other explanation.

Jean-Paul's MO was common knowledge, the fact that his libido had no off switch was not news. The headquarters grapevine buzzed with the whiny voices of the brass who liked nothing better than to repeat rumors and lies. A bunch of old ladies who could give a rat's ass if the stories were true or not.

Nora thinking, Greta Hartmann, oh, man.

"I don't know if I'm ready for this," Nora told him.

"Sure, you are." The chief looked at her without sympathy.

Nora tried to smile. "Paul," she said, "for two days the media treated Max's death like a Kennedy assassination. There were television crews stationed outside my apartment."

"I know."

"I need a rest."

"Do you have a therapist?"

"Jesus," she said, "do I look like I need one?"

"That's hardly the issue. Maybe it would do you good to talk to someone."

"Well, I don't have a therapist but I have a lawyer. As a matter of fact, I've been staying with her for the past few days."

He looked her over again, a softness in his face now. "Look," he said, "you don't need a lawyer. I'm your lawyer, let me worry about IAD."

"Fine, I'll let you worry about Greta Hartmann. As for me, I'm taking another week off. I'm going to get out of town, maybe go and visit my sister."

"You're tired of all this," he told her. "Hell, you should be, but it'll pass. Be patient, it'll all pass."

Nora laughed. A short laugh, hardly pleasant, but a laugh nonetheless. "Listen," she told him, "Greta Hartmann did not earn her reputation by accident, and the woman hates me."

"A chubby lady with no amorous days or nights. She sees you as a star and her own life as sad and deficient. It's a woman thing."

"What?"

"You know what I mean."

"Working IAD is boring as hell," Nora said. "Chasing cops around for wearing white socks, failing to sign in, insurance frauds, that kind of BS would bore me silly. And you want to know something, I told her that. A couple of years ago, at an organized-crime school, I told Greta her job was essentially a great big bore. Screw her."

"Nowadays they do other things, you know that. Nowadays, internal affairs is one busy place."

She glanced at him quickly, trying to tell whether he was joking. "Hey," she told him, "I'm a nice person, I do my job and leave people alone. I'm not in competition with anyone."

"Nora, even nice people have to be brave, smart, and quick on their feet to survive in this job."

"What are you telling me? That they are going to charge me?"

"Not if I can help it they won't."

It started to rain. A wind off the East River cast drops against the enormous restaurant windows. The piano player went on. The waitress returned with another drink for the chief. It seemed to Nora that Jean-Paul wanted to tangle her in conversation and keep her there for hours.

"So," Jean-Paul said, "what's new in Brooklyn? You got this Blaze Longo lined up yet?"

"I think I caught a break. I have someone that can get close to him."

"Great."

"We'll see. Anyway, he's been calling me all week, leaving messages at the office. I haven't had a chance to get back to him."

"Who is he?"

"A street guy out of Red Hook, knows Blaze all his life. He got pinched for assault on a vice cop. I got him paroled. I think he may work out."

"You know," Jean-Paul said, getting dreamy now, going off somewhere, sailing into a swan dive; "sometimes I feel as though I'm twisting this life of mine into a knot of problems that only a magician could untangle."

"You're not the only one."

"Nora, I need help with this Longo character. You'll pull this off for me, won't you?"

"Sure." Nora turned to look out the window, at the Lower Manhattan skyline shrouded now in the pouring rain.

"What are you thinking?" Jean-Paul said.

"I'm going to tell you what I think, but, to tell you the truth, I don't know if I should think what I think."

"Come again."

"Your obsession with this character Longo is like a tongue seeking out a sick tooth. Are you going to tell me what this is really about?"

"I'm employing the necessity defense. It's what I do."

"Try again."

"Well, it means you can commit a lesser evil to avoid a greater evil. Get it?"

"Sure, but what does that have to do with some slimy slug in Red Hook that leaves a trail of inflicted pain? He may be a big deal to the local precinct, but to us, this shitbird Longo is small time."

"He haunts me."

"Look, Paul, I know I'm no longer the *it* girl. In fact the it I am is a target for IAD. I have enough problems, maybe more than I can handle. You have an obligation to let me know if this thing with Longo is personal."

"Define personal?"

"Chief, remember I'm your friend, not your fool. I think you'd better be straight with me."

"Like you're being straight with *me*, huh?"

Nora said nothing.

"I'm going to tell you something that I'm sure you already know. But I'm going to tell you, anyway."

"Uh-huh."

"Who knows better than you do that when you confess you're looking for a way to find trouble. I've got nothing to confess, I'm asking you for a favor. And that's it, no further explanation is necessary."

"I understand. I do."

"I hope so, Nora. In this job a favor is legal tender and ingratitude is unforgivable. As a matter of fact it is the only thing that *is* unforgivable."

Nora thinking, man, this guy can come at you from so many angles he's a circle.

"You know," he said, "that I'm no crook, I've never taken an un-earned dime in my life. But I do do some foolish things, no one has to tell me that. In most businesses, corporations, or whatever, no single incident will break or make your career. That's not true of the department. Screw up once and get nailed, you're history. I'm not ready to be history just yet. And, pretty lady, neither are you."

She looked at him curiously. "I'll tell you what," she said, "if I have anything approaching an ethical belief it is that lying to a friend, when that friend is out on a limb trying to help you, is utterly wrong. That, too, is unforgivable."

"If you're looking for an argument on that one, you'll not get it from me. You're right. Of course, you're right."

"So?"

"So what?"

"You're going to leave it at that?"

"That's precisely where I'm going to leave it. Hey," he said, "what are you doing later this afternoon? Are you busy?"

He was looking into her eyes from a table's width away. He was coming on to her with those eyes. Already! Her husband dead only a week and look out, here comes the ladies' man, the sexual magnet. But such was the nature of the guy whose dick ruled his brain. A five-star super chief, her boss. Christ.

"I'm going home to pack," she said. "What do you have in mind?" As if she didn't know.

"I'm not sure, maybe we should go for a ride, somewhere nice and quiet. Someplace by the ocean maybe."

"I ought to get going, I have things to do."

"C'mon, let's go for a ride."

"You're like chocolate cake, Paul. But right now I'm dieting, and besides, you and me, now that would be just great, wouldn't it? Captain Greta Hartmann would just love that. Talk about your police scandal."

"Nora, a scandal is when important people get caught in the kind of jam that ordinary people do everyday. The operative word here is caught. I don't plan on getting caught. And, be honest, you and Max were history a long time ago. At least that's what you led me to believe."

"You're right. Still. . . ." Nora shook her head and smiled. In fact she was embarrassed, and not because the chief was making a run at her. He pulled that crap every so often, he needed his little fantasies just to keep him going. But what the hell kind of woman does he think I am — that was what she was embarrassed about. A ride in the country. A motel? The way Jean-Paul smiled at her set off an alarm in Nora's central nervous system — *Jerk*. Somehow she knew, based on all her experience, that no matter how clear she had made it before, like a spoiled child in a candy store, Jean-Paul could not accept no.

To Nora's relief, on this day, the chief let the subject drop.

On the way out of the restaurant Jean-Paul stopped for a moment to visit the men's room. Nora glanced back at the bar where the four men from Osaka stood arms folded staring at her.

Under the canopy, protected from the falling rain, Jean-Paul said, "Someday, huh, someday we'll go for that ride."

"I have to admit, you do have a way about you."

"It's only a game, Nora, it's only a game I play."

She laughed. "Well, at least for now, I figure the best way to win at that game is not to play at all."

When the valet came to deliver his car Jean-Paul seemed alert and somber, saying, "That going-for-a-ride jazz was dumb and irresponsible. Sorry about that. Sometimes I have this need to . . ."

"I understand. I feel complimented."

"No, you don't. It's okay, please don't get angry at me. I'm not a well man."

Nora laughed.

"Listen," he told her, "you keep an eye out for Greta the Hun."

After Jean-Paul drove off Nora found herself standing in the rain.

The rain consoled her, she put her head back and looked up at the granite-gray sky. She thought of Max, Greta the Hun, and Sammy. It seemed to her that everything was coming down, that life was fleeting and fluid and could not be grasped. At that moment, listening to the traffic as it rolled over the Brooklyn Bridge, Nora felt as if she were spiraling toward oblivion. And then as part of the same thought, she thought, I need a vacation.

Her beeper went off, she went back into the restaurant and called her office. Nicky the Hawk had telephoned. He had called twice, saying it was urgent that she call him. Perfect, Nora thought, just what I need.

Because the truth was, and she stood frozen in the foyer of the River Café as the rain came now in alarming cascading sheets, the truth was this: Right now there was a gathering of dilemmas circling her head. Her thoughts were focused on Jean-Paul and his transparent personal involvement with this Blaze Longo character. And there was Nicky the Hawk. Dilemmas, yes, but things she was certain she could handle. Thinking of Nicky made her laugh, but in her quiet laughter there was a certain hopelessness.

Nora remembered clearly the self-assured glances of Nicky Ossman. The guy telling her that he was far more at home in the street world than she. Male arrogance. But, a nice smile, childlike almost, and, sure, there was some street wisdom behind it. For a few seconds she had thought, well, maybe. Curious. Denoting what? Loneliness. Unthinking arousal. Need. A new man. Silly. Absurd, really, where this life was taking her. Max is dead, she thought, he no longer exists, died young and for no reason, as if in war. She became very sad, very quickly. Then she felt apprehension.

Greta the Hun, now that woman was no joke, Captain Hartmann could be a serious problem.

Going after Max and Max's lover, using Sam and Ceballos was a serious violation of department rules. Nora was looking at merciless questions from the grim mouth of Captain Hartmann. Questions for which she'd better have some answers. Asking Jimmy Ceballos to come down on Max, two weeks ago, now suddenly seemed incredibly dumb. There was no way to protect herself and Sammy if Ceballos were questioned and told the truth.

Nora understood that once you dance around the rules and regulations and maybe even bend the criminal law a bit, there was always a certain amount of denial. Cops do it every day. Day in day out, you have to claw through mountains of bureaucratic red tape, so sometimes you do a little jig. Speed up the action and put your faith in the belief that you're doing only what you think is right. Denial. Still, even a rookie knew that there were certain people in positions of power just waiting for you to screw up. And when you did they'd come down like the hammers of hell. Rookies knew that and Nora was no rookie.

Once you're in the denial business, though, it's hard to turn it around. Cops routinely ask other cops for favors, ignore department regulations, take shortcuts during an arrest and in court. IAD types say that most cops, especially the superstars, think that they are immune from the petty bull-shit and do what they please: "Hey, I'm too busy taking the predators off the street to worry about the simple shit." But Nora had respect for the destructive ability of the simple shit. Captain Greta Hartmann was every nightmare she'd ever had.

And now, there was Nicky the Hawk.

The rain eased and Nora headed to her car. Less than a mile away, on Poplar Street in Brooklyn Heights, inside the third-floor office of the Internal Affairs Division, Greta Hartmann sat reading a letter from an anonymous complainant. The captain's smile broadened and her eyes twinkled with orgasmic pleasure. The letter was from a woman who clearly despised Capt. Nora Riter. Greta Hartmann nodded her head in what appeared to be total understanding and approval.

Inside her car, Nora went through her notes looking for Nicky Oss-man's telephone number. Her thoughts were like an inventory of things she didn't want to think about. Finding Nicky's number she reached for her cellular phone and tapped it in.

Irma was talking fast. She wore a strange, frightened expression, standing perfectly still, plucking at the skin of her wrist, "Tino was watching me for a long time. I'm lying on my side and the professor from Germany, Jurgen, was doing me, you know. Anyway, I could see Tino over his shoulder and there was the kid, there was Tino in the closet, watching."

Tino said, "Aw, Irma, c'mon."

"Nicky, Tino doesn't understand how this sort of thing could affect me." Now Irma was walking around the kitchen, pointing at her head. Pretty soon she was jumping and her jumping around annoyed the hell out of Nicky. "Oh, this could have a big effect, Nicky. This could have a lasting impact."

When Nicky did not answer, Irma shot him a mean, disapproving stare. "Do you know how I feel? This could give me nightmares. And, you know what, I bet he's done it before."

Nicky said, "Did you ever do this before, Tino?"

Tino, head down, shook his head.

"I don't believe him," Irma said, "maybe you want to, but I don't. This ain't the first time, Nicky. He's been in that closet before. I know he has."

"Tino?"

Tino wagged his head sadly as if Nicky's question insulted him. He looked from the floor to Irma avoiding Nicky's eyes.

It struck Nicky that he never should have given Tino the key to Irma's apartment. Now he was forced to stand in his kitchen and picture the boy sitting on a box in Irma's closet. He had an image of Tino watching the German's head down between Irma's legs. The kid thinking, oh, man. Nicky closed his eyes for a moment, carefully thought about what the kid saw.

Nicky tried to go far, far back in his memory and remember the first time someone had told him about making love to a woman; said something about going down on the muff, it was something like that, the muff. He remembered thinking, saying, not me, uh-uh, not me. Half joking, half trying to imagine what it would be like. Tino didn't have to imagine, he'd seen it in person, and the *oh-man* look in the boy's eyes told Nicky all he needed to know.

Irma looked tortured. Nicky saw her mouth moving, as if she wanted to say something to Tino, but could not manage it.

Nicky understood how Tino's mind worked and figured Tino, intelligent, creative, was probably reliving the experience, just going through it all again, a sort of free-form, life-altering experience.

Since he came home from the street, Nicky had been trying to decide if he should tell Irma of his plans with the woman cop. The fact that Irma was so flighty and silly and out of control encouraged him to let it slide; watching Irma perform convinced him he was right.

Nicky walked over to Tino and pulled the boy in close, saying, "Sometimes we see and hear things we never were meant to. Seeing and hearing things we're not meant to can mess you up. But I'm going to tell you something, Tino. Maybe not tomorrow, maybe not next week or next month or next year, but someday you'll find a woman and fall in love and you're gonna jump for joy. And what you saw and heard in Irma's bedroom this afternoon is not going to seem all that strange and weird and . . . Jesus, Tino, I don't know what to say. Christ, Irma, don't you look around? What was he, two feet from you, didn't you notice?"

"I was busy," Irma said. "I was occupied. But then I saw him, Nicky. I noticed, but it was too late. I will be influenced by this Nicky, this will have lasting impact on my life."

"I know about you, Irma. Okay for you, you'll be fine. Forget you, what about Tino? You have some responsibility here, cousin."

Irma nodded as a woman who has spent some time being shouted at.

Tino was staring at his feet.

Nicky said. "Are you okay, Tino?"

"Oh, baby, oh, baby, oh, baby," Tino said.

"What?" said Nicky.

"That's what he said, 'Oh, baby, oh, baby, oh, baby.' That's what he kept saying, 'oh, baby . . .'"

"Okay," Nicky said, "okay."

He wasn't handling this right. Nicky knew he wasn't handling this right, at all. How did he let this happen? Nicky kept telling himself he was the boy's father. Fathers made sure their twelve-year-old sons didn't sit around watching a hooker earn her keep. Irma kept staring at him but he avoided her eyes.

Nicky had been careful about keeping Tino distanced from Irma's work. In five years, the boy hadn't seen a thing. Nicky wanted him to grow up normally—well, as normal as possible living as he did, with an actor and a whore. Now Nicky felt as though he had blown it; not the best of words to think of just then.

"She winked at me," Tino said. "When the guy was saying, 'oh, boy, oh, boy, oh, boy,' I looked at Irma and she winked at me."

"I did not," Irma said.

"She did Nicky, she did. She saw me sitting there and she winked at me."

Nicky did not enjoy the little flicker of the comedian he heard in Tino's voice. "Go to your room," Nicky told him. "You're grounded. You'll stay in your room until I tell you you can come out."

"Yeah, and what about her?"

"Get to your room, Tino."

Sometimes raising Tino was so tough for Nicky that he could hardly stand it. He sat down in the kitchen chair for a few minutes and drank the rest of his coffee, listening to Irma carry on about Tino and the German. What, Nicky wondered, should I do?

Irma poured herself a cup of coffee and took a seat across from him. Irma continued to talk and Nicky listened. He nodded his head once in a while. Last night in this same kitchen he had listened to Blaze talk about making money, big scores, and had nodded his head a lot because he could understand what Blaze was saying and had wondered what kind of pictures formed inside the guy's nutty head, or even if Blaze saw anything at all. This afternoon he nodded his head and barely listened, wondering about Tino, thinking about Blaze, worried now, listening to Irma.

"His eyes were this big Nicky, this big." Nicky nodding, thinking, the poor kid. Irma said, "Before you came home, you know what he said to me? He asked me if I liked it. I told him hell, no, it's business not pleasure."

Nicky nodded in an understanding way. Kept on nodding as she told him about her own life, how she'd never really been a kid herself, about her starting out young. Nicky knew her story, knew her all her life.

Irma said, "You need to explain it to him, tell him how rough I had it growing up, that I had no choices, nothing for me to do but wait tables, maybe tend bar." It occurred to Nicky that he had forgotten to listen to his new, in-control voice. Irma was rattling on. She had put aside all that he told her. No more hooking, he'd said, she had to lay low for a while, at least until he worked out their problems. She picked up her cup and took a sip and said, "You've got to do something, you've got to explain to Tino."

He said, "I told you no more turning tricks. Not for a while, is what I said. You're on probation, use your head for a change."

She hesitated, giving him a hard cold look. "I am very careful. Jurgen is a regular, I've known him for a long time. A regular."

"Irma?"

"How do I earn if I don't turn out. Who's gonna pay my rent? How do I eat? C'mon, Nicky, be real."

"I'll tell you what's real. What's real is that you're going to find yourself in the street you don't cool your role and start listening to me. I told you, been telling you, I'll take care of things. I'll pay your rent. But you have to listen."

"Maybe I should look for a straight job." Giving him a sly smile.

"Maybe you should."

"You're going to make me stay in the apartment here. I couldn't do that." Irma's hard look now.

The telephone rang.

"That's probably your new friend, Blaze, the guy's been calling every day, your new buddy. That's how you're going to take care of me and Tino, you're gonna join the sporting life, the wild bunch? That's not you, Nicky, you'd make a shitty criminal."

Nicky stood, taking his time before picking up the phone, turning to look back at her. "What?"

"I know what you're thinking, I know you, Nicky. You're gonna run with Blaze and his crew, make some cash, and then you'll split to L.A. Well, what about me, Nicky, what happens to me?"

"What you need, Irma," he said, finishing his coffee, "is a belief in the commitment of man. I gave you my word, didn't I? My word is good. Now go to your apartment, I've got business."

Nicky answered the phone saying, "The whorehouse on the hill."

Leaving his apartment, Irma was scowling.

Nora said, "Excuse me?"

Nicky Ossman stood in the men's lavatory of the Paddock Bar and Grill on Sixty-seventh Street, off Third Avenue. Midtown Manhattan, Friday night, was lively at 5:30. The bar was crowded with TV people from the Fox Television studios across the street. Nicky stood in front of the bathroom mirror, anxious, feeling that he wanted to flee. He'd been anxious all day and through the night after that meeting with Blaze, the guy telling him something solid, real good was coming down. Telling Nicky he could earn, they both could make some money. And then asking some pretty specific questions about Nicky's arrest, the kind of questions Nicky hadn't thought that Blaze was shrewd enough to ask. Nicky thinking about the flat look in Blaze's eyes when he asked those questions. A dangerous bastard this Blaze.

On the wall next to the mirror was a framed lithograph of Saratoga Racetrack. Horses and riders heading for the wire. The way the horses strained, eyes expanded as they raced for the finish, their muscles stretched full out, made the picture suggest a run for their lives. Nicky stood, glancing at the lithograph and then staring at himself in the mirror, wearing his Chicago Bulls leather cap with the long bill, a sweater, and a button-down shirt, his good blue striped one.

As he made his way back into the barroom he wondered if he had time to take a drink before Nora Riter showed up. Vodka and tonic with a wedge of lime, his favorite, probably set him back five bucks in a joint like this. Midtown, probably best to order a beer.

There was Nora, sitting at a table near the window staring out at the street. She turned and looked at him for a long moment, a smile starting to spread. Nicky stood still until he felt silly standing in the middle of the barroom.

He walked in her direction and her eyes followed him, the smile still there. As Nicky walked, he wondered how he looked to her. He stared at that face of hers, the face that had lived behind his eyelids for the past couple of weeks.

And it was that thought, as he sat on a chair across from her, that brought out his best grin. Hoping he looked as good to her as she did to him.

The police captain with all that hair, the thickest eagle's nest of a head of hair he'd ever seen. So much hair in fact, that it was like another presence at the table. He was aware that she was watching him as he rearranged a napkin, a knife and fork, an ashtray. Hesitating, tactful, wanting to do this just right. Thinking, this woman doesn't know me well, doesn't know me at all. Then thinking that Nora probably considered him some mindless, street jerkoff. He was getting charged up, excited, wondering how to play this. Christ, she was gorgeous, those enormous eyes.

As far as Nicky could figure, the suicide of Nora's husband and the shooting of her partner had devastated her. Still, she was cool enough to come off as though she were in control, but he didn't believe it. He remembered seeing the pain there, all of it. Poor woman, all that crazy shit coming down so unexpected, such a shock, at least she made it sound that way.

There was music from the jukebox in the corner, Irish singers doing a rowdy song, laughter and clapping from the crowd at the bar.

"You look like you're nineteen years old. I doubt I'd recognize you if I saw you on the street," she said. "Nice hat," smiling at him, teasing. She liked him, the way she was looking at him, he could tell. Except now she had this serious look on her face.

"How are you feeling?" he asked her. "You've had a helluva couple of weeks, huh?"

"It's never been worse."

He shook his head. "I'm sorry for your troubles."

"Thanks. So, what made you pick this place?"

Nicky shrugged his shoulders saying, "I dunno, it seemed like a good idea. Away from Brooklyn, nobody I know comes here."

"There's a stationhouse right up the street. Cops come in here all the time."

"Really?"

She nodded.

"You should have said something."

"You didn't give me a chance."

She motioned toward the bar. "You want a drink?"

"I'd love a beer." Nicky had to raise his voice over the sound of the music.

She went into her shoulder bag, took out a wallet and removed a twenty dollar bill. "Get me a Bass Ale," she told him, handing him the twenty. "Get yourself whatever you'd like."

He took the money and went to the bar, people gave way, polite, friendly. He ordered two mugs of ale. Returning, he told her, "I like it when women buy me drinks."

"I bet you do."

Nicky felt tongue-tied for a moment. "Hey, c'mon, I'm teasing."

Nora nodded.

"Listen," he said, "if you're uncomfortable in here, we can go somewhere else."

"Next time."

Nicky sipped his drink.

"You've been calling me."

"That's right. I did what you asked. I reached out for Blaze and I wanted to tell you that I've been talking to him for about a week now."

"About what?" She asked with a sly, you could say sexy look. Oh, yeah, she was interested, maybe it was the hat. Women just loved that look. Real understated elegance, rich color and a fine fabric. A leather hat.

A woman wearing a red bandanna played the jukebox and the sound of Enya filled the room. Ooohs and ahhhs from the bar.

Nicky shrugged. "It's not like we had a plan or anything, I didn't know what to ask him."

Her eyes now fixed on his. A little curious, maybe some excitement there, too. He was thinking of what it would be like to kiss her, feeling that sensation spreading through him now, that excitement, that rush. He couldn't believe she wasn't feeling it, too. He was turned on by her quiet, easygoing self-assurance as much as by her beautiful face.

201

Nicky gave her a fast look of discomfort. "I'm not all that clear on what it is you want me to do."

"Sure, you are."

"I can probably line him up for you, if that's what you mean."

His voice carried over the melodious and genteel sounds of the Irish singer. Two or three people turned their heads.

"That's exactly what I mean," she told him.

After a moment she said, "Look, I don't want to screw around with this creep. Put me in a position where I can arrest him and I'll handle the rest."

"Ey, Blaze has some bad people with him. He's not going to be all that easy."

"Ey," she said, mimicking. "I have the biggest damn gang in the city. I call for help they're here before I can hang up the phone. Screw Blaze, he doesn't scare me."

Nicky didn't answer, not liking where this was going. A grim darkness had settled over Nora's features. This woman, this Nora, this captain, was strictly business. She wasn't interested in him as a friend, forget lover. An informant was how she saw him, a spy, nothing more than that. Now she was looking at him in a way that made Nicky feel extremely uncomfortable.

"My dear lady," he said finally, "you don't know what you're talking about. Blaze is a sociopath, he's serious bad news."

"So you've said."

He leaned in close to her so as to get all her attention. "He collects ears," he told her.

"What the hell are you talking about?"

"You heard me. Blaze Longo cuts people's ears off. And whatever else suits his fancy. He's a collector."

Nora seemed to throw every grain of her energy into a great big grin. Her cheeks got all puffy trying to control silent laughter. "Are you serious?" Her happy eyes wandered around the bar then settled on Nicky. "You're serious, aren't you?"

"Captain," he said, "this is no laughing matter. This guy is—what did we used to say—a mad-hatter, a total space shot?"

"That's what we used to say."

Nicky could feel himself losing it. He had wanted to impress her, here in this bar with the music, some drinks, looking good. Giving her a smile that was a look between C'mon, I know what I'm talking about and Do you want to have an affair? He took a breath, maybe he'd try a new tack. "Nora, can I call you Nora?"

Nora remained silent.

"I'll call you Nora. Okay, listen, can't we forget Blaze for now? I don't mean forget, I mean, can't we put him aside for the time being and just enjoy our drinks, listen to the music and maybe get to know each other a little better?"

Nora exhaled heavily, then spoke slowly. "I don't know what you have in mind. Okay, look, I know what you have in mind. I know you're thinking all I have to do is charm this woman, meet her in a bar, have a drink, listen to some music, be calm, smooth, and sensitive and then make a move. Have this woman go ga-ga over my obvious good looks and exceptional charisma, and that'll be the end of it. But it's not going to work out that way, Nicky the Hawk. You are in deep do-do, and you'd better ask yourself, can I handle it. There will be nothing personal between you and me, it's business. Now I have to ask myself, did I make a mistake, was I wrong thinking you could be of some help. I have to think you're not serious, you're screwing with me, or trying to. I have to think—"

"Okay, I understand, enough. Calm down." She was trying very hard to be tough, he thought, and she was succeeding. She didn't seem to be taken by him at all. In all his experience he had never been this wrong about a woman. But then again, what had he been thinking, he hadn't thought at all. It had all been fantasy. Like so many other things in his life, daydreams and illusions. "Blaze wants me to help him do a score," he said.

"That's better."

"Out in Queens. Do you go out to Queens?"

"My badge says City of New York. I go everywhere."

"I don't know what he has in mind, he hasn't told me."

"Nicky . . ."

"He said he'd get back to me. All I know is that it involves some serious money."

"Jesus," Nora said.

"C'mon. Give me a break here. I'm doing the best I can."

"Be serious, will you?"

"I am, what makes you think I'm not?"

"I can tell."

"Well, good for you. You happen to be wrong this time."

"Yeah, well I doubt it. Look," she told him, "believe it or not, I went out of my way big time to help you and Irma get out. Now, I expect— look, you gave me your word and I believed you. Do not, I repeat, do not screw with me. You come up with *bubkes*, I'll send you back to the can."

Nicky didn't answer. They sat quiet and still. The woman in the red bandanna returned to the jukebox and played a Motown tune, The Supremes doing "Baby Love." Nicky felt as if he were snared in the night-time wire, with spotlights and flares and shells exploding around him. He wondered if spending a few months in the joint could be worse than dealing with Nora Riter. Then the old ache came back, the fear of losing Tino. No matter how he sounded, Nicky knew that Tino had no street cunning, he could not be independent. No way he'd leave that boy out on his own. No, not again. He loved that kid.

"I can't believe that you don't believe me," he said at last.

"Sorry," she said. "Don't feel so special, I make it a practice not to believe most people. Does that worry you?"

"Very, very much."

It was wrong for him to be there, that much he understood now. Wrong to be sitting in a Manhattan bar playing the fool for this woman. The music filled the room, the illusions of happiness from the people at the bar, all their phony laughter aroused a kind of alarm in him, his body strained. This was no joke, no game to be found here. No part to play other than what was real. Across from him this frozen-faced police captain plagued by a set of her own problems. She seemed, outwardly, to have chosen him to play a role for which she thought he was prepared. Truth was, Nicky was prepared for none of it. There she sat, upright and unbending and the expression of mild disgust in which her face was set, by his lights, was not about to change.

Sure she was beautiful, he thought; who wouldn't think this woman was a knockout. But she was so tough. Her toughness seemed inflexible to him. She had the ability to make others pay a price.

"I think I should go," he told her.

She nodded without looking at him.

"You must have been very young when you became a cop," Nicky said.

"Twenty-one, just finished college, didn't know what to do. Thought this would be fun, something different."

He wanted to ask if it turned out to be as different as she had once thought.

"You enjoy it?"

"What, being a cop? I don't know, once I did, once it was a whole lot of fun. I was doing something important, I was needed, I made a difference."

Right, he thought, a hippie with a gun.

"Things change, times change, we get older, smarter."

"Tougher," he said.

"That, too."

He nodded.

"I'll tell you," she told him, "as a cop you get to see all the liars for who and what they are. If you have illusions they disappear fast."

"I still have illusions," he told her, "dreams and fantasies. I don't guess I'll ever change, it's who I am."

"If you don't mind my saying so, I find that hard to believe."

"What?"

"That you have dreams and fantasies. I don't mean to insult you, but when I met you, you were stealing meat. A petty thief, then the next time you were protecting a prostitute. Now don't tell me Irma's not a working girl, I've seen her sheet."

Suddenly Nicky realized that Nora was angry. Anger, not sadness, was eating at her. He had figured that she'd most likely be saddened by the death of her husband. Be happy to see him, a smiling face, someone to ease the pain. Right. This meeting was not turning out the way he had dreamed it would. Just the opposite, it made him want to get up and run. This woman was wearing anger like a second skin.

A waitress came by and asked if they wanted more beer. "Two more of the same," Nora told her.

"I was getting ready to leave."

"I'd rather you stayed for a while."

"You'd rather?"

"That's what I said."

"Do I have a choice in the matter?"

"Nope. Well, of course you can leave, if you'd like. I'd prefer you stay is all I'm saying."

The beer came and Nora lightened up a bit. "So, you're an actor. Is that right?"

"I try," Nicky told her.

"Trying is not doing. Do you work?"

Nicky felt as though she were trying to find ways to pick at him now, although she did seem to be easing off. You could fall in and out of love real quick with this broad. Man, he thought, what a lady. He thought of her husband. Christ! His mind was going a mile a minute. Get up and go, he told himself, get out of here.

"I keep busy," he told her. Which, of course, was a lie. He hadn't done a thing in months.

"Would I know anything that you've done?"

"Probably not. I did a car commercial a couple months back."

"That's it?"

"I did something off-off Broadway last summer."

"Did you?"

"Yes, I did. At a small theater on the Lower East Side, called Nada."

She smiled, wagged her head as if to clear it. "A New York actor. I never would have guessed."

"I'm no criminal. Maybe you'd like to see me that way, but I'm not."

"Well actually—"

"I'm not saying I'm an angel, I'm not. When you were born and raised in the Hook, as I was, it's a birthright to hustle. You come from around there no one expects you to stand in line waiting for a paycheck. But that doesn't make me a criminal. You checked Irma's sheet, have you checked mine?"

"Yup."

"And?"

"You were a youthful offender, nothing since you were sixteen."

She seemed happy to know that he didn't have an adult arrest record. At least that was something.

"So?"

"So, what? What are you suggesting? If you're saying all the criminals in this city have sheets? Let me tell you, the smarter ones don't get caught. And it's pretty obvious that you're a smart guy."

"Oy . . ."

"Oy, my foot. C'mon, you want another beer?"

"I haven't started this one." He glanced at her glass and saw that it was empty. "I didn't see you drink that."

"I'm faster than you, Nicky, way ahead of you."

She smiled and seemed to blush a little, tickled pink to toy with him.

Or maybe, just maybe the beers were breaking through. She turned away, then turned back to face him, raising her eyes and looking deeply into his.

"Look, Nicky," she said, "I've been feeling real testy lately. I don't mean to take it out on you."

"Testy? My dear ol dead mother would call you a *baleboosteh*. She was from Sicily, and let me tell you, Sicilians are born with insight, and they have a way with words."

"*Baleboosteh*," she repeated. "Cute."

Nicky downed his beer and they ordered another round of drinks. This time vodka and tonic for him, light rum and tonic for her.

"Actually, I've always had this warm spot in my heart for good-looking Italian guys from Brooklyn. They're sexy."

"Really?"

"No, not really. I don't know any good-looking Italian guys from Brooklyn."

"You know me."

"Ossman?"

"Half Italian. My father was Swedish."

"You do look Swedish."

"I never met anyone who thought I looked Swedish. Irma thinks I look like a hit man. God only knows why."

"She's right."

"Really?"

"Hey, if I were to cast you in a movie, I'd cast you as Michael, in *The Godfather*. The young Pacino."

Now she was grinning, a real broad smile. The smile, that hair, the smell and look of her, small neat breasts, great legs, even the sandals she wore suggested a frank sexuality. The vodka, the laugh. Nicky was smitten.

Normally Nicky didn't go in for hostile, tough women, but in Nora's case, it now seemed okay. More okay after another vodka and tonic. The vodka was turning the entire evening into an antidote for all that came before.

They were both a bit buzzed now and could hear the laughter and singing from the bar. At first all that gay laughter had irritated him. Then he remembered that people, most people can find joy and laughter in their lives and his spirits lifted. Nicky loved happy bars. He enjoyed his independent life, but the minute he was in a pleasant bar with people laughing, singing, he felt a part of something warm, good-natured, and neighborly.

Nora excused herself and went to the restroom.

Nicky looked out the window and saw people moving along the early evening street, a man and a woman with their arms around each other's waists bouncing along, playing at being kids. He followed the couple and in his mind's eye he followed the path of his own life. There, in an instant, was Tino, his life in Red Hook, Irma. Nicky had this strange notion that he was back onstage and all of this was playacting.

Nora emerged from the bathroom with quite a happy look on her face. She had freshened up, now she was trying to be affable, easygoing.

"I want this to work out for you," she said.

"How sporting of you."

"Don't be a smartass. No, really, you take care of this Blaze for me and I'll clean the slate for you and Irma. Then you can get back to your life. I mean, we got off on the wrong foot. Circumstances, not your fault, not your fault at all. I'm going to focus on you, and get this done."

"Focusing on me would be nice. I'd love to have you focus on me." Nicky said, smiling in that lovable, sweet way he imagined Nora would find irresistible.

Nora twirled her finger, making little circles in the air. "I feel a bit tipsy, but you know what, I'd like another drink."

"You're kidding."

"I'm not kidding."

"All right, order up."

"You'll stay?"

"Loving every minute of it," said Nicky, in spite of himself.

"I'm glad. I'm just warming up."

"Good." Nicky didn't know whether he was supposed to appear pleased or what.

She ordered another round of drinks, took a positively amazing swallow and said; "Man, I needed this. This is just what I needed."

"It must be hard to do what you do," he said.

"Hard, yes, it is hard. Impossible sometimes."

"Maybe I can help you relax. Maybe it would be the best thing I could do for you. You know, find a release for all that pent-up hostility. You know, maybe a nice, gentle affair with me would be much more fulfilling than all the cops-and-robbers stuff."

She looked puzzled. "Maybe you're right," she said. Then she said: "Men like you just don't ever quit. It must be in the genes."

Nicky said, "What do you mean, men like me?"

She shook her head, then smiled. "It must be like heroin, cocaine, or some such thing. An addiction. You see a woman, she pleases you, and you immediately want to get in her skirt."

"That's not fair."

"Fairness has nothing to do with it. It's in the blood, you can't help yourself. Am I right?"

"I think you're wrong. At least in my case you're wrong."

"I'm not wrong, I'm right. I'm hardly ever wrong." A great, great grin.

"I do admit that I've been coming on to you."

"Thank you."

"No, wait a minute. I hit on you because I like you. I may be in a little bit of a fix, and sure, you can help me out of it. But I could handle this case on my own. I don't need to be playing Russian roulette with you and Blaze."

Nora nodded. She finished her drink.

"*Comerado, I give you my hand! I give you my love more precious than money, I give you myself before preaching or law; Will you give me yourself? will you come travel with me? Shall we stick by each other as long as we live?*"

Nora smiled, started to say something and stopped. She sat there with her mouth open. "That was very, very nice."

" 'Very nice?' That's Walt Whitman, 'Song Of The Open Road.' "

"A love poem."

"Yes, I'd say that. He wrote a lot of love poems."

"But, you see," Nora said, "I'm not talking about love." Nora told him there were men in her life. Not a great many, but some. And so many men behaved like children. Nicky said he supposed she was right, then again, women weren't much better.

Nora said, "Well, I think, you, like most men, are pretty self-involved. I wasn't talking about you at all. I'm thinking of someone else."

Nicky said, "Your husband?"

Nora said, "No, not Max."

"Someone else?"

Nora nodded.

Just then the waitress returned. "Another round?"

Nicky said, "Nora?"

"Sure."

The waitress brought two more drinks. Nora wrapped her hands around the rum and tonic and stared at it. Her eyes were half closed, she seemed to be off somewhere in her own head. He asked if she'd mind talking about her husband. Maybe she'd rather not get into it. She shrugged, then finished half her drink.

He said, "I'm curious about your husband. What sort of guy was he?"

"Max was a muddle of contradictions, warm and sensitive one minute, cold and quick-tempered the next. The mixture made me crazy. To tell you the truth, I stopped loving him a long time ago. He's been dead two weeks and it seems like yesterday, boy, time gets away from you."

She took another sip of her drink.

"He had another woman. Probably more than one."

"I can't imagine why. What was he, blind?"

"For every pot there's a lid," she told him. "My lid didn't fit on his pot, simple as that. I've never seen such a change in a human being, the kind of changes that came over Max."

"How long were you married?"

"Six years. For the past year he was into drugs, abusive as hell. My partner, Sam, he told me I should have ended it a long time ago. Sam was my best friend . . . God, he's still my best friend. The best man I've ever known, you know? Loyal, honest, strong. You know what? I never once thought of him as a possible lover. He told me, in the hospital, when I went to see him, he told me that he had been in love with me from the beginning. It was probably the painkillers, didn't know what he was saying. Anyway, a seemingly happily married man. What the hell is wrong with you men?"

"C'mon, not all men."

"Really. You have to meet my boss. Now, that's a funny guy. A terrific cop, a great investigator and even better administrator, the man runs the entire detective division. People talk about him like he's a shoo-in for the next police commissioner. A good-looking guy, smart as hell, could get into politics, be the mayor, for chrissake."

"So?"

"Men. See, I know he has a problem. And I'd bet a year's pay it has to do with a woman."

"You know, you're not going to believe this, but I think I know the man you're talking about. He's always on television."

"That's him, a regular media slut."

"A real good-looking guy, blond hair, looks like he could do shampoo commercials."

"He's the chief of detectives."

"Maybe now, but a few years back he arrested one of the neighborhood big guys. I didn't know he was chief of detectives. He's French, right?"

"Canadian, French Canadian."

"What's his name?"

"Jean-Paul Clement."

"Sure, that's him."

"What?" Nora pursed her lips and shrugged her shoulders as if to say, c'mon, how would you know the chief of detectives.

"Where I come from, in my neighborhood there are no secrets. Wiseguys, cops, I don't care who or what you are, you got a secret, you're not going to keep it in Red Hook." There was a moment's silence, Nicky looking around the room. "I'm having a drink one night, about a year ago, me and Irma at the Roma. It's a neighborhood spot over on Court Street. This gorgeous woman comes in, turns everyone's head. I mean, she looks like an Italian movie star, I'm trying to think who she reminds me of. Not Gina Lollobrigida or Sophia Loren, someone else. Anyway, she says something, I don't remember what, but a husky voice, really sexy. And it hits me, Claudia Cardinale! This woman is the spitting image of Claudia Cardinale. You know Claudia Cardinale?"

Nora shook her head.

"She made about a million Italian movies. A few in Hollywood. Do you remember a film called *Once Upon a Time in the West*?"

Nora took her time shaking her head. Her mind seemed to be wandering. She was gazing at him, looking interested and suspicious at the same time. But it was okay; he was becoming more and more comfortable with her. He had a vodka glow on and couldn't imagine that she, too, hadn't felt the bite of the ale and rum.

When she reached across the table and touched his hand, Nicky believed he was falling in love. He wondered what it would be like to make love to a police captain.

She said, "Tell me more about Claudia what's-her-name," her fingers moving lightly over his wrist.

He said, "The movie, *Once Upon a Time in the West*, is one of those Sergio Leone spaghetti westerns, a very long and weird film with a great, great cast. Henry Fonda, Jason Robards, and Charles Bronson. Violent as hell. If you ask me, I think Italian movie makers figure that all American cowboys and gangsters make a habit of killing everyone in sight. Claudia Cardinale was in that movie."

211

Nora speaking softly now, almost a whisper. "Screw the movie, Nicky. I don't care about the movie, tell me about the woman."

"Claudia Cardinale?"

Now a loud voice: "No, goddamn it, not Claudia Cardinale, *the other woman*, the woman that looks like Claudia."

"Uh-huh, you mean Roseann Palumbo?"

"Tell me about *her*."

"Keep your voice down," he said. "Everyone can hear you."

"Nicky . . ."

"I'm sitting with Irma and in she walks, Roseann Palumbo. Now, you know I grew up in the neighborhood, know everyone, everyone knows me? I walk down the street I know who to smile at, who to turn away from. We all know each other since sandbox. I know if a guy's a junkie or a bookmaker. I know if a guy is connected or a wanna-be. Okay. This woman I *didn't* know. I never saw her before. Irma tells me, 'Sure you know her,' I say, 'are you kidding, a face like that I would not forget.' Irma says, 'She's Sally Palumbo's ol lady.'

"Now, Sally Boy, I know. He's from the club. Well, not right now, right now he's playing basketball in the yard at Green Haven. And, and, Roseann is running around on Sally Boy with this big-time cop. The same cop, if you can believe this one, the same cop that sent Sally Boy upstate. It's unbelievable. 'When Sally Boy comes home,' Irma says, 'there's gonna be blood on the moon.' An old neighborhood line. Joey Gallo's sister used it when they killed Crazy Joey.

"Twenty-nine years I'm living in the Hook. I never heard such a story. So how come I didn't know her? Irma tells me that Roseann went to private school, never came out on the street. Her father is this old-timer, a bookmaker, a guy named Alfred Alteri. I know him by Alley Boy. Old-time bookmaker, a degenerate gambler, a bust-out guy, always broke. So this boss of yours, this Clement, he's boffing Roseann Palumbo. And let me tell ya, between me and you, it's craziness. But maybe this Clement don't comprehend that."

"How the hell does Irma know all this?"

"Ey, she comes from Red Hook. You can*not* keep a secret in Red Hook. And, she's a woman. Women know that sort of thing."

"You mean she's a hooker, and hookers find out those sorts of things."

"That, too."

Nora put her arm across Nicky's shoulder and pulled him in close. First she blew, then whispered in his ear. "I hope you can do this for me, Nicky. You handsome bastard, I'm counting on you." It was not the usual tone of her relations with informants. Nicky did a double take, an actor's move—part real, part staged, and part the retreat of a stunned man.

"I'm going to grab Blaze by the short hairs and twist," she told him. "And you, my talented actor, you will put his *cojónes* right here in my hand."

"Nora, maybe you had one too many, huh?"

"Don't call me *Nora*, I'm a New York City police captain. You call me *Captain*, goddamn it."

"Of course," he said.

Nora moved along the sidewalk and tried to make it seem that she was walking down the aisle. She pictured herself a bride going for the altar. The image of a church, she thought, might keep her calm. After a laborious step or two, she was pleased and took pride in being able to walk at all. All in the head, she told herself, control and discipline.

Walking along Sixty-seventh Street, she took Nicky by the arm, telling him that she was positive she had parked her car right there on the corner. She felt herself rock from foot to foot; without warning, her stroll had turned into a kind of ocean-crossing in a dinghy. God, she prayed, don't let me get sick here in the street. The moment she spotted her car, Nora's spirits rose remarkably.

"There's my car. Good ol buddy," she said, patting the roof affectionately. "Where are you headed, Nicky? C'mon," she said, "I'll drop you at the subway; then I'd better get home."

"Tell you what. Why don't I drive *you* home, park your car, and grab the subway from there."

"Come again?"

"Captain, you're not fit to drive. I won't let you, simple as that. Give me your keys and an address."

"Maybe I should take a cab."

"It's up to you. If it was me, I'd want this car off the street and into a garage. You have a garage?"

"Yes."

"Okay, then, give me your keys."

Nora hesitated.

"Nora."

She handed him her car keys. Nicky opened the door then slid into the driver's seat and started the ignition before he unlocked the passenger door.

Inside, adjusting her seat belt, Nora said, "For a moment there, just for a second . . ."

"Yeah, right, you thought, 'what if he just drives off and leaves me.' "

"Actually, I was thinking great, now I have to put bullet holes in my pretty little car."

Nicky drove off into traffic with a small laugh. Nora was laughing, too, all the while wondering why she felt so damn miserable.

"Where are we going?" Nicky asked her.

"Er . . . Seventy-second off Madison. No, wait a minute, I should go home. Listen, take me to Seventy-ninth and Amsterdam."

"I thought I was taking you home?"

"That's where I live, Seventy-ninth and Amsterdam." She struck Nicky affectionately on the shoulder. "Nicky," she said, "this Roseann Palumbo business, are you sure?"

He had stopped the car at a traffic signal. Nora turned to him and found Nicky staring at her. "I mean, you can't be sure Irma knows what the hell she's talking about?"

"Look," Nicky said quickly, "when I first heard the story I found it hard to believe myself. But I asked someone who should know. Believe me, this guy knows everything that goes down in Red Hook. Anyway, he confirmed it. Said it was no secret, everyone knew. It's true, Nora, this chief of yours, this ding-a-ling is sleeping with Sally Palumbo's wife. It's as simple as that."

"Yeah. So tell me, who's this guy?"

"Forget that, you're not going to hear his name from me."

"You'll tell me."

"Yeah, and someday pigs'll fly out your ass." Serious.

"Whoooo, that's funny. You know, Nicky, you should try and not to be so charming."

Nicky wasn't smiling.

"Let's talk about Blaze. What kind of connection could he have to Sal Palumbo?"

"Blaze and Sally Boy, no. I doubt it. Sally's a made guy, a wiseguy, you know what I mean. He don't need to bother with a wacko like Blaze."

"There has to be a connection."

"I'll ask around."

"Do that. I'd like you to do that for me."

"For you, baby, I'd stop a subway with my bare hands."

"Nicky, I can never tell if you're lying or not."

"You have to learn to trust me. As it happens, I've never lied to you."

"Yeah, I bet. Anyway, I have to learn a whole lot of things. And Nicky, do us both a favor, call me Nora if it makes you happy, but don't ever call me baby again."

Nicky looked slightly upset.

"Baby, baby, baby, baby, oooooh baby," he said.

"Give your comedy a rest, smartass, and get me home."

She was feeling that rising tide again, twenty-foot breakers. "C'mon," she told him, "get me home, will you?"

They drove in silence for a while and soon Nora's ocean found its level. It occurred to her that Roseann Palumbo had to be in the mix. A thousand to one, the woman had something to do with her being assigned this Blaze Longo jazz. It made sense. In fact, it was the only thing that did make sense. The question was Jean-Paul himself.

Nicky took Central Park West to Seventy-ninth Street and made a left. He looked good driving her car. Nora thought the Mazda suited him. Nicky in his cap, behind the wheel of her sports car, projected a kind of subtle New York polish. People in the crosswalks turned to him.

The garage was in the basement of her apartment building on

Seventy-ninth, the south side of the street between Broadway and Amsterdam. Not very far away was an Italian restaurant owned by this character, Raymond Sanchez. Raymond was a big-time gambler and drug dealer. Nora, Sam, and a few others had nailed him a few years back.

"I'd bet parking your car here must cost a few bucks."

"It'd be a safe bet," Nora replied.

When Nicky pulled into the garage the nighttime manager, Philip, was sitting at a beat-up old table going through receipts. Philip was a tidy, small man from Trinidad and he was still in shock over the armed robbery that had taken place the past week. Two boys, a couple of kids, had worked him over pretty good and threatened him with guns, automatic weapons. As Nicky pulled to a stop, Philip's eyes moved nervously about and his hand went for a baseball bat that he now kept handy. The investigating detectives had told him he should not have a weapon of any kind. "Give it up," they had said. "If they come for you again, just give it up." But Philip's upbringing had been tough and he had been half hoping the kids would come back.

Philip did not recognize Nicky, but when he noticed Nora he smiled. And when Nicky handed him the car's keys he said, "I was sorry to hear about your husband, Mrs. Riter. Dat's de truth of it, he was a nice mon."

She thanked him and turned to Nicky saying, "Listen, there's a subway station just across the street. C'mon," she told him, "I'll walk with you."

They said good night to Philip and made their way out to Seventy-ninth Street. As they walked Nicky took hold of Nora's elbow.

"How you doing, Captain?"

"Okay," Nora said.

"You seem fine, considering."

"I shouldn't have drunk that much. Believe it or not, I hardly ever drink."

"You could have fooled me."

Nora reached inside her shoulder bag and removed a card. "My beeper number is on that card. It's the quickest way to reach me."

"How about your home number?"

"I don't think so."

"Okay. Listen," he said, "are you going to be around?"

Nicky was tapping the card against a thumbnail as a hodgepodge horde of pedestrians moved along the nighttime street. One group of twentysomething Wall Street-types followed a young woman in a silk suit who held theater tickets aloft in both her hands. There were four well-dressed black men who stared with delightful bewilderment at a Hispanic teenager selling watches from a box. An Indian woman wearing a dazzling blue shawl and a diamond-shaped red mark on her forehead offered lamb kebob on sticks. There were taxicabs and buses. Boys on bicycles blew whistles at the intersection where a wino, it seemed, was having a convulsion while speaking in tongues. On warm Manhattan nights there were always more people who preferred to watch than intercede.

Nora said, "I was thinking that I might take a few days for myself. But I've changed my mind. Sure, I'll be around."

"You know what, it's too bad you just can't relax and let this Blaze stuff slide for a while."

"It's too bad I can't go dancing, it's too bad I can't go to the theater or to a movie or read a book. You know it may sound pompous and corny, but I don't have the time to do a damn thing other than my job. Sometimes," she said, "sometimes when I look in the mirror, there's nothing there."

"Meaning what?"

"You tell me."

They stood on the corner of Seventy-ninth and Broadway amid the sounds of buses and cars, horns blaring. Nicky didn't answer her. He stood still, arms folded, staring at her. Nora didn't know what else to say or even what to do with her hands. Then he leaned toward her and kissed her. A quick, sweet, small kiss. Nora turned away saying, "Hey, hey. C'mon."

Nora's response was hasty and resolute but she knew her face was flushed.

"I've been wanting to do that all night. Forget all night, I've been wanting to do that since the day we met."

"So you did it, good for you. Stay in touch." Nora said. She felt rattled. But she was not angry at all, and that surprised her.

Nicky looking at her with a schoolboy look, lips pursed, head nodding. "You were curious, too. Weren't you?"

"Curious about what?" Nora said, her face reddening. That kiss was a delight, a freshness, the good feeling of a perfect fit. But, hell, she'd be damned if she'd let him know. "Don't do that again."

"Really?" He bent forward and kissed her again, this time on the forehead, and she could feel the tiniest flicker of his tongue.

Nora didn't like what that kiss did to her. She was annoyed. Nicky came at her again and brushed his hand along her cheek. In a hurry her dim uneasiness flared into visceral anger. She took hold of his wrist, saying, "I have a black belt in judo, I could toss your ass right out into the street. Now cut it out."

Nicky closed his eyes and wagged his head. "You mind telling me," he said, "what I have to do to get you to chill out?"

"Nicky you're going to be trouble for me, and I don't need it."

"So you're saying, what you're saying is that you don't want me to come up."

"Come up? What, where?"

Nicky rolled his eyes toward her apartment building.

"Hey, Nicky," Nora said. "Go home, will you. You've been a pal, a good drinking buddy tonight, now go home."

Nicky gave her a little Cary Grant. "If we get out of this alive, let's go back to New York on a train together. All right?"

"That was terrific, what was that?"

"Cary Grant, *North by Northwest.* You know that man was truly an underrated actor."

"You're not bad yourself."

"There's no convincing you?"

"Stay in touch, okay?"

"It's your call. See you around, Captain." Then he turned and walked away.

When Nora went into the vestibule of her building, she saw the doorman waiting for her, wearing a look of uncertainty. He handed her a business card saying, "There were two people here looking for you, ringing your bell. I told them you weren't in, but they didn't listen to me."

Nora glanced at the card, prickles of anxiety ran up her spine right across her head. The card said, CAPTAIN GRETA HARTMANN NYPD, INTERNAL AFFAIRS DIVISION.

Remo Caruso, Nora's doorman for the past five years, claimed to be a former cop from Cleveland. There had been a time when Nora considered checking his story, then decided against it. Remo was quiet, friendly, discreet in the extreme when it came to Max and his often daft behavior.

"How long ago were they here?"

"They just left."

"They left?"

"It couldn't have been more than five minutes ago. They were standing right here, saw you on the corner, couldn't miss you. I was going to say something, then decided, what for?"

"Did they say anything?"

"The woman said something about a camera. That she wished she'd had one. Ringing your bell like that, then looking at you on the corner. It seemed foolish to me, them being police officers just like you."

"Not like me, Remo, they're not like me, at all."

"Well, it just seemed kind of ridiculous to me. If you know what I mean. Silly."

Nora walked past the doorman and into her apartment building, thinking, I suppose silly is as good a word as any.

Waiting for the elevator, Nora decided that she would shower, change into some comfortable clothes, and then send out for some Chinese food. Yes, a shower and something to eat, all the better to clear her head. Then she planned to telephone Chief Jean-Paul Clement at home.

Muttering unhappily she fumbled into her apartment. Roseann Palumbo and Greta Hartmann were the dynamic duo of ill omens, making her miserable, a misery she planned to share with her chief.

Later that night, thirty-five miles south and east of the city, in the town of Old Westbury, Jean-Paul Clement turned his back to his wife Bridget and tried to find sleep. As was his way, he slept facing the bedroom window. When he was a child his mother used to say to him, "Paul, before you fall asleep search the night sky for a shooting star. If you find one, you can make a wish and be guaranteed it will come true." Jean-Paul didn't believe it then, and he didn't believe it now. Still, he always slept facing a window and before he went off to asleep, his eyes would search the pitch-black sky. In any case, Jean-Paul felt he could use whatever luck was available to him.

"Are you sleeping?" Bridget whispered. "I'm awake and I'm feeling restless."

Christ, what did that mean? It was early, a little before ten, but he was bushed, tired from day-long meetings with the police commissioner and the other super chiefs. Crime was at record low levels in the city, but meetings were at an all-time high.

"Tired," Jean-Paul said, "I had meetings today."

"I'm wide awake," Bridget told him, "and I shaved my legs."

"Sheesh, honey, I'm wiped and tomorrow I need to get an early start."

"Paul," she told him, "it has been a while."

Jean-Paul hearing that, eased toward the edge of the bed. It was sleep he wanted, not sex or conversation. And man, it had only been a few hours since he'd gotten a magnificent blow job from the hairdresser. His wife's hairdresser, and she'd drained him. That wanton little suburban chippie could suck your dick till you had short-term memory loss. Joyce had dropped to her knees in his den while Bridget slept peacefully under the hairdryer in the kitchen.

Jean-Paul knew he had been reckless, the twins in their bedroom watching a video, Bridget two rooms away, but this woman was the best, unquestionably the most skilled. Joyce, breathy, speaking barely loud enough to be heard. "C'mon, it'll only take a minute." Giving him that weird sensation, exciting, risky. Joyce in that blue T-shirt and white shorts, not that it was such a warm night, good-looking legs and great, well-kept hair, the back of her head going up and down like a wounded puppet. Jean-Paul afraid to look at anything but the closed den door, hoping the fucking hairdryer didn't go off.

He had been frightened but it was an eerie, thrilling kind of fear. Joyce Rose humming away, playing a tune—heaven, or what heaven should be. Bringing that tension in his groin to the point of eruption and the eruption itself, beyond bliss. Still, what a sick, wicked, what a detestable and amoral thing to do. But Jean-Paul couldn't help himself.

Not that doing sick, wicked, and amoral things was at all unusual for Jean-Paul. Nevertheless, the past year had been exceptional, herculean.

Two, sometimes three times a week he would see Roseann. If she were depressed and irritable they would simply drive to Queens, sit and talk and watch the sun fade over Jamaica Bay. When she felt cuddly and warm they'd head to the motel in New Jersey. Lately Roseann had been so raving mad that the Jersey trips had become fewer and fewer.

In the early part of the year, not a whole lot came his way. It was in March when his luck shifted. Jean-Paul had taken off a few pounds, started working out, did daily leg raises and sit ups, and began to run in the mornings. And bingo, just like that, for the past four months he could not turn around without bumping into a woman who wanted to screw. Since Jean-Paul did not have much going for him in the way of discretion—forget resistance—he found himself waist deep in women. If one included Bridget and Roseann, Jean-Paul was sleeping with five women. Herculean.

There was the WASP assistant district attorney in the Bronx who wrote poetry and wore her blond hair in cornrows. Her name was Susan and she had a studio apartment near Van Cortland Park. The apartment was dominated by a poster of a bull fighter and a pull-out sofa, on which they would make love to Beatles songs. After a day of tossing street beasts into the slammer, sweet Susan would screw like a mink to "Hey Jude."

Jean-Paul was screwing a four-foot-eleven Chilean law student named Carole. Carole looked Japanese and, he was certain, had no green card. The distance around Carole's tits was amazing for such a small woman. She lived in Astoria among the Greeks and had a smell about her that was pure wildcat sex.

Then there was the young, green-eyed FBI agent from California, whose husband was with the CIA in Panama and who had loved a lecture Jean-Paul had given at the FBI academy. Her name was Loren and Loren had a fully equipped gymnasium in her apartment. A stationary bike, a treadmill, and free weights. Loren was built like a young boy and was as horny as a toad. She would really give it to him, Loren really let him have it.

Not one of these women had proved to be difficult. No unwanted phone calls at the office, no pressure at all. Not a thought that any of them would come to knock at his door. Then there was Roseann.

Roseann was threatening and dangerous. That had been apparent from the minute she found her father among the missing. And lately it was not going at all well between them. But how to end it? The way she responded to things was frightening.

In the meantime, as Jean-Paul grabbed at the pillow in his bed, Bridget's breasts doing hot-cha, hot-cha, circles on his back, he wondered if Nora Riter would come through for him.

Bridget said, "I was dreaming a wonderful dream. Italy, Rome, the Trevi Fountain, the awesome soft tints of the buildings, the size and texture of the grapes and the cheeses. Remember the restaurant in the wall near the Via Veneto."

"Uh-huh."

"Our honeymoon."

"Maybe," Jean-Paul suggested, "you shouldn't talk, it'll keep you awake."

"Remember how we walked and walked and listened to the fountains. God, we were so much in love."

Jean-Paul pretended sleep.

"Remember the taxi driver from Brooklyn. The young man that took us up to the restaurant in the hills?" She put her hand on Jean-Paul's shoulder and pushed. "Don't kid me, I know you're awake."

"I am now."

"It astounds me, staggers me that I love you as much today as I did then."

Her hand slid from his shoulder to the back of his neck. Jean-Paul knew that if he squirmed one inch farther away, he'd fall on the floor. He was ready to jump out the window.

"Come on Paul."

"It hasn't been *that* long." He was indignant because she was right. It was true that his marriage was riddled with lies and false gestures of affection. Nevertheless, if there was any guiding principle in Jean-Paul's married life, it was the old ladies'-man standby: If you can't take care of business at home, you've got no right to play outside.

Bridget made soft sounds, sweet buzzing sounds, and nuzzled his back with her breasts.

"Honey," he whispered, "how about we send the boys to your sister's for the weekend?" Jean-Paul did not want to think about sex right now. Postpone, postpone, cut the bullshit. He had always been the kind of man more inspired by the women of his thoughts than the woman in his bed.

Bridget had believed for quite some time that his professional life had taken a serious toll on their love life. Jean-Paul had encouraged her to believe it.

"You know," she told him, "it's four o'clock in the afternoon in Rome, and I want to be in Rome."

"I'm tired, honey."

Bridget was not discouraged.

She nuzzled him again. Easing her thighs up against him and rolling her assbones in a small revolution, a series of tiny circles then a gentle push. A calling card, a hint, an announcement. "Paul," she whispered, nibbling at his ear, putting Jean-Paul into a cold sweat. But, man, he was drained and weary and, man, oh, man, he hoped the ginseng would kick in. He was considering the paradox of unappeasable hunger and the eternal reality of a cock under grave pressure and strain. Then the telephone rang.

Jean-Paul's first reaction was relief. Thinking, so there is a God, isn't there.

Nora had been glancing at CNN on the television in her bedroom, at the same time reading the intelligence folder on Blaze Longo. Larry King had said something about a woman named Paula Jones, something to do with the Arkansas state police, the president, and a blow job. It was not unusual for her to read and watch CNN at the same time.

After her shower and Chinese dinner she had been sorely tempted to telephone Jean-Paul at home, but decided to wait until morning. Now it was near 10:00 P.M. and it occurred to her that the names of Roseann Palumbo and Greta Hartmann would certainly pollute her peaceful dreams. Nora decided that she'd make that call.

She went into the bathroom to put some cold water on her face, then had a look at herself in the mirror. Nicky Ossman was four years her junior, but, she supposed, the age difference made no difference. She realized that she was attracted to him more than she should be. He was a head-turner, he sure as hell was. And, he was far brighter than she had believed at first.

Nora's reflection encouraged her.

Before calling Jean-Paul she had a quick glance at the Longo folder. In the background she heard a guest of King describe sexual intimidation in the workplace. A condition she was not unfamiliar with.

Longo's file made no mention of any organized-crime connection.

He was a street gorilla, a tough guy, with a series of arrests for assault and robbery. And there was one for narcotics, possession of heroin with intent to sell. The arresting officer, Det. Timothy O'Grady. Well, well, now, how about that. She knew O'Grady, had worked with him for a short time when she was in narcotics. A good guy, straight, and hardworking. It was said that O'Grady had once studied for the priesthood. She'd have to remember to give him a call.

Sitting on the edge of her bed, she picked up the telephone and tapped out Jean-Paul's number. He answered after two rings.

"I know it's late, I'm sorry," Nora told him.

"It's okay, what's up?"

"Can you speak freely?"

A long pause, and then, "Er . . . No."

"How about, yes and no?"

"C'mon, Nora, what's up?"

"You arrested Salvatore Palumbo a few years ago, is that right?"

"I arrested him five years ago."

"I have to ask this question."

"Go on."

At first she thought it would be best to project the maximum degree of courtesy and deference, and then decided, screw it. "There's a rumor," she told him, "that you're having an affair with his wife, Roseann Palumbo."

"Is there any good reason why this could not wait until tomorrow, Captain? Look, tomorrow is Saturday, it will be quiet in the office, come in and see me, okay?"

Jean-Paul referred to her as "captain" only when he was irritated. "I'll be in the office in the morning," he told her. "Come on by."

"How about a yes or no, it would help me sleep."

"Nora, there is no yes or no. I'll have to explain the situation to you."

"The situation?"

"Is that it?"

"Captain Hartmann and someone else stopped by my apartment building this evening."

"Did she?"

"Yes, she did."

"Did you speak to her?"

"I wasn't here."

"Nora, don't let this IAD business get you down. You know you can count on me. 'A bridge over troubled waters,' and all that. I'll call Chief Powers myself and find out what IAD has in mind. Powers worked for me at OCCB, he's not a bad guy."

"You know, Paul," she said, "I'm getting tired."

"Get a good night's sleep, Nora. Bear in mind just who I am and remember, I'm here for you."

His speech, the way the chief spoke was soft and laced with care and concern. Jean-Paul was stroking her, easing her along, playing with her head. Nora had been around long enough to understand that Jean-Paul was trying to take something from her. Something, she considered, that might already be gone. His tone made her weary.

Nora could hear Jean-Paul take a deep breath and blow out some air, when he gently said; "You ever think that maybe we're in the wrong line of work?" Nora said, "Ummm," and nodded, completely exhausted now. "Chief," she told him, "I'll see you in the morning."

Lying there, Nora began turning out schemes, angles of approach, game plans, thinking this man Jean-Paul Clement may be a bit murky on some things, but he was as poised as they come. The guy's play at arrogant innocence amazed her.

Nora knew Jean-Paul well, better than most people, and understood that for all his good looks, smarts, and celebrity, the man had a startling amount of contempt for most women. Suddenly, from nowhere, she felt a stirring of loneliness and anger. She thought of phoning Nicky the Hawk. She tried to put herself in Nicky's place and wondered just how far he would take this Blaze Longo business. Thinking, too, about what it would be like to allow Nicky to take that long walk from the street, to her apartment, to her bed. Nora got rid of that thought, there and gone.

Nicky fully intended to telephone Tino the minute he found a pay phone, but as soon as he entered the subway station and dropped his token, he heard the train and scooted to make it, telling himself he'd be home in a half hour.

He took a seat in the train, anxious, his heart banging away like thunder. Nicky was trying to envision Nora grabbing Blaze by the short hairs. What a joke, a stupid, dangerous joke. Thinking of Nora and Blaze made him cold and he wished he'd brought along a sweater. Despite himself, he ran a scheme or two through his head. Wild thoughts in and out and gone. He found a copy of the *Atlantic Monthly* and thumbed through the pages.

He turned up the collar of his jacket as he read a story about India's bandit queen, murder, rape, and revenge, a tale of Indian politics. For some reason the subway was practically empty, a few Orthodox Jews heading back to Crown Heights and some black guy who was a Denzel Washington look-alike. Denzel Washington, Nicky considered, would not be riding the F Train.

He exited the subway at Ninth and Court, stopped in the Roma, and made his way through a pimple-faced gathering of neighborhood hip-hop types hooting for Michael Jordan on the TV above the bar. Nicky found a spot at the corner of the bar and shouted for Jackie O.D. to get him a double espresso. Container in hand he headed on home.

Nicky moved on autopilot toward home. It was getting late, near eleven o'clock. When he walked past Charlie Chan's social club, he slowed for a moment, considering. Charlie's car was parked at the curb, the man never rested.

If he went in to see Charlie what would he say to him? That he was spending time with a police captain? Better yet, that he was hooked up with Blaze-fucking-Longo? Stop me, before I do something totally insane? That was a real possibility, that'd he'd throw all caution aside and shoot the moon. In happier times he would have found all this a life experience, a little grist for the actor's mill. But the way things were shaping up it was more likely he'd find himself in a trick bag with no way out. Nicky stood motionless in the center of the sidewalk. He found himself thinking about Charlie; of how, when you said something stupid, the Chan could stare at you silently, without sympathy.

Unnerved, he turned into his street and when he did he spotted a parked car he thought might be Fat Paulie's.

The sight of a car that looked like Fat Paulie's brought Nora back to him quite clearly. Around that woman all the chemistry in his body went haywire. He could hear himself babbling about this and that in the self-mocking tone he hated. The old Nicky speaking without thinking. Nicky felt momentarily overwhelmed by a feeling of self-disgust. Stealing a kiss, throwing his eyes up toward her apartment, as if to say, *How about it?* Amateur night, amazed at himself for all his silly gestures. The woman must think him an idiot.

Then as part of the same thought, he wondered, could a woman so attractive and smart really take down the likes of Blaze? You bet, he told himself, bet your ass, that is one tough broad. Telling himself, you see this train coming and, man, oh, man, you jump right onto the tracks. Brilliant.

Nicky had the feeling that his relationship with Nora and Nora herself was like a hovering tornado, she'd yank him up higher and higher. He figured that the longer it went on, the farther he'd drop. So, speed was the answer, get it on and get it done, and don't be so damn terrified. You're Nicky the Hawk, a character actor, a man with a myriad of talents. Then the new voice screamed from his brain, the new Nicky, resonant with remorse and regret, you mentioned Charlie Chan, not by name but you hung it out there. Nicky thought about it, the way Nora said, "You'll tell me."

He started to put his key in the door and stopped. Voices from inside, laughing, Blaze's voice and Fat Paulie, too. He slid in his key, turned the knob, and went in.

He saw Blaze sitting at the kitchen table with a beer, legs up and feet resting on a chair. He saw Paulie standing in front of the kitchen sink, arms crossed, a great big smile on his face. Tino sitting at the table turned to look at him, his expression, hard to tell, he seemed happy enough.

"There's no school tomorrow," Tino said. "It's okay."

"Yeah, school's out so tough Tino, here, figures he'll be a night owl. You know what, Nicky? This kid, your boy here, he's been telling us about his love life." Blaze mellow and relaxed, hanging out with a buddy. "We knocked and Tino let us in. You told him we might be around, huh?"

"That's right, I did. But not at eleven o'clock at night. Where'd you get the beer?"

"Irma's fridge is always full, Nicky," Tino said. A cool dude, one of the boys, hanging out with the big guys.

"Get your ass in bed," Nicky told him.

"Aw, c'mon."

"Tino!"

"All right, I'm going."

"Good talking to you, Tino," Blaze said. "Now do what I told you. What you do is get yourself some flowers and bring them to the girl." He brought his steel-tipped boots off the chair, stood up, hands on his hips. He wore a zippered leather jacket over a black turtleneck sweater, freshly creased jeans and boots. He looked well kept and serious. He looked like the bastard son of evil. "Tino's got a thing going for this Puerto Rican chick in the next building."

"He never told me," Nicky said, looking at Tino, following him as he left the room. "Since when do you stay up past eleven o'clock?"

"C'mon, Nicky, it's our fault," Fat Paulie said. "We came by to see you, the kid said you should be home any minute. You know, time flies. We're here, what? an hour, an hour and a half."

"I had to be polite," Tino said. "You tell people to come over and you're not here, what's with that?"

"Now, now," Blaze said, "your father was busy. He had things to do, places to go, people to meet. Nicky is a busy man."

"I had to go over to Manhattan to see about a job," Nicky told them.

"See, I told you he was busy," Blaze said.

Blaze wrapped an arm affectionately around Nicky's shoulder. "I want you to take a ride with us. I got something I want to show you."

"What? Now?"

Blaze's eyes went to Fat Paulie. "You figure our boy here is tired?"

Fat Paulie shot Nicky a quick look of curiosity. "Could be," he said. "A tough night in the big city, maybe he got laid. Had some actress lady blow on his balls a bit."

Nicky laughed.

"This ain't funny, Nicky," Blaze said, "we've got business and I want you to come along."

"Business. At eleven o'clock at night?"

Blaze watched him quietly for a moment.

"It's not Chase Manhattan you work for, Nicky. We don't do nine to five," Blaze said.

"I understand. I do. But I have the boy and I don't know where Irma is."

"So go and tuck him in, give the kid a kiss goodnight and let's get going. It's no big thing, no one's going to steal him."

Nicky thought about Irma and where she could have gone off to.

"Nicky, it was *you* that came to me looking to do some work. Now look at you, you're acting hinky on me. Nicky, my boy, you confuse me. Whadaya think, Paulie?"

"Hinky. I think he's a confusing kinda guy. This Nicky is a jester."

Nicky rushed to offer an apology.

Blaze said, "No one's twisting your arm here, you wanna come, come along. You don't, we'll see ya later."

Nicky knew he was being tested. It would be the second time he turned Blaze down. He doubted the guy would give him a third chance.

"Sure," he said, "I'm game, let's go."

Blaze looked thoughtful for a moment, then his icy, treacherous features filled out in a broad smile.

"Let's do it."

"Let me talk to Tino a minute, I'll meet you guys downstairs."

"We'll wait," Blaze told him. He seemed genuinely happy.

Nicky moved past Blaze quickly, walked through the hallway, went into Tino's room and closed the door.

"Nicky," said Tino, looking concerned, "you know, Blaze and Paulie don't seem all that bad."

Nicky sat down on the bed next to Tino's feet. "Have you seen Irma?"

"Uh, yeah. She had a date."

"A date?"

The boy gave him a little nod of the head and a grin that said, "Got me. You know Irma."

"Tino, I have to go out for a while."

"Where are you going? It's late."

"I have to go with Paulie and Blaze."

"Nicky, these guys are—"

"Shhhh," said Nicky. "Look, I won't be long. You'll be okay, huh? Just keep the door locked and don't open up for anyone."

"What about Irma?"

"Go to sleep. If I know Irma she won't be home till morning."

"Hey, Nicky," Blaze called out, "hey, Nicky boy, time's flying."

Tino sat up watching Nicky. Nicky looked at the boy, saying, "Tino, do you know how to use a telephone beeper?"

Tino wagged his head.

Sitting quietly in the bedroom they listened to Blaze and Paulie laughing, joking around in the kitchen. "If I write it out for you, do you think you could do it?" said Nicky.

"I don't know. Sure, if you write it out I could."

Nicky took a pad from Tino's desk, tore out a page, and searched around for a pen. Finding one in the desk drawer, Nicky took Nora's card and wrote, "1–800 first, then the number, then hit the pound sign on the phone. After a beep, tap in the number and wait." Nicky handed Tino the paper and said, "Can you do this?"

"Yessir."

"Good, good. Listen, if I'm not back in a few hours, phone that beeper. You'll get a call back from a woman. Her name is Nora. You tell Nora that I went out with Blaze and Fat Paulie. Can you do that, Tino?"

Tino nodded at the paper.

"Nicky boy," Blaze called out.

"On my way," Nicky said.

"That Blaze, he's strange, Nicky. I mean, sometimes he seems like a cool guy, but, man, is he strange." A funny smirk got Tino's point across.

Nicky looked away. "They're not my new best friends, it's business. When I get the business done we won't be seeing much of those two."

Nicky smiled, and he had never been more serious in his life. "I won't be long."

"Nicky?"

"Sleep. I promise I won't be long."

It was a clear night and cool; a stiff breeze came in off the harbor weighted with the smell of the sea and the moon shone happily off the windows of the tenements and markets along Columbia Street. A nice eerie night to cat around. In Fat Paulie's car there was a stirring expectancy about a promise of dark deeds that would be made plain before long. Nicky, tired and antsy, inhaled a strong scent of danger coming from Blaze and Paulie.

"Remember what it was like along these docks?" Blaze said. "It usta be bustling down here. Now, nothing."

Nicky said things change, times change. Hell, they even changed the name of the neighborhood.

After a few minutes of silence, Blaze caught Nicky's eye in the rearview mirror. "You're nosy, I bet, huh? I bet you're dying to know what's happening, where we going, shit like that?"

"I figure when you're ready to tell me, you'll tell me."

Blaze poked Paulie with an elbow. "He's not going to believe how sweet this is. What we got going here is pure gold, Nicky. The perfect score."

"The perfect score," Nicky said. He leaned forward, feeling strange riding alone in the backseat. "So tell me, what's the perfect score, Blaze?"

"Sit tight, you'll see. There's a couple of people I want you to meet, people that want to meet you." Blaze turned his cheek to the rearview, checked the side of his face. "And there's this place, this spot I have in Sheepshead Bay. You'll see, you're gonna like this, Nicky. I know you, you're gonna like this."

Blaze seemed to feel that they were buddies; the guy coming on friendly, as if they had been crime partners for years. "Paulie," Nicky said, "no hard feelings, huh? That business with my cousin Irma."

"C'mon, c'mon, c'mon," Paulie said, "water under the bridge, a misunderstanding was all that was. Hey, I've known you for years, and Charlie the Chan vouched for you. What's better than that?"

Blaze nodded his head in quiet affirmation. "It's not like we don't know you, Nicky. Like you're a stranger or something. You're a neighborhood guy, one of us. And shit, you've been vouched for."

Paulie turned to him, saying, "We need your head, Nicky, you're a weird fucker, but you're smart. Always have been."

Nicky felt overwhelmed with the urge to press the subject, find out what these two loonies had in mind. The impulse stronger than any thought of being patient.

"Tell me about this perfect score."

"Perfect," Blaze said, glancing into the rearview again. Nicky said, "Fine, I'll sit back, wait and see. You guys'll tell me soon enough."

Nicky wondered if he should ask about Roseann Palumbo and Sally Boy. "Let me ask you guys, you know Roseann Palumbo, Sally Boy's ol lady? What's with her?" Just lay it out there, see where it goes.

The car slowed and Blaze turned to glance back at him. "What about her?" A menacing sound creeping into his voice.

Nicky hesitated, thinking, go for it, then thinking, cool it, cool it. "Nothing," he said, "I just haven't seen her around much."

"Where you gonna see Roseann around?" Paulie said. "She ain't never around."

"I guess you're right, Sally Boy doing time and all."

"Yeah." Blaze said, "Poor Sally, he's upstate married to his right hand and Roseann is giving it away to some cop. She's fucking this cop, Nicky. You know that? Roseann is fucking the same cop that busted Sally Boy."

"I heard. But I find it hard to believe. I mean, how do you do that, sleep with the man that put your husband in jail?"

"Tell him, Paulie."

"Ask Charlie," Paulie said, "everybody at the club knows. Sally's gonna know the minute he comes home. And let me tell ya, knowing him, he's gonna go and cut her fucking head off."

"Humm," said Nicky, and that's all he said.

"You know her old man, her father?" Blaze said.

"Alley Boy, the gambler. Sure I know him."

"That sonofabitch," Blaze said, "he owed us money for months. Like we were some kind of dunces or something. Like we were nobodies."

"Nobodies," Paulie said, shaking his head.

"Now that you mention it," Nicky said, "I haven't seen him around, either."

Blaze turned to Fat Paulie and Paulie smiled. "You ain't been looking hard enough," Paulie said. "He's around, he's all around. Alfred is all over Brooklyn, is where he is."

Nicky was not ready for Blaze and Fat Paulie's laughter. At that moment he was swamped by the clear assessment that these two jokers had killed Alley Boy. They were saying, what? Alley Boy was all over the place. In pieces, right? He wondered how the Chan would feel about that? Charlie and Alley Boy went back a long way. His new Nicky voice told him to mind his own business. *But that was his business, that was just what Nora wanted to know, what he promised to deliver.* Don't push these characters, he thought. Be cagey and leave it be for the time being. Should he ask about Nora's boss, the big-time cop? No, he didn't think he should.

Fat Paulie's car found the Gowanus Expressway, the road rose beneath them and before long they were tooling along the Belt Parkway, Blaze saying they were going to Sheepshead Bay, to an apartment he kept down near Emmons Avenue, about a block or two from the ocean. "Man," Blaze told him, "wait'll you see this spot."

The apartment house was on a dead-end street at the end of a row of vacant buildings, off Bay 8th Street. The neighborhood was on the rise, making a comeback. The way Nicky saw it, city masterminds had skipped over this street.

In front of the building was one of several streetlights that threw off a misty mustard glow, setting the street into a grotesque gloom. A vacant lot took up half the block with a burnt-out, abandoned car parked in the center; toward the dark end of the street, a battered refrigerator stood at attention among beer cans and slabs of cement, its great yellow-and-white door open in a comic salute.

Blaze parked the car under the streetlight and they walked into the apartment building, pausing at the foot of the stairway. The illumination inside the building came from smoky ceiling fixtures that flickered with half-life.

Somewhere above them there was loud music, a woman shouted in a language that was not familiar to Nicky, and a second woman shouted back in heavily accented English. A door slammed. Blaze started up the stairs, turned to Nicky, saying, "The building's condemned, but there are people here and they get some electric power. Don't ask me how, I got no idea."

"Russians," Paulie said, "can pirate anything. Russians are slick."

"Yeah, it looks it. They certainly turned this place into a marvelous little oasis," Nicky said.

"Ever been down to Brighton Beach?" Paulie said. "Ever go to one of the Russian clubs?"

"Can't say I have," Nicky told him. "When I go to a club, I usually go to the city."

Nicky had been born and raised in Brooklyn and took a certain pride in knowing the borough. *I know Brooklyn.* But in fact he knew almost nothing about Sheepshead Bay, Coney Island, or Brighton Beach. He did know that recently those Brooklyn neighborhoods had taken in thousands of Russians.

Blaze shook his head. "Well, man, you should go and see this joint, the Paradise. I'm telling you it's like nothing you've seen before. Ey, Paulie, the Paradise, it's something, ain't it?"

"I don't like it," Paulie told him. "Too many Russians."

"A Russian nightclub," Blaze told him, "what'd you expect to be there, Frenchmen?"

"They're weird," Paulie said.

"Like you're not," Blaze told him.

"Me? Shit, I'm just a South Brooklyn kinda guy. Nothing weird about me."

The air in the stairway was so hot that it seemed to Nicky that the building's furnace was going full blast when it should have been off. And there was a mighty odor. The atmosphere was fragrant with the reek of uncollected garbage and other smells he could not begin to identify.

On every landing they passed cracked and broken plastic garbage pails that stood, or lay on their sides overflowing with rubbish. The building was full of noise. Loud, verbal brawls behind closed apartment doors.

Instinctively Nicky followed Blaze and Paulie trailed behind him.

Nicky was scared shitless, wondering what in the hell he had let himself in for. Thinking, a place like this would scare the shit out of anybody. He fingered the pocket of his jacket where he carried his knife, and remembered that he had left it at home.

Blaze took the final flight of stairs two at a time and Nicky had some trouble keeping up. When they reached the top-floor landing, Blaze stood for a moment his hands on his hips, looking down the length of the hallway. There was dim light and the heat was so intense that Nicky felt as if he'd just stepped into a steam room. But there was something worse than the heat; the stench was powerful, oppressive. Nicky blew out some air, tried to be casual about it, holding his nose and grinning.

Fat Paulie had been hit the same way. "Somebody's dead in this joint," Paulie said. "Somebody is rotting around here."

Nicky said, "What in the hell is it?"

"It's down below somewhere," Blaze said, "not where we're going," as though that were all right.

They walked along the hallway, Nicky feeling the tension building in his legs and arms and fingers. If I had to fight for my life in this pit, he wondered, could I survive barehanded. He could do it, if it came to it, he felt certain he could and he would. Nicky felt a little sorry for himself, thinking that a few months in jail could not be worse than this.

"Fucking top floor," Fat Paulie snorted, wheezing, reaching for a breath of rotten air.

They were moving along a long hallway, Nicky relaxing a bit. It didn't last.

At the far end of the hallway, just in front of an apartment door, was a small, white trash pail chock-full of battered containers of old Chinese takeout. There was movement in one of the boxes, and it took Nicky a moment to realize it was a rat.

Oh, man, he was in no mood for rats. He could remember very clearly his time working the docks with rats climbing the pilings at the change of tide, the way the creepy bastards turned his blood cold.

The rat came out of the pail about five feet from him, stood for an instant head held high sniffing and looking about. Cornered, Nicky thought. The closed apartment door behind him, Blaze, Nicky, and Paulie in front. Nicky thinking how he would tell Nora about this night. See how much of a rise he'd get out of her when he painted the scene of the building, the Russians, and the rats. Whoa, she'd say, and then what happened? This rat made a funky little dance step, spun around, and dove into a hole in the hallway wall. See, he'd say with some bravado and conviction, see the places I go for you, the psychos I am forced to deal with, just for you? Thinking of Nora made Nicky feel close to her. His mind flashed on when they had walked in the street, the way she held on to his arm. And, man, the way she threw her head back when she laughed. He could not help thinking of her. Wondering if Nora was thinking of him. He was falling in love. The ebb and flow of this day was wearing him down.

Blaze pointed at the rat and smiled. Nicky smiled back, saying, "Jesus, man, oh, man, how'd you find this place?"

"It's perfect," Blaze said, "condemned and perfect." Then he knocked on the door. Once, then twice, then once again. It was a signal and he'd done this before. Blaze turned and looked at Nicky, saying, "What are you looking at?" Nicky said he wasn't looking, he was thinking, and Blaze said, good. Blaze turned to knock again but as he did the door opened and a man stood with a chicken leg in his hand, waving them in.

It was the living room of a big apartment, high ceilings and wide, double-hung windows looking out onto Bay 8th Street. Nicky was struck by a new odor, a combination of incense and a backed-up toilet.

"Where's Montonero?" Blaze said. "I want him to meet Nicky. I brought Nicky the Hawk, the guy I told you about."

Nicky stepped to the side, squinting. The light in the room coming from four scented candles, one set in each corner. The dim light hurt his eyes.

The man who stood before him was black with a shaved head. He wore darkened granny glasses, and was barechested under his blue bib overalls. One diamond stud earring flashed in the faint light. A big, warm, and friendly grin. Twenty-six, twenty-seven years old. He took Nicky's hand telling him his name was Morgan. Morgan's hand was soft and smooth, with long fingers. Nicky thinking the guy could be a musician, or a poet, a thinker. Nicky said, "How in the hell can you live here?"

"I don't live here, buddy, I'm just passin through. Whadaya think, because I'm black I'd live in a shit-hole like this?"

Nicky tried to keep his voice neutral. "Sorry," he said.

"Another fucking bigot. I'm kidding, calm down."

"Montonero?" Blaze said. "Where is he?" Morgan didn't answer, he watched Nicky. "What'd he do? Take off on you?"

"He's checking on something," Morgan said.

When Montonero came into the room he held his hands in the air as though he were surrendering. "Blaze," he said, "where the hell you been? We've been waiting, you got any idea what's it's like to sit around and wait in this garbage dump? This place stinks to high heaven, man. It's nauseating, repulsive. To top it off, the whole goddamn joint is filled with Russians. Did you know that?"

"Sure," Blaze told him. "They mind their business."

"You know," Morgan said then, "this place wouldn't be half bad if you hadn't gone and killed those two dogs."

"Is that right?" Montonero said then.

"He shot our neighbors' dogs," Morgan said, "two of them, big fuckers, threw them in the cellar."

"They were barking, growling, showing me their teeth. Fuck those dogs and fuck the Russians, too."

Morgan nodded. "In case you haven't noticed, the two mutts been laying down in that cellar a week now. They're getting ripe, giving the rats a feast."

Nicky looked past Morgan toward Montonero. He tried to swallow but he couldn't. Morgan was still watching him. Morgan saying, "He shoots em right in the first-floor hallway, and then this bozo waits around to see if any of the neighbors would make an appearance."

"Well, they quit barkin," Montonero said.

"And nobody came out of the apartments," Morgan told him.

"See," Blaze said, "I told you these Russians mind their business."

Montonero nodded as though he understood the Russian mentality having to do with secrecy and concealment. He was of medium height and quite thin. His hair was long and tied behind his head and he had a big, droopy Pancho Villa mustache. Nicky thinking he was interesting to look at, a mean sonofabitch in leather pants and motorcycle boots.

Nicky looked around the room, saying, "We're gonna stand here and bullshit, or is there a place we can sit?"

The room they were in was without furniture or fixtures, just the candles in the corners.

"There's a table and chair in the other room. We can go in there," Montonero said.

"I guess right here will do as good as any place," Nicky told them. "So, let's get to it. Why don't you tell me what you guys got in mind, then I'm out of here. Nothing personal, but this is one smelly, fucking depressing, ugly place. I don't know about you, but I don't plan on staying here any longer than I have to."

"If this is the guy you've been telling me about," Montonero told Blaze softly, "then things should be looking up."

"Nicky," he said, "meet Montonero, the whole name, the whole package."

Montonero came away from the door to shake Nicky's hand and Morgan said, "Say hi to Nicky the Hawk."

"Nicky the Hawk, huh? Good to meet ya. How you been doin?"

"Tell you the truth, it could be worse, though I don't see how," Nicky told them.

Everyone laughed.

Morgan sat cross-legged on the floor. Montonero, Blaze, Paulie, and Nicky remained standing.

Blaze said, "Nicky is lookin to earn, he wants to join the crew. And like I told you, this is one smart sonofabitch. He's got some fucking weird ideas, but, hey, he's one of the toughest and smartest guys you ever gonna meet."

"If he's so smart," Morgan said, "what the hell is he doing with you?"

Blaze laughed softly.

"Same as you, buddy, same as all of you."

Nicky looked at Blaze, avoiding Morgan's eyes. Morgan, it seemed, was quite taken with him.

"So let's get to it, Blaze," Nicky said, "it's getting late. I don't have all night."

"I know you, Nicky," Morgan said then. "I can't figure from where, but I've seen you somewhere."

Nicky had no answer.

"You've seen him on television," Fat Paulie said, "Nicky's an actor. The car commercial, Nicky." He winked at him. Nicky saying then, "I doubt it."

"I told you he had some weird ideas," Blaze said, "Nicky wants to be an actor."

"You're an actor?" Montonero said.

"You could say that."

"A man of the stage and screen," Montonero told them. "Perfect, Blaze, perfect."

Fat Paulie nodded generously.

Morgan looked uncertain.

Nicky blew out some air thinking that Blaze was a psychopath, but he was not stupid. His trouble was that he was too much of a neighborhood guy, a street guy, an enforcer, and it ended there. He was not stupid but he certainly was not smart. For all his cold-blooded craziness, there was no way Blaze could pull anything off that took more thought than shooting or stabbing someone. And he was a terrible judge of character.

"What do you have in mind here, Blaze?" Nicky said.

Blaze turned to stare at him, giving him a hard look, thinking.

"You ready to hear this?"

"No, I'm here in hell in the middle of the night because I love your company. C'mon, get it on. If it's a piece of work you want to get done, let's talk about it."

Blaze smiled.

Montonero said, "He knows nothing?"

Blaze shook his head.

Morgan said, "Oh, man!"

Blaze said, "You know me and Paulie were into this and that. We were putting some money in the street. You knew that, right?"

"It's no secret that you're a loan shark, Blaze."

"Ancient history, brother. Too much work, chasing people around for nickels and dimes, keeping records and shit. History. I'm through with that."

Morgan said, "How the hell can you bring somebody here to meet me and Montonero, and them knowing shit about what we do? What's with that? Are you nuts?" He patted Nicky's arm. "Nicky here seems like a good guy. You must work out Nicky, a helluva arm you got there. Say Nicky, here, this good-looking sonofabitch with muscles, don't want none of this? Say he got no heart for it? Say he tells us to fuck off. Huh? What do we do then, Blaze?"

And Montonero sounded like a man that meant what he said, saying, "That's the easy part. Nothing personal, Nicky, you turn on me, on us, I feed you to the rats."

Nicky grinned. "Now you're threatening me? I just met you guys and you're threatening me. I love it."

"Oh, yeah, bet your ass. No threat, a promise is what it is," Morgan told him.

Nicky trying to remember something Charlie Chan had once said about tough guys. That real tough guys never threaten, never warn. With real bad guys you never see it coming. And Nicky knew that had some meaning here.

241

"C'mon, c'mon," he said. "Let's get with it, what do you guys want from me?"

"Tell him what we want," Montonero said. "You brought him around, Blaze, you tell him."

"No, you tell him. Explain it," Blaze said, "I love the way you tell it."

"We have a word in Argentina, *chupado*. You know *chupado*, Nicky? Ever hear that word?"

"You're kidding me, right? The only word I know in Spanish is, *por favor*."

"No reason you should know, *chupado*. Nice accent, by the way, *por favor*, very nice. In my country if someone is *chupado*, it means he's sucked up, disappeared."

It was a simple Spanish word, *chupado*, but it gave Nicky a queer buzz.

"All right. So?" Nicky said, getting antsy.

"Sucked up. I love it," Blaze said then.

Morgan was biting his thumbnail.

"Let me put it this way," Montonero said, "when you suck somebody up you snatch em. Take em, stash em. Maybe scare em a little. Maybe scare em a lot. Maybe scar them a little."

"You're talking about kidnapping people and cutting their ears off." Nicky turned to smile at Blaze. "I saw his collection," he told them.

"Ears, fingers, what's it matter? You know what I'm saying," Montonero said.

"Yessir." Now Nicky wondered if it was possible that all four of these characters were wacky. What were the odds on that? What were they trying to tell him? Now Montonero was getting to it.

"In South America," Montonero said, "they do what they call fast-food kidnapping. Businesspeople, politicians, film and TV stars. These people get taken off for quick money, twenty-five, fifty, a hundred grand. A quick snatch, a fast payday."

Nicky stood, arms crossed, and went off into his thoughts, not paying attention anymore, only vaguely aware of what this screwball was talking about; thinking about Nora, knowing that she had no idea of what she had asked him to get involved in. He felt sorry for himself, sorry, and scared silly, because maybe he talked a good game, but these guys were for-real crazies. They were into shit that was way beyond any of his experiences. When he finally snapped back and looked into Montonero's face, the guy was smiling as if he could read his thoughts.

"Nicky, this is not as crazy as it sounds. Hey, all you gotta do is pick your spots, your targets."

Nicky said, "You know, with all the Spanish-speaking people in Brooklyn, sometimes you can get confused. But in case you haven't noticed, this ain't South America. You kidnap somebody famous here, you disfigure them, maim them, you'll do about a million years. Thanks for asking, but I think I'll take a pass."

"Hey, Nicky," Blaze said, "let him finish. *Famous* people, I know you think I'm bent, but take my word for it, I'm not. *Famous* people? Tell him, go on, will ya, tell him all of it."

Montonero nodded, a quiet, self-assured look coming into his face now. "We jump outlaws, Nicky. People that can't go to the cops. Nobody famous. Drug dealers, big-time gamblers, people that got nowhere to go. Outlaws with fat boxes of cash."

"They got boxes of cash," Blaze said, talking soft and firm, focusing. "And they stole it. We're just going to steal a little from them. They'll pay, they'll have no choice but to pay. Always remember that they got nowhere to go."

Morgan came in from the shadows, walked over to Nicky, and put his finger on Nicky's chest. "Let me tell you, you take some guy off, rip off his ear and deliver it to his ol lady, it gets their attention."

Nicky turned to him, smiling. "Man," he said, "I don't even like going to violent movies."

"This is not theory, Nicky," Montonero said, "it works. It works in Chile, Mexico, Colombia, and it works in New York. This is perfect, no risk. We make the people we deal with believers. And, like we've been saying, what are they gonna do, they're fucked."

"Yeah, but Jesus, Blaze," Nicky said, "I can't believe these people won't go to the cops."

"We tell em," Fat Paulie said, "gahead, go to the cops. You got a little package with an ear, the next package you get is going to be big, and square, and it's gonna contain the head of your loved one. Whadaya think they're gonna do?"

Nicky raised his hands. "You tell me."

"Pay," Blaze said, "they'll pay. C'mere, I want to show you something. Paulie," he said, "check the time. Make the call." He turned to Morgan and then to Montonero. "If everything is everything, you two go and make the pickup."

"And if the ol lady goes hinky on us?" Montonero said with a faint smile.

Blaze went into his pocket and came out with a straight-edged razor. Razor in hand he made a gesture of thoughtful surrender. "I'll have no choice," he said, "but to remove from his head, one ear."

Blaze turned and looked toward the darkened hallway beyond the living room, he crooked his finger. "C'mon, Nicky," he said, "you come with me."

Nicky followed him down the hallway into a second room, Blaze waving his hand in a dramatic gesture. "C'mon," he said, "c'mon." Then Blaze turned and passed through a doorway, Nicky followed, all the while thinking, man, oh, man, this is some weird shit. Nicky looked at Blaze and turned and looked into the room.

There was no light, no candles, nothing but the sole refracted glow of the streetlights that came in through one large window. Nicky moved forward and saw a man tied to a chair and he approached him and stood staring at him. He turned to look into Blaze's face and asked, "What in the fuck are you doing?"

Blaze just stared at him stupidly. "You seem confused," he said, "what's the problem?"

In the dim light, it seemed to Nicky that the man was dressed all in white. He was bound so tightly to the chair that no movement was possible. Duct tape around his chest, legs, and wrists. A black bandanna kept his mouth shut. "Blaze," Nicky said, "this is not funny, this is no joke. Who is this man? What in the hell are you doing to him?"

Blaze sighed with frustration. He took Nicky by the elbow and brought him across the room. When he spoke, Blaze spoke warmly and slowly. "May I present Hector Santiago," he said. "This guy is a full-fledged doctor, and a half-assed priest, and a walking bank vault for fucking drug dealers."

Nicky glanced at Hector's face, the bandanna covered his mouth and chin. Nicky could not make out any marks or wounds. "Are you all right?" he said.

Hector rolled his eyes.

"Of course, he's all right," Blaze said. "No one is going to hurt you, Hector," stroking Hector's hair as he spoke. "Your wife comes through, you're home free."

Hector gestured with his chin, pointing toward the hallway.

"Don't be shy, speak up," Blaze said.

There was a garbled sound, then a hoarse whisper. Nicky thought he heard, "Bathroom."

Hector put his chin to his chest, then raised it, pointing again toward the doorway behind them.

"He needs to use the bathroom," Nicky said.

"Well, ain't that the drizzling shits," Blaze said. "Sorry partner, the toilet's busted."

Hector sucked in his breath and held it for a moment then let out a startling sound, his face straining, the sound coming out stronger, building to a drawn-out, garbled shriek.

Nicky began working at the duct tape, saying, "For chrissake."

Blaze fixed him with a tight scowl. "The hell you think you're doing?"

"What's it look like," Nicky said, mainly to himself, since he expected no rational answer from Blaze.

Hector dropped his head onto his shoulder and let out a deep, mournful sigh.

"Well, now," Blaze said, "check that out. He went potty. Atta boy, Hector, atta boy."

Paulie called out, "She's ready, they're gonna go and make the run."

Blaze clapped his hands in delight.

Watching Blaze, Nicky began to think of another conversation he'd had with Charlie a few years back. There were kidnappers around then, too, crazy bastards who snatched one of the Gambino kids. It made all the papers. The kidnapper and his buddies were a tough, Irish crew from the West Side of Manhattan. Nicky had heard just how tough these guys were and he mentioned their toughness to Charlie. Charlie had told him that he was right; they were tough, killers, badasses. But then again, Charlie had said, everybody cries before they die. And they did, too.

"What I wonder, Blaze," Nicky said, "is why you need me here?"

"I guess I may as well come right out with it."

"Maybe you should."

Blaze nodded and turned and stared at Hector. "The Chan loves you, Nicky, everybody knows that. And I figured that if you're serious about making some serious bread, we could use that connection. You know, you and Charlie."

"What are you talking about?"

"Ey, Charlie knows people with mountains of money. People who are no friends of his. You talk to him, come on to him, nice, nice.

Explain how easy this all goes down, he might just want to back us. He would. I'm sure he would."

Nicky thinking that Charlie hated kidnappers more than he hated turncoats, and nobody hated informants more than Charlie the Chan.

"The hell you talking about, Blaze? You talking about kidnapping wiseguys, connected guys. Whadaya got, a death wish?"

"Ey, most of those guys are old and slow and sloppy, they don't scare me."

"Uh-huh."

Blaze twisted his mouth into a smirk. "I know you and Charlie are close. What I'm trying to figure is, just how close?"

Blaze took Nicky by the sleeve and brought him to the window. "Look," he whispered, "turning a dollar here is about as easy as it gets. You should be convinced."

Nicky looked at Blaze without seeming to hear what he'd said.

"Nicky?"

"Convinced of what?"

"That the Chan should back us, set people up. You can influence him, Nicky. You can do it. Charlie can give us people."

Nicky trailed off, thinking, man, this guy is just dying to die. "Who knows?" Nicky said. "Who knows what Charlie would do?" For a moment he thought of telling Blaze exactly what he thought Charlie might do. But he decided to let that pass, saying, "Are we through here?"

"We have to wait for payday, brother. Payday is coming and maybe if you're nice I'll give you a taste." He still held Nicky by the sleeve; Blaze tightened his grip and pulled him in close. "You'll talk to Charlie. Because when you get right down to it, ol Charlie Chan ain't no different than any other money-grubbing greaseball. If he's convinced he'll earn big here, man, he'd suck your dick."

"Uh-huh."

"I know him, he don't fool me. Maybe he has you bullshitted, but not me, buddy, not me."

"I'll talk to him."

"That's the spirit."

Blaze's eyes were merry as he patted Nicky's cheek. "Bet your ass you'll talk to him. You wanna know why?"

"Tell me."

"Because when you get right down to it, brother, all that matters is the cash. Me, you, Charlie, everybody, cash is what it's all about. What the fuck else is there?"

Moving briskly, Blaze walked over to Hector Santiago. He stood still for a time, studying the man seated before him, trying to decide. He took the razor from his pocket and turned it in his hands. "How about a little nick," he said, "a little slice off the top."

"Hey," Nicky said, "come back here."

"Just nod if you can hear me, Hector," Blaze said. "Your ol lady, she gonna show with the beard or what?"

Hector nodded, he nodded many times.

"Gotta make em believers," Blaze said, and turned toward Nicky with an amused little grin.

Nicky figured that events had been heading this way for a while. Blaze building to a meltdown. Thinking, this is nothing but degenerate evil. "Hey," he said, "c'mere, will you? I want to get something straight."

Blaze studied his razor, the smile fading. He seemed to be unhappy. Blaze spun around and crossed over to Nicky.

Nicky said, "What you're saying, you're saying you want me to ask Charlie Chan to finger targets for you?" Nicky smiling, admonishing himself: Just make this clown happy and get out of here. His new Nicky voice telling him, look, look at the way he holds that razor in front of his face, as if the blade was something he liked to smell.

Blaze's smile returned. "That's right, that's right. We're talking big-time money here. There ain't a wiseguy in the world that will turn away from big-time cash. All you gotta do, Nicky, is point Charlie's nose in the right direction."

Blaze seemed to be losing it a little. His jaw trembled. "These guinea bad guys don't scare me, Nicky. They don't."

Nicky was overwhelmed with a mixture of panic and relief, telling himself that Blaze had gonorrhea of the brain and that he deserved what-ever wicked shit came his way. Look what he's done to that man. Look at Hector! Look at Blaze, crazy bastard, evil prick!

"Whadaya think," Blaze said, "maybe I should go over and nick the spick a bit."

"I don't think it's necessary," Nicky said.

"Maybe not. But still."

Nicky wanted to grab Blaze by the back of the neck and bang him off a wall and slap his face. He wanted to see him put away for a long, long time. His new Nicky voice telling him, look at *you*, *you* worked at avoiding these schmucks all your life. Now you're up to your eyeballs in assholes and you got no one to blame but Nicky the fucking Hawk.

Nicky's mind was trying to find some magic trick. Some way to get the hell out of that room, that apartment, away from the lunatics.

"Phew!" Blaze said, "let's go. This room stinks. You know what, I think ol smelly Hector shit his pants again."

Nora woke up at five o'clock in the morning trying to shake off the sound of her beeper and the fragments of a bitter nightmare about Max and Sammy. Max crouched in a shooter's stance on the boardwalk, a cowboy hat on the back of his head, wide-eyed and crazed, Nora's heavy-barrel Smith clutched in both his hands. Sam backing off, his arms criss-crossed in front of his face.

Five hours earlier, Nora had slid beneath her comforter and crashed. Her exhaustion the consequence of drink and of conversation with Jean-Paul Clement. A man she now considered an unequivocal dipshit.

Although she almost never left her beeper on her nightstand, she had that night, thinking Nicky might call. And now, five o'clock in the morning, beep-beep-beep. Jesus, it's five o'clock in the morning, beep-beep-beep. Jesus, it's five o'clock. Nora double-checked the flashing number, lifted up the receiver and poked out the numbers.

"Is that Nora?" The voiced sounded like a child to Nora's ear. "I'm Tino Ossman, Nicky's son. And, ah, Nicky told me he said to call you if he didn't come home. He didn't come home."

"Nicky Ossman's *son?*"

"Yeah. Yes, Nicky's son. And, ah, it's real late and he's not home, and he didn't call, and he never does that, stays out and doesn't call. And you know, you know, he said, he told me to call you."

Nora yawned into her fist, tried to clear her head.

"Nicky has a *son?*"

The boy was silent for a moment. "He told me if he didn't get back I should call you."

Nora rolled on her side and closed her eyes.

"He went out with those two guys. Last night, Nicky left with these fellas and he hasn't come home. He told me if I got worried I should call you."

Nora felt a slow surge of heat rising into her stomach. "Told you to call me?" she said.

"If I was worried, I should call you."

"And you're worried?"

"Sort of."

"Tino," she said, "can I ask how old you are?"

"It's okay," he said, "Nicky told me to call you and I did."

"Tino . . ."

"No, no. It's okay." He hung up the phone.

Nora had to think about it for a minute. "Damn," she said, "so Nicky the Hawk has a son."

Nora tapped out Nicky's number again, the boy answering after one ring, saying, "Nicky?" Nora saying, "It's me, Nora. Tell me who were the men that came for Nicky?"

Silence. Then a sound, a sob, a terrible sobbing.

"I thought you were him. C'mon," he said, "where is he? Where is Nicky?"

"I don't know where he is, Tino. But I know that wherever he is, Nicky knows how to take care of himself. He'll be fine, don't worry, your dad will be okay."

Silence.

"Do you know the names of the people he went with?"

"Yes."

"Tino?"

Another long moment of silence and then, "Blaze and Paulie."

Montonero handed an attaché case to Blaze, saying, "She showed like clockwork. Dropped the bag and split." Moving around the room like a flamenco dancer, slapping his fingers off the heel of his hand.

Morgan said, "Perfect, brother, perfect."

Fat Paulie added, "We made those chumps believers, they gave it up, Blaze. They gave it up."

"Anybody see you?" Blaze said.

"Not hair one, nothing," Morgan told him.

Blaze saying now, "That is perfect. Hey, Nicky, how you doing? You don't look surprised."

"Listen, since when you surprise me, Blaze?"

"Seventy-five thou for three-days' work," Blaze told him. "Not bad, eh?"

"You're a foxy guy, Blaze, a man of talent," Nicky said.

"Foxy, naw, I'm not foxy. C'mere, you come with me." He handed the attaché case to Paulie and took Nicky by the elbow, leading him along through the hallway, into Hector's room and said to Nicky over his shoulder, "A fox, fuck, no, I'm a wolf." Blaze put his hand in the pocket of his jacket.

Hector had his head down, his chin resting on his chest. Blaze pushed Nicky off to the side, paused a moment and said, "Hector, your ol lady came through. Stand-up broad, that woman of yours."

Hector made a sound, a quick whisper of protest.

"What?" Blaze said, "talk fucking English, will ya?" Turning to Nicky, saying, "Man, we fucked up. This guy has heard a lot, way too much."

Nicky saw it, the pistol coming out of Blaze's pocket, saw Blaze steady himself, extending his arm. "Blaze," Nicky said, "what in the fuck?"

Blaze shot four times. The window behind Hector exploded. Blaze fired again, walked over to Hector and fired again, shooting a dead man.

"Jesus, Blaze, Jesus."

"Nicky, shut-the-fuck—up. You wanna hang around here with the dead dogs and dead Hector and the fucking Russians and cops on their way, or come with us?"

"What?"

"Think about it, Nicky. With us or what?"

Blaze had a concerned look on his face. Nicky watched him glance at Hector then look around the room. When their eyes met, Blaze's look of uneasiness turned into a smirk.

"You're going to take me home?" Nicky said in his softest voice.

"Yeah, sure. We got some things to take care of here. A little cleanup. I'll have Morgan run you back." Blaze found him somehow funny. "You talk to Charlie," he said pleasantly, "work this out and you can split to L.A. with some real cash in your pocket."

"I'll talk to Charlie tomorrow, how's that?"

Blaze said, "Atta boy, Nicky."

Nora sat on the edge of her bed in the darkness, thinking of how that boy Tino sounded, how he sobbed. Nicky had never mentioned he had a son. She had never thought to ask. She walked through the apartment trying to think of what she could do. She knew she had to do something. It was between five and six o'clock in the morning. The night team of detectives was covering the office. She could call, at least let them know what she was doing, and then head out to Red Hook.

She dressed quickly in gray slacks, red silk blouse, and blue blazer. When going into the office Nora carried her gun in her attaché case. When she went into the street, she wore it on her hip. For a fleeting second she considered calling Jean-Paul, waking the bastard up. But checking the time, thinking he *is* the chief of detectives, she lost her nerve and telephoned her office.

Five minutes later, Det. Mike Rogers of the chief of detectives' office hung up the phone, read the notes he'd just made and turned to his partner, Frank Sena, saying, "You know who that was?"

Sena smiled, "Sharon Stone. It was Sharon Stone, right? C'mon, tell me she's on her way over here to be interrogated, wearing that skirt, no panties. We'll make her sit right there, those gorgeous legs crossed and every once in a while she'll give us a peek. How's that for the horny, thinking-man's policeman?"

Rogers said, "That's not bad. It was Captain Riter."

"Wouldn't mind peeking at her, either. I'm one passionate bastard in the morning. What she want?"

"She's working a case, on her way to Red Hook, said she'd like to get backed up."

"I'd like to back her up, all right."

Rogers looked at the notes. "I wonder what the hell she's got going in Brooklyn at this time in the morning?"

"It could be anything."

"Of course, it could be anything," said Rogers, "but I wonder what?"

Rogers kept looking at the notes. "Fourth and Court Streets, down there. Wasn't the boss fucking someone down there?"

"Down where?"

"In Brooklyn, in Red Hook," Rogers said.

"He's fucking someone everywhere. He's the chief of detectives, you'd think he'd show a little ingenuity. On Thursdays he tells the day men that he has to go to the dentist. The man goes to the dentist every Thursday and comes back to the office smiling, like he just had his dick polished and his balls flossed."

"Someday," Rogers told him, "somebody's husband is gonna drop the hammer on the good chief."

"Personally, I'm counting on the fact that the man's been lucky. I got three more years to do and let me tell ya, he's the best boss I ever worked for."

"A great cop."

"And a helluva man."

Rogers said, "I told her we'd hang loose here. If she needs us, we'll be here."

"I'm off at nine. Shit happens, it better happen before nine. I got a fishing trip planned."

"Are you kidding me, a fishing trip? Since when you go fishing?"

"It was the only thing I could think of."

"Well, you'd better come up with something better than that. A fishing trip?"

Driving through the quiet, morning Manhattan streets Nora was thinking that this job of hers was a lonely and dangerous business. It was absurd.

Fifteen minutes later, she was crossing the Brooklyn Bridge; the sun was rising and the view of lower Manhattan, the river and ocean beyond, was spectacular. Nora's outlook lifted as she crossed Atlantic Avenue and turned into Court Street. Being there in Brooklyn, heading for Nicky's apartment, gave her the cheerful feeling that came when a case was moving. Her instincts told her that this one was starting to give.

At Fourth Street, right off the corner of Court, she found a place to park. Nora got out of her car and put her hand on the roof. Smooth and hard. She walked half a block before she found Nicky's number. Up three steps and through the door into the foyer. There were six apartment buzzers and mailboxes, two of the boxes had been pried open. It took her a minute to find OSSMAN.

She pushed the buzzer, and waited. While she was waiting, an elderly woman dressed entirely in black, came out through the inner door, dragging a shopping cart. Nora held the door open for her, wondering, who the hell goes shopping at six-thirty in the morning. The woman smiled, saying, "Thank you. Whadaya doin here?"

Nora said, "I'm looking for Ossman, Nicky Ossman."

The woman looked her up and down, still smiling. "There's no Oss-man here," she said.

"His name is on the bell."

"He don't live here. There's no Ossman here."

"I'm a friend of his," Nora said.

The woman shot her a look as though she felt sorry for her. She pulled the door closed and made sure it was locked, then stepped out onto the stoop. Leaning her cart against the building, she called out, "Nicky, Nicky, hey, Nicky, you up?" She had a strong voice.

A boy's head popped out of the top-floor window, Nora waved, "Tino, it's me, Nora."

"I'll buzz," the boy said.

Nora walked back into the foyer, when she turned to thank the woman in black, Nora found that she was gone. The door buzzed open. Now, this, Nora thought, is what I'd call a close-knit neighborhood. There was a staircase and Nora went up four flights, saw Tino in the hallway. The boy said, "He's still not home. And he hasn't called me." His eyes were brimming.

He was a thin boy of average height with black shoulder-length hair. He stood staring at her with big, almond eyes, and olive, almost brown skin. He was wearing baggy blue jeans, a black T-shirt. Eyes black, as well, shiny, bright black eyes. He looked nothing like Nicky the Hawk.

Nora walked through the apartment doorway that opened into a fairly large kitchen. Three windows faced the rear yard and there was a skylight.

"So he still hasn't called?" Nora said.

Tino shook his head. "You know," he said, "Nicky told me to lock the door and keep it locked and not let anyone in. Then he said if he wasn't home in a few hours, I should call you."

"Okay."

"But I don't know who you are. I figure you're a friend of Nicky's and you have a beeper. Nicky showed me how to use it, it's easy, just tap the numbers. Who are you?"

"Just a friend."

"I never met you before."

"No, this is the first time."

"Look at the time," Tino said, "it's almost seven o'clock. Nicky never stays out like this."

"It's all right. I'm sure he's okay," Nora said, and the boy smiled and nodded, pretending he believed her.

"I don't trust Blaze and Paulie," Tino said, "they act okay sometimes, but I know they're losers. Nicky hates them, I don't know why he went with them."

"Irma lives in this building, doesn't she?"

"Cousin Irma, sure, she lives across the hall. And you know what, she's not home either."

"Well, Irma is probably out a lot, busy girl that Irma"—Nora said—"in her line of work." She was suddenly embarrassed that the boy would think she was condescending and arrogant. "I don't mean her line of work . . . I just mean, I don't know what I mean. Listen," she said, "is there any coffee here?"

"I'll make coffee, I know how to make good coffee, Nicky showed me. I make his coffee. It's okay about Irma. I know she's a hooker, but she's a good person," Tino held out his hands palm up. "Irma is Irma."

The boy turned away, watching her out of the corner of his eye, then he shrugged his shoulders. Nora thinking that Tino seemed a gentle kid, thoughtful, and kindhearted. She didn't know how to answer him and she could feel herself blushing. Coming on like a cop in front of this boy who probably thought she was some kind of hardass. "I'm sorry," she said. "I don't know Irma, she probably is a good person."

Tino looked at her and nodded his head, straight-faced, as if to say, "Sure, she is." He made an exaggerated blowing sound. "When Nicky gets home and sees she's this late, he is going to be pissed. I don't want to be Irma when Nicky finds out." He took a saucepan off the stove, filled it with water, then adjusted the flame under the pan. "I'll make you the best coffee you ever had," he said. Tino turned and looked at her, "You like real coffee, strong, and all?"

Nora smiled, nodded her head. "Mind if I look around?" she said.

"Sure," Tino said, "I mean, no, I don't mind."

Nora found herself wandering aimlessly through the apartment. Although there was nothing particularly unusual about her pace as she walked through the hall and peeked into each room, she was, however, extraordinarily changed as she moved. Nora was more impressed with each step.

The apartment was spotless, picked up and neat. It was decorated very nicely with old, tasteful furniture that most likely had been bought in second-hand or antique shops. The walls were covered with film posters and tasteful reproductions and lithographs of old Brooklyn and Paris. And, there were books, a lot of books in hand-made shelves. Two bedrooms, one bath, a small living room, and large kitchen. This apartment, Nora considered, would be at least two thousand dollars, more, in her building or anywhere else in Manhattan. Here, in Brooklyn, it was most likely rent-controlled. She doubted that Nicky paid more than five hundred dollars a month.

Somehow, she could not resist the urge to examine Nicky's bedroom. The closet door was open, slacks and shirts hung neatly, and the bed was made. One poster, Bogart and Bacall in *The Maltese Falcon*, hung on the wall over the bed. NO Bacall

Nicky the Hawk, there was the slight smell of him in the room. And for a moment she imagined Nicky in the bed quietly making love, as Tino slept in the next room. There were no photographs, no family, no women, not one of Tino or Nicky, nothing.

She made her way back to the kitchen and stood behind a chair. Tino was taking a container of milk out of the refrigerator. On the table was a French coffee pot, the kind with a plunger, and one cup and a sugar bowl. "You take your coffee with milk?" he said.

"Black is fine."

Nora poured her coffee and looked up at the clock over the stove. Seven o'clock. Nicky had been gone, what? Eight hours. Now scary pictures were starting to form in her head.

"Do you drink coffee?" she asked.

"Oh, no, not me. I don't like it. And, Nicky don't let me."

"Your father won't let you have coffee?"

"No way." He was facing the stove and she thought he was crying.

"Tino, may I ask where your mother is?"

Tino gave her a quick glance. "How good a friend of Nicky's are you?" he said.

"I don't know, I think of him as my friend."

"Then you better ask him about my mother."

"I'm asking you."

"It's okay, you'd better ask Nicky."

Nora nodded. She glanced again at the clock and pulled out a chair and sat.

Tino stuffed his hands in his pockets, he turned and looked around the kitchen. "You know," he said, "you can take off your jacket. It's okay, I've seen guns before."

Nora laughed, then stopped laughing when she heard the key in the door.

Shit, man, he'd just walked through the door and the phone was ringing. Like the man knew his every move, like he could see through walls and read his thoughts. The Wizard was a magician.

When he picked up the phone there was a moment of silence and then the Wizard said, "Blaze, how you doing?"

"Jesus Christ, I just got in. I've been out all night, I'm beat, man, wasted."

"No rest for the weary, buddy. Look, number five, in ten minutes, okay?"

Number five was a phone booth near the precinct house on Union Street. Early on, it had been in Blaze's mind to ask for a beeper. When he'd asked, the Wizard told him, shit, no, no beepers, beepers are dangerous. Public phones, different public phones, one through five. I give you the number you go to that phone. Easy, safe, I know what I'm doing, the Wizard had told him.

The Wizard said, "Get moving, Blaze." Then he hung up.

This running to phone booths was getting to be a bunch of bull. Who the hell would tap his phone? Shit, the cops got more important business than bugging and watching him. The cops didn't know shit about him. How could they?

Better safe than sorry, the Wizard said, said it over and over. Better safe than sorry. He couldn't imagine why, the guy saying the same thing over and over, like Blaze was stupid or something.

Blaze walked quickly, every once in a while looking back over his shoulder, just checking. He walked up President to Court Street then down Court to Union. Not a whole lot of people in the street, just a couple of cops in front of the precinct. When he got to the booth, the phone was ringing. "Je-sus Christ, I'm tired," Blaze said.

"So you said. A busy night, huh?"

"We picked up seventy-five suits."

"It should have been more."

"I don't think so. I think we got what they had."

"They're a flourishing company. They could deliver a half-million suits easy." The Wizard groaned in exasperation.

"I don't think so."

"You're not supposed to think."

"I'm not stupid."

"If I thought you were stupid, I wouldn't be talking to you."

"And I wouldn't be sending you this fat envelope. Same place, huh?"

"Same place. So tell me, how did it go? Easy or what?"

"A little problem, nothing I couldn't handle."

"Uh-huh."

"Guess what? That guy was no voodoo priest, he went poof like everyone else."

"All right. I don't want to hear about it."

Blaze decided that he would risk a tough question. "Hey look, can we get together? There is something I want to talk to you about. You know, face-to-face."

"What did I tell you? Do you remember what I told you?"

"Yes, sir," Blaze said in anticipation.

"So, is there any reason you can't talk to me now?"

"No."

"I'm waiting."

"Anyway, I've come up with something, had a thought of my own. If you can believe that."

"You're scaring me, buddy, scaring me bad."

"If I say so myself, this is brilliant."

The Wizard said, "I bet it is."

Blaze took a moment, trying to think faster than he'd ever thought in his life. He was scared silly and the silence from his end of the phone gave him away.

"C'mon, will ya? It's okay, you can tell me. So what's this brilliant idea?"

Another long moment of silence, Blaze trying to come up with some way to explain. The Wizard always making a point of being careful on the telephone. So careful you couldn't talk fucking straight.

"There's a company, a major supplier, right down here in the Hook. And I recruited a guy who can deal with them."

"What in the hell you talking about, *you recruited a guy?*"

"I was going to talk to you about it."

"What do you mean *you were going* to talk to me about it? When were you going to talk to me about it? You don't talk to me after the fact. Are you fucking stupid? You don't recruit anybody, I do. I send you the right people, people I've spent time checking out, you moron."

Blaze was quiet, listening.

"You take somebody in off the street, could be anybody, could be a rat. You can't be that stupid. Maybe you can be. I don't know. Maybe you want to go to jail."

"Wait a second, I know this guy all my life. He's a neighborhood guy. I know him like I know the fat man."

Blaze felt as though he were being smart, calling Paulie the fat man. The Wizard should appreciate that, him being cool, using his head on the phone.

"Okay, so tell me, who is this guy and what do you got cooking in that bizarre brain of yours?" Keeping his tone easygoing, almost pleasant.

"Can I speak plain?"

"May as well."

"Nicky Ossman."

The Wizard, speaking slowly now, listening, maybe writing something down. Telling Blaze, give me his name again.

"Ossman," Blaze said, "Nicky Ossman."

The Wizard saying now, "All right, go ahead, what do you and this Ossman got in mind?"

When Blaze said, "The Chan, Nicky is like a son to the Chan," the Wizard said, "I don't think I'm hearing right, did you say Charlie Chan?"

"Yup."

It seemed to Blaze that the Wizard was laughing for effect, for the sound of it. The guy sounding hysterical over the phone, like he'd lost his mind or something.

"You stupid bastard, are you fucking crazy?"

Blaze said, "I've been thinking about this move a long time." Putting that even, casual, thinker sound in his voice. Blaze assumed in this moment that he had risen to something special. An important man discussing important business.

Blaze said, "I know I can bring the Chan in. The man is out to make money and I can show him the way. The Chan can make us all rich."

The Wizard said, "Buddy," sounding like he wanted to make this clear, but no big deal. "Charlie Chan will cut you up in little pieces and feed you to whatever fish are left in the Gowanus Canal."

"I don't think so."

"I don't think you think at all, buddy. I think you've gone and lost your fucking mind."

"I think I know what I'm doing."

"Yeah, right," said the Wizard, then he hung up the telephone.

Recently, Blaze had been taken by the word, think. He used it repeatedly. Why the hell not? all these mutts throwing the word in his face. People like the Wizard and Montonero and Nicky the Hawk, using the word all the time, trying to insult him and make him feel stupid. The truth of it was, he'd spent time thinking this perfect score through. Nicky would lead him to the Chan, and the Chan would find him a hole in a wall where he could put his hands on a treasure map.

Heading for home, head held high, a nutty little grin on his face, Blaze imagined tying some guinea gangster in a chair. One of those greaseballs with silver streaks in his hair. One of those guys in a thousand-dollar suit and a car trunk full of money. Lay that razor against his cheek, see how fast the ginzo would pay.

What he needed was one, maybe two real good scores. Serious cash. Three, four hundred thousand. Why the hell not? It was out there and he could get it. Lean a little on one of the old-timers, maybe take an ear or two, send a little package to the wife and kiddies. See how fast they'd show with bags of cash, then it'd be, see-ya time. He'd head south, way south, live in Mexico, get himself a couple of those brown-skinned little girls. Or, maybe, just keep going to Argentina where Montonero came from, anywhere. Blaze ran those pictures through his head, telling himself the world could be his. There rose in him a kind of glow of expectation, a primeval belief in the power of his razor.

Blaze stood in front of his bedroom mirror with an expression of indignation. Naked from the waist up, he kept his gaze fastened on his reflection. He flexed and did bodybuilder poses. Sure, Nicky the Hawk was smarter than he was. Blaze was no dummy, he had always respected and hated the guy for his cool smartness. Blaze had been thinking about Nicky. About Nicky and the Wizard, all the people that liked to play with his head, turn him around and use him. What he wanted, he realized, was to tie them all in chairs, tape them down, cut their ears, and put all those slick bastards' ears in his pouch. What he wanted more than anything was to wear that pouch around his neck.

Such thoughts made Blaze shudder, made him wonder if he was in fact a little bent. From the time he was a kid, people always telling him he was a crazy fucker. Blaze took his nipple between his thumb and forefinger and twisted. He had always been aware of a subsurface channel of something spooky in him. A few years back a shrink told him that once that shadow took over the brain, all hope was gone. That he must fight the shadow, that increasing presence. Blaze smiled at his recollection, thinking, it might be true. It just might be possible that he was nuts. Thinking, yeah, so?

Two hours earlier, as Nicky sat with Nora in his kitchen drinking coffee, listening to Billie Holiday do "I Loves You, Porgy," he realized how unlikely it was that he would ever meet another woman to whom he would be more attracted. Her face, those dark, dark eyes that had brilliant spots of light in them. Eyes that were wide open and staring at him. Wide-open eyes that were vacant of any compassion.

"I was tired, it was what? about eleven when I got home. Blaze and Paulie were waiting for me."

"You were gone eight hours," she said. "The boy was panicked, I mean he was really frightened. Nicky," she told him. "It's after seven o'clock in the morning."

Nicky looked at her a half second, then turned away, not saying a word.

"Nicky?"

"Hang on a minute. I'll tell you why I'm so late."

As he got into it, tried to explain, every so often she'd give him a little knowing look, cocking her head. He'd glance at her and see that she was not very pleased with what he was saying. It came to Nicky that telling this woman half-truths would probably not work. She was smart, and being a cop made her suspicious and untrusting. Living with a woman like this, he thought, would not be a stroll in the park.

There had been other women in his apartment, he reminded himself, plenty of them. Early Saturday morning, after a hot Friday night, the smell of them still on his fingers when he lifted his cup of morning coffee. It had been a while, sure, but there had been other beautiful women seated across from him at this table. Women that he told half-truths to. And the feelings he had for these women lasted, even if the memory of who they were and what they looked like did not. They all had a lot to say about commitment, about tomorrow and the day after tomorrow, about wanting and needing love. About needing, always about needing.

Women he'd met at clubs in the city who just wanted to spend the night and get it on; neurotic models walking around naked wanting to impress; acting students who rapped endlessly about the new Woody Allen open casting call; even, once, one of Tino's teachers, chubby and bawdy—she was the one he had had to hide from Tino, sending the boy across the hall to spend the night at Irma's. All of them big-time talkers, with a whole lot to say about the crazy turns of their lives. Now it was his turn, a witness to murder—try and dance around that one.

Nora hadn't said anything much, at least not up until now. Her face intense, staring at him as he explained the night in Sheepshead Bay. But, fuck it, not the whole night, not about Hector. Blaze and Paulie and Montonero and Morgan—that's all. Try to explain to a cop that you were in a room where someone was murdered, it wouldn't be long before you'd be explaining to a lawyer, a judge, a cellmate. Fuck that. But, man, she had a way about her, the way she looked at him. As if she knew, as if she had him nailed.

"Blaze and Paulie took me to this building in Sheepshead Bay," he said. Then what?

"What building? You get an address?"A firm teacher's voice.

"No. I'm sorry, it was dark and I couldn't see. How could I ask?"

"So, what did they want?"

"You should have been there, it would have been something for you to see."

Nora smiled and nodded, "You were there," she said, "you're my eyes and ears. You come up with something? Hell, Nicky, by now we should be able to put Blaze down."

"He's a kidnapper, they're all kidnappers."

"Really?"

"You know," he said, "as soon as I met the other two, Morgan and

Montonero, got a close look at what they were up to, I said to myself, these guys are into things way beyond what Nora's thinking. Let me tell you, all right? One, Blaze is a stupid man, crazy, and out of control, but stupid. And two, between the four of them they couldn't put together the kinds of scores they got going. I figure someone out there is directing them. Morgan, the black guy, he drove me home. When I asked him how he'd come to hook up with Blaze, you know what he told me? He said, a friend put them together. What do you think of that?"

Nora said, "I don't know what to think." She finished her coffee and looked around the kitchen. "Where's Tino?"

"In his room, reading."

"What, no TV?"

"It's Saturday morning, what's he going to watch, cartoons?" He spoke as if he were flinging an accusation at her. "Listen," he said, "this jazz with Blaze, it gets better. Ever hear the Spanish word *chupado*?"

"What's wrong with cartoons?"

"They're stupid and violent as hell. Besides, he's twelve years old. He doesn't need to waste his time watching robots shooting robots. Tino's got good books to read, let him read his books."

Nora watched him for a moment, thinking, it's possible you've completely misjudged this man. "Where's his mother?" she said.

"He has no mother," Nicky said quickly. Annoyed. Then going on, no pause. "Of course he has a mother, we just don't know where or even who she is."

"You're kidding me."

"I don't want to talk about it," Nicky said wearily. "Nora, are you listening to me? I asked if you've ever heard the word *chupado*?"

"What are you talking about?"

"It means sucked up, disappeared, vanished, kidnapped. In Chile, Argentina, Colombia, Mexico. Anyway, it's what they call people who've been kidnapped. People get snatched and their families pay ransom. It's what Blaze is doing, him and his crew, they're kidnapping people. Cutting off ears and sending them to family and friends. A sort of greeting card, like, guess what?"

"And the building where they brought you last night, that a spot where they stash these people?"

"Wait, let me tell it, okay?"

"Go on. Wait a minute. Can I ask you something? You're telling me that Tino is not your biological son?"

"Excuse me, but what's important here, Blaze or Tino's pedigree?"

"Sorry. I'm curious, go on."

"So Paulie and Blaze pick me up and bring me to the spot."

"Was somebody there? Did they have someone stashed?"

"Will you let me tell it? Man, you're a pain in the ass."

"Go on."

"You ready?"

Nora nodded.

After a long moment, Nicky said, "I'm in this building that's supposed to be abandoned, but there're Russians living on every floor. Now, I'm scared, I'm thinking what if Blaze brought me here to whack me? Who knows what these crazy bastards got in mind, you know what I'm saying? These guys are demented, certifiable. Anyway, Montonero and Morgan are waiting there, waiting to meet me. *Me*, like I'm important, like I'm somebody."

Nora filled her cheeks and blew out some air. "Sooo," she said, "they brought you there for a reason. What was it?"

Nicky grimaced, "Look," he said, "this is getting way out of hand. To be honest, I'm thinking maybe I'd better let you drop the cuffs on me, maybe I'm better off."

Nora straightened in her chair. "They had someone there, didn't they?"

"I'm not going to lie to you. Things happened, things were said. But I'll need time to think this through."

"You don't have the time. And let me tell you, neither do I. So why don't you fill me in on exactly what you heard, what you saw. Get to it. You were gone seven, eight hours, that's more time than people usually need for a little conversation."

"Hey, look, I'm serious. I'm thinking I'm better off just letting you cuff me for belting a cop. I'm thinking that might be wiser than getting involved in this insanity. You understand me? A few months in jail is preferable to forever at the bottom of the Gowanus Canal."

"I appreciate how you feel," Nora said. "But, Nicky, you've gone too far. You hopped on the back of a tiger and grabbed him by the ears, you try and jump off now, he'll eat you up."

"It's a she-tiger you're talking about. You mean you'll eat me up."

"Whatever."

"Wait now, you're telling me I have no choice in the matter? I'm not stupid, Nora, I can go to a lawyer, I can get help." Nicky closed his eyes. He saw Hector taped to the chair again.

Nora nodded her head. "Of course you have a choice. I'm not saying that. I am saying that if you don't come straight with me, you'll go to jail. You've never done time, I know you haven't. It's no joke, you know it's no joke. And, tell me, you in the can, what happens to your boy? What happens to Tino? I'll tell you what happens, he becomes a ward of the state. Hey, look, don't make me your enemy. Right now, I'm on your side. You can get through this. You and I together, we can nail the creep and put all this Blaze crap behind us. Then we can get on with our lives. So, Nicky, why don't you stop bullshitting me and tell me what happened? If you don't, believe me, I *will* drop the cuffs on you. Think about it, Nicky, take your time, I'll give you ten minutes."

The room was quiet. Nora got up and walked into the living room to inspect Nicky's collection of movie posters.

Nicky said, "Okay, whadaya say I make this a hypothetical. What if I told you I saw Blaze kill somebody?"

Nora said, "Is that a what if, or are you saying, you saw Blaze Longo kill somebody?"

"A hypothetical, I'm saying, what if I saw that, what happens to me?"

Nora said, "I'm a police officer, I don't deal in maybes and what ifs. If you're telling me you were a witness to a murder, I'm telling you that you give a statement to me and the DA, you testify. Or, Nicky, you'll end up being a material witness, a coconspirator, acting in concert with murder. You'll be charged. You're telling me you saw Blaze Longo kill someone? Is that what you're telling me?"

Nicky said, "It was only a hypothetical. But, say it was true, how exposed would I be?"

Nora said, "You kidding? You'd be exposed, big time."

Nora walked back into the kitchen. "Is that what happened last night? You saw Blaze kill someone?"

"I couldn't stop it, there was nothing I could do."

"Blaze Longo killed someone. Is it true?"

"Yes."

"And you saw him, you were there?"

"Yes."

"Do I have to explain to you the jam you're in now?"

"It's driving me crazy," he told Nora. "It's making me sick. I can't believe I saw what I saw."

"The fact that you don't believe it is not the best defense."

"I guess not," Nicky said.

"Where did it happen?"

"I told you, at that abandoned building."

"The one you didn't get the address for."

"Right."

"What happened, this guy didn't pay the ransom?"

"No, he paid."

"Blaze killed him anyway?"

Nicky stood up, he stretched, trying to shake off his weariness. "Boom, boom, shot him dead."

Nora said, "Let me ask you something, if you and I took the ride, could you find this place?"

Nicky seemed surprised now. "Sure. Yeah, I think so. Maybe after it gets dark. Anyway, it wouldn't do any good. They cleaned the place up. And, let me tell you, knowing these guys, nobody is going to find that body."

"I'll pick you up here, say nine o'clock."

Nicky shrugged. "Okay," he told her. "bring your gun, that place is a zoo."

"I'm wondering about something," Nora said, "they bring you to this place to show you a killing. That doesn't make any sense."

Nicky turned away and shook his head. "Will you give me a little room here?"

Nora sighed.

"Wake up, will you? You can't play these kinds of games."

They stood in silence for a while. Hands on his hips, head back, Nicky stared at the skylight.

"Maybe I should know how to handle this," he said, "what to do next, but I don't."

"You can't hold anything back, Nicky, don't try."

"Can we talk about it tonight?"

"All right." She looked at him for a moment and took out her pad. "Give me the names again, there was Blaze, Paul DiMaria, a guy you call Montonero, and the black guy, Morgan. That right?"

Nicky nodded.

"And the man they killed, you get his name? Or was it too dark?"

"C'mon, Nora. Please give me a break," he said softly. "We're talking about my life here."

"Yes, we are, and it's about time you took control of it."

"I'm going nuts," Nicky said.

Nora stood tapping her pen on her pad. "The dead guy, what was his name?"

"Hector, Hector Santiago," Nicky said dully.

"Okay, anything else?"

"Blaze said he was a doctor, a doctor and a bank vault for drug dealers."

"A doctor?"

"That's what the man said."

"This just gets better and better," she told him.

Nicky tapped once on Tino's bedroom door, opened it, and then he and Nora went in. There was Tino on the bed propped by two pillows, sitting with his head down, reading a book. He looked up quickly, great big eyes open wide. "It's gonna take me ten years to read this book," he said.

"Tino, Nora wants to say goodbye," Nicky said.

"What are you reading?" Nora asked him.

"*Streets of Laredo.*"

"Do you like it?"

Tino dropped the book and leaned on an elbow. "It's great," he told her. "But it's a big book. Ya know, real long."

"There's a video," Nora said.

"Let him read the book," Nicky said, "then he can watch the video."

"It's on video?" Tino said, "Nicky, why can't I watch the video?"

"Because Larry McMurtry is a terrific writer, what you'll find in that book, you're not going to get from the video. Nora's leaving, say goodbye."

"You're leaving?"

"Yup, I've things to do."

"You'll be back?"

"Tonight."

Tino stared at Nora, flicked his eyebrows. "Will you stay over?"

Nora said, "I don't think so. But nice of you to offer."

"Nicky will make breakfast tomorrow morning. Sunday mornings, Nicky makes the best breakfast. Irma will come over, we'll have a party."

"Sounds great," Nora said then.

"No one has heard from Irma," Nicky said. "Right, Tino, she didn't call, did she?"

"Cousin Irma is being Irma," Tino said, smiling. "She'll call. Right, Nicky? Irma will call or come home soon, right?"

"Sure, relax. Irma is probably on her way home this very minute. Some big night out on the town. She's probably in the city. This time of the morning, it's tough to get a cab that'll go over the bridge," Nicky told him.

Nora looked at the small, nervous smile on Nicky's face. She knew that nervous smile.

Nora walked toward the apartment door, followed by Nicky.

Nicky said, "Nine, you figure, you'll be here by nine? Listen," he said, "you don't have to come up. Just beep, I'll come down, then you don't have to worry about parking."

"Parking my car is the least of my worries. Anyway, nine, right about then, look for me."

"Nora," he said, "I've got myself in deep here, haven't I?"

Nora stopped, turned around, saying, "I'm willing to give you the benefit of the doubt. Probably you're telling me the truth."

"Not probably, for sure."

"All right."

"Absolutely. Look," he said, "you give somebody a little room, have a little faith and trust, someday somebody gives it to you."

"I guess in a perfect world, Nicky, that's just the way things would work."

"Irma," Nora said, "do you have any idea where she is?" Nicky turned away, he seemed to be listening for something.

"No," he said, "none."

"Well, don't panic."

"I'm not panicked, I'm worried."

Nora walked down three flights of stairs and out into the early morning sunlight. So Nicky kept a clean apartment, and obviously he was doing a great job raising that boy. Under her breath she told herself, don't close your eyes and shut your ears, this guy was a witness to murder and God knows what else. Thinking, Nicky's an informant. Think of him that way, she told herself. Only way to go.

There was her car, untouched and waiting. It was almost nine o'clock but seemed much later. She'd get to the office and make some calls. Maybe take a run out to see Sammy. You believe it, Nicky witnessed a murder. Saw Blaze Longo kill a doctor, for chrissake. What she should do was call the Sheepshead Bay precinct. Have them send some detectives right over there. But where? She didn't have the address, and besides, she had this feeling of wait and see.

She got in her car, headed for the Brooklyn Bridge. Bright white clouds drifting slowly overhead on even light winds, allowing all that sun to come straight down. In that dappled light from the bridge's superstructure, Nora knew that in her life nothing was as it seemed. Thinking, you're not handling this right, not by a long shot. She couldn't wait to see Jean-Paul, watch him spin in place when she gave him the news.

Nora figured that if she considered Nicky the Hawk in a way other than as an informant, she would lose herself in an ocean of confusion.

She said out loud, "But, there is something about this guy, this Nicky; the way he looks at that boy, the way he looks at me."

A smart, handsome, brown-eyed man would play hell in her life right now. The boy Tino saying, how about spending the night. Sure. Perfect. Driving, her spirits rose and fell. Thinking, dearie, you'd better get this business with Blaze Longo finished.

Jean-Paul was waiting in her office. He smiled as she came in, telling her, "Look at this, a Saturday morning when normal people are at home with spouse and kids, and here we are."

He seemed calm and relaxed, as if he had nothing to hide. Roseann Palumbo came into her mind, a glimpse of what she must look like, an Italian movie actress; saw Roseann and Jean-Paul eating pasta in some small romantic restaurant somewhere. Some place with blue velvet wallpaper and red cotton tablecloths. The two of them playing footsie under the table, listening to Sinatra tunes.

"Sorry about calling last night," she told him.

"Goes with the job. I called *you* early this morning, got your machine."

"I was out."

He put his hand on her arm. She drew it away quickly. "You're angry at me, aren't you?" he said this as if he were being humorous, joking with her. "You're wondering about Roseann Palumbo. I'll tell you," Jean-Paul said. "But first, how are things going with the Longo case?"

Nora said, actually, she'd like to hear about Roseann Palumbo first. So he told her about this five-year-old investigation, a job he did when he was on special assignment with the U.S. attorney of the Eastern District.

Nora listened.

He arrested Salvatore Palumbo. At Sal's arraignment, he met Roseann.

"This woman threw herself at me," he said.

Nora sat behind her desk, folded her arms as she listened, interested, even more than usual, paying close attention. Thinking, this man is such a charmer, look at him, smiling, wagging his head, like none of this is any big deal.

"All right, so, you began seeing her."

Jean-Paul shrugged and nodded. His face was a little red. Maybe, just maybe, she thought, he's embarrassed.

"For five years you've been having an affair with Sal Palumbo's wife, a made guy in a Mafia family."

"I guess you could call it that."

"Is there something I'm missing? Probably there is, because, I can't figure what else you would call it."

"Nora, you're a woman, you of all people should understand. I met her and my head spun, I had one of those moments, you know, like maybe-this-is-the-start-of-something, moments. Suddenly I felt twenty years younger, I felt attractive, I was jolted awake, I came alive. Let me tell you, back then I was pretty indifferent about my marriage. Bridget and I, you know, there was nothing going on."

Nora was thinking, back then, who you kidding? But she said, nice and easy, "Are you sure you want to get into all this?"

"You want to hear about Roseann Palumbo, I'm going to tell you about her. I thought about it all night. Didn't sleep a wink. I've decided to be straight with you, lay it out there. Be a man, right?"

You'd have thought the man would waltz around the story a bit, but you'd have thought wrong. Jean-Paul Clement walking around her office, describing a love affair as if they were buddies, drinking at a bar somewhere, sharing the stories of the exotic conquests of their lives.

Everything happened quickly, deliriously, he told her. Jean-Paul was trying to explain that before long he was in over his head.

"This crazy woman," as Jean-Paul proudly told her, "loved me. I know the difference. She's in love, and you know these Italian women, they love, they love with everything they have. Hate too, you know, love and hate are a close call. They take it in their head to hate you, man, they pull out all the stops, come at you with two guns blazing. Roseann wouldn't care if I went up in smoke, she just wouldn't care, all she would want is for me to pay, for me to go down.

"She threatens me Nora," he said, "you know, with exposure to the press, the department, she'd ruin me in a heartbeat."

"Didn't you just tell me that she loved you?" she told him. "Why would she want to hurt you?"

Jean-Paul said, "It's not that she is not totally in love with me, she is. Or else she's put on one hell of an act. No, Roseann loves me, I have no doubt, only she loves her father more. Roseann is completely devoted to her family, and her family is her father. No brothers or sisters, the mother died when she was a kid."

"What about her father?" Nora asked. "What's his story?"

"Wait, wait, let me finish. Roseann's married to this bum, Sal, for years. And this ace, he's using her like a punching bag. I come along and put him in the can. He'll stay in the can for a long, long time. That makes me her hero, I'm all she has, except, of course, her father.

"And look," he told her, "the best I can tell, her father treated her like she was a princess. Roseann never said a word about the beatings, afraid the guy would confront Sal, and Sal, you know, he's a badass, a killer. Who knows what would have happened?"

Jean-Paul gave her a look and she gave him a shrug.

"So," she said.

"See, what happened," he told her, "the father, his name is Alfred Alteri."

"They call him Alley Boy," she said, "goofball kid names, these Red Hook street boys. A really creative bunch."

"How do you know his name?"

"Listen, why don't you just get to it? No offense, but up till now, you haven't exactly moved me."

"I've made my point, haven't I? I mean, about Roseann. You understand, don't you?"

"I understand that you're married. Never mind, forget it, tell me about the father."

Jean-Paul looked over and seemed to notice her for the first time. He stared, no expression, then a small, sad smile, saying, "You're right, I'm married. But Bridget understands me."

"She knows about Roseann?"

"Of course not."

"But knowing her, you figure she has this enormous sense of humor, and . . ."

"All right, cut it out. I'm just staying she knows me."

"Tell me about Alley Boy."

"He's a degenerate gambler. Bets on everything, sports, the horses, the weather, his blood pressure, for chrissake, anything."

"And," Nora said, "he loses."

Jean-Paul was nodding his head. "Always. You know a gambler who doesn't? Anyway, he was into the bookmakers, couldn't pay his rent, couldn't buy food. Busted out, period. So he goes to a shylock and the loan shark turns out to be Blaze Longo." Hissing in disappointment, Jean-Paul saying now, "The poor schnook gets ten grand and anybody that knows him, knows there's not a chance he'd pay it back."

Nora met Jean-Paul's gaze for a moment and didn't say a word.

"Alley Boy makes a payment or two, then blows them off, et cetera, et cetera. A little while later Blaze and some other guy grabbed hold of him, cut off his thumb, told him the next week they'd be back to take his head."

"The other guy was Paul DiMaria, they call him Fat Paulie. And he is."

"What?"

"Fat."

"You know all this?"

"Some. With the rest, I'm guessing."

Jean-Paul stared at her mournfully. "Okay, Nora, look, what happened here, Roseann's father took off. The best I can figure, he took off. Roseann goes batty, thinks because I am who I am, I can fix it. You know, slam-dunk Blaze Longo so good ol dad will feel safe to come home."

"What makes you think that they didn't kill him?"

"Naw, they wouldn't kill him. What for? They kill him, for sure they'll never collect."

"These guys would waste him for the fun of it. For the exercise. Do you have any idea just who we're dealing with here?"

"I told you, remember?"

"I remember, it's you who seems to have forgotten." Nora could feel him watching her, waiting for her to say more. Finally, he said, "Christ, I hope not. I hope you're wrong. God only knows what Roseann would do if her ol man shows up a corpse."

Nora didn't say a word.

"You know," he told her, "sometimes I feel so guilty and like such a bad guy. But the truth of it is, how bad a guy can I be if I feel guilty. I mean, if I truly was a terrible husband and father, I wouldn't feel guilty. Isn't that right?"

"You don't want an answer."

"Maybe not."

Nora nodded her head.

"Tell me, go on, tell me what you're thinking," he said.

"I'm thinking you don't want to hear me."

"Sure, I do."

"I'll tell you what I think. I think Bridget devotes herself at home to raising your two boys. But don't kid yourself, she's a smart woman, she knows what you're up to."

"And?"

"A woman knows when she is being gypped and suckered, that all the vows you made her are lies. A woman knows when her marriage has turned into a joke. Bridget figures she's better off keeping up appearances, she hangs in to keep the family together, while you go around partying with the likes of Roseann Palumbo. She's trusting that sooner or later, you'll wise up. I know how she feels, believe me, I've been there."

He stood up and turned away from her, saying, "The truth of it is, you don't know Bridget, at all. The woman trusts me and, strange as it may seem, she loves me."

"You asked me what I thought," Nora said, "I told you. Maybe you're right, maybe your wife does love you. I don't know, it's a shitty world, I don't expect much from it and maybe Bridget doesn't, either. You tell me Bridget loves you, I'll say sure, why not, I've learned anything is possible."

"Don't be so fuckin tough on me."

"Tough on you? I don't think I'm being tough on you. You want to see tough, wait till Roseann finds out her dear ol dad is history."

"You know that for sure."

"A guess."

"Christ."

Nora said, "How much time do you think you have before this affair of yours falls apart? Before Roseann loses her patience, goes batshit, and starts looking for a publisher."

"I don't know, five days, a week, maybe."

"I'll nail Longo before that."

"You sure?"

"Positive."

Nora got comfortable, placed the Blaze Longo intelligence folder on the desk in front of her. She said, "Let's talk about Blaze."

Now Jean-Paul got uncomfortable, took a chair and sat, glancing at his watch. "Yeah, sure, show me what you have. Except, I don't have a whole lot of time. I've got a ton of paperwork and a meeting uptown, around noon. Which happens to be with the commissioner." Jean-Paul grinned, "I do have thirty-five hundred detectives that I supervise. You understand me, this Longo thing is important. Right. Of course, it is. You told me you'll make a case soon. Okay, I'm telling you, I trust you, I leave it all in your hands. What do you have there?"

He opened the folder, glanced at a page or two then handed it back to her.

Nora loved the way Jean-Paul put it right out there. The way he cupped a hand to the side of his mouth, saying, "Go on and do whatever you have to do, don't bother me with the trivia."

His head was in the clouds half the time. Nora wondered how Jean-Paul ever got to be where he was. He would have been a good yacht salesman, who could bullshit you right out of your shoes. Always in the right place at the right time. Touched both by the gods of good looks and good fortune. A natural, a born politico who knew how to cultivate powerful friends. What's more, she reminded herself, he was *her* yacht salesman, *her* strength in the department. And she had hung on to him without fear or favor. She had been very clever, she thought. Jean-Paul had given her the kind of freedom few others enjoyed in the department.

Of course, that kind of career support came at a price. The question was and always had been, was she willing to pay? She had always had an answer: definitely. For better or worse, success in the NYPD was contingent not on what you knew, but who you knew. Jean-Paul had changed things for her; changed the treadmill, precinct rat race into a first-class, well-respected, headquarters detail. The best way to go through the job.

The trick was, she thought suddenly, just how much humiliation you were willing to swallow. This guy was a total phony. That's the rub, because you had to figure there was only so much of your self-respect that you could surrender for the enticement of an easier life.

Nora smiled at him. "I'll handle it," she said.

"Do you have something tangible, enough to bring to the DA? You've been at this awhile. I'm counting on you. You're my star, I expect you to come through." He was pressing her, laying a little guilt on her. So she told him about Nicky the Hawk, that he had managed to get himself close to Blaze, and Jean-Paul nodded as she spoke, interested but preoccupied, glancing at his watch. The sneaky bastard had a date, she'd bet a month's pay on it. "I have this feeling that I'm getting close," she told him. "But you never know."

For a moment she caught his eyes, then he turned away, looked down at his watch again. "Okay," he said, "lemme hear it."

"My informant, his name is Nicky Ossman, anyway, he gave me something that I need to look at. It pans out, I've got a case."

"What kind of case?"

"Unlawful imprisonment, kidnapping, and murder one."

"Oh, fr chrissake, you're kidding. Ossman told you about a murder?"

"Yup."

"You believe him?"

"I don't know. I think so."

"Yeah, well, listen, that would be great. You put a murder case together against Longo, I'll be very happy."

"I'm going to try. I need a body and a location."

He sat up straight and looked at her. "You need some help? You know we have people around here sitting on their hands, you need help, ask."

"I might need some help tonight. I'm taking Ossman and we're going to make a run out to Sheepshead Bay, see if I can come up with a place of occurrence."

"You make sure you have some backup. I don't want you going out there alone."

"I appreciate your concern," Nora said. "But I couldn't bring anyone new in. No, I've had enough trouble with this guy."

"Well, you work it out. Just make sure you don't go out there by your lonesome. Have the night team back you up. All the other BS aside, I don't want to see you get hurt. You hear me?"

Nora nodded, "I'll work it out." There, *there* was Jean-Paul Clement, everyone's favorite boss, a look of concern on his face. Meaning it.

Nora said, "I'm just going to nose around a bit. See if I can come up with something."

"What are you looking for?"

"I don't know, but I'll know it when I see it."

"So you're positive there was a killing?"

"Positive? No, but it certainly looks that way."

"Where did it happen? The 161?"

"That's what it sounds like."

Jean-Paul spoke now with overstated calmness. Asking Nora if she'd checked with the precinct. Nora saying, No, not yet, realizing that it sounded negligent, she gave him a faint smile.

Jean-Paul said, "What are you doing today?"

"I've got a ton of calls to make."

Without taking his eyes from Nora's face, Jean-Paul stood up. "Nora, I don't mean to push you, but, Jesus Christ, I think you'd better get on the horn. Shit, murder one, excellent. Have you determined if it is true or not?"

"I just found out about it."

"Check CB, see if they got any calls."

"I will, Paul. Look," she told him, "if you want to know the truth, I'm not so sure it happened. I don't fully trust this guy Ossman. He's, I don't know, he's strange."

"Well, I suggest you look into it. I don't have to tell you how important it is to move fast in a murder case. Things blow up and disappear. I've seen it happen too many times. Whadaya mean strange?"

"I don't know, strange, different. The guy's a freakin actor."

"Aren't we all. Okay, listen," Jean-Paul said. "I think you'd better get a move on."

Nora didn't think that time was all that important in this case, but she nodded.

"Look," he told her, "I'm here, whatever help you need, just ask."

"I'll be fine," Nora said. "But there is one thing I'd like to ask you."

Jean-Paul said, "Ask," with a small smile.

Nora took a moment. She said, "I'd like to know if you're serious with this Roseann Palumbo?"

"What do you mean, serious?"

"It sounds to me as though you have genuine feelings for her. That you in fact care for this woman, that maybe you're ready to leave Bridget."

"Are you kidding? Look, make your calls and keep me informed, all right? Leave Bridget? For God's sake, do I look that stupid to you? Nora, I thought you knew me better than that." Cold, and as hard as stone.

"One more question?" she said then.

Jean-Paul kept watching her and nodding, "Go on," he said, "let's have it."

"I'm curious, has there ever been a woman you've met socially or professionally, that you didn't want to sleep with? I mean, do you know how bizarre this Roseann Palumbo thing sounds?"

"Don't be silly," was his answer.

"I'm many things, Paul, but I'm not silly. I just don't know what to call . . . what it is that you do."

"Well, then, if that's the problem, I suppose you could call it re-search, a sort of intelligence gathering. I've always been known as a great detective."

"Listen," she said, "I'm your friend, your colleague, in many ways, your fan. But, I have to tell you that it's a dangerous game you play. I just cannot figure you out."

Jean-Paul laughed. He paused, took a confused step toward her, paused, and said, "Work on it, maybe you can figure it out for the two of us." Then he turned and left her office.

That morning Nora stayed at her desk, checking her notes, making phone calls, and running faces and places through her mind. Around eleven o'clock she called the 161st Precinct for the third time and found the switchboard was still busy and it stayed that way for another hour. Wandering the headquarters corridors, looking for a fresh pot of coffee, she noticed that all the fourteenth-floor offices were active. People were waiting in the hallways, detectives, various commanders. Nora thought she recognized an assistant district attorney or two. Headquarters, generally quiet on a Saturday morning, was bustling.

Soon after the noon hour she telephoned the 161st Precinct detectives again, got through, and found that they had no information regarding a Hector Santiago, no missing persons report, zilch. The detective squad commander, a tough old-timer by the name of Leyden, was curious and pushed her for more information. Nora surprised herself, telling the captain she would stay in touch, would get back to him before the end of the day. That was a call she had no intention of making. This case, she figured, had way too many elements in it that had best be kept with her.

She put in a call to Nicky, hoping he'd somehow remembered something about the building in Sheepshead Bay. Tino answered and told her Nicky was out, that he'd be back later in the day. Out, Nora thought, does this guy ever sleep? And Irma? Yes, Irma came home. Irma is in her bed, resting.

Tino letting her know that Nicky had shouted at Irma, and then Nicky had made a point of explaining to Tino that there was nothing more tragic than a woman like Irma, facing her bed in the morning.

"I don't know what he meant by that," Tino said. "But he had a red face, I'll tell you that. Nora, you don't want to see Nicky get mad."

"Sometimes," she said, "the people we love make us angry. Sometimes, they make us angrier than anyone else could."

"It's Irma, she makes Nicky mad all the time. Listen!" Tino shouted. "Tomorrow morning, Nicky makes pancakes from scratch. The best you've ever had. We have room, you should sleep over."

Nora thinking, a sleep over, that does sound inviting. "So tell me, Tino, what are your plans for the day?"

"I don't know, hanging around the house, I guess. Why, you want to go to a movie or something?"

In her softest voice, "Thank you, Tino, I don't remember the last time I was asked out on a real date."

"A date? I'm twelve years old. I don't have any money. We go to a movie, you pay." There was silence and then some giggling.

"Of course," Nora said, "that would be fine."

"Whooops, I'm sorry, I forgot."

"What, what did you forget?"

"You're a cop, right? Nicky said that cops are like crime, they don't pay."

"Very funny."

Tino made a whistling sound. "You're a cop, huh?"

"That's right, but I don't think we want a whole lot of people to know that."

"Nicky told me you're a police captain. I spied your gun the minute you came through the door."

"Did you?"

"Your jacket was open. What kind is it?"

"I don't know anything about guns."

"You don't know what kind of gun you have? I bet it's a .38, one of those police specials."

"Actually it's not, it's a Glock, a nine millimeter."

"I thought all cops carried .38s?"

Nora wondered how a twelve-year-old knew so much about guns.

"Not anymore," she said, "but I did have one once." Words seemed to fail her for the moment. Discussing the gun that killed Max gave her stomach the jitters.

"Don't worry, I'm not telling anybody you're a cop. Around here a lot of people don't like cops. I do, I think that maybe someday I'll be one."

"Really?"

"Yeah, or a movie actor. Nora," he said, "don't worry, I won't let anyone know that you're a detective."

"That's probably a good idea. Listen, Tino, when you see Nicky, ask him to give me a call, Okay?"

"I'll tell him."

"And, Tino, I'll take a rain check on the movie."

Nora phoned Sam Morelli, just checking, and Julie, his wife, told her that Sammy was resting, doing fine but resting now, and maybe, if Nora could find the time, she should telephone later. "Ever been to England?" Julie asked her. Nora told her that England was one of the many places she'd never seen. Julie thought that England was beautiful. A trip to Ireland, Scotland, and Wales would blow your mind. Nora said she imagined it would, I bet you get that sense of belonging, the mother country, and all . . . That's it, Julie said, that's at the heart of it, that feeling of being related somehow. Actually, she'd made that trip twice. Sammy had missed out, too busy. Or so he said.

"It must be great to be in a European country where they speak your language," Nora said.

"Sam continues his recovery, I'm going to take him. He may not want to go, but I plan on pushing him." Nora saying now that she didn't think Sam would need a lot of convincing. "He'll love it."

"I'm really looking forward to this trip," Julie said wearily. "You know, like when you were a kid and summer vacation was coming nearer."

Nora didn't answer.

"You're a Manhattan woman, aren't you, Nora, you love the big city?"

"Yes. I guess that's me. Julie," she said, "tell Sam I called and I'll call back later, okay?"

"How would you like to come by for dinner?" Julie asked her.

At the point of quickly declining, Nora felt a sudden urge to somehow relieve all those terrible questions that she suspected were banging around in Julie's head. "Thanks, but I'm busy tonight, work. But, listen, there is something that I have been meaning to say to you."

Silence.

"I want you to know that Sam Morelli is the most decent, honorable man I've ever known. This job, the department, was a tough place for a woman like me. But I'll tell you what, that husband of yours got me through. If we had the time I would explain all of the ways he sustained, defended, and protected me. He is very special to me, and I suppose I am to him, too. At least I hope I am. But the affection we share is not the kind of devotion that you two have. I hope you understand that."

"He had a crush on you. I think that maybe he still does."

"You know, Julie, with all the painkillers the doctors gave him, it's possible he remembered it that way. I don't know. All I know is that we worked together for ten years. And in all that time, all those nights together, he never once dishonored you, or made me feel in the least uncomfortable."

After a long, long moment, Julie said, "Sam is a good man."

"And lucky to have you," Nora told her.

"Thank you, Nora. Listen," she said, "you're welcome here any time. I know that Sam would love to see you. Do you know what he calls you?"

"I'm afraid to ask."

"The mistress of can-do, that's what he says, Capt. Nora Riter is the mistress of can-do. He once told me that he sees you as a person who's larger than life."

Nora shifted in her seat uneasily. She took a big swallow of her coffee. She couldn't help but wonder how much Sam actually did tell his wife.

After a moment Nora said, "You know, some of the jobs we did together were pretty intense. Close friendships develop, it's unavoidable. But, Julie, there's a difference between friendship and, well, you know what I mean."

"I'm sorry, I'm so ashamed," Julie said. "I feel so stupid."

"Forget it, Julie, I understand."

"I sent an anonymous letter. I did that, I was going to tell you anyway. I may as well tell you now."

Nora gave out a low groan. "It was *you* that sent the letter to Internal Affairs?" she said.

"Things are bad enough for you in that damn job. I made them worse."

Nora nodded to herself, thinking, so there it is.

"Don't worry about it," she said. "And besides, things aren't all that bad for me. I'm the big city woman, I know how to handle myself."

"It's not funny," she told Nora. "I was so jealous and angry that Sam would put his life on the line for you. Jeopardize his career, his pension. So I really fucked up, didn't I? Please, whatever I can do . . ."

"Take care of that man of yours, everything else will work itself out."

"I'm tired."

"Boy, me, too."

"Nora, come and see us, don't be a stranger, we'd both love to see you."

"Thank you, Julie."

"No, thank you."

Nora recalled her day at the hospital, how she had stood next to Sam's bed and how he had grabbed her arm, held it tightly. She remembered thinking, the man's dazed and bewildered, the painkillers doing a tap dance in his brain. Poor Sammy thinking that maybe he was heading for the light. The second Julie left the room, Sam dropped it on Nora, whispered that he loved her, that he had been in love with her for a long time. Years, he'd said. Nora remembered feeling that cold rush in her belly, that sliding sensation, her mind doing flip-flops, not knowing what to say. She said, Okay, okay, sure. What else cold she say? Saying anything else would have made them both feel like shit, and poor Sam was feeling shitty enough.

Nora made herself another cup of coffee and stood by her office window. The sunny day was beginning to darken, towering masses of thunderclouds were converging over the city. It was weather not unlike the day of Max's funeral. Gloomy and ominous clouds, one of those days when dusk sets in at noon, and then the rain.

Nora recalled how she had stood on the sidewalk outside the chapel, not far from Max's parents, Carol and Michael. It had been a weekday but Nora had not remembered any cars passing. All during the service Max's father and mother had not spoken a word to her. On the sidewalk, Carol lingered and held out her arms and people came to her; some were family, some were family friends, others were colleagues of Nora's. Many held and hugged her and whispered encouragement, some gave her small, sad smiles and passed her by. A whole lot of rolling eyes and shaking heads. There had been a great deal of stomach churning during that one. Later on, she spoke to Max's father and tried to describe to him, as best she could, the recent madness that had taken hold of Max's life. But Nora had sensed then, as she did now, Michael had not believed her. The way the man looked at her, the way he shook his head, repeating over and over, "I don't believe you, why the fuck should I believe you? It was your gun, your gun."

Max's mother had always disapproved of Nora, could not imagine her son married to what she called a city employee, especially one, who on occasion, wore a uniform. A cop, she thought, was a blue-collar worker not a lawyer, doctor, a college professor. The sort of a woman that would have made a more suitable wife for her son. Whenever Nora and Carol were forced together at family social gatherings, the woman never bothered to conceal her disappointment. She saw Max's mother's face now, and realized that the woman had not uttered a word to her since the day of Max's death.

A little shaken with the memory, Nora returned to her desk, opened the Longo case folder and glanced at a printout of Blaze Longo's yellow sheet.

There was a narcotics arrest without a disposition, the arresting officer was Det. Timothy O'Grady. She had been meaning to contact O'Grady and check that out. The arrest report consisted of a couple of nonchalant sentences about possession of an ounce of heroin with intent to sell.

It was sometimes around two o'clock when she put in a call to the Narcotics Division office.

Nora and O'Grady had never worked a case together, but for two years they had been assigned to the same narcotics division office. Nora thought that ought to count for something. O'Grady was your typical overworked and underrecognized narc, and had a reputation for scrupulous, even hardheaded honesty. In fact, everyone she knew considered Tim O'Grady just about the straightest cop in the department.

"No," the narcotics clerical officer told her, "O'Grady's not due in until Tuesday." Nora saying, "Okay, how about his home number, this is important, I'm Captain Riter from the chief's office."

The narcotics guy playing it totally deadpan, saying, "I'm sure you are, but, Captain, I can't give out a home number, you know that."

Nora saying, "Okay, okay, look, you call him, tell him to phone me, I'll be waiting right here."

After a long moment of silence, the officer working the narcotics division phones gave in.

O'Grady said, ''Captain Riter, it is really nice to hear from you. How have you been? I heard about your husband, a terrible thing. I lit a candle for the two of you."

"That's very nice of you, Tim, I appreciate it."

"And Sam Morelli, how's he doing?"

"As a matter of fact, I just spoke to his wife. Sam is coming along fine. Tim, I have a question about an arrest you made a year or so ago. A guy named Blaze Longo, you remember him?"

"Sure. Sure, I remember Blaze."

"There's no disposition on the yellow sheet."

"There wouldn't be. The case is not disposed of. It's still pending, but not really pending. It's done, oh, yeah, it's over, he'll get a walk." Then he added in a low voice, "Captain, he's working. Blaze is a CI, a confidential informant, he's registered."

"Really? You registered him, you're using Blaze Longo as an informant?"

"Me? No, not me. I don't use informants, never liked working with them, don't trust them. Don't need the headache. I'm a wire man, bugs and wiretaps. Wires, the best informants in the world, they don't play with your head, lie, or get you jammed up. If you know what I mean."

Nora laughed. "You got that right. So tell me, who is Longo registered to?"

"Captain, when we took this guy down, this Longo, he was part of a sweep, a broad case that involved three or four teams. After the collar, I did the paperwork. I was up, my turn for an arrest, so they gave me Longo. I guess he flipped. As far as I know, he works for Jimmy Ceballos."

"Jimmy Ceballos?"

"Yeah, I figured that would get your attention. Jimmy arrested your husband, didn't he?"

The question was so plain-spoken and candid that for an instant Nora didn't know how to answer. "Yes," she finally said, "he did." She thought about what Tim had said for a second. "Blaze Longo is a registered informant for Jimmy Ceballos?" she asked.

Tim speaking now in a placid, firm tone. "Captain, Jimmy Ceballos has a ton of informants. The guy's been in this business a long time."

"Yeah, you're right. Maybe a bit too long."

O'Grady's reaction was slight, but it was there, a sound like psssst, coming from him. Then, in the way he said, kind of slow and easy, "You know, when Jimmy arrested your husband, it was the talk of the office. That's not something you could keep quiet."

Nora nodded, "It's complicated, Tim. Max was a real human tragedy. The man lost his mind. To be honest, I don't know how it happened. He started doing drugs, coke. I didn't know what to do."

"Captain, shit happens, who's to explain it. After all the years I'm working in narcotics, nothing surprises me. You'd like to think that smart people don't do drugs, you'd be wrong, right? I mean, anybody can get caught up. For chrissake, we've been trying to figure this out for years, losing our kids, some of the best and brightest we have, and what have we learned?"

There was a pause, a beat or two, Nora thinking, right, she had heard this all before, none of this was new to her. She had made the same speech herself a hundred times. But this time, hearing O'Grady, thinking of Max, she was moved almost to tears.

"If you knew me," O'Grady said, "you'd know I have no use for drug dealers or drugs, period. But I'll tell you, it's time we put a new spin on things, because what we've done up till now sure as hell ain't working."

"Tim," she said, "I'm going to throw some names at you, okay?"

"Shoot."

"Paul DiMaria, they call him Fat Paulie."

"Never heard of him."

"He's a Brooklyn guy, hangs with Longo, runs an afterhours gambling club in Red Hook."

"Don't know him."

"All right. A guy named Montonero?"

"I know him, if it's the guy you're talking about. His name is Raul Mora, they call him the Argentine. Montonero, too. It's a nickname, don't ask me where it comes from, I don't know."

"That's him."

"Yeah, right, what about him?"

"What can you tell me?"

"I don't know. He's a major violator, or was. Doing big-time drugs, coke, mostly, and pills, out of Mexico. We've had him listed as a major drug violator for a long time. Ran with a black guy, some dude named Bobby Morning. Listen, we had them both slated as the targets of the month for a year, and nobody was able to bring them down. A couple of slick rascals, both of them. And nasty bastards, too."

Nora said, "Tell me about Bobby Morning?"

"Bobby, I think, was born and raised in Germany. His father was with the military, something like that."

Nora glanced down at her notes, telling him, "Tim, do you know how to say morning in German?"

"I could find out real quick."

"I think it's *morgan*. Spelled different, but that's how you say it, Morgan. Like *Guten Morgen*."

O'Grady had to think about that one. "So?" he said.

"What I'm getting at, I'm thinking that if Bobby Morning wanted to use an alias, Morgan might be a good fit."

"Sounds reasonable."

"You have files on these guys?"

"Oh, yeah, big ones."

"Tim, you could do me a helluva favor."

"If I can, sure."

"Pull those files for me, bring 'em down to the office here. That would be great. I'd really appreciate it."

"Today's my day off, I go into the office, it'll seem a little strange. I might have to answer a question or two."

Not sounding annoyed, put off or anything, just thoughtful. "Will you be there all day?"

"All day. But look, you feel uncomfortable coming here, I'll come out and meet you somewhere."

"That might be better. Tell you what, Captain. Give me a couple of hours, I'll call you back."

"Look, why don't you take my pager number. This way if I'm out, away from my desk . . ."

"Good idea."

"Tim," she said, "Hector Santiago? You ever run across him?"

"The doctor?"

"Yeah."

"Sure, everyone in the office has worked that guy. He doesn't sit on any drugs or anything, just mountains of cash. He's a stash plant for these big-time dealers that are into Santaría. Santiago is a Santaría priest, if you can believe that. A doctor, some kind of voodoo evangelist."

"Santaría is not voodoo, Tim, it's a legitimate Caribbean religion. Well, some people think it's legitimate."

"You have an altar and on that altar you cut up live animals, I don't know about you, Captain, but I'd call that voodoo. Anyway, this guy, this Hector Santiago, he's a priest or something, and these dopers, I think they think the guy is trustworthy, safer than a bank. They have him hold their money. What I think happened, I think the office turned over our information to the feds. The FBI, the IRS, they're yapping at his heels now."

"From what I hear, they're going to have to yap pretty loud to get *his* attention."

"How's that?" The sound of his voice predictably curious.

Deciding to sidestep the question for the time being, Nora said, "You worked this Santiago?"

"I, ah, yeah. I took a run at him. Sat on him for a while." His voice dropped. "I applied for a wiretap, they turned me down. I didn't have enough and the guy being a doctor and all."

"So that was it, then you guys turned it over to the feds?"

"No." O'Grady's voice dropped even lower, a whisper. "I worked him six months ago. Last I heard, Ceballos was on him."

"Jimmy Ceballos, again?"

"Amazing isn't it? The guy is the most active detective here. I'll tell you what, Jimmy Ceballos has no family life, this job is all he has, all he does. Seven days a week. He's a first-grade detective, has nothing to prove, he's done it all. Still, the man stays out there in those streets, amazing, really."

"Hey, that's why he's a first-grade detective," Nora said. Sounding positive, upbeat, feeling rattled. Tim's story making her believe that this case of hers was acquiring some bizarre elements.

Nora gave Tim O'Grady her pager number, hung up the telephone and finished her coffee.

She was feeling spooked. Something was going on in her head now, and not anything comfortable or good.

Fat Paulie slithered down in his seat like a whale traveling tailfirst beneath the surface of the sea. He looked away, watching Nicky out of the corner of his eye as he stood in front of Charlie Chan's social club and waved to someone just inside the door as if the Hawk was expected. Blaze and Paulie had been sitting here for half an hour, waiting for Nicky to show and had seen Vito, Charlie's man, out in front of the club, walking around with his hands on hips, nodding to people as though he was king of the street.

Blaze was slouched, arms folded behind the wheel, a contented guy at last getting his way.

"I'm telling you this is gonna work. I figured it out, I know what I'm doing. Don't I know what I'm doing? I'm not stupid, I spend my days fucking thinking, how can I be stupid if I'm thinking all day long? I know what scares these guinea bastards, I know exactly how I'm gonna put it to em. I know just what to say, how to say it, too. I know what kind of cash they got stashed. You snap one of these fat fuckers up, get em when they're alone, coming out of their house in the morning, put a fucking hood over their head, some tape on their mouth, watch em fuckin blubber and moan, cause they know, always have known that someday, somebody is gonna pull their plug. I'm a stupid bastard, eh? A crazy son of a bitch, huh? I'm alert, man. My mind's going like this and like that. I pay attention to these fuckers, been around them all my life. This guy implies I'm nuts and I don't know what I'm doing. 'Charlie will toss you into the Gowanus Canal.' Look out, maybe I'll toss *his* sorry ass in the damn canal. Maybe I'll just put Charlie on the top of my target list of greaseballs. I'm supposed to be scared of these guys, right? Half of them, rats for the feds. That guy in Jersey, you read about that guy, and Sammy the Bull? It's unbelievable. Charlie tells me to forget the number, embarrassed me in front of those *mooks* at the club. You know what I'm saying? They ain't so tough, maybe they was once, but they ain't no more. This guy doesn't understand that, thinks their reputation is what's real, when it ain't nothing but old news. Fucking Charlie, fuck him. And this other guy, smart prick, I'd like to meet him face up, I tell ya that, this guy thinks he can call me stupid and crazy. Smart bastard sits back and I send him fat envelopes of cash. I make my mark I get rid of him, too. If I could only figure out who the fuck he is, this guy, this fucking ghost that calls me. What the hell do I need him for?"

"You got em all running for cover. You're the man, you're Blaze."

"I'm talking to this fuck on the phone, listen to this."

Fat Paulie, half asleep, glanced away from Blaze and looked down the street. There was the Hawk and Charlie walking arm in arm like a couple of fags. "Lookit that."

"I see them. I'm on the phone with this guy, right, I'm telling him we got seventy-five suits, he tells me it shoudda been half a million. A half a million? I don't think so. And then I happen to mention that I popped this voodoo asshole and he tells me, ya know what he says? he says he don't want to hear it. Like he wants to stay cool, and far removed, he don't want to be involved."

Fat Paulie held up his hand then pointed. "Look out, look out," he said.

Paulie looked at Blaze. "You gonna get outta here or are you going to let em walk right over us? C'mon, start the car, let's get going."

"I don't want to lose Nicky, I'm telling you we're gonna stay on this phony, slick piece of work and see what he's up to. Because, you know, he's up to something. Imagine that, a stupid guy like me, ain't so dumb not to see that Nicky the fucking Hawk is up to something."

Making a quick U-turn, roaring down the street, circling the block, driving in silence until he spotted Nicky and Charlie. Blaze wanting to drive right up on these two jokers, maybe join the conversation. But it was Paulie telling him to pull over, pull over, don't let them see us: "You wanna tell me what Charlie sees in this guy? Look at him, with his arm around Nicky's shoulder. You'd think they really have something going, those two."

"The Hawk can talk you right out of your shoes," Blaze said. "That's what Nicky does, he bullshits."

"I'd like to hear it, man, I'd like to know what they're saying. You figure Nicky is laying it on him? Maybe asking the Chan if he wants to back us."

Blaze was thinking about Nicky and Charlie but he said, "What we shoudda done was have Montonero cut that bitch. What we shoudda done was send Irma home short one ear."

"She carried the message, that's all we needed. Who's to say we can't go back there? Who's to say we can't snap her up again?"

Charlie and Nicky vanished from Blaze's mind and he was thinking about how Irma would look topless, taped to a chair. Slice them nipples from those little titties. Make Nicky a true believer. Sometimes when he was not expecting it, the shadow in his mind worked its will with Blaze conveying sparkling images of amazing creativity.

It lay like a snake coiled in his chest.

The vision of the first woman he would tape to a chair.

Irma would be fine. But the truth was, any woman would do.

"Blaze," Paulie said, "this guy, this ghost, the Wizard, you know, you ever think he could be a cop?"

Blaze thought that was funny, gave Paulie a quick short laugh. "Nah, think about it, cause, let me tell ya, I've thought about it a whole lot. If it was a cop into this shit, he'd do it himself, why would he need us?"

"The other two, Morgan and the other guy, they think it's a cop."

"He ain't no cop, Paulie. I don't know who he is or what he is, but he ain't no cop."

"How can you be so sure?"

"I'm not, I just don't think so. But, I'll tell ya what, the man's voice is familiar, I notice it more every time he calls, a sound I heard before. The way he talks, you know what I mean?"

Blaze felt himself yanked out of his thoughts, Paulie, that big fat arm of his giving him a jab. "There they go." Paulie extending his arm, pointing at the windshield.

Paulie said, "Man, that Nicky can really talk. Lookit him go, the man's a talking machine."

Blaze looked at Paulie and shrugged. "That's what we told him to do, ain't it? We told him to talk to Charlie and that's what he's doing. Maybe we should just trust him. Whadaya think Paulie?"

"Nicky the Hawk's a schemer."

"A schemer, you're right."

"And an actor."

"Uh-huh," Blaze said.

"You tell me what's worse than that," Paulie said, "a scheming actor. This fuck is up to something, and that I would lay my life on."

Blaze nodded his head, keeping an eye on Nicky and Charlie, watched them walk around the street, arm in arm, every so often a little laugh. Suddenly, from nowhere, Blaze felt the shadow fly through his brain and it frightened him. A long time ago he had learned to pay attention to that cool darkness, a tingling feeling at the base of his neck. He had learned what it forecast. As soon as he felt the cool, Blaze jumped.

"Are you awright?" Paulie said. "You okay?"

Blaze put his hand on Paulie's shoulder and squeezed, when the cool shadow came, sometimes Blaze would feel as strong as an ox and almost ready, it seemed, to fly off to secret places. Blaze asking Paulie now, "Whadaya care how I'm feeling? Why do you give a fuck?"

"C'mon," Paulie whispered.

"What?"

"C'mon."

Two hours earlier, it was Irma again. This time strolling through the door around ten o'clock in the morning with a big silly-ass grin on her face, handing Nicky a sealed envelope containing what looked like a greeting card.

Irma was a picture in red, color-coordinated in red stretch pants, and red shapeless blouse of some flimsy material hanging down just above her ass. And her headband, a red headband. And on her arms coil upon coil of glittering silver bracelets.

"You mind my asking where the hell you been?" Nicky shouted.

"Listen to you," Irma said. First she turned sideways to look at him. Then she turned toward the counter and took the saucepan, went to the sink, and filled the pan with water.

Nicky waited.

After Irma put the pan on the stove, talking to herself, as though she were trying to get something straight in her mind, she turned to face Nicky directly, breathing in and out, calming herself. "You know exactly where I've been."

"Really?"

"Stop playing with me, Nicky."

"You've been drinking. I can tell you've been drinking."

"I had a glass of wine and took some hits off a joint." Her pale, wary face spread into a hint of amusement.

299

"I'm making coffee," she said, "you want a cup?"

Tino came walking in from his bedroom. Nicky thought he would say something to Irma, but he said, "I made coffee for Nora this morning."

"Who's Nora?"

Nicky said, "Tino, I want you to go back to your room. I need to talk to Irma. Now! I'm not going to say it again."

"Good morning, Irma," Tino said, "and where have you been?"

"Go to your room, you little pervert. So," Irma said, "who's Nora? Tell me."

"I don't need to tell you, you know. And if you don't mind, I'm asking the questions. You got exactly three seconds to tell me where you were last night. One, two. . ."

"Whaddaya gonna do, hit me? Don't *tawk* like a tough guy, Nicky, trying to scare me, shit like that. I know you wouldn't hit me, so don't *tawk* like that." She turned her back to him, reached up and took a coffee can out of a cabinet.

"Maybe I was sitting here all night waiting. Did that possibility ever occur to you?"

"Oh, bullshit. You weren't waiting for me."

"How the hell do you know that?"

"Your friend told me, that's how I know."

"What friend? I have no friend that talked to you."

This time Irma spun around, put her hands on her hips, and looked at Nicky as though everything he'd said was just too much for her. "Your . . . friend . . . Montonero . . . your . . . friend!"

"*Who?*"

Irma took a chair from beneath the kitchen table and sat. She turned to Nicky, then dropped her head into her hands as though something had made her suddenly sad.

"Why are you doing this to me?" she said. "Trying to make me nuts?"

"Start from the beginning," Nicky told her. "Don't leave anything out, okay?"

"You know a guy named Montonero, right?"

Nicky nodded.

"Awright. He found me at the Roma. He told me *you* told him he would find me there."

"And you believed him?"

Irma held her elbows in, arms extended straight out, her bare palms facing upward in a sign of appeal. "Why not?"

"Because it wasn't true. Irma, have I ever sent anyone to see you?"

Irma shook her head.

"Haven't I always told you that I'm not your damn pimp? Do you ever use your head for anything other than bobbing over some guy's dick?"

"You didn't send him?"

"No."

"Wow."

"Yeah, right."

"That's weird, Nicky. This guy took me to the motel out in Sheepshead Bay, the Golden Door, and he gave me five hundred dollars."

"So tell me what happened."

Irma sounded excited, which was annoying as hell.

"You know Friday night is a madhouse scene at the Roma. And last night was even worse because somebody was having a birthday party. I'm sitting at the bar, chatting with Jackie O. D. And there is this guy smiling at me. He says, Irma, for Christ's sake, I've been looking all over for you. I'm Montonero, a friend of Nicky's."

The sound of the guy's name coming from Irma's lips gave Nicky the shivers.

Nicky never knew this girl to show the slightest amount of common sense, none. It was amazing.

"He comes over and throws his arm over my shoulder, gives me a hug. Tells me he's a friend of yours. I'm thinking, well maybe. I mean a good-looking guy, clean and neat, a cute ponytail. Could be an actor. He says his name is Montonero, I'm thinking, man, that's a pretty name, probably is an actor. I tell him I know all of Nicky's friends and you ain't one. He says you don't know me. You can't know all of Nicky's friends, now can you? He takes out his roll of bills, buys me a glass of wine, buys Jackie O. D. a drink, like, he's friendly to everybody. You know what I'm saying, a real nice guy. Right then he said, I want a date for the whole night. I'll give you five hundred. I go, I'm your girl. But you say I shouldn't've, huh? I mean, when you think about it, what am I doing out there? That's what I do, right?"

Irma did a little something with her eyebrows, "Sometimes," she said, "I get confused."

"Did you ever think to check with me?"

"Check with you, how? You weren't around, Nicky. You were out gallivanting with Blaze and Paulie."

"When did he give you this card?"

"I was getting out of the car, he handed me that envelope, saying, in a soft voice, but real serious, "I got a card for Nicky." He made me promise to make sure you got it. So I gave it to you. See, I was a little nervous at first, I mean like what is this guy up to? Look, I'm almost never wrong about a trick, this was a really nice guy. Nicky, he paid me five hundred dollars to watch a little TV, eat some Chinese food, and sleep near the ocean, and, are you listening? We didn't party, nothing, *nada*. The man left me alone for the whole night, perfect."

"You liked it?"

"Loved it."

"Would you like it more if I told you that Montonero is Blaze's guy?"

"Nicky, he is interesting."

"He's demented. Like Blaze he's deranged, a psychotic, and you find him interesting."

The silly smile on Irma's face caused the tension in Nicky to go away. He felt tired and sat down. From his bedroom down the hall Tino's voice called out, "I told Nora she should sleep over and have your special breakfast tomorrow morning."

"Nora's the cop, right?"

Nicky nodded.

Irma stared at him. "You got something going with her, don't you?"

Nicky said, "Don't worry about it."

"Awright. So what's in the card?"

At eleven forty-five that morning, walking across Court Street toward Charlie's club, Nicky saw Vito Vizzini in the doorway and gave him a quick wave. As he approached, Vito eyed Nicky doubtfully, as if he knew, but didn't know, that Nicky was expected. Nicky saying, "Is he around?"

"Is he expecting you?"

"No."

"Then you better just wait a minute, let me go check and see if he's here." Smiling, an impatient, contrary sort of smile.

This guy Vito never seemed to trust him. Nicky had always figured it was wiseguy paranoia. If-you're-not-with-us-you're-the-enemy kind of thing. But he always made a phony pretense at friendliness. When it came to Nicky, Charlie Chan had made his feelings clear. "Hey," he told Vito, "hey. From the time Nicky was a little shit, playing stick ball out here in front of the club, I've always liked the guy. You be nice to him, he's a good guy, someday he'll be a famous actor." Still, Vito remained skeptical, always looking at Nicky as though he knew things.

Vito was a tall and powerfully built man. Nicky knew enough about Vito, and his reputation with a pipe, or a bat, or a gun, to know that if ever there was such a thing as a real Mafia enforcer, Vito was it. He was Charlie Chan's main slammer.

Nicky looked at Vito wondering what made guys like him the way they were. Looking at you the way they did, always seeming at ease, standing on the sidewalk in front of the club, arms folded, checking the street, checking the people passing by, knowing that you knew they could wreak havoc in a heartbeat, maybe use an ice pick, or a hatchet, and then go have a pizza, mushrooms with extra cheese and onions.

Vito led Nicky into the social club, one large room, with a table and chairs, a sofa, and countertop bar. The walls were painted pale green, decorated with eight-by-ten, black-and-white photos of Italo-American sports and show business celebrities. It seemed to Nicky that Tony Bennett held a place of special regard. His painting, a shrine to the tuxedoed singer, hung just above the coffee machine.

Vito headed for the back room leaving Nicky standing alone.

The early morning sun fought its way into the club through white-washed windows giving the walls an uneven glow. These ancient wooden walls, Nicky considered, contained ghosts of quiet, menacing conversations that went back close to a hundred years. The dampish, musky smell of the carpet and aged wood gave Nicky the feeling of being in a place that had deteriorated, old and worn-out.

Nicky was pouring himself a cup of coffee as Vito came back into the room, he nodded to Nicky saying, "He'll be right out." There was the sound of some disappointment in his voice, giving Nicky a look that said, "Why are you bringing your troubles here?" Nicky saying now, "The weather's been good, huh?" Vito gave him a fast shrug, then went out the door to his post on the street.

Charlie stood in the doorway, saying, "Hey, Nicky, how you been, buddy?" He seemed to be studying him, cocking his head. "Boy, I don't see you for I don't know how long, now it's like you're one of the guys."

"Geeze, Charlie, I need to talk to you."

"Things going good?"

"I feel like the world is falling in on me."

"That good, huh?"

Vito came back into the club and glanced at Nicky and Charlie with a broad and friendly expression.

Charlie was in one of his typical running suits, navy blue with a white stripe, and he was wearing new tennis shoes. No Italian-designer clothes for the Chan. John Gotti's fate taught a lesson.

Charlie put his finger across his lips and pointed to the walls and ceiling. Then he turned to Nicky and gave him a defiant, far off, harassed look as though he were sadly dealing with problems that were beyond his control. "It's a beautiful day. Let's go for a walk and talk, buddy."

On the way out, Charlie stopped to whisper to Vito. Vito nodded, threw a quick look at Nicky, and smiled.

Walking along the sidewalk, Charlie held Nicky by the arm, directing him slowly. Nicky debating with himself if he should simply grab the bull by the horns, and lay it all out there. He didn't know what to say, or how to say it, so he said, "Are you afraid to talk in your own club? Think someone's listening?"

"I know someone's listening, the fucking government is like bird shit, they're everywhere."

"Why do you stay there?"

Without answering, Charlie turned to look in a store window at some men's shoes. He was smiling and Nicky wondered why? He thought it had something to do with why Charlie didn't leave the neighborhood. That in the end there were only so many places a man like Charlie could go. Charlie pulled him in close still holding on to his arm. Nicky could feel the strength in his hands, the smell of his aftershave. "Tell you the truth," he said, "I've got one or two things going. When they're done, I'm gone, I'm out of here. Just like the rest of the old-timers around here, I'm history."

"Speaking of history, I understand that Alley Boy, the gambler, he's an M-I-A."

"Sez who?"

"Blaze. That's who."

"Really?"

"That's what he told me, he told me Alley Boy's all over Brooklyn. Like, you know, he did the guy."

"Wrong. Alley Boy's fine. Well, not fine, they cut his fuckin thumb off, those jerkoffs. You know, I told him and I told him, stop the gambling, stop borrowing money. But you know Alley Boy, hasn't changed in thirty years. Anyway, he's fine, he's in Vegas, like he died and went to heaven. Vito talked to him last week. Those guys, Blaze and Paulie are all talk, Nicky."

"They cut his thumb off."

Charlie was silent for a long time, staring at him. Finally, he said, "I know, you're right. Of course, you're right. You're not really a street guy, Nicky, sometimes, you know, there are things that maybe you don't understand."

"I guess you're right. Sure you're right." Nicky sounded helpless. "Code of the street, all that stuff."

"What I'm saying . . . look, Alley Boy's not with me, not under my flag, and he was warned a million times. They cut his thumb, it's true, he pushed his luck, you know your thumb is better than your head. Maybe he learned that now, maybe that's all he learned."

Nicky didn't say anything.

"I know Alley Boy for years," Charlie said, "we came up together around here. He's a guy I know, a harmless guy, but he's not one of my people, understand? Anyway, as far as Blaze is concerned, I had Vito promise Alley Boy he'd have the last word. And let me tell you, staying alive is a distinct advantage in that regard. Alley Boy has just got to bide his time."

Nicky said, "Roseann, his daughter, is that one beautiful woman, or what?" Nicky paused and said, "She's a story, ain't she?"

"A story, she's a fuckin' mini series. Let's not talk about Roseann. I don't care to discuss Roseann, that's about a ton of dynamite waiting for a match."

Captain Nora Riter came into Nicky's mind, her boss and Sally Palumbo, Roseann's husband. He pictured Sally Pallumbo's face now and said, "I don't want to be around when Sally Boy comes home."

"There you are," Charlie said, "you see the problems I have to deal with? So," he said, "tell me, what problem did you bring me this time? I know it's not Blaze and Paulie. I sent word, I sent Vito, believe me, they got the message."

"Let's walk," Nicky said.

They strolled through the old neighborhood that was now split, old and new. New families, new faces, now claimed the streets as their own. Nicky noticed that a block or two from the club, people stopped smiling at Charlie.

"You know when I left you the other day, I got pinched," Nicky told him.

"I heard about it. You hit a cop. That's funny, Nicky, you shouldn't do that. You can get in trouble you throw a punch at a cop. So, that's what it is, you need money for a lawyer?"

"I don't need money, Charlie. No disrespect, but I wouldn't ask you if I did."

Charlie laughed. "Nicky," he said, "don't talk to me about respect, that kind of bullshit. What are you, a wiseguy? You're no wiseguy, you're an actor, an artist, for chrissake. You know what I'm saying? What you should do is take your kid and lose yourself. Get the hell out of here, lose yourself and go to L.A."

"I can't leave the city, I have this case."

"It's not serious, right? I mean, taking a poke at a cop can be serious, but this isn't serious, is it?"

"Serious enough, I can lose the kid. I could do a little time and they'd take Tino. I couldn't let that happen, Charlie."

"Of course not. How can I help?"

They walked along and Nicky tried to explain about Irma and the cop. He told the story of the lamb, of how he met Nora. And Charlie remained affable and smiling and squeezed his arm signaling all's well. Shaking his head, laughing out loud. As he talked, began to describe his meeting with Nora in the city, how he agreed to help her nail Blaze, Nicky began to sense some discomfort from Charlie, a certain tension in the air.

They stopped at Court and President Streets. Charlie saying, "You want to see the house where I was born? It's right down here, fourth house from the corner."

"Sure."

In fact the house was familiar to Nicky. Everyone talked about Charlie Chan's house. From the outside no big deal, nothing really out of the ordinary, a somber brownstone. Inside, they said, amazing imported marble and carved mahogany everywhere. Persian carpets, good ones, it figured. And, original paintings, museum quality: a Picasso and a few Modiglianis, those big eyes staring at you. That figured, too.

When they turned into President Street, Charlie asked him, "So you agreed to, what, hook up with this woman police captain?"

Nicky heard himself trying to explain and it sounded to him like an apology. Christ, he didn't know what to do. When you considered the options, go to jail, lose Tino, or jam up Blaze fucking Longo, shit, man, he didn't want to be a stool pigeon, or anything like that, far from it, "But what the hell was I going to do?"

"I hope you're not coming to me to ease a guilty conscience," Charlie told him. "I don't want to hear you're an informant for the police. Please, spare me that, that's the last thing I want to hear."

The way he looked at him, somber and nodding, Nicky figured this was the way Charlie looked when he was about to tell Vito just what to do with the legs or the head of a traitor. Nicky considered that maybe, just maybe, he'd done it all again, jumped straight onto those tracks.

They were standing on the sidewalk in front of an impeccable three-story brownstone. There was no one on the street and except for a breeze that came in from the harbor there was absolute silence.

"The first time I saw you, you were coming out of that house," Nicky said. Pointing to a large stoop with a painted, black wrought-iron banister that led to double oak doors. "You were carrying the biggest cake box I ever saw. I was with this guy Frankie Shay, and he told me, he said, 'You know who that is . . .?'"

"I was born in the basement apartment of that house," Charlie said. "I still live there. This is my home. All three floors are mine."

"I know," Nicky said. "it's a great house."

And that it was, with its high stoop, Italianate windows, and door hood above the entrance. The entire building was extended into the rear yard, a massive structure, built of Jersey freestone.

"It's empty now, my kids are gone, my wife, too. She got on an airplane and flew three hours to see her grandchildren. I don't fly on airplanes. But maybe in a couple of weeks I'll take the ride. Ever been to Florida, Nicky?"

"Twice."

"Yeah, on the west coast, the Gulf of Mexico, it's nice."

"It's not bad, but way too hot in the summer. Charlie," he said, "I think we've had this conversation."

Charlie stood for a long time, nodding his head, arms crossed, staring up at the brownstone. "These fucking cops," he said, "wherever they go they give rise to rats."

"I'm no rat, Charlie."

"I know you're not," he said. "Since you were a little, street-running kid, you've had a good heart."

That made Nicky smile, thinking of Charlie Chan thinking of him.

"You know I have two children, right? Girls, and three grandchildren, all girls. I love them, let me tell you, they are terrific, all of them. They're in Florida. C'mon," Charlie said, "whadaya say we sit on the stoop for a minute."

Nicky sat on the stoop with Charlie's hand on his shoulder. "If I did have a son," he told him, "I'd like him to be like you." Charlie stared at him a long moment, and Nicky wondered who he thought he saw.

Ah, Charlie, he thought, I'm not your missing son. His new Nicky voice telling him, his son? you're an informer for the police, you fucking goofball, you're his enemy.

Nicky looked up into a high and clear sky. A jet, a silent, tiny silver cross was sailing through the vault of heaven, trailing its tendrils of white. On the stoop, shoulder to shoulder with Charlie, Nicky's troubles seemed miles away, and for a moment he could imagine himself sitting in the window seat on that airplane, heading west.

Nicky turned to Charlie and considered him a minute, the way he sat hands behind his head, the dreamy look in his eyes, watching the disappearing jet plane. He told himself that Charlie must have a multitude of problems. One only had to read the paper to see that Charlie's—and people like Charlie's—days were numbered. He thought he understood Charlie's problems better than his own.

"Ever think about living in Florida, Nicky? I mean, the boy, Tino, would love it. And Irma, no reason she can't start over, you know, a fresh start."

He'd never thought about Florida, and could not imagine living there. "Who knows?" Nicky said. "You never know what life holds, how things work out."

Nicky looked at him ashamed. "Charlie," he said, "by you, can you ever see a valid reason for someone to hook up with the police, the cops?"

"Nicky, for Christ's sake, are you nuts? Don't you know who I am?"

"I saw Blaze shoot a guy last night. He killed a guy."

"You actually saw him?"

"I was there, I was standing right next to him."

"There you go, Nicky, a real life-and-death experience, a little grist for the old actor's mill."

"The guy's an animal, Charlie, a fuckin mutant." Nicky took a deep breath and exhaled it slowly. "If there are rules, Charlie, and to tell you the truth, for someone like me, I'm not so sure there are. Anyway, for creeps like Blaze and his crew, those rules don't work. You got to protect yourself from animals like that. And if it means going to the cops . . ."

"That's bullshit. Who are the cops? They're people, all kinds, sure there're some good ones, but there're some I wouldn't trust as far as I can throw this house."

Something about the way he said it alarmed Nicky.

"I saw a man killed for no good reason, for no reason at all."

"Don't misunderstand me, Nicky, don't take this wrong, but, let me tell you, there are people who need killing."

Nicky stood, then moved to a step above Charlie and sat down again. "This guy was a doctor, a Cuban guy, supposed to be holding money for big-time junk dealers. Anyway, they kidnap him, his wife comes up with the money, and Blaze still shoots the guy. I was there, Charlie, I saw it, I saw Blaze, and let me tell you, he liked it."

"Of course, he liked it. So, you see that, and now you're gonna go and tell the cops? Maybe testify against the sneaky bastard, get your name in the news, that kind of shit. Kidnappers, I hate fucking kidnappers."

Charlie was staring at hm.

"Look," Nicky said, "look what they sent me."

Nicky went into his pocket and carefully removed the greeting card Irma had given him, the card she got from Montonero. He handed it over to Charlie who took the card and stared at it, stone-faced.

Charlie studied the caricature of a pig with a gigantic ear, the words ARE YOU LISTENING? across the top.

Charlie opened the card and in script, a child's scrawl, was written, *Hurry and have a chat with your friend, time's a wasting.*

Charlie smiled, saying, "You want to tell me what is this silly shit?"

Nicky wasn't sure how to say it. "This card," he said, "came from Blaze. It's a warning, I don't go and talk with you, these schmucks . . ."

"With me? Why do they want you to talk to me?"

Nicky said it quickly, just to get it out, knowing as he spoke what Charlie was thinking, seeing Charlie staring at him as if to say, "What in the hell are you talking about?"

"Hey, Charlie, it's simple. Blaze wants me to ask you if you'll hook up with him. What he wants, he wants you to finger targets for kidnapping. You know, people that you know, guys with big cash."

Charlie said, quietly, quickly, "I'm gonna kill this motherfucker. End of story."

"Charlie, I'm going to give him over to the cops. Think about it, I kill two birds with one stone. I get out from under that pinch, and Blaze does about a hundred years in the joint. Two for one, it makes all the sense in the world."

Charlie listening, but he didn't seem to hear. Charlie stood and stretched his arms, Nicky could see that he was pissed and upset. "Look," Charlie told him, "better I kill this piece of shit than you label yourself a rat. I like you, Nicky, I like our conversations, I think of you as a friend. Now, listen to me, I cannot have a friend that's a stool pigeon."

"With this guy, Charlie," Nicky said, "if ever there was a good and valid reason to rat some bum out . . . I mean, it's Blaze fucking Longo."

"Nicky, Nicky, Nicky, what universe do you live in? Not in mine. There is never a good reason to throw in with the cops. C'mon, you know that."

"Charlie, I have to tell you that the cops are all over this guy now. It's only a matter of time, he goes down."

Calmly now, walking in circles in front of the building where he was born, Charlie said, "You know this character Blaze and that blob friend of his, that Paulie, they came to see me. I told you that, right?"

Nicky nodded.

"They came to me, over at the club one day and tried to hump my leg with all this respect bullshit, and I told them, I said, 'take a walk, what do you think this is, the fucking movies. I look like Brando to you?' Nicky," he said, "you're so far beyond these shitheads, how did you allow yourself to get involved with them? I'm disappointed, I am. I understand, still I'm disappointed."

Nicky felt himself blushing, knew he was turning red, thinking, man, now you've done it, you don't want to lose Charlie, you lose Charlie, you dumb shit, you'll really be out here alone.

Nicky said uncertainly, like an embarrassed kid. "Charlie, I hope you're not pissed off at me. I mean, in your eyes, I hope I didn't really fuck up here."

Charlie smiled, saying, "We'll work it out. Just promise me, okay, you're not going to be anybody's stool pigeon."

Nicky, feeling sick now, flashing on Nora now, wondering how the hell he was going to manage this. He nodded his head, saying, "I promise, I give you my word, Charlie," thinking, oh, boy, atta boy, you've done it now.

From half a block away, Charlie saw Vito Vizzini standing in the doorway of the club, his head bowing into an open newspaper. Vito glanced at him as he cleared the corner then turned to look inside the club. As Vito turned back to look at Charlie he was smiling, Charlie thinking, it is the wrong time for a smile.

"What the hell's so funny?" Charlie said.

"You ain't gonna believe what happened," Vito said. He called into the club, saying, "Bobby, Richie, come out here."

Bobby and Richie were two brothers from Bath Beach who belonged to Vito. They were young guys, not made members, so Vito called them "the kids."

"Well, the kids were down in Atlantic City last night, doing whatever they were doing. I don't know. Anyway, they decided to stop by. You know, just to say hello, see what's goin on. Shit like that."

When the kids came outside, Vito and Charlie walked off toward the corner, near the shoe store with the big plate-glass window, the kids followed.

Vito said, "What happened was, when you took off with the Hawk, I spotted this Buick, it was familiar. You know I'm out here every day, I know who's moving around. Some cars are familiar. Anyway, it was Fat Paulie and that psycho, Blaze."

"Yeah? And?"

"They were following you."

"Following me? And you just—what did you do?"

"Charlie, my car's in the lot. I mean, for a second there, I panicked. I mean, I could of run after ya, but, man, ya know. And then, ba-bing, the kids pull up. Bobby," Vito said, "c'mere, tell him."

"Vito, you tell me."

"I jumped into their car and we tailed ya. Christ, ya know, Charlie, I don't have a piece, I don't have anything. Good thing, these kids they got a couple of pistols in the trunk, you know, I felt a little better."

Charlie looked from the kids to Vito standing there with his arms folded. He wondered if Vito had told these kids that he had set the law down, no guns near the club? The brothers standing there, hands in their pockets, heads bowed.

"And then?" Charlie said. "C'mon, Vito, you're driving me nuts here. What happened?"

"Nothing happened, thank God. You went walking and talking with the Hawk, they followed ya, we followed them. When you're sitting on the stoop, they parked up the street, just sat there. I tell ya, I'm going nuts trying to figure what the hell to do they decide to get out of the car and take a walk."

"It would've been a problem," Charlie said.

"No problem, Charlie, you told me to tell these two assholes, what was it? a week, two weeks ago, I told em both to stay away from Nicky. Now here they were stalking the guy, stalking you. No problem, Charlie, if they get out of the car and head toward you, I shoot em. Simple as that."

"Where are they now?"

"Tell him, Bobby. C'mon, tell Charlie what you saw. How after you dropped me you scooted back and spied the Buick parked up the street from Nicky's place. C'mon, tell him. Charlie wants to hear it from you, tell him."

Charlie folded his arms and glanced around the street, thinking, man, thirty years of this shit.

Bobby said, "Me and my brother, we spied the Buick parked up the street from Nicky's place."

"Both guys still in the car?"

"Both of them."

"Good. Listen," Charlie said, "you got a phone?"

Bobby nodded. "In the trunk," he said.

"I want you to hurry up and get back there and keep an eye on those two, all right? Stay with them until you hear from Vito." Charlie never spoke on a telephone, any telephone. "Vito," he said, "you got their number, you can reach them, right?"

"Yeah, sure."

"Before they go," Charlie said, "ask these kids if they can make those pistols they got quiet?"

"They can."

"How do you know?"

"Charlie, I'm their boss."

"Okay," Charlie said, "who's coming around today?"

"The usual. You know it's early. Five, six guys be in this afternoon."

"Where's the Turk?"

"You told him to stay away, Charlie. I dunno, he's probably home."

"Get in touch with him. If I need him, I want to know where I can reach him."

"You sure?" Vito said.

Charlie stood still for a moment, then he turned away, taking his time before coming around enough to look back at Vito. "A crazy bastard, this Blaze. He likes to scare people telling them how nutty he is. He likes crazy, I'll show him crazy. Get in touch with the Turk, okay."

Detective Tim O'Grady was in the last booth of Peter's Pub, a joint over in Jamaica, about four or five blocks from the Queens narcotics division office. Nora had come to meet him and found Tim sitting alone, looking around the room as if he were planning to paint the place.

As soon as she stepped through the door, Nora waved like an old friend or a date, doing her best to give the impression that there was nothing heavy going on. It was four o'clock, a Saturday afternoon, the bar was busy, all men. Some of the weird-looking ones could have been narcs.

She sat down with him.

"Hey," she said, "it's nice seeing you. What's it been, two, three years?"

"Got to be a couple of years. You look the same, maybe your hair's a little longer."

"More than a little. Listen," she said, "aren't we only a few blocks from your office? We could run into people here."

"It's possible. I'm not worried, it's not like you work for IAD or anything, right?"

Tim may have been somewhere in his late thirties, but appeared much younger. His close-to-the-scalp haircut, his baggy jeans, sweat shirt, and tennis shoes made him look like a graduate student from a nice town in Connecticut.

A career narc, Tim O'Grady had made his reputation when he was a rookie doing undercover work at East New York Vocational High School. All his features soft and boyish, he had a gentle and good-hearted look to him.

"No," she told him, "I don't work for IAD, I'd never work for IAD."

"Really?" he said, "and why's that?"

"I don't know. I wouldn't enjoy the work, I suppose."

He made a hand movement to show that was neither here nor there. "If they asked me," he said, "I would go. Let me tell you, this narcotics jazz has gotten real old."

"You've been at it for a while."

"Ten years. Ten long years."

"How about it," she said, "how would you like to have something to eat on the city?"

"I'll have a beer."

"Good."

"Listen, Captain, I went to the office, there was nobody around, I checked the files. Nothing."

"No fooling? How about that?"

"I looked everywhere, the files are gone."

"I don't mean to sound paranoid, but don't you think that's a little strange?"

"Strange, yeah, I'd say strange is a good word for it. Captain," he said, "I'd like to help you, but I don't think I can. I have no idea what happened to those files."

"They have to be around," Nora said.

"Yeah, I know they have to be, of course. But I couldn't find them. And let me tell you, I know where to look. I'm in those files all the time. I mean, that's what I do. I check the files, run down names, put things, you know, names, faces, places together. I don't use informants, I dig out my own stuff. So I'm in there all the time, browsing for this and that. The Mora and Morning files are gone, nothing on Longo and no file on Santiago. The kicker is, I was in the Santiago file just last week. Pulled it Monday or Tuesday, I don't remember, anyway, it was an inch thick. It is very weird. Look," he told her, "I'd like a beer. Can I get you something?"

"No. Listen, sit here a minute. Call me crazy, Tim, but I find it a bit hard to believe that those particular files grew legs and walked out of your office."

O'Grady sat still, staring at her. "The funny thing is," he said, "say somebody wanted to lift those files. Why wouldn't they simply make photocopies and return the originals? See, Captain, what I'm thinking is that there's nothing sinister here. Somebody just borrowed the files."

"Ummmmm," Nora said.

"I'm gonna go get a beer."

Tim slid out from the booth and walked to the bar. A moment later she heard him order a Bud Light from the bartender. All the while Nora was wondering, thinking that official police department intelligence files do not disappear. She marveled at how this happened, how a nothing case on a dipshit like Blaze Longo had turned into a bad dream.

She found herself thinking of Jimmy Ceballos. He was somehow a link here, he was the connection, he was the bad dream. No real proof, just the feel of it. The memory of him, that sly grin. Jesus.

"H'lo," Tim said as he returned from the bar, "where are you, Captain?"

Nora shrugged. "Thinking," she said. And then she took Tim's glass of beer and took a sip. "Listen," she said, "you tell me Blaze Longo is a registered informant for Jimmy Ceballos, and Jimmy Ceballos was working Hector Santiago before your office turned Santiago over to the feds. Now, what you wanna bet, I check your confidential-informant file, Jimmy has Montonero and Morning registered, too? He's protecting these people. And I think I know why."

O'Grady looked at her a long moment, making her feel a bit uncomfortable, making her turn away. "It wouldn't shock me," Tim said. "What are you saying?"

"You tell me."

Tim O'Grady shrugged.

"What does that mean?"

"Captain, I'm not going to put any jacket on Jimmy Ceballos. The guy's been in this office longer than I have. He's out there every day trying to catch death. You have to start with that understanding. The guy's been kicking in doors forever, you know, you kick in enough doors sooner or later one is going to kick back. This is a dangerous business. It wears you out, changes you. Once you understand that, then everything else falls into place. I don't like Jimmy Ceballos, but I won't judge him."

"I'm not asking you to judge him. I'm asking what you think."

"I know what you're asking. Look, Jimmy has tons of informants. It's his way, it's the way he works."

"I'd love to see your office's informant file," Nora said.

"Well, I can't get it, that file is locked up. Only the boss has access. That's why they call it confidential."

Nora leaned across the table so close to O'Grady their foreheads almost touched. "Between me and you and the table here," she whispered, "give me your gut reaction to Jimmy. No bullshit, the straight scoop. I'm not in internal affairs, you know that. I'm a detective like you, I want your feelings about the guy. It goes no farther than this bar."

Tim pushed himself away from her, smiling. "First of all, that's bullshit. Okay, excuse me, I don't mean to be disrespectful. But, Captain, you are a captain and I'm a detective. There's a difference."

"Your gut feelings, Tim?"

"My gut feelings, between me and you and this table here?"

"That's all I'm asking."

"You're not going to quote me?"

"You have my word."

"Jimmy Ceballos is one hell of an active cop, he locks up a whole lot of drug dealers. He is also a pure outlaw, so far round the bend that no one can reach him. Jimmy's gone, he's one of them, been that way for quite some time. I mean, you worked with the man, you know him."

"I never worked with him. Sure, I heard the stories, but anyone as active as he is, there'll always be stories. My partner Sammy didn't think of him as such a bad guy. And I'd trust Sam's opinion."

"Sam Morelli was wrong, he didn't know him. Well, he knew him, but not really. When people meet Jimmy, they like him. He's a likable kind of guy. When I think of Jimmy Ceballos, I think of a relentless gutter fighter, an obscene, malicious, angry man who is extremely intelligent, a guy who presents his disregard for any sort of morality as an act of some crazy kind of manliness. He is everything we worry about in this police department come true. You want to know what I think, that's what I think."

"Capable of what?"

"If you're asking my opinion, I'd say, anything. Now all that said, Captain, I think it's reasonable to ask why you would choose a man like Ceballos to arrest your husband?"

Nora had the feeling that this was a question she'd be answering more than once in the near future. A shivery, apprehensive feeling, not unlike that of a cheater caught cold, crept into her nervous system. She felt frightened.

"I didn't choose him. I wouldn't have."

"Do you know Frank Rawlings?"

"Sure, Cellballos's partner."

"Right. He and Jimmy are in the office, they're standing by the switchboard, you know by the message desk. I'm one of maybe five, six guys standing near the desk, getting an overhear, as Jimmy tells Frank about a hit they were going to make that night. A hit coming right out of the chief's office. Frank was saying that was bullshit, they had other work to do, and they're going back and forth and finally Jimmy apparently had had enough and raised his voice saying that Sam Morelli asked for a favor, and if Sammy's asking, it's important because everybody knows who Sammy's hook is, his rabbi. It's you, right? And, it's not like you're just any other captain, Captain, you're the chief of detectives' favorite captain. That's no secret, it's common knowledge. And so what would you think if the next day Captain Nora Riter's husband is collared with a broad and coke in some crib in Queens? You'd figure that Captain Riter set this up, right? So that's what everyone in the office thinks. Can't blame them, we're narcotics detectives, maybe a bit warped, but we're not stupid."

Nora didn't say anything.

"If you were to ask me, I'd tell you that wasn't too smart, Captain."

"You don't have to tell me, I know it. But then I'd tell you, you'd have to have been there to understand," Nora said.

"I guess you figured you'd ask a favor, it'd get done, and that would be it. You know it doesn't work like that in this job. You get a big favor, you owe. Now, from the questions you're asking and the answers I'm giving, it doesn't seem to me that you're looking to do any favors for Ceballos. It seems to me that, if anything, you're looking to jam him up. Then again, maybe I'm wrong. What's going on, Captain?"

Nora stared at Tim O'Grady, there was no mistaking the curious and inquisitive gleam in his eye. Not knowing how to answer that question, wanting now to get out of the moment, Nora said, "I got myself a situation here and it's important I deal with it."

Tim smiled at her and did not turn away. Nora held his look, feeling the tension rise. Finally, she turned away, saying, "Shit."

At that moment the beeper went off in Nora's shoulder bag.

"I've got to use the phone."

Tim motioned toward a pay phone in the back of the pub near the juke box. Nora went from the booth back to the telephone on the wall.

A young man in a suit and tie was studying the record selection, frowning. As Nora passed him he looked at her a second and did not speak or smile, then went back to searching.

Nora called her office, and Officer Howard, her clerical man, said the chief wanted to talk to her. Before Howard put her through, he asked her if she'd heard the news.

"What news is that?" Nora said.

"It's all over the radio, about the PC."

"What about the PC?"

"The commissioner is resigning, didn't you hear? This place is a madhouse, the brass and the media they're everywhere. You must have seen the crowds this morning."

"As a matter of fact, I did. But I don't remember seeing any media there."

"They just arrived, loads of them."

"Captain," he said, "everyone's saying the chief is the top contender."

"For what?"

"Police commissioner. It's on the radio, they mentioned his name as the leading contender. Said the mayor loves him."

Howard put her through to Jean-Paul's office.

"Nora," he said, "Nora, Nora, Nora, you hear what's going on?"

"Just now, from Howard. Did you have a clue about any of this?"

"None. He told me today at lunch, said he's getting out. He's been offered a huge job at Microsoft, chief of international security, something like that, at four times his present salary."

"Is it true?" she said.

"Of course, it's true, you should see this place."

"No, I mean, that they are considering you as the next PC?"

"Lemme tell ya, it's a surprise to me. But, man, can you believe it?"

"Sure, I believe it, the truth is, it doesn't surprise me at all. I mean f'r chrissake, it's perfect."

"Jesus, Nora, if that party were to go to the press now, you know there are people out there always looking to embarrass the mayor . . . Nora?"

"I understand."

"Do you?"

"Yes, of course."

"We have to find out . . ." Jean-Paul hesitated, Nora heard an enormous puff. "Look," he told her, "I have to know is the father alive, or isn't he? Nora, she just called me sounding crazed, sounding like . . . You know what I mean."

"Paul, you're the chief of detectives, try and calm down. I'll do what I can." Nora stopped, and considered what she'd just said, how it sounded to Jean-Paul. "Look," she told him, "relax, by the end of the day I should have a handle on this."

"You will, right? I mean, I'm counting on you. Nora," Jean-Paul said, "I've arranged to have the night team come in early. I want you to have backup when you go out to Sheepshead Bay."

"Good, as long as they hang back, don't get in my way, it'll be fine. Paul," she said, "there's a bit of a hitch here."

"A hitch? Whadaya mean, a hitch?"

"There may be a cop involved with Blaze. Tell you the truth, I don't think there are any maybes, I think for sure there's a cop involved with Blaze Longo."

A long, long, moment of silence. And then, "Don't tell me that. I don't want to hear that."

"Okay."

"Who?"

"A detective named Jimmy Ceballos."

"Where've I heard that name before? Nora, isn't he the guy that arrested Max?"

"Yessir," Nora said. The phone went quiet again. "Captain," Jean-Paul said, when enough time had passed. "Why do I find that so hard to believe? I mean, talk about a coincidence."

"Not as much as you might think."

"Tell ya what I think, I think I'm getting a massive headache."

Nora was looking around the bar for Tim O'Grady when she answered, "Join the crowd."

By the time Nora hung up, Tim O'Grady had gone to the bar to order another beer. Nora's head was spinning. She was wondering just how much of what she said to Jean-Paul was real, how much was fake; all of it, she thought, pure performance.

Once, centuries ago, she knew precisely what she was doing. Now, she could hardly walk across the room without her mind exploding with what-ifs and maybes.

At the bar Nora said to O'Grady: "The PC resigned, there're going to be changes at headquarters."

"I heard it on the radio this morning. They're talking about Clement as the next PC. Good for you."

"Good for me? Well, maybe."

"How can you miss? It's perfect. You're hooked to Clement's train and from what I hear the man's going right to the top."

"Hooked is a good word, Tim, that's exactly how I feel. Hooked."

O'Grady looked puzzled.

Tim had always impressed Nora with his seeming willingness to take things as they came. He kissed no one's ass, didn't seem to have this burning need to score points with the bosses, trying to get ahead. Nora felt as though she had failed herself in that regard. At that moment, she felt envy and a bit of admiration for Tim O'Grady.

"Tim," she said, "I have something I want to run past you."

"Sure."

"I have an informant," she said. "He told me that last night he was with Blaze, when Longo shot and killed Hector Santiago."

"Whoa!"

"That's not half of it. Listen, this guy, my informant's saying that Blaze, Morning, and Montonero along with some other dipshit named Paul DiMaria are running a kidnap ring."

Tim raised his eyebrows. "You believe this guy?"

Nora frowned at him, "Wait, wait, we're not there yet. This guy, my guy, he tells me that Blaze and the others don't have the smarts to put this together. You with me so far?"

"It doesn't take a genius to kidnap people."

"Hold it," she said, "it's not the kidnapping, it's coming up with the targets. He figures that somebody is controlling these guys, directing them to the scores."

Tim frowned, it was a kind of sympathetic expression, as he asked, "You don't think it's Jimmy Ceballos?"

"Yes, I do."

"Jesus Christ."

"What I'm asking you, now this is confidential, truly, between me and you, no bullshit. What I'm asking, do you think it's possible?"

"What does it matter what I think?"

"It matters to me.

"You flatter me, Captain. But how the hell would I know?"

"You've been around Ceballos more than anyone I know. I'm interested in what you think. Help me here."

O'Grady stared at her, half smiling. "You're serious?"

Nora didn't answer him.

"You're asking me to be a stool pigeon, that's what you're asking, Captain. You want me to be an informant like your friend."

She knew he was right but had to take a moment, then she broke into an impulsive and unashamed smile. "I am something, ain't I?"

"Yes, you are. Well, everyone always said you were a hardass, I guess everyone was right."

"Well," she said, "at least we got that out of the way. Soooo, whadaya think?"

Tim O'Grady finished his beer with one long swallow. After he put the glass on the bar, Tim smiled at Nora who was all eyes, nodded knowingly, and said, "You want me to tell you if I think Jimmy Ceballos, a man I work with, is capable of kidnap and murder?"

Nora nodded.

"You betcha."

"See," Nora said, "what's making me crazy is that none of this shocks me. I mean, all this, or anyway most of this would blow the average person's mind, even the average detective's mind. And me, I'm thinking, so, what's next? Like it's business as usual. Christ, I've gone round the bend."

Tim looked at her sullenly. "Look," he said, "no offense, but you're pretty insulated down there at headquarters. It's been a while since you've been in the street. The war is still in high gear, we don't talk about it much anymore, but the battle still rages."

"What are you saying?"

"Guys like Ceballos are important. I mean, you may not like what he does, hate it even, but maybe it's not so bad to have guys like him on your side."

Nora was watching Tim with a sad smile.

"I mean," Tim went on with a laugh, "there's a whole lot of psychos out in those streets, when we have one of our own, it sort of levels the playing field."

Nora looked away.

Tim said, "I guess it depends on how you think."

"Tim," she told him, "if I believed that you really held to any of that baloney, I wouldn't be talking to you."

"Well, maybe I said some dumb things, but you get my point."

She said, "I think you're burnt-out and tired." Nora told him that was not a good thing to be. O'Grady nodded and that's when she said, "You need a change. Maybe I can help."

They sat in silence, Tim finished his beer. "You're a good person, Captain. No, really, you are. Listen," he said, "I don't want to get involved with Ceballos, his problems, your problems, but I will give you a little tip. It might be nothing, then again, who knows?"

"You can never tell," Nora said.

"That's right," O'Grady said. "Jimmy loves gadgets, bugs, shit like that. He bugs his informants, he bugs everybody."

"You don't say."

"Outlet bugs are his favorite. They have their own power source, put one in, it lasts forever. You know, you stick one of those little beauties in the wall, the conversation, all the sound from that room are yours. All you need is an FM receiver."

"I've seen them."

"Yeah, they were real popular in narcotics. We used them for years."

"Popular and illegal."

"Not always, you can get a court order."

"Oh, excuse me. So now you're going to tell me that Jimmy Ceballos gets court orders to bug his informants?"

"Oh, for Christ's sake, Captain. Come on."

"Anything's possible."

"Sure. And O.J. Simpson was an innocent man, falsely accused. Look," Tim said, "all I'm saying is that you check Blaze Longo's apartment, chances are you'll find an outlet bug. Maybe even fingerprints."

"Well, it's a thought. But I doubt you'd get prints," she said. To herself she thought, Ceballos is one slick piece of work, a real slimeball. Doing deals with Blaze Longo, what the hell does that tell you? Sam, she thought, Sam, what were you thinking? What the hell were they both thinking? Going to a guy like Ceballos for a favor, man, they weren't thinking at all.

"You put Ceballos on your husband, didn't you?" Tim said.

"Guilty."

"This is no can of worms you got here, Captain, this is a bucket of snakes."

"You don't know the half of it."

Nora was scared to death to confront Jimmy Ceballos, going head-to-head with an evil bastard like Ceballos could ruin your week. Sooner or later, though, sooner or later, she'd have to face it. What else was new? Christ, the things Ceballos could say, embroider, turn this way and that. Forget her, she wasn't worried about herself, it was Sam. Nora didn't want to think about how many of the department's rules and procedures she and Sam had bent. Enough, she knew, to jeopardize Sammy's pension, his income and life's work. Nora was thinking that Jimmy Ceballos might be a contemptible and dangerous clown, but he understood department rules. He knew he had her, had her so good, she could cease to be a threat to him, period.

"What the hell have I done?" Saying it as if she were talking to herself. "Sam put himself way out for me. Put himself right in the jackpot." Sometimes what she was feeling was so obvious, anyone could see it.

Tim O'Grady smiled, saying, "Hey, Captain, my feeling is that, first of all, Sam Morelli is no rookie, he's a big boy, he knows what he's doing. Second, if I were in your position, I wouldn't be worried about Jimmy Ceballos, he should be scared of you. *You* know what *you're* doing, Jimmy is running wild, he's out of control."

Nora looked around the bar while Tim emptied his glass. O'Grady was staring at her, seeing the look on her face, trying to read her. It was a while before they spoke.

"I'm going to nail them," Nora said. "If there is evidence to support any of this, I'll put Jimmy Ceballos and his merry band of so-called informants in jail."

"And, that's exactly what you should do," Tim said, and smiled a little. His smile was more an expression of apprehension. "Just don't ask me to help. All bullshit aside, I don't expect internal affairs to chase drug dealers. No one should expect me to chase a cop."

"Ceballos is not your problem, he's mine."

"Thank you. Did you ever consider that maybe, he's not really yours? Why not let IAD handle him."

"Man, I'd like to, but I don't think I have much choice here."

"We always have choices, Captain. You're smart, you'll figure out what to do."

Nora folding her arms now, stared at Tim, biting the inside of her mouth, a habit she'd picked up as a teenager.

"I'll take care of this," she told Tim. Feeling the certainty of it pass more deeply into her, knowing exactly what she had to do.

"I'm sure you will. I know you will. Like everyone says, you're a hardass, and the thing about hardasses, they don't go away." Tim O'Grady touched her shoulder, gave her a little squeeze. "Tell you what, Captain, you are the real deal. I wouldn't want you after me."

Why, she told him, would I ever want to be after you? Tried to tell him. In the end she kept still and nodded her head.

The **second thing** Blaze said to the Wizard was, "Why'nt you go and fuck yourself." The first thing he'd said was, "Man, I knew it was you. How did I know it was you? Guess I'm getting spooky like you, seeing things before they happen. I walk through the door, the phone's ringing, it's gotta be you." When the Wizard said, "Okay, Blaze, now you listen to me, you go to number three." That's when Blaze said, Why'nt you go and fuck yourself.

"Listen to me, you fucking moron, you go to number three."

Blaze exploded. "Moron. Moron! Who do you think you're talking to? I'm always thinking, my mind figuring things, I know stuff nobody knows. I'm no moron."

Blaze was standing in his bedroom, looking out the window. It was 8:00, still bright, a cheery, radiant quality to the ending of the day, there were plenty of people walking about.

There was silence on the other end of the phone, when the Wizard spoke again his voice was under control.

"I need to talk to you, my friend, it's important. Please, do me a favor, do us both a favor and go to number three."

"Fuck you."

"Christ."

"Hey, I'm into something here, I've got things going, I only have a

327

minute. You got something you wanna say, you'd better say it, time's a-wasting."

"I'm not going to talk on this phone. What is wrong with you, are you crazy? Of course, you're crazy, I've always known you were crazy, but I didn't think you were stupid."

Blaze nodded, smiling, feeling the cool, light breeze on the back of his neck, the shadow creeping through his mind, thinking, I'm crazy, huh, stupid, too.

"I made you rich, you prick, and what do you do, you call me names. You wouldn't call me names to my face, not you, not the Wizard. You're a punk, come into my face, I'll cut you, cut you good."

A loud, deep, mournful sigh came through the phone. It made Blaze's smile grow. "Yeah," he said, "you gonna say something, say it, man, say it."

"All right, awright. Your friend, your buddy, your crime partner, the Hawk?"

"What about him?"

"Oh, man, don't make me talk on this phone. Christ, please, go to number three."

"I'm gonna hang up, one . . . two . . ."

"Okay, okay. What did the Hawk tell you? He told you he got pinched, right? What else did he tell you?"

"Nothing else."

"He told you he made bail. Am I right?"

"So?"

"He was paroled, no bail. Understand what I'm saying? He's an informant, he's a stool pigeon, a rat, Blaze, and you're rolling right around in his nest. You fucking moron."

"Nicky the Hawk is a stool pigeon," Blaze said, and then repeated the words under his breath. "I'm going to kill him," Blaze said.

"I think that would be wise."

"That would make you happy?"

"Oh, yes."

"Maybe I *should* go to number three."

"It's a little late for that. No, what I think you gotta do is pray that no one's listening."

"C'mon, be serious, why would anybody be listening to my fucking phone? I'm a nobody, man. I'm nothing, you said it yourself, I ain't shit."

"Well, there you have it, the story of your life in a nutshell."

"You're a cop, you sonofabitch. That's how you know all this shit. Everybody's been right about you. It was only me that didn't see it. I guess I am stupid."

The Wizard hung up the phone, Blaze was still smiling, he kept on smiling as he stared out the window. He went to his dresser, took the nine millimeter, the pistol he called his guinea gun. His shiny Baretta. Made sure the clip was fully loaded. Looked through his drawer for the other two clips, turned back to look at the phone, thought that maybe he should call Paulie on his cellular, make sure that Montonero and Morgan were set up on Nicky. That's when he thought, no, screw that. Blaze the thinker, he wasn't about to use that fucking phone.

Blaze tucked the automatic into his belt and headed for the door. It was 8:15.

Nora spent the remainder of the afternoon and the early evening at home. Most times, when her investigations began to pick up heat, Nora found that her appetite would all but disappear. Tension, dread, and the mood of the hunt made eating unthinkable. But this night, she figured, should be nothing more than a little cruise out to Sheepshead Bay, to run down an address. Simple. So, with plenty of time before she was to meet Nicky, Nora patiently made herself a modest feast of a broiled lamb chop, sautéed onions and mushrooms, with a cucumber and tomato salad.

She ate the meal in her kitchen, then took her coffee into the bedroom, and settled down to watch the evening news. The commentator was a bright, attractive Asian woman, whom Nora had met a few years back. It was a homicide investigation of a seventeen-year-old NYU student. There had been some suspicion the death might have been cult-related. The young man had been an introverted loner, a genius, a computer wiz at the top of his class. The homicide turned out to be a suicide. When they were hanging from a tree, it was always suicide.

"Earlier today, the mayor announced the resignation of Police Commissioner Marcus Black. A new commissioner will be appointed within the next several days." So spoke the woman, serious and hard-faced. She pointed out that there were several men under consideration for the post.

"The leading contenders," she said, "are former FBI agent Vincent

Wexler, and the current chief of New York's detectives, Jean-Paul Clement."

Photos of the two men flashed on the screen. In his blue blazer and striped tie, Jean-Paul looked more movie starlike than usual. There was Jean-Paul and then there was Wexler, a stern-looking, puffy-faced man, with a brush cut, no chin, and gloomy eyes.

The woman commentator pointed out that inside sources at head-quarters took it for granted that the appointment would go to Clement. She admitted that it was a natural next step in an already-illustrious police career.

"Is that man gorgeous, or what?" she asked playfully. She made no comment regarding Wexler. Probably, Nora decided, Jean-Paul had already worked his way up the TV commentator's skirt.

Nora went into the kitchen and made herself another cup of coffee. Sitting at her table she tried to collect her thoughts. It was the PC, after all, who approved all promotions above the rank of captain. With Jean-Paul commissioner, Nora had no trouble seeing herself promoted one, two, maybe even three ranks. "You're the chief's favorite captain, Captain." That's what O'Grady had said, and Tim was right. In the world of police-department politicos, Nora knew she could write her own ticket. Her demented sense of loyalty could pay off. But to who, to what? A weak man who was a cheat and a liar, that's who, that's what. Nora sitting, thinking, telling herself, it's the world's oldest story, you gotta go along to get along. A spiritual malaise, but it works. Loyalty, in her world, she knew was the principal feeling, and loyalty would always be the overruling emotion. Stop kidding yourself, she told herself, an allegiance to amorality is nothing to be proud of.

Nora checked the time; saw that it was 7:30. She was meeting Nicky at 9:00. Jean-Paul had used her and she was using Nicky, both of them coconspirators in the chief's soap-opera life. Nora deeply resented being played for a fool. Jimmy Ceballos, Blaze Longo, she and Nicky, all actors in the chief's show. Somehow, she thought, there is a terrible justice in all this, but she was not in the frame of mind to take pleasure from it.

Nora had been so focused on Ceballos, so pumped to nail him, that she had all but forgotten Nicky's role.

She had thrown Nicky out there, too, hung him right in the bull's-eye the way she had with Sam. All this, all of it, because Jean-Paul Clement couldn't keep his dick in his pants. So now they would make him the chief executive officer of the New York City police department. What a country.

An hour later, in the underground garage of her apartment building, Nora started her car. She checked her gun and her cellular and for a split second she considered calling Sammy, give the guy an update. But then she thought, let it be, let the man rest, she'd talk to him soon enough. It was 8:20 P.M.

Nora drove out to Seventy-ninth Street, hung a left, and then drove down through Central Park. Her heart was beating with a slight adrenaline rush and she felt a little weary. The evening was pleasant, cool and clear. Bugged all day by the mystery of what she would do about Ceballos, Nora felt thankful for the opportunity to clear her head. She'd drive out to Sheepshead Bay with Nicky, poke around a little, find the crime-scene location where Hector Santiago was murdered, then get the homicide squad to come in and do their thing. When she hit the FDR Drive, she telephoned her office and told the waiting night team to meet her out in front of headquarters. She'd be there in ten minutes.

At **8:45, only** five minutes after falling in behind Nora's Mazda, detectives Mike Rogers and Frank Sena were sitting in the center traffic lane on the Brooklyn Bridge, two cars separating them from the funky little red car. Mike behind the wheel of the unmarked police cruiser, Frank riding in the shotgun seat.

Mike felt antsy in the fading evening light, sensing ominous signs in the twilight, telling Frank, "I hate this time of day, the gloaming, depresses me."

Frank swallowed a yawn, "Just don't lose her."

Mike sat staring at the swelling Saturday night traffic, all the cars heading for Brooklyn, the Mazda inching along ahead of them in the right lane.

"So," Mike said, "what did the chief say?"

"Whadaya think he said? Anything happens to her, it's your ass."

"He's fucking her," said Mike.

"Well, sure," said Frank.

Thirty seconds passed.

Mike said, "Do we know where we're going?"

"She's picking up a CI at 777 Fourth Street. Right off Court Street. You know the neighborhood?"

"A little."

"Hey, you're the reader, brother, the educated end of this team, tell me something about Red Hook."

Mike wasn't saying a word. The concerns of his existence were tightly focused. At this moment his entire life had but one purpose: Tail the captain. Below him was the East River, green, black, reflecting the lights of lower Manhattan; the shimmering golden light of the great Big Apple; the massive pillars of the Brooklyn Bridge, as Detective Rogers watched, holding you high in the air. The steady procession of cars, vans, taxis, limos, trucks all moving in endless streams, headlights, taillights, the very lifeblood of the city heading for Brooklyn.

"What do you want to know?"

"Why they call it Red Hook, for one thing."

"*Roode Hoek*, it's Dutch, because of its shape and back then, a long time ago, the color of the soil on the Hook was red."

Frank looked straight ahead at the road and shook his head slightly. "Nowadays," he said, "the only red dirt you'll find in South Brooklyn is where some poor bastard was left bleeding."

"You know, Al Capone lived there once," Mike said, "did his act around the docks. You saw the movie, *On the Waterfront?*"

"I don't think so."

"You're telling me you didn't see that movie? *On the Waterfront's* a classic. With Brando and Eva Marie Saint, I coudda been a contender. You didn't see that fucking movie?"

"No. No. I don't think so. Was Clint Eastwood in that?"

"Clint Eastwood! Rod Steiger, you asshole. Jesus, why am I talking to you?"

"I dunno, it's probably not such a good idea. You being the kinda guy has trouble doing two things at once. You just missed the turnoff."

"Shit!

Nora would always drive the right lane, scoot over the bridge and hang in that exit lane that hooked around and came out onto Court Street. A left and then a straight run down to Atlantic, across the avenue, shoot down to Fourth Street, easy. Crossing the Brooklyn Bridge from Manhattan you could drive the center lane, get a good, friendly look at both midtown and downtown Manhattan, and the lady in the harbor, at least that was the theory. But, you had better be on your toes. Look out, before you knew it, you'd blow past the exit and find yourself on Tillary Street.

Ever since they reached the halfway point of the bridge, Nora had been trying to figure what in the hell the two detectives had in mind in the center lane. See, she told herself, you make em get off their asses, shake them out of their comfortable tree, and these headquarters detectives couldn't find their dick with either hand. Glancing in the rearview, watching them talking, one of them aiming a finger out toward the river, pointing toward the docks, grinning, the two of them laughing at each other. When she hung that right, she saw the cruiser charge right on by and Nora said, "See ya," out loud and watched the two detectives disappear into the night.

A minute later her cellular went off, she picked it up saying, "Yeah, where the hell you two going?"

"Captain, we missed the turnoff."

"You don't say? Look," she told them, "you have the CI's address, I'll be there in five minutes. I'll wait for you."

Nicky sat on the stoop between Tino and Irma eating a slice of pizza. The white cardboard box with big black lettering, ROMA CAFE, on a step beneath them. He spotted the red car the minute it turned into his street, Nora behind the wheel with all that hair, a small sad smile on her face, pulling in and parking at the curb right in front of him.

Nicky had been haunted by the afternoon's conversation with Charlie Chan. He had sorted out all his options and had made a decision. But, he also had a feeling, one of those scary ones, that made you think maybe this time you screwed up in such a spectacular way that you're fucked for life. Now, he stood up slowly and handed Irma what was left of his slice of pizza. Irma took what Nicky gave her, turned it this way and that, then offered it to Tino.

"I don't want any more," Tino said.

Earlier, Nicky had showered and shaved, with schemes bouncing around his head. He read a little and watched some TV. Couldn't believe what he saw and heard on the evening news. It was then that he'd decided, man, are you kidding me, screw this.

Now he was braced for a blowup with Nora. Nicky looked up then down the street, he turned toward Nora, smiled, and waved. In his fidgety state, he imagined himself having to take a collar. Just the thought of being arrested put snakes in his stomach, making him feel like grabbing Tino and hitting the highway.

"I'm going to say hi to her," Tino said.

"Go right ahead," Nicky told him.

Tino stepped off the stoop and walked over to Nora's car, his thumbs hooked into his jeans, a swagger to his step like a gunslinger's.

Nicky dropped a hand on Irma's shoulder, saying, "I'm going, you stay put and keep an eye on Tino." Irma swatted his hand away telling him, "Wait a minute, you want to go out and party, Okay, go ahead. But I'm no baby sitter, Nicky. I'm staying home tonight because I want to."

"You're staying home because, in your heart, you're a good person, Irma." But she didn't seem to hear him.

Nicky started down the steps toward Nora's car, his head buzzing, wondering just how to play this. Play it straight, his new Nicky voice telling him, spell it out, brother, tell her you want out of this scam, this stool-pigeon role she cast you in. He stopped on the curb of the street and looked around, imagined seeing heads in parked cars at the far end of the block. Then he actually saw one.

Irma called out that she was nobody's baby sitter, Nicky tuned her out, savoring this decision he'd made to take a stand, wondering now what Nora would do. Bring him to the precinct? Arrest him on the spot? Or maybe just tell him fine, Nicky, fine, let's forget the whole thing.

Yeah, right.

"Tino," he said, "you get going. Go on in with Irma." The boy did a little be-bop two-step, then broke into song, *"That's the way I like it, uh-huh, uh-huh, that's the way, that's the way, I like it."* Then he spun around and casually jogged back toward the house. Throwing Nicky the thumbs-up sign as he went.

Nora laughed.

Nicky walked around the car, opened the door, and sat in the passenger's seat, rolling down the window. "C'mon," he said, "let's go."

"That boy is hysterical, you won't believe what he was telling me."

"Yeah, he's a regular comic genius. Now, come on, let's get going."

"Sure, so you okay?"

"Fine, let's go."

Nora adjusted her rearview mirror, turned it once, then put it back exactly the way it was before. "I can't," she said, "I have to wait here a minute."

Nicky rubbed his eyes.

"The thing is," Nicky told her, "I want to tell you something, let's move, I want to get out of here."

Nora looked over at Nicky, saying, "What do you want to tell me?"

They looked at each other, then Nora's cellular rang. She reached out, slowly picked up the phone, and raised it to her ear. Nicky was careful not to seem to be listening, in fact he was looking out the window, past Nora, at Tino and Irma, trying to get their attention, wanting to be sure they both went inside. Feeling a deep uneasiness, almost panic creep into him. Hearing Charlie say something like, basically you can't trust a cop, no matter who it is.

Nora said, "Now, where are you?" Detective Rogers saying, "We made a couple of bad moves here, we're kinda turned around." Nicky saying, "Who are you talking to?" Nora raised her hand to quiet him. Like that, making Nicky furious.

"Hey," he said, "either we go right now, or I'm out of here. You understand me, lady, you wanna see how fast I get out of this car and bug off."

Nora drove off saying into the phone, "Hold on a minute, Mike." She turned to Nicky saying, "I need to tell them where we're going. I can see you're upset, now calm down a minute."

"Who are these guys you're talking to?"

"They work with me."

See, more cops, Nicky's thinking, keep hanging with this broad, you'll be up to your ass in cops, which is what you deserve, shithead.

"Just go down and around," Nicky told her, "when you get to Atlantic Avenue, make a left and head to the expressway. Screw these guys," he said, "what the hell do we need more cops for? What is this, a damn convention?"

Nicky sat back with his head against the cushion of the seat, his arms folded. Nora had to drive with one hand, the other holding her cellular, she was getting annoyed, too, saying first into the phone, "Mike, go find the Gowanus Expressway. We're heading out toward Sheepshead Bay, taking the Belt Parkway." Putting her hand over the mouthpiece, asking Nicky, "What exit?" Nicky saying, "We're just going to take a ride past the building, right?"

"Nicky, for chrissake."

"Tell them to get off at Emmons Avenue." Nicky couldn't think of anything to add until Nora said into the phone, "Get off at Emmons Avenue, we'll wait for you there." That's when he said, "*You* wait for them. I'm telling you, when you stop this car, I'm getting out and heading home. I've had enough of this bullshit, I ain't kidding."

Nora turned left under the BQE overpass, headed in the direction of the Gowanus Expressway. The Mazda took a hard bounce from a pothole, veered left to avoid a second one, and quickly managed to cut off a black van with tinted windows. The driver of the van leaned on his horn. The blaring horn dodged the Mazda and flashed past them. "Careful," Nicky said.

Nora had no comment. Nicky glanced at her. She was looking straight ahead, hard-faced, grimly moving the Mazda in and out of the chaotic Saturday night traffic.

"Are you going to tell me what's wrong with you?" Nora said finally.

"Yes, goddamit, I'm going to tell you what's eating at me. And if you don't like it, then too bad, take me off to the slammer. You know, hey, fuck it."

"The way you're talking to me, is that supposed to shock me? It doesn't, nothing shocks me, Nicky. So calm the hell down, and tell me what's bothering you."

In a few minutes they were driving by the Fort Hamilton approaches for the Verrazano Narrows Bridge, Nicky sat back looking out at the bay and the lights of Staten Island.

"This started out as a prank, a gag," he told her. "But it's not funny anymore."

"Funny?" she said. "This case is a lot of things, but it was never funny."

"Well, you know what I mean, something of a joke. The beautiful police captain, the aspiring actor, smitten and moved by the woman's good looks and knockaround ways. When I think of the lost possibilities I shudder."

Nora smiled at him, saying, "What the hell are you talking about?"

"Hell, man, you had to know I had a bit of a crush on you," he said.

"Had, past tense, how sad," Nora told him. "I'm very hurt, Nicky, your love faded so quickly."

"I didn't say anything about love. A crush is not love, it's anything but love. It's fascination, pure animal attraction."

Innocently, Nora said, "And I thought you would love me forever. What a fool I've been."

"Nora," he said, "this is not funny. Blaze came along and all the laughter died."

"Blaze," she said, "good ol Blaze."

"As far as he's concerned, if somebody dropped that guy in a hole and put a lid over it, I'd throw a party."

"I am going to drop Blaze in that hole, Nicky. So what's the problem? No, wait a minute, what you're saying is that this romance you dreamt up is not working out and you're disappointed? Poor Nicky."

"Don't be so goddamn cocky, that's not it at all."

"Yeah, then what is it?"

"You got me involved in something here that's foreign to my nature, that's not me. I'm no stool pigeon, not for you or anybody else, I'm nobody's rat. But that's what you want from me, that's all you ever wanted from me, just to turn me around and into a stoolie. Well, screw that."

Nora laughed in frustration. "There is the small matter of punching a cop."

"C'mon!"

"And, and," she told him, "the slightly weightier circumstance of witnessing a murder. What's wrong with you? I could put your ass in jail for a long time."

"Hey, look, lady, I happened to be with Blaze because you forced me to be with Blaze. Not for you, I wouldn't have spent two minutes with that creep. It's your fault I was in that building, your fault I was there when he shot that poor bastard."

She agreed absolutely. He was right, of course he was right, but it didn't change anything. Somehow, she thought, Nicky failed to understand that his problem was real. She reached over and shoved his shoulder, trying now to get his full attention. "Nicky," she said, "do you really think you can walk away, like timeout, game's over? Too late, way too late, buddy."

"You're telling me I'm in serious trouble?"

"That's right."

"I was watching the news, and you know what, I see that they're going to make your boss the police commissioner. That right?"

"It looks that way."

"Looks that way. The fact that he's fucking a made guy's wife is no big thing, huh?"

"C'mon," she told him, "be serious."

He shook his head. "Oh," he said, "I'm serious, real serious."

"You were a witness to murder, Nicky."

"And, your boss, if you understand anything about these streets, he can cause one. When Sally Boy Palumbo comes home, he's going to cut Roseann's head off. Now you tell me, what's worse?"

"You have a point, but who's to say? Anyway, that's not your problem, Nicky. And let me tell you, nothing much is going to matter if you're upstate breaking rocks."

Nicky laughed a little but he looked sad.

"Yeah, well, I'm going to show you the apartment building, and then I'm gone, I'm out of it."

"That's your decision to make. But let me tell you, turning your back on me is the wrong decision."

He smiled at her then, a mean little smile. "It won't be the first time," he told her. "I'm the king of wrong decisions. Get off at the next exit. Let me ask you something," he said. "Say you and I happened to meet somewhere else. I mean, what if we weren't involved the way we are now, say we met somewhere in the normal people's world. Tell me the truth, would I have had a shot?"

"Another time, another place, in the world of normal people?" she said. "Hummmm, let me tell you, Nicky, under the right set of circumstances, I'd be all over you like you were a great big birthday cake."

"Really?"

"Maybe. It's an interesting thought though, huh?"

He nodded enthusiastically. "By the way," he said, "Roseann's father, Alley Boy, he's alive and well and living in Las Vegas."

"What?"

"I'm telling you. I spoke to someone who told me they'd talked to him just last week."

"Who?"

"Somebody local, somebody who doesn't like you."

"That's interesting, why's that?"

"Get off here," he told her.

"Roseann's father is alive, well, isn't that something. Hey," she said, "this is not Emmons Avenue, it's Knapp Street."

"Get off here."

"Didn't you tell me that Blaze said he killed him?"

"Nora, the man cuts people's ears off, he shoots people. I don't think that lying is any great stretch for a guy like Blaze."

Nora thought about Roseann, about Jean-Paul for a moment. Then she remembered the backup team and reached down to pick up her cellular. Nicky grabbed it and tossed it out of the window. "Just you and me now, babes, all alone together. How's that?"

"You're a putz, you know that? What if we need some help?"

"You have me."

"Ahh, yes, my hero—the handsome putz."

Blaze got to Fourth and Clinton and peeked around the corner. Halfway down the block, on the far side of the street, Paulie's Buick was tucked in at the curb. He had parked behind Montonero's van. Turning to look back toward Court Street, Blaze spied Nicky on the stoop and for a second he was startled. Blaze stepped back into a doorway, agitated and pissed off.

He had spent most of the day sitting in the Buick with Paulie. It wasn't until late in the afternoon that he had reached out for Morgan and Montonero. Now he had to tell them, all of them, the whole posse— Nicky the Hawk was a rat. He seemed to feel that shadow arrive again, though he wasn't sure. The skin on the back of his neck trembled and he was feeling sick to his stomach. He tried to relax, breathing deeply. The light was fading and for that he was pleased.

Blaze waited for several slow-moving cars that were passing down the street. He crossed between them, and got to the far sidewalk and scooted along the building line up to the Buick.

Paulie opened the passenger door, shouting, "Get in, get in."

When Blaze slid into the front seat, Montonero grabbed his shoulder from behind. "You wanna tell me what's going on?" he said. "Why the hell are we sitting here like a bunch of cops, watching Nicky?"

Blaze turned to look back at Morgan and Montonero then he bent his head toward Paulie. "We're gonna do this guy, we're gonna do him tonight."

Paulie cleared his throat and said, "Why's that?"

"He's a rat, I got a message from the Wizard, he's sure Nicky's working for the cops."

"And you believe him?" Morgan said.

"Nicky lied to me," Blaze said. "When he was busted he lied, telling me he'd made bail. What happened was, he'd been paroled. Now, you don't get parole for punching out a cop."

"He's a rat," said Paulie.

"Fuckin A," said Montonero.

"I don't know," said Morgan. "I met the guy, I liked him. He didn't seem the rat type to me."

Blaze met his eyes. "Tell me, Morgan, what type is that, the rat type, what's that?"

Morgan shrugged his shoulders, saying, "Ey, tough guy, you're the one brought him around."

Blaze glanced back at Morgan again and smiled at him. "That's right," he said, "and I'll be the one to put a bullet in his fucking head."

Morgan looked sad.

"So, what's happening?" Blaze said.

Paulie pointed down the street with his chin, "They've been on the stoop for about twenty minutes. It was me, I'd go and snap the fucker up, take him for a ride out to the bay."

"Just like that?" Blaze said. "And what would you do about Irma and the kid, Tino?"

Paulie shrugged, saying, "I dunno, I'll think about it."

"Why'nt I take a walk down the street," Morgan said. "They don't know me, I could walk right up on Nicky, tell him to come along, he'd come along easy, 'cause we're buddies."

For a moment, Blaze pictured himself driving up the street to Nicky's house with guns blazing. Shoot all three of them, do one of those California drive-bys. That was exactly how he felt, but he knew that was a dangerous way to feel. See, he told himself, you're not stupid and you're not crazy, but man, you have every right to be pissed off.

"We'll sit tight," Blaze said, "it's still early, give Nicky some time. I gotta believe the guy's going out. It's Saturday night, he'll go out, maybe up to the Roma, something like that. Then we'll snap him up."

Blaze watched Nicky silhouetted in the fading light, Nicky sitting, then standing, moving around the stoop, impatient, maybe waiting for someone. Cars were moving down the street, horns honking, a couple of guys playing stick ball, pains in the asses, stopping traffic. Blaze shook his head, picturing Nicky taped to a chair. Yup, yup, since the morning at Paulie's club, Blaze knew that sooner or later, he'd have Nicky taped to a chair. A guy like Nicky, too slick, too smooth, too fucking smart.

A little red sports car pulled up in front of Nicky's building, and the kid Tino got off the stoop and walked over to it.

"Who's that?" said Blaze. And Paulie said, "I have no idea." From the backseat, Morgan said, "what's goin on?" and Montonero said, "what's happening?"

"Nothing's happening," Blaze said, "Shut up, everybody. Just shut up a minute. Who's that, Paulie, you know that car?"

"Never seen it before," said Paulie, "looks like a broad."

Blaze looked up the street, trying to get his eyes adjusted to the gathering dark. He could feel his mind shifting, moving to the dark side. His mouth went dry and he was beginning to tense up, eager, more aroused than usual. Bizarre sounds repeated, strange songs played in his head along with a ceaseless chatter of unrecognizable voices.

Paulie said, "Look out, Nicky's getting in."

"They're gonna leave the neighborhood," Blaze said. "Nicky's going out on a date." He grinned in triumph.

From the backseat came a steady riff of "What, who, what's happenin?"

"Okay. Heads up, they're pulling out," said Blaze. "Don't lose em Paulie, and don't let em see us."

The Mazda rolled straight at them, Blaze could see the woman driver, she had moved the car back into traffic, talking on a car phone. From what he could make out, a broad with a mountain of hair and knowing Nicky, Blaze figured she must be a looker. For a moment he thought the woman had glanced their way.

Paulie allowed for two cars to come between the Mazda and the Buick. They were tailing them closely, but the prospect of losing the little car seemed worth the risk.

When the Mazda made a left at Atlantic Avenue toward the Gowanus Expressway. Blaze slouched down in the seat, when they made the turn onto the expressway, he glanced up at Hicks Street. Off the corner of Van Brunt and Hicks was a burnt-out and abandoned Chevy where Hector Santiago had been left in the trunk. When they passed the access roads to the Verazzano Bridge, Blaze was bouncing up and down on the seat. He spread his arms balling his fists and stretched his neck right and left.

"The fuck you doing?" Montonero asked him suddenly. "You okay, what the hell's with you, Blaze, you stoned?"

"I'm gonna fall back," Paulie said.

"Fall back," Blaze told him, "don't let them see us." Blaze bent in the seat and thrust his clasped hands between his legs. "Where they going, Paulie?" he said. "Tell me."

Blaze heard Paulie say, "They're pulling off at Knapp Street. Nicky wouldn't be taking her to the stash plant, would he?"

"Of course not," said Montonero.

"What for?" said Morgan.

Blaze closed his eyes and put clasped hands over his face. "Yes," he said, "of course," he said, "the rat is taking the rat master to the stash plant. I'll bet that broad's a cop."

"C'mon," said Paulie, "that ain't no cop car. Whoa," he said, "they pulled over."

Hands still over his face, Blaze saying, "Where now, Paulie, where are they?"

"Could be . . ." Paulie said, "Well, I don't know where the fuck they're going. She just pulled out again, looked like Nicky threw something out the window. Christ," he said, "they're getting close to our spot."

"Classless bastard," said Blaze, "a man without self-respect. A stool pigeon. Nicky, Nicky, Nicky, you tried to fool me." He turned to Montonero and then to Morgan. "Are you two ready for this?"

"For what?" Montonero said, "You talking about killing a cop?"

"I'll tell ya what," said Morgan, "maybe she's no cop at all."

"How about you?" Montonero said. "What are you thinking?

Blaze saying now, "I think I gotta kill em both. Tape em in chairs and . . ."

"They're parking," Paulie said, "right in front of our building."

"Perfect," said Blaze.

Charlie Chan sat in Vito's car in the parking lot of the Bay Front Diner. It was Larry San Martino's spot. Larry was a friend, though Charlie hadn't seen him in years. He sat looking out the window toward the bay, listening to the Yankee game, watching a pair of seagulls stroll in the light of a streetlamp.

"You know, the Turk and the kids," Vito said quietly, "are getting a big kick out of this."

Charlie turned to look at him.

Vito, smiling now, "I mean you gotta admit it's funny, ain't it?"

Charlie didn't answer, he turned and looked back out the window, thinking that it had been years since he'd traveled to Sheepshead Bay. And the place so close by, what, fifteen, twenty minutes on the highway. Used to be some great places to eat down here, and the smell of the sea.

"Not for nothing, but do you have some plan, some idea about what you wanna do here?" Vito said a few minutes later.

Charlie turned to Vito again. "No," he said.

"It's okay, good, good, be a little loosey-goosey, play it as it lays, see what happens, that's the idea."

They had tailed Paulie's Buick out of the neighborhood, the kids and the Turk in the kids' car. Vito and Charlie coming behind, staying in touch by cell phone. Everyone brought a pistol, everyone except Charlie.

"So, who is this broad with Nicky?"

"A friend of his," Charlie said.

"A nice car," Vito said, "the broad, she's got a nice car there. But, I don't like those little cars. I don't think they're safe."

"Sporty."

"Yeah, you're right, and easy to park."

Charlie glanced down at the cellular on the seat and Vito watched him. "How long have they been gone?" Charlie said.

"Five minutes, that's all. It goes slow, ya know, sitting here, waiting, it goes slow."

"We shouldn't have been so far behind," Charlie said.

"Couldn't get too close, Charlie, they would have spotted us."

"They're junkies and assholes, they couldn't spot their hands and feet on a clear day."

"You're sure you can call them?" Charlie said. "If we need to reach the Turk, can we call him?"

"Sure, you want I should call em?"

"No."

"This kid, Nicky, he's got a nice life, huh?" Vito said.

"He hustles, this kid, nice-looking kid, he's smart. He's got a good heart taking that boy Tino off the street. Taking care of that wacky cousin of his."

"She's a hooker, huh, that girl, Irma? She works, right?"

"What do I know? She's doing something stupid, that's for sure."

The cellular on Vito's car seat went off.

Vito picked up the phone, he nodded and repeated the conversation to Charlie. "Bobby's telling me that Nicky and the woman musta gone into a building on Eighth Street. Their car's parked on the street. Paulie's car is parked there, too, just sitting there, empty."

Charlie was alarmed and looked it. Vito saying, "It's okay, they tell me there's just two buildings on the whole street. If we gotta, we'll go to every apartment, fuck it."

"What are you, nuts?" For a moment Charlie considered it, thinking that maybe, if they had to. "We got no idea what building they went into, right?"

"You know which building they went into?" Vito said into the phone. Telling Charlie now, "They don't know. There's two big apartment buildings, could be either one." Vito could see the anxiety growing on Charlie's face, he shouted into the phone. "What building they go into, for chrissake, can't you find out?"

"How they gonna find out?" Charlie told him. "Calm down, it's all right. Tell them to sit still and wait. Tell them not to hang up, keep the line open. Vito," he said, "you still think this is funny?"

Into the phone, Vito said, "It's okay. Sit still. And listen, don't hang up, we need the line open. No, Charlie, I'm sorry, it's not funny. I know how you feel about that kid, Nicky."

Charlie wagged his head saying, "But you don't know why, right? You're confused."

Vito shrugged.

"It's okay," Charlie said, "so am I."

"I'll tell ya, Charlie," Vito spoke while holding the cellular to his ear, "I ain't had this much fun since that thing we did over in Jersey. I mean, sometimes it's good to get out, you know, move around a little, work the kinks and rust out. If we knew where the kid was, this wouldn't be half bad. Wait a minute," he said, "Paulie and the two other hard-ons just came out of one of the buildings. Blaze ain't with them."

"All right, Okay. Tell them to grab those three, grab em now, and tell em to bring them here."

"Bobby," Vito said, "snatch those three half-a-humps. I don't care if you heard him, I'm tellin you, grab those three hard-ons, then you and the Turk meet us by the diner."

Ten minutes later Bobby's Caddy rolled quietly into the Bay Diner parking lot. Bobby, the Turk, and Richie in the front seat. Bobby pulled up alongside Vito's car.

Charlie leaned forward slightly to see inside the car. There was a black guy in the backseat, his eyes open wide. Seated next to him, some freaky-looking dude, with long hair and a strange smile on his face. Charlie thought it was a smile of recognition. A kind of smile he'd seen many times before.

Charlie stepped out of the car saying, "C'mon, Vito, you come with me."

The Turk joined Charlie and Vito in the parking lot, saying, "Nobody tried to do anything or nothing. They didn't run, put up a fight, nothing. Not that they could have put up much of a fight. I mean, we ambushed em. Ba-bing, just like that."

Charlie said, "Good, that's good. Where's that fat fuck, Paulie?"

"No room," the Turk said then, "we hadda shove him in the trunk."

"He fit?" Vito said.

"Just about," said the Turk.

"Vito," Charlie said, "I want you, the Turk, here, and the kid, Richie, to take care of this." Charlie turned to the Turk, put a finger in his chest, "These three pieces of shit are kidnappers, I never want to see them again."

"Kidnappers," the Turk said. "Okay, fine, good. That's good."

Charlie Chan walked to the back of Bobby's car and leaned his hands on the trunk. "Bobby," he said, "C'mere, come out here, and open this trunk."

The trunk opened and Fat Paulie's voice came out to Charlie. "Jesus, Charlie, Jesus, gimme a break here, will ya?"

"What's your crime partner doing with Nicky and the woman?" Charlie said.

"He's fuckin with them, Charlie, you wouldn't be happy. No, I don't think what Blaze is doin would make you happy at all."

"What apartment they in?"

"Top floor rear."

"You better have a key."

"Here," Paulie said, "here in my jacket."

"Don't get up, you fat prick, just stay there. Get me the key, Vito."

"Charlie, can I say that I wanted no part of this? Blaze is one weird fucker, you know that. But not me, Charlie, not me. I walked away, turned my back on him. C'mon, Charlie, give me a break here, will ya?"

Charlie, with Vito and the kid Bobby close beside him, stared at the absurd figure of Fat Paulie stuffed into the trunk of the car. "Look at him," Charlie said, "he takes up the whole fucking trunk."

"And this car has a big trunk," Bobby said, "this trunk is huge. I mean, it's one of the reasons I bought the car, you don't find trunks like this anymore."

Fat Paulie's hands covered his face, frightened to look at the people that would kill him. When he took a peek through his fingers he groaned, "Charlie, a break, some consideration, huh?"

"Like you gave Alley Boy?" Charlie said amiably. "He's an old man, you fucking bum, you cut his thumb off. You freak."

"Blaze," he shouted, "it was Blaze." Paulie began to tremble, he was trembling all over. "Charlie," he said, "you can't do me like this, let me outta here. Charlie, you can't do this."

"Of course I can," Charlie said. Then he slammed the trunk closed.

"Bobby," Charlie said, "I want you to think of this night as a learning experience."

The kid Bobby solemnly nodded his head.

From Bobby's trunk came the sounds of kicking, thumping, the panicked screams of a terrorized man. A moment of silence, then whimpering, sobbing, pleading.

"See," Charlie said, "what you'll learn here tonight is that even the toughest guys cry before they die, especially kidnappers."

"What can I say," Bobby said. "I'm here to learn."

Nora didn't cry. Ever. Sometimes she wished she could. As a child she could remember crying, what it was like, the feeling of it. It was unattractive, the effect was inelegant and ugly. Ugly was the term her mother had used. Many years ago her mother had told her, be a good girl and behave yourself, and you'll never have reason to cry. Her mother had never encountered some dipshit who seemed to have come up out of a sewer, like something foul that rose from the core of the earth. Her mother had never met the likes of Blaze Longo.

Nora sat stunned, battling to get her mind working. Think of something, she told herself, try to do something. There was the punch, and then the slaps, hard, vicious, jolting her. The blows took her instantly back to Max, the way she'd covered up, the way she had been unable to fight back, the look in Max's hot, crazy eyes, not unlike the look in the eyes of the lunatic standing before her now. When she had glanced over to Nicky, he had met her gaze with unmistakable gloom. Unlike her own, Nicky's mouth was taped. "Oh, Nicky," she said as though she were humiliated.

Feeling lost and angry, fighting like hell not to give in to tears. Nora turned to concentrate on Nicky. He was taped down and bleeding from a slash across his cheek. There were tears in the creases of his eyes. His head was still, his eyes boring into hers. Something else, too, Nora thought, can you believe it, the guy's smiling, an attempt at bravery. At that moment, the comic actor she'd told only minutes before to shut up and disappear, made the dingy room, the maniac, Blaze, the terror, drop away, and Nora felt close, almost safe, with Nicky the Hawk.

Earlier, Nicky had been unable to get through to her. If only he had, if only she'd listened, this all might have been avoided. Nicky had told her he was not going into that building, and that she shouldn't, either. The place is a pit, he'd said, it stinks to high heaven, there's no electricity in there, no power, no lights. Well, there was some, but not enough to see well. And there are rats, big ones. Rats, he'd said, big fuckers, like cats. You wanna go, he'd told her, you go ahead, I'm staying right here, maybe catch the end of the Yankee game.

That's when she'd said, You can stay in the car, or disappear, but do me a favor and shut up. She had to think it through. Nora had to go into the apartment building, no question in her mind.

When she stepped from the car Nicky had tried very hard to sit still and wait. All right, he'd called, wait up, I'm coming. "Man," he'd said, "you know, sometimes I wonder if you're a sane person."

They hadn't gone far beyond the doorway, through the foyer to the foot of the stairs when Nora sensed something behind her. And when it happened, it happened fast, like in a horror movie, only worse. Later, she'd remember that it was a proven fact, when the worst moments of your life arrive, they have a habit of arriving at the speed of light.

Blaze and the others came through the door behind them and they came in screaming, and to Nora's surprise and embarrassment, she threw her hands in the air.

They did all have guns, and their guns were aimed at her and Nicky. And there was the screaming and shouting, "Put your hands up, up, put em up." That's when the terror seized her, and she threw up her hands. Nothing to be ashamed of. What could she do? What could anyone do? Cop or no cop, when guns are in the hands of madmen, and those barrels are shoved into your face, you throw up your hands.

Nicky tried, did a little of, "Whoa! Fellas, take it easy. It's okay, you'll see this is okay, it's no big deal." It didn't work.

They grabbed them and took them under the stairwell where they searched her and roughed up Nicky. When Blaze discovered her gun and then her ID, he had giggled. To Fat Paulie and the others it was not so funny. There was a lot of, Oh, shits, and whadaya-gonna-do-now chatter.

Morgan said to Nicky, "I'm disappointed. I thought we were buddies."

When they led them up the stairway, Nora looked around and was hit with the feeling that she'd never get out of this disgusting building. She followed close on Nicky's heels, and it was between the second and third floors that he reached behind him and squeezed her hand. When they brought them into the top-floor apartment, through the apartment to the back room, and taped them side by side in two chairs, when Nora noticed the smell, she was positive that this was where it would end.

First Blaze put tape across Nicky's mouth, then he set about lighting candles. A lot of them, there were at least ten burning in the small room.

Fat Paulie and the other two men seemed to want to avoid eye contact. They moved about the room whispering to each other, and after a while, right after Blaze had taped Nicky's mouth, Fat Paulie said, "Buddy, you gotta think about what you're doing here."

"This is serious shit," the black guy they called Morgan said. "I don't want anything to do with this, I'm telling you right now, I'm not down for fucking with a cop."

"And she ain't just a fucking cop," Montonero said, holding her golden badge in his hand. "This broad is a captain. Fuck man, they'd hunt us forever, we pull some shit like this."

It was lucky, Nora thought, that three out of the four, at least, were thinking.

Fine," Blaze said happily, "why'nt you all cut out. You, too, Paulie, go, the three of you, beat it, it's okay." A little too happily, Nora thought. With a little too much drive and anger.

Feeling a small wave of confidence rise, Nora decided to speak. As it turned out, it was not a wise decision.

"What you're doing is stupid," Nora told them, "stupid and crazy. You're right," she said to Montonero, "there's a backup team following me here, they'll show any minute now, you'll be in deep shit."

"We should go," Morgan shouted. Montonero nodded in agreement. "I don't know about you guys," he said, "but I'm out of here." Paulie just walked around in circles, muttering.

Nora said, "I'm telling you, now listen to me, I could use your help. You all could help me and that would carry a whole lot of weight."

Blaze shouted, "The rat master speaks."

"You're not thinking. None of you are thinking. It's not smart," she told them.

Blaze gave her a look of such hatred and fury that Nora felt as though her stomach had turned completely over. She could tell now what this guy was about, and why Nicky was so fearful of him.

"Stupid," Blaze said, "you think I'm stupid, you think I'm crazy? Who's in the chair, you smartass bitch? Me, or you?"

Blaze moved in front of her, switched the pistol he carried from his right to his left hand. He punched her, a short quick jab of a punch, strong, snapping her head back. With his left hand he went into his boot, and came out with a straight-edged razor, which he displayed in front of her eyes, then he quickly, with a certain amount of grace, slashed Nicky's cheek.

"Nicky!" Nora shouted.

And Blaze hit her again, this time open-handed. A slap that was fierce and spun her head.

"Nicky," she said again, hardly able to speak.

"Oh, man, fuck this," Paulie said, "I'm gone, you guys coming? It's a woman, Blaze, and a cop. What the fuck are you doing?"

"This ain't no woman," Blaze said then, "she's a rat master, a cheese feeder. By the way, how come you're all still here?"

After Paulie, Montonero, and Morgan had left, Blaze shoved his pistol in his belt, his razor he stuck in his boot.

"Tell me," he told her, "how'd you turn the actor around? There was a time Nicky was a stand-up guy. How'd you do it? Spread those pretty legs of yours, I bet."

Nora didn't answer.

"Nothing to say, huh? Well, well, now, let's see. Maybe what I should do is open that blouse and get a look-see at some real tits."

"Blaze," she told him, "there is nothing you've done up till now that we can't work out. You read the papers, DAs and cops work things out with people who've done far more than you."

Nicky was trying to speak, making sounds.

Blaze set about dancing around the room, he shuffled and did a two-step. "You can work things out for me, I'll find myself free and clear. Is that what you're telling me, I can walk away free and clear?"

"I give you my word."

"Oh, get out of here. You don't know what I've done, how can you clear me of what you don't know? See, you lying bitch, playing with me, treating me like I'm stupid. But I ain't stupid, not me, bitch, not me, ho." His inflection now was in some sing-song rap tune, it was as though he were trying his hand at amusing and entertaining. He was giddy and wild-eyed.

In an attempt to stop the bleeding, Nicky turned his cheek into his shoulder. But his eyes were locked on Nora, encouraging her, or trying to.

Looking into Blaze's eyes, Nora had a picture of herself as if she had been at the mercy of some serial killer. Somebody like Jeffrey Dahmer or John Wayne Gacy. Often, when she had read the headlines and studied the details of sexual assault, mutilation, even cannibalism, she'd imagine herself there, dealing with the beast. It happens so fast, she thought, so fast.

Blaze shocked Nora by grabbing her breast and twisting. "Ow," she cried, angry. Blaze snapped his fingers then pointed at her. "You've been showing Nicky these tits, haven't you?" He tapped his head, "I ain't stupid, flash tits like this in his face a man will weaken."

"Keep your fuckin hands off me," she snapped.

Blaze went up on tiptoe, "A toughie, huh, a fighter. You could die in here, bitch. I could cut your throat. You'd better be nice to me. Speak nice, cause I could kill you both, slow and long." Then he did it again, seizing her breast, fondling this time, a gentle squeeze making Nora nauseated. "I could set fire to this place, you know they don't call me Blaze for nothing. Burn the whole joint to the ground. Oh, man, I'm a genius, ashes, ashes, ashes, all the evidence gone up in smoke."

Nora imagined the scene and was frightened now, terrified, knowing she had only minutes left before this creep went completely off the edge.

Seeing Blaze's eyes spread, the way he looked around the room, looking for what? Paper, rags, things that would burn? She took a deep breath, gearing up for a last shot, "You're important, Blaze," she told him. "But there are others, more important than you. Help me." She threw everything she had into the punch line, "It's not you we want, not you at all. Help me nail the man making money off your back and you'll do short time—maybe, just maybe, no time at all. It's been done, Blaze, you know it can be done."

Blaze looked off then muttered, "Fucking cheese feeder, rat master." Blaze raised his hand like a traffic cop. "I am not stupid," he screamed.

"Oh, sure, you are."

Charlie Chan walked in without breaking stride, "You're a moron, but you're smart enough to know you'll die you don't drop that gun."

Blaze worked his mouth soundlessly, dropped his gun, and stepped back. Charlie followed him across the room, his own gun jabbing into Blaze's chest. Charlie quickly glanced over at Nicky, turned back to Blaze, "You're a dead man, you piece of shit."

Blaze was bouncing his back off the wall, shooting desperate looks around the room. Charlie back-stepped to the chair Nicky sat in and tore the tape from his mouth. "Charlie, man, it's good to see you, pal."

"I bet," Charlie said.

"Who's this?" said Nora, her eyes still on Blaze.

Charlie kept his gun on Blaze and busied himself taking the tape from Nicky's wrists.

"Who are you?" said Nora. "I mean, it's great to see you, whoever you are, but who *are* you?"

When Nicky was free he moved to the edge of the chair Nora sat in, and stood for a moment.

"I got a flash for you, Charlie," Blaze said. "This here bitch is a cop. Your boy, Nicky, is a rat. He's working with the cops. I'm just doing the right thing here."

"That right?" Charlie said. "Nicky's working with the cops? You helping the cops, Nicky?"

Nicky shrugged without answering.

"Who are you?" Nora said.

"Do me a favor," Charlie told her, "be quiet a minute. I get the feeling you like to talk, you talk a lot, I bet. It's all your talking that put everybody in this room. Got Nicky that cut on his face."

"Please," she said, "take this tape off me." When Nicky put his hand on her wrist, he felt her trembling. "You'll be all right," he said, "you're going to be fine."

"Me?" she said. "Me? Look at you."

"It's not so bad," he told her. "I don't think it's bad."

Without taking his eyes off Blaze, Charlie walked over and gave Nicky a hand with Nora's tape.

"She's a cop, a police captain," Blaze said. "I warned you, Charlie."

"Listen," Nora said, "whoever you are, there're three others, they could come back here any minute."

"Fat Paulie," Nicky said, "and two other guys, they can't be too far away."

"Oh, they're far away," Charlie said. "Just like Elvis, they left the building, had their tickets punched, and took a powder. As sad as it may be, my bet is that we'll never see them again."

"Serves em right," Nicky said softly, working at the tape around Nora's ankles. When Nora stood she put her hand on Nicky's cheek. "This doesn't look too good. We have to get you to a doctor. Where's my gun?" she said, turning to look around the room. Charlie was silent. He looked at Nicky's wound, studied it for a moment, the way the cut came from the corner of his eye to the edge of his mouth; the bleeding had almost stopped, the wound was not deep.

Nora turned to look at Charlie for a second. "Hey," she said, "hey, am I crazy or . . . aren't you Charles Conti?"

"Nora," Nicky said, "calm down."

"Charlie Conti, you believe it." Nora said, "You're Charles Conti. Charlie Chan Conti, that's you. Christ, go back a few years you were running everything around the docks. I came close to working you myself. Charlie Chan Conti. No kidding, Charles Conti. Man, I'll bet you punched those guys' tickets awright, I bet you did just that."

"What can I say?" Charlie said. Charlie was half turned now looking around the room. "That your gun over there?" he said.

Nora spotted her gun lying in the corner, walked over and bent to pick it up.

That's when Blaze made his move.

Blaze braced himself against the wall, then uncoiled and flew across the room. He shoved Charlie aside and grabbed Nicky, laying his razor across Nicky's neck. "I'll cut his fucking throat."

Blaze looped his arm around Nicky's neck and held Nicky in front of him like a shield.

"I'll kill you," Nora said.

"Yeah, sure you will. Gimme your gun," Blaze said, "you too, Charlie, gimme them guns, man. I don't care if I die, I don't give a shit. I got no win here, anyway. Gimme them guns or I cut Nicky boy's throat. Watch me."

Charlie glanced at Nora and Nora shook her head. "I'm not putting a gun in that man's hand, not me."

"I'm telling you," Blaze screamed, "I'll cut him deep." Blaze's body stiffened in a sudden spasm. "You fucking dopes, you don't believe me?"

Nora took a deep breath, swallowed, and raised her pistol.

Nicky shut his eyes. "Please," he said, "will somebody please kill this motherfucker."

Blaze's face was just beneath Nicky's shoulder. Nothing much showing at all, a bit of forehead, his hairline. Really bad odds. "Do it!" Nicky shouted. Charlie said, "Wait a minute, hold on now. Listen, Blaze, there ain't nothing in this fucking world that can't be worked out."

Nora exhaled, turned away as if she were confused, turned back and fired. She knew her luck was good when Nicky fell forward and Blaze flew backward.

Then it got better, much better, Blaze hit the wall and slid to the floor, a clear shot now, and although he was dead, a nine-millimeter through the forehead makes you very dead, Nora kept shooting, pow-pow-pow. Man she loved these Glocks, accurate as hell and smooth as silk.

Nora took her time leaving the building, made sure that Nicky and Charlie were a long-time gone. She drove to Emmons Avenue and found a place to park near the docks. The nighttime fishermen were coming in, crowding the wharf. A couple of old geezers and a pair of teenage boys coming off the *Valiant Two*, smiled and showed her their buckets of bluefish. A good sign. At the end of the pier, across the street from Lundy's, she found a working pay phone and telephoned the local precinct. After speaking to the night duty, detective-squad commander, giving him a rundown, a sort of rundown, and getting a whole lot of "Jesus, man, what the hells?" Nora told him she'd meet him at the scene, then she telephoned her office.

Detective Frank Sena answered the phone.

"Captain," he said, "man, it's good to hear your voice."

"I'm sorry, Frank, we lost touch, my fault."

"We tried calling, tried and tried. Oh, Captain, man, it's good to hear your voice. You're okay, huh?"

"Fine. Is the chief around?"

"Yes, he's in his office talking to Mike. Captain, he told me he's going to give me this dream assignment guarding a city dump in the far end of Staten Island. Captain, I live upstate in Rockland County, we're talking a three-hour trip."

Nothing was worse than living in Rockland County and working in Staten Island, Frank said.

Nora thought about worse things: being taped to a chair in a foul-smelling building, a maniac with a razor, a husband that shoots himself with your gun.

"Don't worry about it, Frank," she told him. "I'll explain. Could you get the chief for me."

"Sure, Cap. Can I ask, everything work out okay? I mean, everything go down, nice, nice? You got what you needed?"

"Well, I guess you could say I got what I needed. But as far as things going down, nice, nice, I think that would be stretching it a bit."

"Oh, no, you better not tell me."

When Jean-Paul Clement came to the phone, he came to the phone screaming. "Jesus Christ, Nora, you know what time it is?"

"No."

"It's two o'clock in the morning. I'm the chief of detectives, next week I might be the police commissioner, I have no business being in the office this time of night. Where the hell are you? What are you doing?"

Nora wiped a curl of sweat from forehead and cheek, and jumped. Her cheek was swollen, the whole side of her head had puffed up. A present from Blaze.

"Right now I'm watching some fishermen load their cars." She spoke very precisely.

"Are you all right?"

"No, I don't think so."

"What's wrong? Look, where are you, I'll come get you."

"Paul, the 161 squad is coming to meet me." Suddenly Nora's knees began to vibrate. "Paul, I just shot Blaze Longo. He's dead."

"Whoa! Where? How? You okay?"

"No, I'm not okay. But I'm all right, if you know what I mean."

"I'll be right there, Nora." His voice was unexpectedly calm and sympathetic. "Do not talk to anyone."

"Chief, it was a legit shooting. It'll be awright."

A long, long moment of silence, "I'd better get out there."

"You're the boss. But, listen, you'll just bring more attention than I want to deal with right now. I got a whole night of paperwork ahead of me. I'll come in first thing in the morning. How's that?"

"It was a good shooting, huh?"

Sometimes a good shooting meant different things to different people, but on this one, Nora knew, there was no doubt at all. "He had a gun, a razor, it's a long story. But the shooting was totally legit."

"Was anyone else there?"

Nora gave the question a moment, but answered before she had her story fully worked out. "No."

"I'll meet you at the precinct. Look, I want to."

"And I appreciate it. But let me get this paperwork done, I'll come in first thing. We'll talk then."

"Screw this guy, Nora."

"You got that right."

"And Nora, listen, I'm only bringing this up to maybe, you now, ease your mind. I entertained Captain Greta Hartmann half the night. She was here, we talked, wait till you see her."

"I'm not looking forward to it."

"Look forward to it, she'll be here in the morning, too. It's going to be fine. Nora, you were on the money with Ceballos. What's more important, as far as that business with Max is concerned, you're out of the woods."

"Good."

"Anyway, wait until you see Greta, you're in for a shock."

"One more shock and they'll take me away in a net," she told him. Still surprised at her decision not to mention Nicky or Charlie Chan.

"I can be there in twenty minutes," he told her.

Nora looked off, scanning the docks, all the boats at their moorings. "I appreciate the thought, but I can handle this."

"I can't imagine what it would be that you couldn't handle."

"I'm tired," she told him. The fishing boats, the sound and smell of the sweet sea air, making her think of her sister, her sister's country house in Rhode Island. "I need a break," she said.

"You come in tomorrow, we'll have a little chitchat with Captain Hartmann, then you can take as long as you like. As long as you like, does that sound good?"

"As long as I like," she repeated.

Around ten o'clock the next morning Jean-Paul Clement, Capt. Greta Hartmann, and a lieutenant named Frank Russo were seated in Jean-Paul's office. Because it was a Sunday stacks of opened morning newspapers. A basket of bagels and muffins, and a coffee urn, were arranged on a table that had been set at the far end of the room.

They were talking about the mayor and about the retiring police commissioner, when Nora walked in. All three stood and smiled, Russo made silent applause. The entire scene was congenial and clublike, friendly.

Coming off the elevator Nora had seen it in the faces of the headquarters cops: She was a star, a heroine, her name a headline in all the morning papers.

"Sit down, make yourself comfortable," Jean-Paul said.

He introduced Nora to Russo who nodded his head, smiling and still applauding. When she turned to Greta Hartmann, Nora said, "Wow, what happened to you? Greta. You look fantastic."

"Medifast." Greta said.

"How much?"

"About fifty pounds. I run and bike and go to the gym, it is a new me. Forget me, how about *you?* A helluva night, huh?"

"One for the memory book," Nora told her.

Greta had an exquisite haircut, her blond hair had gone a brilliant, summertime white and was very short. She wore an expensive blue suit with silver jewelry, elegant stuff. Nora knew the difference. There was about Greta, and her outfit, a kind of professionalism that Nora had never been able to achieve. Looking at her, Nora could see the reason for Jean-Paul's enthusiasm.

Getting right to it, Greta said, "Let me tell you why we've been trying to reach you. First of all, there was this anonymous complaint, it came in soon after your husband killed himself."

"Excuse me," Nora said, "don't I get a read of G.O.15? I mean, no offense, but I know my *Patrol Guide*, you have to give me my rights. And I haven't had my coffee yet."

Nora went to pour herself a cup of coffee, she could sense that despite her new look, Greta Hartmann would never shake Greta the Hun. It was in the genes.

Captain Hartmann sat up straighter, the old Greta making an appearance. "You're not a target, Nora, I thought that Paul had filled you in?"

Nora nodded her head theatrically, "That's a relief," she said.

Paul, she thought, well, well, now.

Jean-Paul got up from behind his desk, walked to the table for another coffee. "I meant to fill Nora in last night. But, the good captain was pretty busy. Hell, we've all read the papers."

"Of course," Greta said, "naturally. A helluva thing. It's amazing, really, the situations you get yourself into, Nora."

They drank. Nora thinking, who am I kidding? I hate this bitch.

"As I was saying," Greta said, "IAD received a complaint, it was well written, well written as those things go. Clearly, it was sent by a cop, a cop's relative. We get, by the way, a ton of those and they're always anonymous." She took a long sip from her coffee. "The writer called two days ago, identified herself and withdrew the complaint."

"You know who sent it, Nora," Jean-Paul said. "It was Julie Morelli, the woman was a wreck, her husband had been shot, almost killed. It's understandable."

"Perfectly understandable," Nora said.

"The thing is," Greta said, "in the letter there was a mention of Detective Ceballos, that he had arrested your husband. We knew that, of course. By the way, if you have information regarding a narcotics violation, it's expected that you would notify the narcotics division. Officially, or unofficially." Greta threw a small grin at the chief, like, we're in this together. "It's your intentions that we are most concerned with, and in your case, they apparently were honorable."

Nora looked away.

Well, Nora thought, she had a new body, and maybe a new soul, but she was a politician, no question she knew how to play the game. Jean-Paul's newest best friend. She didn't like Greta the Hun very much, not the fat one, not the thin one. "So," Nora said, "is that it?"

"Hardly," Greta said. "Tell her, Frank, better yet, show the captain."

Lieutenant Frank Russo went into his attaché case and removed a cassette player and a tape. "Wait till you hear this," he said. He sounded nasty.

When the lieutenant snapped the tape into place and hit the play button, Nora glanced at Jean-Paul. He gave her a reassuring smile.

"I made you rich, you prick, and what do you do, you call me names. You wouldn't call me names to my face, not you, not the Wizard. You're a punk, come into my face, I'll cut you, cut you good."

"I guess you know that voice," Greta said.

"Intimately," said Nora. "You had a wire on Blaze's phone?"

"That we did," said Frank. "We've been on Ceballos and Blaze for the past six months, we know their game. Tell me," he said, "how about this?"

"Oh, man, don't make me talk on this phone. Christ, please, go to number three."

"I'm gonna hang up, one . . . two . . ."

"Okay, okay. What did the Hawk tell you? He told you he got pinched, right? What else did he tell you?"

"Nothing else."

"He told you he made bail. Am I right?"

"So?"

"He was paroled, no bail. Understand what I'm saying? He's an informant, he's a stool pigeon, a rat, Blaze, and you're rolling right around in his nest. You fucking moron."

"That's Ceballos," Nora said, "that's him. You got him."

Jean-Paul said, "Nicky the Hawk, that's your informant?"

"That he is."

"And he left you out there in Sheepshead Bay by your lonesome, a real hero, this actor."

Right, Nora thought. A genuine hero. There in Red Hook, raising that boy, living his life, an authentic good guy.

"I told him to leave, it was my decision," she said.

Lieutenant Russo smiled and Greta Hartmann, too. Then Russo's face darkened, "I have a search warrant, and an arrest warrant in here. We're going to take Jimmy Ceballos down this afternoon. Maybe you'd like to come along?"

"Maybe not," Nora said.

An **hour after** the meeting, Nora sat behind her desk, testing her new cellular phone when Jean-Paul came through her door.

"Your face doesn't look too bad," he told her. "But it's swollen, I can see it."

"I iced it all night, I'm okay."

"It's amazing those two didn't notice. Well, maybe they did, but they didn't say anything."

"I guess they had other things on their minds," Nora said. "Greta looks incredible, the woman went from Roseanne Arnold to Cindy Crawford, the magic of modern medicine."

"She's hardly Cindy Crawford and Roseanne Arnold is not Roseanne Arnold anymore."

He gave her that smile that had turned a thousand heads, more maybe. "Speaking of Roseann," she told him, "I understand that her father's fine. He's living in Las Vegas, everything you touch is coming up golden. It's going to be okay."

"I guess. You know, it does look fairly certain that they'll appoint me PC."

He gave her a rundown on the various political shenanigans taking place at city hall. He told her what he knew about the numerous changes that would take place at headquarters.

"Administratively speaking," Jean-Paul said, "no one understands this job better than I do. From the cop on post to the brass at headquarters, I understand what makes them tick, what pleasures and pains them. I have all the political savvy to run this department. You know that Nora, you know. Hell, man, if I had a mind to, I probably could take a shot at the mayor."

Nora took a deep breath, out of weariness, or stress, or to keep from screaming.

Jean-Paul leaned forward and lowered his voice. "I'm serious," he said, "there are people talking me up for the next mayoralty, can you believe that?"

"Hell, Paul, if you ask me, I'd say, why stop there? Personally, I think as slick as you are, you'd make a great president."

"I'm serious.'"

"And so am I."

"Don't laugh at me," he told her. "But later on today I plan on stopping in at St. Andrew's in the Plaza, at least I'm going to try."

"Right," she said. "Religion is the answer."

Nora hurried now, telephoning her sister, calling Nicky. Neither one was home. Before leaving headquarters she tried Sam Morelli.

When Sam answered the phone, Nora could feel that moment all over again, the moment when she was told that Max had killed himself and shot Sammy. That dropping sensation, she slumped back into her chair. "Sam," she said, "how are you feeling?"

"I'm reading the paper right now. I can't believe this. I leave you for a few days, and you head to the O.K. Corral. What in the hell happened?"

"Sammy, it's a helluva long story."

"Are you awright, Christ, how are you feeling? How you handling this?" The first person to ask, she thought, always, forever, my partner. "I'm okay, really, I'm okay."

"You're famous. In the newspapers, you're everywhere, The *Post* has a great picture of you."

"And this, too, shall pass," she told him.

"You're telling me you're awright. Personally, I have this feeling that you're bullshitting me."

"So, what's next for you and Julie?"

"We're leaving for England on Tuesday." There was a long pause. "I'm going to miss you."

"I'll be here when you get back, call me." She decided to improve on that. "When you and Julie get back, we'll have dinner. I'll cook."

"No offense, but why'nt we just go out to dinner."

"Thanks."

"I'm going to miss you."

"Well, as you can see, I sure as hell miss you."

Leaving headquarters, driving over the Brooklyn Bridge, she tried them both again. Lilly was home, had no plans for the next couple of weeks, and she'd love to see her. At the foot of the bridge, Nora tried Nicky. Tino answered, saying, "Hey, where are you?"

"Let me speak to your father," Nora said.

"Wait until you see Nicky's face, you won't believe it," Tino said. Nora agreed, she wouldn't believe it.

"He got fifty-eight stitches."

Nora flushed. "That's terrible, is he there?"

"Captain," Nicky said, "how goes it?"

"Listen, cowboy, ever been to Rhode Island?"

"Been through on my way to Boston, never stopped."

"Wanna go?"

"When?"

"In about a half-hour. I've got to make one stop, after I do, I'll come by and beep."

Nicky laughed. "We can't all fit in your car."

"All, what do you mean, all?"

"You don't expect me to leave Tino, and there's Irma."

Nora was quiet for a long moment. Then, "Listen," she said, "maybe

374

you'd better go and rent a car." Thinking, Lilly, you and the people of Wickford are going to love this.

"You're serious?"

"You have half an hour. Can you get a car?"

"In a half-hour, I could get an airplane."

Nora came off the bridge, made it to Atlantic Avenue in seconds, downtown Brooklyn, a ghost town on Sunday. As soon as she turned into Court Street she spotted him.

He was standing on the corner near his club, arms crossed, sniffing the air like a wolf. She pulled right up in front of him. Nora got out and walked to the corner.

"Hey," she said.

"Hey, yourself."

"I'm glad I ran into you," she said.

"I'm glad you're glad. So, what's up?"

"I want to thank you for last night, you don't show, it's nightmare time. Nicky and me, we're rat food."

Charlie nodded noncommittally and cleared his throat.

"Anyway, I wanted to stop by and thank you. I also want to make something clear."

Charlie stood, stone-faced and arms crossed, staring at her.

"The way I see it," she said, "we're even now."

"That the way you see it?"

"Hey, there was Paulie and the other two, I figure all three are part of a construction site somewhere. Under a highway, maybe a football field."

"That what you figure? Well, I figure that maybe you're wearing one of those gizmos, a wire or something. You got some fantasy going here, lady. I don't know what the hell you're talking about."

Nora thought about that, nodded her head. "All right," she said, "okay, I understand, but you understand, too. You and me, we're even. I don't want Charlie Chan thinking he can come to me for a favor. I'm nobody's whore."

"No need to be sarcastic," Charlie told her.

"Okay, I apologize, I just don't want any misunderstandings between you and me. We're on different teams, that's the way it's been, and that's the way it will stay."

"It's incredible," Charlie said, "what you can get away with when you're beautiful. That's the truth."

"I'll take that as a compliment. But it's not true, it's more important to be smart. And I don't think it would be too smart of me, not to let you know how I feel."

"More truth," he told her.

"Charlie," she said, "for guys like you the truth is always so simple."

"It is simple, it's only people like you that try and make it complicated. It's pride, you see, you either have it or you don't."

Nora looked at him, then up and down the street. She shook her head. "Different teams, Charlie, same game, different teams."

He smiled. "Fine," he said, "I understand. Let me tell you something, Captain. I know who and what I am. In that respect, there is no confusion in my life."

They smiled at each other like children whose game had ended in a tie.

Nora stood now next to her car, going through her shoulder bag, searching for her keys. Charlie was standing beside her, looking around the street as though he were expecting someone. Nora said, "Thanks again, huh."

"Don't mention it."

"You understand, I had to make my point."

"Sure. By the way," he told her, "that whore line was good, but you're wrong."

"No, I'm not."

"Yes, you are. I'll tell ya, it's been my experience that everybody is a whore to somebody, but not everyone has the courage to admit it. You're no different than anyone else."

"Like I said, Charlie, simple answers."

"Easy questions," he said.

They left Brooklyn via the Brooklyn Bridge and followed the FDR Drive northbound, the Willis Avenue Bridge out of Manhattan, into the Bronx and the Bruckner Expressway. From there it was a straight shot on to the New England Thruway. Connecticut and then Rhode Island lay dead ahead.

It was an unclouded and crystal-clear day, and Nora drove with the top down. For a Sunday, traffic was unusually light and Nora had little trouble keeping Nicky in the rearview. Tino, next to Nora, wore a rather nifty cowboy hat. Nicky and Irma, staying more or less on their tail, rode in the biggest, blackest, Cadillac Nora had ever seen. The Caddy had tinted windows and carried registration tags that Nora planned to check.

They followed I-95 North past New Haven and the sporty towns of southern Connecticut. Oftentimes, on the long ride, Tino would turn in his seat, making sure Nicky and Irma had not been lost.

For Tino's benefit Nora summarized all the possibilities for a boy his age in Wickford. "I have a niece your age, her name is Maggie and she'll show you around," Nora told him. "You'll go fishing, swimming, hiking in the woods, how's that sound?"

"Maggie, what kind of name is that?"

"It's a nice name, a girl's name."

"I never met anyone called Maggie."

"Well, you'll meet one soon. Ever been on a boat?"

Tino shook his head.

"Think you'll like it?"

"I don't know, I might get seasick."

Tino pulled his hat down just above his eyes, Nora could see that he was grinning with pleasure. "Maggie?" he said. "You know what Irma said, she said they better have sidewalks, she doesn't want to go anywhere where they don't have sidewalks."

"There're sidewalks," Nora told him. "In town, there're sidewalks."

"And out of town?" Tino said, turning in his seat, checking the highway behind him.

"Out of town, there's no need for sidewalks," Nora said then.

"Oh, boy," Tino said, "you better tell Irma."

Just north of Charlestown, right past the state line, Tino told her he needed to use the john. Down the road there was a rest stop. Nora drove in and parked. Nicky and his Caddy pulled alongside. Tino and Irma made it to the restrooms.

Nora and Nicky walked to a wooden table that sat under a stand of white pine. Beyond the pine trees was a fenced-in, freshly cut field, where sheep were grazing and a horse. The sky was high, cloudless, and altogether blue.

Nora stood watching with some amusement while Nicky walked to the fence and whistled for the horse. When she joined him at the fence, he smiled and touched his cheek, "Fifty-eight stitches," he said, "I hope it leaves an interesting scar."

She brushed his cheek with the tips of her fingers. "There is nothing that could ruin that face, Nicky," she told him. "I can't get over how brave you were."

"Me? You were incredible. I think a lot about that guy Hector Santiago, that could have been me, that could have been you."

"Yes, I know," she said. "Thank God for Charlie."

"Charlie," Nicky said, "go figure."

"He likes you . . . more than likes you."

"The truth is, I really don't know him all that well. But he knows a lot about me. I mean, he's a whole lot older than I am. For chrissake, he went to school with my mother."

"Maybe it was a long-ago, never-forgotten love. Who knows? Your mother, was she beautiful?"

"Very."

"See, it could be something like that. Your father, he was a Swedish seaman, right?"

"And, always at sea," Nicky told her.

"See that."

"Christ," he said, "don't you ever stop playing detective?"

"Yeah, well, it makes for a great story. I'm a romantic, it works for me."

"So, is this it?" Waving his hand at the field, Nicky said, "is this the other place, the other time, the real people's world? Can we pretend that we just met?"

She laughed at him. "Anything's possible."

"How many bedrooms does your sister have?"

"Enough."

"Nora," he said, leaning on the fence, "I should let you know, I've been known to walk in my sleep. I could get lost."

"You? Never. I'd find you."

"Whoooo," he said, "where's Tino and Irma, I want to get going."

Nora's beeper went off.

"You have got to be kidding," Nicky said. "You're on vacation, toss that sucker. Or do you want me to? I can do that, I've done that, I hate those gadgets."

"I know, I was there, remember? Look," she told him, "it's my office, let me make this call, and then, in the trunk it goes."

Jean-Paul's voice said, "Nora, I got the call."

"You're the police commissioner."

"Yup."

"Well, well, now, congratulations. Really, that is something."

"Nora, how long you plan on being gone?"

"Paul, you said as long as I like, that's what you promised me."

"I did say that, didn't I? Well, you certainly have earned it."

"Thank you."

"Greta and Russo checked in just a little while ago. They hit Ceballos, his apartment, one or two other addresses they had for him. Guess what? He's gone, skipped, his closets are empty."

"Paul, Ceballos is not my problem."

"He left a note, you believe it, a greeting card. You want to hear what it said."

"No."

"Fuckyaall. One word, fuckyaall."

"Really? Ummm," she said, "a creative guy this Ceballos, a student of words."

"Give me a week," he told her, "two at the most, you're an inspector."

A two-rank jump, Nora stammered a little, "Oh," she said, "That's great. Thank you."

"Girlie, no one deserves it more than you."

"Paul, for chrissake, there are a whole lot of things you can call me—girlie, is not one of them."

"Sorry, c'mon, you know what I mean."

"That's the point, isn't it, I *do* know what you mean."

"Nora, I'm the police commissioner, *holy shit!*"

Nora let what he said sit there a minute. "It is something, Paul. It truly is."

"So," he said, "how long do you plan on staying away?"

"Give me a week," she told him.

"Atta girl."

Charlie Chan was right, she thought, of course he was right—that everyone is a whore for someone, sometime. Then again, Charlie was a criminal, a guy who committed crimes both out of tradition and principle. But, out of greed, too. He was a killer, pure and simple. What the hell does Charlie Chan know?

If you don't take your fate in your own hands, you're screwed, was what she was thinking. Look, she told herself, despite all your pretensions at worldliness you remain naïve. Sure, things have changed, but it remains a man's world, sister, they still make the rules. Fornicating suits with smiling faces.

She started for her car, there were Nicky, Irma, and Tino, the Red Hook trio.

"Nicky," Nora said, waving him over, "can I talk to you for a minute? Listen," she whispered, "can't we do anything about Irma's get-up."

"What's wrong, you don't like red?"

"No, it's not the shorts, or the T-shirt, for that matter. It's the fishnet stockings. Talk to her, will ya?"

"You don't like fishnet stockings?"

"Nicky, with shorts and sneakers? All right," she said, "let's get going, time's a-wasting, we're off to visit the real people's world. And, let me tell you, they are going to freak."

Nicky threw out his arms, it was quite a graceful gesture. *"O wonderful, wonderful, and most wonderful, wonderful!"* he sang.

"Oh, that's great, now you're doing Lawrence Welk."

Nicky rolled his eyes, rapped his head. "That was *As You Like It,* Captain. *Shakespeare.*"

"Inspector, Nicky, it'll be inspector now," she said.

"I'll call you sweetie," Nicky told her. "I'll call you babes."

"You will, huh?"

"Yes, yes, I will."

Nora grinned.

"And, maybe if I get real lucky, Irma will let you borrow her fish net stockings."

"I had something just a little less obvious in mind."

"You plan on surprising me?"

Ummmm, why not? She liked him, for God's sake. And, it had been a while, I mean, you know, hey . . . It had been a long while. "Who knows," she told him, "maybe I'll surprise the two of us."

Nora got into her car and started the engine. Tino slipped into the seat beside her. "Pancakes," Tino said, "in the morning Nicky will make pancakes from scratch, he is the best. I'm telling you, he will amaze you."

"I'm counting on it," Nora said enthusiastically. "Tino," she said, her eyes casually glancing to the rearview, "Nicky hasn't failed me yet."